DAUGHTER
OF THE
SHINING ISLES

DAUGHTER

OF THE

SHINING ISLES

VOL. I
THE MAGDALEN TRILOGY

ELIZABETH CUNNINGHAM

STATION HILL

BARRYTOWN, LTD.

Published by Station Hill / Barrytown, Ltd.
in Barrytown, New York 12507.

E-mail: publishers@stationhill.org
Online catalogue: http://www.stationhill.org

Station Hill Arts is a project of The Institute for Publishing Arts, Inc., a not-for-profit, federally tax exempt organization in Barrytown, New York, which gratefully acknowledges ongoing support for its publishing program from the New York State Council on the Arts.

Excerpts from *Carmina Gadelica* by Alexander Carmichael are used by permission of Lindisfarne Books, Hudson, NY 12534.

Design by Susan Quasha
Photo on jacket front by Barbara Leon
Photo of author by Maureen Beck

Library of Congress Cataloging-in-Publication Data

Cunningham, Elizabeth, 1953-
    Daughter of the shining isles / Elizabeth Cunningham.
       p. cm. – (The Magdalen trilogy ; vol. 1)
    ISBN 1-58177-060-X (alk. Paper)
       1. Mary Magdalene, Saint–Fiction. 2. Bible. N.T.–History of Biblical events–Fiction. 3. Christian women saints–Palestine–Fiction. 4. Women, Celtic–Fiction. I Title.

PS3553.U473 D38 2000
813'.54–dc21

00-036072

Manufactured in the United States of America

CONTENTS

For Douglas
in spite of—and because of—all.

DAUGHTER
OF THE
SHINING ISLES

BOOK I

THE ISLE OF WOMEN

1

THE BIRTH OF BRIGHTNESS

You have all heard of his birth in Bethlehem in a stable—though his mother told me it was really a cave, and she's vague about the location. You know the story of the attendant animals, the bedazzled shepherds, and the Magi who followed the long-tailed star. But did you know that the star had a twin? The sister star chose a tiny island in a northern sea. Its long tail lashed cold waters. Far from that holy birth in the hills, brightness rose from beneath the wave.

That was me.

I had a full head of red hair exclaimed upon, as I crowned, by the seven midwives, my foster mothers all. I had no need of awe-struck shepherds. My mothers kept sheep and pigs and goats besides. And listen, even though it's midnight, the mourning doves lift their heads to make soft, wondering noises, almost obscured by the raucous chorus of ravens in the wood and the cry of seabirds from their nests in the cliffs. And yes, if you pay attention, you can hear the walrus and seals barking for joy on the rocks. Wild horses answer, and a she-bear roused from sleep adds low, grumbling praise. Now if you look very carefully at the island's heart between mountain breasts, you can glimpse a moonlit flash of gold as the salmon of wisdom leaps from its pool.

And what need had I of visiting wise men when I was already surrounded by the Warrior Witches of Tir na mBan, the Land of Women? Ah, I see that name stirs some forgotten memory. Just as everyone is a little bit Irish, who has not dreamed of the Shining Isles always to the West? The Summer Land. The Apple Isle. The Isle of Women. The Land of Youth. The Isles of the Blest. Dangerous, paradisiacal places where a hero could be made or undone. The greatest heroes—Cuchulain and Fionn MacCumhail—received their training in the arts of war and the mysteries of love at the hands of women who dwelled in island strongholds of ancient, female power.

At least, that's how it was in what my mothers called "the good old days," lamenting the lack of heroes in these slack modern times. Maybe it was the times. Though none of us knew it then, ground zero (actually 4 BCE), when he and I were born, was the meeting place of history and myth, of time and time out of time.

Wait. Before you mourn the passing of myth, think what it might be like to live in one. Or to embody it, as my mothers did. For every great adventure,

5

told and retold as a stirring tale, there is a vast and smooth eventlessness, like the featureless sea surrounding the quirky surprise of an island. The story is always biased towards the hero. When Cuchulain leaves the Isle of Skye, you follow him. You don't hear what Scathach and her daughter did for the rest of their timeless lives. Well, I can tell you. They waited, like my mothers, for the next trainee, scanning the curve of sea and sky for a glimpse of a phallic mast. Not that they wouldn't have welcomed a girl hero.

(Yes, I know. Girl hero is awkward, like woman doctor. It's the qualifier that makes it so silly. But I balk at the word heroine. A personal quirk. I don't mind some female forms: goddess, priestess, and waitress are all right. They sound somehow more substantial, even more splendid, than their male counterparts. But the "ine" on heroine is too tacked-on. Tacky. And besides, these days it calls to mind the drug you shoot into your arm, and if you are doing that I hope you are at least using a clean needle.)

Anyway, my mothers did welcome me. I was the great event of their elemental lives, washing up on their shore from the inward seas of my mother's womb. See their fierce, hungry gladness as they bend over me in my birth mother's arms. Notice how the curve of their backs echoes the curve of our round wattle and daub hut built in the shape of a beehive, the shape of a breast. See them examining me, admiring the delicate rosebud of my sex. At my first cry, colostrum spurts from—count them!—sixteen breasts. Though to the sorrow of seven only one could carry me in her womb, they all succeeded in their determination to lactate. So my first meal was a sumptuous, seemingly endless feast as I was passed round and round from breast to breast.

I imbibed, with that magical abundance, a desire that grew, as I grew, to be not the setting of a narrative, but the teller—better yet, the protagonist. To be, in short, the hero of a story with a plot. In this determination, my mothers inadvertently encouraged me. For I was their nursling, their fledgling, their ready-made and only pupil for their many arts.

∞

All parents affect the climate of their children's lives. You could even say they create it. My mothers did—literally. They were weather witches as well as warriors. Picture us on our mythic island at the rim of the world, leagues away from the mainland (if any of the British Isles can be called that). We couldn't leave the success of the crops to chance. On a clear day, sister islands floated just in the range of vision to the Southeast. I spent hours gazing out over the sea, seeking that ephemeral line of land-blue. The back of a whale was a more common sighting. Or the undulating curves of a migrating sea monster.

Weather magic was also needed to maintain the fragrant garden that blossomed and bore fruit all year round. You see, it was essential that perfumed breezes waft from this garden at all times in case the nose of a hero might be passing nearby. Perhaps now is the time to mention that the Shining Isle of Tir na mBan resembles the shape of a woman lying on her back, thighs sloping down into the sea. You can imagine where the garden would be.

I have to admit that my mothers did not work weather magic out of necessity only. Just because men have hoarded the more obvious forms of power for several millennia doesn't mean women are immune to its seductions. To say that my mothers abused their power may be too strong. Their isolation and wildness gave them innocence. In temperament, they resembled the weather, which can be bad and destructive from a purely human point of view yet has no malevolent intent. In any case, they could not resist playing with the weather. On our island, it was both entertainment and sport, a competitive sport at that. Each one had her jealously guarded area of expertise. I'll introduce them to you by way of their meteorological specialties. Never mind if you can't remember them all. Think of them as a collective maternal force.

Fand presided over fogs and mists. She regarded them as an art form and had hundreds of different names for her creations that only she could remember, all very poetic: The Seventh Veil of Danu; The Silkie's Cloak; Filigree of Gull's Wing; Crane's Wedding Day.

Emer, Etain, Deirdru, and Dahut, sisters in blood as well as art, commanded the four winds, as they liked to put it. They were usually good about taking turns, but occasionally conflicts arose that resulted in twisters. Once they created an enormous whirlpool off shore that so delighted them they forgot their quarrel.

Liban came into her element in spring when softening rains were needed to ready the fields for planting. Since they both dealt in moisture, there were occasional border disputes between Fand and Liban.

Boann ruled storms and extended her realm to include hard frosts and the odd snowfall. (Weather witchery notwithstanding, we didn't get much snow, being such a tiny land mass so far out to sea.) Boann was impulsive and impatient and had a special fondness for hail, which could be disastrous if dropped on the crops at the wrong time.

Of course, we all liked a good storm. (Even my womb mother, Grainne. I will tell you more about her later.) And if Boann was reckless and needed to be restrained at times, she was also the most generous about sharing her turf. Often everyone got into the act, and together they created some really first-class squalls. These joint ventures had a tendency to coincide with my mothers' collective PMS.

PMS! I hear some of you protesting. But I thought they lived in harmony with nature! Sure they did. But who says nature is always nice? Yes, they cycled together (more or less according to the moon's phases) which made it all the more companionable and efficient. And they were not as depressed as some modern women, because they didn't believe in holding anything back. They reveled in bitchiness. Like everything else they did, from chariot racing on the beach to wild blue body painting, they bitched with verve and their own peculiar style. Just listen for a moment.

"Deirdru!" someone snaps. "Either tune that thing or hang it up!"

(The above, you understand, being a loose translation of what scholars call Q-Celtic.)

"This harp is in perfect tune," Deirdru insists, as she twangs off key, giving new meaning to the word harpie. "Besides. Even Mabon Ap Modron would have a hard time keeping an instrument in tune in this damp."

Here she casts a speaking look at Fand.

"You call this delicate hint of moisture—designed to preserve your rapidly deteriorating complexion—damp! Well, if you want to look your age, dear, I'm sure one of your sisters would be happy to call up the siroccos."

"We all know the problem isn't the air, it's the ear." Boann jumps in to escalate the conflict. "You either have it or you don't. And it's no secret, Deirdru, that the great druid Cathbad laid upon your father a *geis* of danger and destruction if he should so much as open his mouth to sing another note, and as for your mother—"

Now all four sisters are on their feet.

"Is it our lineage you're impugning then?"

"Now, ladies." Liban has an aggressive habit of attempting to soothe people just when they're fully roused for a good fight. "I'm sure we're all a little on edge, it being *that* time of the moon. I'm going to make us all some of my delicious Dragon Slough tea—"

There follows a collective gagging.

"No offense intended," Etain lies shamelessly. "But I'd rather go milk the billy goat."

They can be wonderfully crude, my mothers.

"It did help my cramps last time," puts in my tender womb mother Grainne, seeing the wounded look on Liban's face.

But by this time it's too late to placate anyone. Boann has gotten her drum and something perhaps best described as Q-Celtic rap is about to begin. Anticipating Boann, Etain is already sauntering center stage, rapping as she goes:

> Well, my name is Etain
> and I sprang from the breeze.
> My daddy met my mama
> in the sacred oak trees.

As Etain takes a breath, Boann jumps in.

You're hot air for sure,
there's no denying.
The Dagda spread his cheeks,
and Etain went flying.

Now Etain is back, on a roll.

Well, I'd rather be a fart
from the good god's ass
than a half-assed witch
without any class.

So don't you dis my lineage
or I'll tell you 'bout yours.
When your daddy met your mama
she was down on all fours.

Boann doesn't miss a beat.

All four feet of Macha the Great Mare.
When a goddess is your mama
you got class to spare.
And if you call me a bitch, girl,
I'll bite your behind.
Takes one to know one.
We're all the same kind.

This could go on all night: brag capping brag, insult rivaling insult. Doing
the dozens was my mothers' favorite martial art. All Celts, left to their own
devices—that is, without Roman legions massing on them—preferred single
combat. To this form, lengthy, verbal challenge was essential, a fine-honed
wit and quick tongue as important as any other weapons. So my mothers
kept in practice. When they'd exhausted their store of words, they'd let it rip:
air masses would collide, lightning split the sky, winds tear and tumble like
huge kittens play-fighting. Finally rain or sleet or whatever was in season would
come sluicing down.

The next day we'd all go down to the shore to watch the storm-whipped
waves crash on the rocks, sending up spray shot with rainbows. If it was
warm enough, we'd strip, my mothers bleeding richly and freely, often using

their blood for ritual finger-painting on flat stones. All quarrels would be temporarily forgotten—if not forgiven. They didn't believe in forgiveness, my mothers. I think they feared it would blunt the edges they liked to keep sharp, blur the shapes of personalities they preferred to keep distinct—even if it meant they chafed. But if they held onto ancient enmities, no one ever loved her enemies with such fierce devotion as my mothers.

Life on Tir na mBan was not all storms. (Though I later learned that the erratic weather patterns surrounding our island had attracted the attention of druids, who advised voyagers to give it a wide berth.) My womb mother Grainne—the youngest of the eight and the shyest—had the power to coax the sun. Do you remember your mother bending over your baby self? Did you think all warmth and light began in her? Imagine my mother, standing on a rock, overlooking a lackluster sea, shrouded in one of Fand's lingering fogs—let's call it Walrus with a Toothache. She is wearing a green tunic gathered at the waist with a gold cord; a gold torque circles her neck; and her hair, a cloud of gold, floats around her head, lifted on the eddies of air she stirs with her body's heat.

I am a small child—maybe three or four years old—crouching nearby, playing with smooth, cold stones that are beaded with moisture. My heavy cloak is heavier with damp.

Now see my mother lift her arms. She is making a cup. She is a light-bearing chalice. Her radiance spreads out in ripples. Feel that heat touch your skin; feel it enfold you as it enfolds me. I close my eyes. The world swims with hot gold. When I open my eyes again, the fog is gone, the sea leaps with light, and my mother is so bright I can't look at her. But I know she's there, all around me. And there is nowhere I can go in the whole world that she is not.

Some of you may have noticed that my mothers' names belong to Celtic goddesses, *Bean Sidhe*, hero women. Whether they were those mythic figures or were merely named for them, even I don't know. Reincarnation makes everything so complicated, don't you find? I do know that old female archetypes never die; they just retire to the Shining Isles, as the Celts well knew, and as I know better than anyone.

There was some controversy among my mothers over what to name me. There is a Celtic custom of giving a newborn a childhood protective name. If the fairies or the *Sidhe* knew the child's true name, they might spirit her away. Some of my mothers wanted a childhood name for me, my womb mother Grainne among them. Looking back, I can see that tall, blonde Grainne was more Celtic than the other mothers. They were smaller and darker and looked like the queens of earth they were reputed to be: remnants of the old people who were native to the Holy Isles long before the Celts came and more or less conquered.

"But we don't have to worry that anyone will steal our babe, Grainne," Fand insisted. "Don't you understand? For all intents and purposes, we *are* the *Bean Sidhe!*"

Though no one ever admitted any such thing, it occurred to me later that my womb mother herself might have been a stolen child. I never knew much about any of my mothers' lives before they came to Tir na mBan. Oh, they told stories, lots of stories—with no concern for consistency whatsoever.

"But it's traditional, Fand," argued Liban. "It can't do any harm."

"Let's give her a child's name now," suggested Boann, "and let her true name come to her when she's ready for it."

"Make it a powerful name of protection," urged Grainne.

Fand took a deep breath, as if absorbing all the air so that no one else could use it. Then she spread her arms in that flashy liturgical way of hers and pronounced:

"She shall be called Bride's Flame!"

With that, she expelled all her breath and fixed each one with a glare, daring anyone to dispute her poetic inspiration, her prerogative as prime namer.

So it was that I came under the protection of Bride, also called Brigid, mother and/or daughter of the Dagda, goddess of smithcraft, poetry, and healing, who survived the coming of Christianity by turning into a saint—(I told you, they just won't quit, those old girls)—and not just any saint. According to lore, Bride was the foster mother of Christ, which makes him—don't you see?—my foster brother.

In my lifetimes, I have been called by many names. Or, you might say, certain names have called me. More than one of those names begins with the letter you know as M, a compelling shape in Latin script, echoing the shape of breasts, mountain peaks, sea swells, the wings of birds spread in flight. And if you take the Latin letter B and tip it on its side, you see that shape repeated. But it was many years before I learned any form of writing or inscription. Raised in the oral tradition as I was, I'm still not convinced that the written word is any improvement over the spoken. After all, talk never killed a tree.

Meanwhile, despite Fand's authoritative naming of me, my womb mother called me Little Bright One, and the others soon fell into the habit. And that is how I knew myself in my earliest years.

2

WIST YE NOT?

What amazes me about the time my foster brother stayed behind in Jerusalem playing child prodigy at the Temple is not his nerve or precocious wit, but the fact that nobody missed him till they'd gone a day's journey. Cosmic twins separated before birth, we grew up so differently. Compared to me, he lived among throngs. Also the child-parent ratio was different. Her perpetual virginity notwithstanding, Mary did have more than one child. I had more than one mother. He had a whole country to lose himself in. I had one small island. So my determination to give my mothers the slip and be about my own business required more ingenuity. Oh, I know, I know. He wasn't just being a bratty, worrisome kid. *He* was about his *father's* business—and he didn't mean Joseph's. "Wist ye not,"—I love that word wist; that's why I'm using the King James version—"Wist ye not," he said to his dazed, uncomprehending parents, "that I must be about my Father's business?"

It wouldn't have occurred to me to go about my father's business. He seemed to have matters well in hand. The tides went in and out on schedule, and he often left gifts of whelks among the rocks. Though I had never seen him in the way you understand seeing, he was not invisible in that annoying, omniscient way of some gods I could mention. We were surrounded by his kingdom, Tir fo Thuinn, Land under the Wave. He was no less than Manannán Mac Lir, god of the sea.

On this point, at least, my mothers were agreed. They loved, of an evening before the peat fire, to narrate my conception. The details varied considerably, depending on whose turn it was to tell the tale. There were always some interruptions and corrections, but, in general, poetic license was granted. A tale was "true" if it was well told.

Manannán Mac Lir was a god who lent himself to invention. He was a night prowler, visiting women in the dark "as the dew visits the earth, making it moist and fertile," so Fand liked to express it. And he was a shape shifter. Yahweh with his angel messengers and Zeus with his swan feathers had nothing on my father. See the bone-white gleam of that twelve-point rack of antlers? That's him. Feel a sudden gust of wind from a rush of wings? There he is again. And that huge white seal slipping from the rock into the sea? Now you see him. Now he's gone.

In some stories he came to Grainne—whom the others described with utter lack of envy as the loveliest of all—on the shore, taking shape from sea foam. Sometimes he appeared in the oak grove. In yet another story he entered our round hut, his greatness expanding the walls to the breadth of sky. Then he and my mother became the earth and the moon and the others, the circling constellations.

Only Grainne made no contribution to the vast store of conceptual lore. At the time I took this omission for granted. She'd had the glory of being my womb mother; let the others be the myth makers. Not until much later did I have cause to consider that her silence might have had another meaning.

Did I miss having a mortal father? Did I long for my immortal one to appear and stake some claim, whisk me away from the world of my mothers to some great adventure? In one sense, I did not miss him at all. As I've said, he surrounded me and any male animal potentially housed him. In another sense, I did not know what I was missing until much later. I had never seen a human male, much less sat in a male lap, breathing the scent of musky sweat or rubbing my cheek against stubble or beard.

Yet perhaps I intuited something. My mothers told a story of my father's magical bag made from the skin of a sacred crane. This bag contained odd wonders: the shears of the king of Caledonia; the King of Lochlainn's helmet; the bones of Assail's swine; Goibne's smithhook; Manannán's own shirt; and a strip from a great whale's back. When I was a little girl, I longed to see these treasures, and more than once I slipped out at night to wait for Manannán Mac Lir on the Western bluffs. (I was sure he would come from the West.) I have vague memories of being carried home half asleep in some mother's arms.

On the whole, I lived happily in the female hive and lacked for little, certainly not for attention. No one ever said to me: Get lost, kid. If I wore out the patience of one mother, there was always another to take up the slack. They all had something to teach me: herb lore, weaving, animal husbandry, bareback riding, elementary—and yes, elemental—magic. They all had the knack of making work indistinguishable from play. I roamed within reason, usually with some mother following in my wake to make sure I didn't fall into a bog or jump off a cliff. You see, I had ambitions to fly. I'd seen the birds plunge into the air. Why couldn't I?

(I'm going to leave that an open question. You may think the answer is obvious, but you haven't heard my whole story yet.)

Year by year, my mothers extended my circle of freedom, as a tree grows, in widening rings. They enforced these boundaries with binding spells—the original invisible fencing. By the time I was twelve, with fresh, green hormones beginning to rise like sap, I'd developed a positive ambition to get lost.

Who knows? Maybe my know-it-all witch mothers had it all figured out ahead of time. They must have known that if they made one thing forbidden, that would be the one thing I'd want. So there was one place I was not allowed to go. "Until the right time comes," they said with maddening maternal vagueness. "Then we will take you there ourselves." I had very early learned the knack of getting one mother to say yes, after another had already said no. The united front was not their strong suit. But on this prohibition, they were each and all immovable.

The forbidden place was the valley between Bride's Breasts, two mountains on the northern side of the island. As my own breasts began to rise from the once flat plain of my chest, I became obsessed with finding that hidden valley. On my own.

One Spring morning I woke early and went outside to the trench to relieve myself. I enjoyed the contrast of my steaming pee and the chilly dawn air. (Life is full of small, unmentionable pleasures.) As I squatted, I gazed toward the mountains. Milky light dripped down their eastern curves. Mist ringed one nipple. Far away, and so tiny I could barely see it, a bird floated down into the forbidden valley. My new breasts ached. I slipped a hand inside my tunic to cup one of the soft mountain shapes.

Growing pains, my mothers had explained the aching to me. How big would they get, I wondered? They already overflowed my palms. And when, *when* would I bleed? My mother's stock answer, "all in good time," was worse than no answer at all. I also did not appreciate their jokes about torches flaming at both ends. That's right, my pubic hair had grown in as bright as the hair on my head. I can only be thankful that they did not know the story of Moses and the Burning Bush or I never would have heard the end of it. Clearly they were guilty of great parental crimes. They did not take me seriously enough or regard with sufficient awe the volcanic changes in my body. Worst of all, they knew things that I did not, things that they could not or would not teach me. Today, I resolved as I shook the last drops from my fiery thicket, nothing would stop me. I was going to find that valley. I'd waited long enough.

Luck was with me. After we milked the goats and ate our stirabout, my mothers fanned out: two planting barley; another two pruning the orchard; two in the forge mending spears; and two more out on the moors gentling the wild horses. I took care to spend some time with each pair. That's the advantage of having so many mothers. By the time I'd made my rounds, each pair could assume I was with another. Before midday, I was on my way, the pockets of my tunic stuffed with flat, round oat cakes. By the middle of the afternoon, I had reached the edge of my known world.

The boundary place was mysterious enough itself: a grove, primarily of oak, that had been growing in the sheltered center of the island ever since this isolated bit of earth had surfaced from sea into air. Who knows how the acorns got there? The spoor of some prehistoric flying boar? Or perhaps a voyager had landed, traveling with a herd of swine. Our own pigs rooted about in this wood from *Beltaine* to *Samhain,* and I'd helped drive them back and forth. The day I ran away, the trees were not yet in full leaf, though some had baby leaves, perfectly formed, that looked almost comical in contrast to the massive limbs and trunks.

I decided to rest for a moment and eat some of my oat cakes. I'd need all my strength to cross the invisible border. It was very quiet in the oak wood. When I'd been here with my mothers, I'd noticed that our voices had sounded unnaturally loud, yet also flat, as if the wood absorbed any floating vibrations. Or as I'd put it then: "The trees are listening to us." Eavesdropping. Now the sound of my own chewing roared in my ears. I was glad of the burbling indiscretion of a small stream that meandered nearby. Politely offering part of my oat cake to the grove, I took a drink, then rose. I made my body as compact and unyielding as I could and marched straight to the edge of the grove. Twice the power of my mothers' spells hurled me backwards. The third time, I dropped onto my belly and slithered through like a snake. I stood and looked back. "Don't tell!" I whispered to the trees. Then I turned, my breasts pointing towards Bride's, and walked on.

Hers were more massive than I'd imagined. They loomed above me, endlessly pouring blue-white milk into the bowl of sky. Still a child in my perceptions, I thought I must be almost there. For hours I scrambled up a long, gradual slope through patches of heather and clumps of furze, leaping many brackish tarns, and still the mountains remained incomprehensibly remote. Nor was I prepared for the way they appeared to shrink from me when I did get close. I felt disoriented, and the path seemed much less obvious. When I turned and looked back over the way I'd come, I got a shock.

The oak grove had disappeared behind a swell of land. I could not see the orchard or our fields. I had never been so far from the sea in my life. The distance made it appear strangely silent and motionless. A cool wind sprang up, and a huge storm cloud moved inland and swallowed the sun. The cloud's shadow rushed over the way I'd come like a black wave. For a moment, I wavered, picturing myself running back home, back down to sea level, away from the naked slopes of Bride's breasts to the safety of the sixteen breasts that had given me suck. Then the sun found a break in the cloud. A cuckoo called, always a good omen. I scrambled up the ridge and then—Ah, look.

⚮

Did you know? Maybe you've seen this place in a vision or remember from some dream of your own. Between Bride's Breasts is a green valley. The light there is gold. People have spent lifetimes trying to paint that light.

They'd fill skies with it and place the earth-colored robes of saints before it. Or birds would fly there, delicate specks of darkness. Painters would take that gold and put it around his head and his mother's. But to me the light in the paintings looks too heavy and dead, gold cooled to metal, something you can take off and put on.

This light isn't like that, though I won't say it isn't heavy. Its heaviness is warmth and sweetness and languor. Living gold. It lives in that valley. You can taste this light. It's food, you see, and drink. You can feel it flow through the rivers of your arteries and veins. In the heart of the valley wells a pool. Nine hazelnut trees grow around it, bending their branches over it, dropping their wisdom-ripe nuts to the salmon swimming there. Five streams flow out from the pool into all the holy rivers of the world.

The more literal-minded among you may be wondering how this spring on this tiny (and, I bet you're thinking, fictitious) island in the Outer Hebrides (that's where you've decided it must be) could give rise to any rivers besides a creek or two on the island itself? Moreover, Celtic scholars have located the Well of Wisdom in Ireland. Listen, it's not my job to explain the mysteries. But I will say this much: Did it never occur to you that all the sacred rivers—the Ganges, the Euphrates, the Nile, you name it—might be connected? That there's a sisterhood under the earth's skin of holy waters and wells? It didn't? Well, it will have to do.

Now, see me walk down the soft, grassy slope. Imagine how it feels to my bare feet. When I reach the pool, I kneel beside it, just as you would. I have enough sense to hesitate to touch the water. I was raised by eight witches. I know strong magic when I see it. And I am, after all, in the heart of the forbidden place. So I just stare into the water for a long time. Stare and stare.

First the water seems black, as if it gave onto the bottom of the world—or led to another world. Then it turns into a mirror, reflecting the hazel branches and the golden light. I lean farther over, and there's my own face. The surface is smooth and unruffled. The image holds, and I can even see the hazel of my eyes. Maybe it's the strange light that seems to come from everywhere, from the air itself: the light has gotten into my hair. To compare it to fire is no longer hyperbole. My hair flames. Talk about halos! The wimpy piss-yellow lights around the saints pale by comparison. The fire around my head is the real thing.

And it is *hot.* Something like an electric shock begins in my crown and spreads through my body, concentrating most powerfully in my hands. It streams through my fingers as if each hand were the source of five holy rivers of fire. I don't know what to do with these hands—mine and more than mine. I gaze at them: the backs, the palms, and then the backs again. They burn, and though the burning is not pain, exactly, it's no less unbearable for that. Finally, I hold my hands out over the water. The pool's surface shivers and ripples in response. Then the blackness returns. I pull back my hands and use them for balance as I lean over the pool again, peering into its depths. I want to see to the bottom, but all at once, my face forms again, except—

Except that it isn't my face. Eyes, almost as black as the pool, meet mine. Eyes alive in a face I've never seen before. Yet, somehow, I know this face, strange as it is, as if it were my own. The image grows sharper. Now I can see black hair. My hands tingle as I grip my own bit of earth to keep from falling headlong into the world opening before me. I see a whole figure now, though the eyes still hold me. Whoever it might be is standing in a brown, thirsty-looking world of walls and what could be dwellings. (You must remember, my knowledge of architecture is limited to our hut.) The figure wears what I take for a tunic, its color a mixture of the dust that coats his feet and the glaring white sky of that world. All these details hover at the periphery. The eyes are the main event, dark and curious, looking out of a face that is lean but unlined. The skin is browner than any I've seen; the nose is narrower. The mouth almost smiles.

Suddenly, I know what it is that's different. This is not a grownup face. This body has no breasts! It's as flat as mine was a year ago. For the first time in my life, I am seeing another child. Tremendous excitement rises in me and, with it, recklessness. I am about to hurl myself into the pool, when the eyes, that have held mine until now, lose their focus.

The figure looks around in mild confusion. Then it shrugs, as if the coming and going of fiery visions (such as I must have appeared) were an intriguing but not uncommon event, not a matter for undue concern. Then, very casually, as if it were the most ordinary thing in the world, the figure does something extraordinary. Turning, so that I now see the profile, it hoists its garment and takes hold of some strange apparatus between its legs.

Then, behold: a golden arc, caught in the light of that other world, streams from that amazing appendage, darkening the dry ground like a tiny rain-storm.

Are there alarms going off in your head, shrieking: Blasphemy! Obscenity! For, of course, you've figured out that this is it: my first glimpse of Jesus of Nazareth. Well, did you think he came down from heaven to earth and held it for the duration? Listen, whether you think he was the only begotten son of god, or a great ethical teacher, or a failed Jewish revolutionary, while he was here, he ate and drank and shat and pissed with the best of us—and with the worst. Because we're all incarnate. That's what it means.

For me, this vision of my foster brother pissing in an alley was an epiphany, an encounter with my other self. I was not entirely ignorant of male anatomy.

I'd seen the penises of rams and goats, boars and stallions. But I'd never taken penises personally, so to speak. Here was a personal penis, attached to someone my own age—somehow I knew we were age mates. A person who had locked eyes with me across worlds. A young, male person. I did not even know the word "boy." But immediately I wanted to know all about such persons. No, I did not develop a sudden case of penis envy. Fascination, yes. Instantly, utterly. I couldn't wait to get my hands on one. On that one.

I can see it so clearly: the tender, oh so vulnerable male member, held in those strong brown hands, as he gives it a final shake. Shedding what shreds of caution remain, I plunge in my hand and make a grab for it.

I can still feel the shock of that water, my hand burning now with cold. I can still hear my own cry as the world in the magic well is lost to me. You know it is. You can see the dark water, the ripples made by my hand catching the light, which is now beginning to fade. You can feel my confusion. It was so real—not the mere watery reflection of some fancy. The veils of water, the veils between the worlds had parted for an instant.

My frustration is mounting to rage. I have been cosmically thwarted. I don't take things lying or even sitting down. I am on my feet, wading into the pool up to my thighs, ignoring the sharp, slippery stones. I bend over, reaching in with both arms, as if I can seize the vision with sheer force of will.

My hands do close on something. It is smooth and round on the top, but full of jagged holes on one side. Diverted by this encounter with something I can actually grasp, I lift the thing from the water into the air where it gleams eerie and unearthly as a daytime moon.

Have you guessed what it is? Wist ye not?

Even though I've never seen one before, I know with a shock of recognition: it's a skull. In my hands I am holding a human skull.

3

THE BLOOD OF THE MAIDEN

Yes, that's right, a skull: the brain case, the hard nutshell that protects the mysterious meat called mind. What was it doing there? I didn't have a clue. Regardless of what you may think of my mothers' eccentric rites and the unconventional education I was receiving at their hands, believe me, they had not schooled me in the niceties of headhunting—though maybe they were saving the best for last.

You probably know more about the cult of the head than I did. No? You don't believe that collecting the heads of your enemies gives you access to their powers? Then why do you still speak of heads of state, and heads of household? Head is still synonymous with power and control. When you want to procure someone's powers for your own purposes, what do you do? You hire a headhunter.

As for what the skull was doing in the well, if you wanted to send a messenger to the otherworld or to appease its powers, where would you look for entry? I know. You're more sophisticated than that. You know all about underground springs and the strata of the earth. More than that, you know that the underworld is just code for the collective unconscious. Wells and caves are archetypal symbols. Right. And you've never tossed a penny into a wishing well.

Okay, you admit, a penny. But a skull is not exactly loose change. True. Votive offerings may be the one commodity that's gotten cheaper. If you're still wondering whether my mothers hurled that head into the Well of Wisdom, I still can't answer you. But consider: with a population like ours and a birthrate of one child to eight women, human sacrifice was hardly practical. Though my mothers were dedicated to the warrior arts, I had never seen violence. My childhood was, in fact, sheltered beyond ancient or modern comprehension.

So here I was, hip deep in a magic pool with night approaching and a skull giving me the hairy eyeball. It was that sense of personal confrontation that prevented me from dropping the skull like a hot potato. The skull had presence. It gaped eyelessly and grinned with its remnant of tooth and jaw, as if I were the best joke to come along in quite some time. I decided against putting it back in the pool. If something unnerves you, it's best to keep an eye on it. Finally, I tucked the skull cozily into the crook of my left arm, then, using my right arm to balance, I made my way out of the pool, my feet and legs numb with cold.

Back on dry land, I placed the skull on a flat stone and took stock of my situation. The sun was setting. I was cold, wet, and hungry. I had eaten all my oat cakes, and, to top it all off, I had succeeded in my goal: I was alone; there was not a mother in sight, which, at the moment, I considered gross maternal negligence on their part. Moreover, I had just been seized with cramps. Thinking that the cold water might have brought them on, I peeled off my damp tunic and hung it on a hazel branch. Then, careful not to take my eyes off the skull, I backed up a few paces and squatted.

Just as I was about to loose a stream, I remembered my vision of the dark-eyed stranger and the elegant golden arc that had poured from the appendage. It must be so much fun to stand and aim instead of crouch and flood. Of course I had to try it for myself. And so I rose and grabbed hold of what I could—with predictable results. But as I gazed in disappointment at my hands and thighs, I made a great discovery: blood.

It was the blood, my woman's blood. I was bleeding! I felt a shock of joy as sudden, bracing, and pure as the cold water of the spring. Maybe you can't fathom the absoluteness of my elation, unmixed with fear, confusion, or dismay. As for shame, you may already have gathered I did not know the meaning of the word. Well, you've met my mothers. Their own blood was no onerous secret suffered as a curse. They had not taught me that the coming of the blood would mean the end of my freedom. Unlike other mothers, they probably never considered the reproductive repercussions of menarche. There are advantages to living on the Isle of Women. Among my mothers, blood was an openly declared mystery, an occasion for abandon and celebration. Now, I exulted, now I was initiate.

I might have missed my mothers more in this momentous moment, except that the whole world seemed to be celebrating with me. The sky turned from gold to brilliant red. The Well of Wisdom shone red in reflection. A flock of cranes circled the valley, the curve of their wings catching the color. Even the skull took on a pinkish glow and seemed to regard me with greater respect.

I walked, stiff-legged with the newness of it all, back to the edge of the pool. Kneeling, I rinsed the urine from my hands and legs. Then I sat down, knees drawn up against my breasts, to examine myself. As you may know from experience, it's hard to see much. But fingers can go where eyes can't. I thoroughly explored those petal-like folds, enjoying their smooth, watery feel. Then I found the hidden opening. Talk about springs and caverns and gateways between the worlds! My fingers slid deeper, and my mind filled with images of red, iridescent caves and strange, bright fish, swishing their tails, riding the red currents.

When I resurfaced from the inner world, the red had drained from the sky, leaving it that nameless color—not silver, not blue, not purple—that lingers an instant before sheer night. Stars came out to keep me company, and the skull glimmered faintly.

On impulse I rose and approached the skull. Crouching before it, I dipped my fingers into my blood and began to draw swirling patterns on the skull's crown. I don't know what prompted me or why I heeded the urge. I can only tell you that it was a deeply satisfying act. So absorbed was I in this task that I did not notice when approaching light chased away a portion of the night, except to take pleasure in a clearer view of my handiwork: mostly spirals and groupings of circles. (Let me tell you, in case you've never tried it: forefinger and menstrual blood are a crude medium.) Still, I admired the look of blood on bone. Then the light leapt and flickered in response to a gust of wind. I started and looked up.

Beyond the skull I saw a grey robe, stopping just above bare feet, the most beautiful feet I had ever seen, surely the feet of a goddess. Hardly daring to breathe, I lifted my gaze and a flash of fiery beauty almost blinded me. Imagine if lightning walked the earth and took a form. That's what I saw in the split second before I shielded my eyes. When I summoned the courage to look again, the robe was the same, but the feet were gnarled and knobby. A bent hooded figure stood before me, holding a torch in one hand and a walking stick in the other. I could not see the face, but I knew absolutely: this was not one of my mothers. It occurred to me that it might be the spirit of whoever once inhabited the skull, wrathful at the liberties I'd taken. Patting the skull on the head, so to speak—the way you might say "nice doggy" to a Doberman—I rose to face whatever face or facelessness the hood concealed.

What I saw was almost as much a revelation as the vision in the pool. If the person I'd glimpsed across the worlds was younger than anyone I'd ever seen, the one standing before me was infinitely older—though at that time I had no concept for age any more than I did for boy. My mothers, as you will have gathered, were not menopausal. Though I know now that they may have ranged in age some twenty years, then they were all old to me. I had never given much thought to anyone's age or aging but my own. I did not think "old" when I saw this face, but I was fascinated by the intricacy of the thousands of tiny lines, by the sheerness of the flesh that barely concealed the bone. (At the moment, I was all too aware of the bone beneath the mask of face.) But here was no glaring emptiness like the skull's sockets. The eyes that met mine were as gold as the Salmon of Wisdom. In these eyes I saw again the living light of the Valley. That light had not disappeared with the sun but stored itself in these eyes, eyes as dangerous and promising as the sacred well.

A shiver ran through me as I guessed: This must be Bride, Bride herself taking form before me. Gods and goddesses are famous for shifting their shapes. They can be animals or trees, young or old, beautiful or ugly. It's a form of sport. And if you know a god when you see one, that's score one for you. If you don't, you not only miss that point, you miss *the* point: divinity is everywhere. Beware. Never scorn an old woman or a beggar. Listen carefully to what children tell you, and never hurt an animal.

I glanced from the goddess' face to her breasts. Her eyes may have matched the well of wisdom, but her breasts did not seem very mountainous. They were hardly visible beneath the loose, grey tunic. Still, appearances can be deceiving. That's their point. I looked back, wondering when or if she would say something. Then it struck me: she's waiting for me. It's my move.

"So," I said with a brave show of nonchalance, "are you the goddess of this place, or what?"

The response was a low laugh that sounded at first more like a growl. Then she said, quite distinctly, "They told me you were a precocious brat."

Brat? Me? But the way she said the word did not sound pejorative. I even detected a note of approval, which, I confess, I considered no more than my due.

"Who told you?" I ventured.

"Who else but your poor mothers, whose hairs are turning grey even as we speak. Did you give a thought to the grief you would cause them when you ran away this morning?"

Whoever she was, she seemed to know more about me than anyone, even a goddess, had a right to. Still, my conscience—something I'd been about as aware of as my liver—prickled uncomfortably.

"But they would not have let me come if I had told them," I pointed out. "Besides, Liban will make walnut rinse for the grey hairs. She and Fand and Deirdru already use it every dark of the moon."

"And do you know why they would not allow you to come here?"

"No. They would never say."

But I was beginning to wonder if maybe they were right. I wasn't sure I liked being alone in this valley with this goddess person before me and a bloody skull at my feet—never mind that it was merely my blood. Where *were* my mothers? Why hadn't they warned me properly? And look here: they'd gone and told this personage all about me and told me nothing about her. Her shining eyes were unsettling. Predators had glowing eyes. Suddenly I wondered again: How *did* that skull get into that well?

"And what have you found, now that you have defied your mothers and come here alone?"

I hesitated. I wanted to know more about the pool and the vision I'd seen, where it had come from, and why it had vanished. But I also didn't want to tell. Others had secrets from me. I needed a secret of my own. That vision was mine, and the person with the wondrous appendage, my secret, mine.

"I found a skull in the well." I indicated my find with a gesture.

"And you have honored it with your first blood," she observed. "It was well done. I must say, they have brought you up to have nice impulses." She said it as someone else might say nice manners. "Though clearly they haven't managed to curb your impulsiveness, which I'm afraid may land you in a lot of trouble one of these days."

Like it hadn't already?

"The skull," I said, getting back to the point. "How did it get there?"

"She has persistence, too," the personage observed, "which may help to balance the rashness. But then again it may not. Combined, rashness and persistence may become merely foolishness and obstinacy."

She seemed to be running down a checklist, making notes to herself. I was, in short, being weighed in the balance, and I didn't like it. Until now, I had never questioned my own utter perfection—nor had anyone else.

"But the skull," I persisted, proving her point. "The skull, did *you* put it there?"

"Direct." She spoke again to herself. "A refreshing quality but not always a wise policy. Listen, honey, rule number one: if you want to keep your head, don't lose it. And the second is like unto it: don't ask too many questions."

But I had rules of my own. Growing up with eight mothers, number one was: never listen to advice.

"Who in *Abred, Gwynfed,* and *Ceugant* are you?" I demanded, naming all the circles of existence. A sort of formal, Celtic way of saying: who the hell are you, anyway?

"Listen, Little Bright One, Bride's Flame." She knew my mothers' names for me. "Listen well, and I will tell who I am."

She thrust her torch into the ground and raised her arms, still holding the stick in her left hand. "I am the Cailleach," she began. I recognized at once the shift from ordinary speech to chant.

> I am the Cailleach.
> Mountains are made of me.
> Mine is the cauldron
> that heroes seek.
> No one is sovereign
> who shuns my kiss.
> I am the Old One.
> Some call me Hekate,
> some Kali Ma,
> some Black Annis,
> some the Blue Hag.

Blue for the night sky
wounded with stars.
Hag for the haggard moon
wakeful at dawn.
I drift down the darkness
In my silver boat.
I fill the seas
when I drain my cup.

Maiden, look well.
I am your mirror,
Your true other self,
ash to your flame
and earth to your flower.
Blessed be, blessed be
Blessed be your maiden blood.

"Anoint me," she commanded. "Anoint me as you did the skull."

For the first time in my life I felt shy, but it did not occur to me to refuse. So I bloodied my fingers again. First I made a sign on her forehead, three dots within a circle. Then, renewing the blood, I touched her cheek and lost my shyness in wonder. Her skin was so soft, softer than mine, as if time and the elements, working in those thousands of lines, had made her into finer stuff, just as beaten gold is finer than metal that has not been worked. I did not draw designs on those cheeks but gently smoothed in the blood so that the beauty of the designs already there showed more clearly. Just as I was putting on the final touches, I was startled nearly out of my skin by *bean sidhe* screeches resounding in the valley.

"The mothers have arrived," announced the Cailleach, unperturbed.

I looked around and saw the swiftly bobbing lights of their torches. Soon they had surrounded us: the Cailleach, the skull and me. And their shrieks gave way to a silence even more unsettling. My mothers were not quiet types. Usually they all talked at once. I would have expected loud, competitive up-braiding from them. Instead they just stared, but when I tried to catch anyone's eye, each one looked away from me—all except Grainne, who looked so stricken that I felt my first thoroughgoing pang of remorse. The Cailleach did not speak at once, but her eyes glowed, and her mouth twitched.

"So," the Old One spoke at last, "shall we begin by stating the obvious? She is here."

"Yes," said Fand. "And what do you intend to do about her? She's broken the one *geis* we laid upon her!"

"Now, Fand," Boann objected. "It wasn't exactly a full fledged *geis*. We didn't say anything about danger and destruction coming upon her and all that. It was more like a rule—"

"Whatever it was," put in Emer, "she broke it."

"And had us all in a tizzy," chimed in Dahut.

"Well, but we knew where she'd gone," Etaine pointed out.

"No we didn't!" Deirdru was heated. "With that one, you never know. That's why we went to the cliffs first!"

"I always said that was stupid," grumbled Boann.

"You know we had to," Grainne spoke up. "We knew she'd at least be safe here—"

Did they? I pricked up my ears. Then why the so-called rule?

"But she has run off to the cliffs before, and you know how dangerous they are—"

"And with that storm coming," broke in Liban, frowning at Boann. "We had quite a time heading off that storm, once we realized—"

"And it was going to be a doozy," Boann sighed wistfully. "I sort of hated sending it out to sea. What a waste of a good head wind."

"Well, what else could we do?" Liban was getting huffy. "With Little Bright One off on her own somewhere, exposed to the elements."

"I keep saying," Etaine was exasperated, "we *knew* where once we thought about it."

"It doesn't matter now." Fand cut in. "The point is whether you call it a *geis* or not, she broke it willfully. Knowingly. Damn it all, on *purpose*!"

"Well, of course she did!" Boann threw up her hands.

The sound of my mothers arguing was as soothing as the lullaby it had often been. And the outcome would be the same as ever: whatever I'd done, I'd get away with it. My mothers could never reach consensus about punishing me. Never.

"You will see if you look: the maiden was not mistaken in her timing." The Cailleach spoke quietly, but all dispute instantly ceased. She gestured towards my bloody thighs.

Then another cry rose from my mothers, a soft one, full of tenderness and reproach. As one being, they planted their torches and swarmed around me.

"Little Bright One!"

"Why didn't you tell us?"

"We would have taken you here!"

"In solemn procession."

"With drums and singing."

"And a bright red tunic!"

"And wreaths of flowers on your head."

"And mead to drink."

"Ah, Little Bright One. Our baby. A woman."

Then I understood. Of course. That was the "right time" they kept referring to: my first blood. They'd been saving the Valley between Bride's Breasts for my initiation. It was to be a surprise, a present, a revelation of mystery. And I'd jumped the starting line and raced here on my own. In effect, I'd eloped with myself, cheating them of the ceremony.

"I didn't know." I spoke for the first time, and two tears—one from each eye—overflowed and started down my cheeks. "When I ran away this morning, I didn't know that the blood would come today. I just wanted to do something that you wouldn't let me do. By myself. I'm sorry." I wasn't used to saying those two words. My tongue felt stiff and strange with speaking them. "I'm sorry I caused you grief." I borrowed the Cailleach's phrase.

"Grief!" There was a collective snort from my mothers. "Do you suppose she even knows the meaning of the word?"

"She'll learn," the Cailleach stated flatly. "Oh, yes, she'll learn." Her eyes swept the circle of Mothers. "It's time she came to me, you know."

"Oh, surely not yet!" gasped Grainne.

"She's only twelve and a half," added Liban.

"She has her blood," countered the Cailleach.

"Wait a minute," I interrupted. "Do you mean—"

"Hush!" said the Cailleach and all the Mothers together.

"Haven't you taught her all you can?" The Cailleach put it to them.

"Not really," said Boann. "Her aim with the *laigen* needs work. We haven't even started her on chariot driving. And she's only now developing the upper body strength she needs for serious work in the forge."

"You are assuming that she is going to become one of you."

There was a shocked silence that I shared. My craving for adventure notwithstanding, I had never imagined being anything other than a warrior-witch like my mothers. What else was there?

"Do you know something you're not telling us?" demanded Fand.

"I do not," said the Cailleach, "but it may be that the young one does, though she may not know what she knows."

What? What did I know? Even as I asked myself I knew what: my vision in the pool. And if I hadn't run away—upsetting everyone and losing out on a new red party tunic—I never would have seen the vision. I did not know how I was going to do it or what it would mean, but someday, somehow, somewhere I was going to find the Appended One. I had a destination now. A destiny.

"But we're not ready to let her go!" cried Grainne.

"Look here. It's just too sudden." Boann was blunt.

"Very well," said the Cailleach after a moment. "We will wait till *Samhain* when she has lived thirteen years. That gives you the bright half of the year to teach her all you may. Consider well what she may need to know, and give her your manifold gifts. Meanwhile, it may come to me what lessons I must prepare for her. Is it agreed among us, then? Among the Nine Witches of Tir na mBan?"

You might need to be a Celt to know the jolt I felt to hear the Cailleach call herself and my Mothers the Nine Witches. Nine is the number of numbers, the sacred three times three. I did not simply learn to count like any child with fingers and attentive parents, I learned the meanings of numbers, the stories connected with them. I had always considered myself all the more special, because I brought—so I thought—the human population of the island to nine. I brought my mothers' number to mystical completion. Now it struck me with the force of a blow: There were already nine, had always been nine. I made ten, a dangerous, dubious number: an overflowing, a new beginning, a change, change of pattern, change of fortune.

"We are agreed. We are agreed." My mothers' voices circled around me, and I felt dazed and dizzy.

"Now," resumed the Cailleach. "We are all here. And the maiden bleeds for the first time in the dark moon of Shoots-Show. Little Bright One, Bride's Flame. Do homage to your mothers as you have done to me."

Can you see us? We stand beside the Well of Wisdom between Bride's Breasts, their massive blackness edged with stars. My mothers surround me, their faces lit by torchlight. They are so well known to me. These are the faces that crowded over my cradle, vying for a turn to rock me and nurse me. Yet tonight they are also unknown, new, strange. For the first time I am separate, not just their child. I am a woman bleeding as they are bleeding. One of them, but no longer theirs. The Cailleach has retreated into the circle. I am left alone in the center with the painted skull. I am standing naked in the midst of the women who made me.

And I am beautiful.

I begin with Fand, anointing her forehead and cheeks, and make my way slowly from mother to mother. Their tears mix with my blood, and we are all wordless. The last one, standing next to the Cailleach, is my womb mother, Grainne. As I touch her face it blurs, and I can't see anymore. Then in one dark rush, the mothers wash over me, and I am fully enclosed in a warm, dark woman place that tastes of tears and smells of blood, as one more time I am cradled and rocked.

4

WHAT'S IN A NAME?

In many times and places, there's been no such thing as adolescence. The change from child to adult is as sudden as the turning of day to night at the equator. Blaze then blackness. The transition is sudden, dramatic, maybe even violent. I thought it would be that way for me when my blood came. And hadn't I looked a skull straight in the eye? Hadn't I traced the map of time in the Cailleach's face?

In the far North, where I lived, twilight lingers during the bright half of the year. There are hours and hours when it is neither day nor night. Those last months with my mothers, I lived in a kind of twilight, suspended between my child self and whatever was to come, enduring the awkwardness and indignity of metamorphosis in process. No wonder caterpillars spin a cocoon. You need a little privacy. You certainly don't want the running commentary of eight mothers.

In fact, they were as confused as I was. One day they would schedule activities to the minute, even going so far as to announce change of classes with a blast on the bagpipes. Another day they'd turn me loose with my pockets full of oatcakes and send me off to wander. I suspected them of wanting to get rid of me the better to kibitz about my fate. Or maybe they just wanted a break. I certainly did. I got tired of their teaching, especially since they couldn't—or wouldn't—tell me anything I really wanted to know.

"The people with the appendages, you know, like the stallions and the stags, where are they?" I asked not long after my excursion to the Well.

"People with *appendages*!" My mothers looked at each other and tittered. Really! Who were the adolescents? "They're all over the place. Why, most of the world is theirs!"

"But why don't they come here?"

"We have been wondering that ourselves," my mothers sighed and looked broody.

"But why don't you know?"

"We don't know everything, Little Bright One. Not quite everything."

"You don't even know my name," I informed them. "I am *not* Little Bright One anymore!"

On my roaming days, I searched all of Tir na mBan for a new name, and as much of the sea and sky as I could scan from atop one or the other of Bride's breasts. (Would you believe? The open rock faces on the peaks were

28

indeed a brownish pink, especially at sunset.) I was constantly on the alert for a sign or omen. I greeted every animal or bird that crossed my path as a potential messenger. You may wonder why I did not go to the Well of Wisdom again. I can only say that an uncharacteristic restraint, even shyness, inhibited me. Perhaps the Cailleach put a warding spell on the place to keep me at a distance until it was time for me to go to her.

I did not find my name on my ramblings, but I gained an intimate knowledge of Tir na mBan, learning every curve and fold, every cliff and hidden cove. I did not know then how soon I would leave or for how long or how far away I would go from my mother island. But I carried the Shining Isle of Tir na mBan in my body: the blood, sinew, and bone the island had fed and formed. In a sense, I was Tir na mBan. No matter where in the world I went, I could always re-member.

∽

Not all changes and exchanges between my mothers and me were frustrating. Some I welcomed. Now that I had my woman's blood, my mothers had spiced their repertoire with tales of Queen Maeve of Connacht. These stories were my mothers' idea of sex education, and I, for one, think every pubescent girl ought to have a chance to hear them.

(I know I haven't helped much with pronunciation. But this name, as you will see, is important. So remember this: Maeve rhymes with brave, as in Maeve the Brave. And Maeve rhymes with a host of other wonderful words like wave and cave. Got that?)

Queen Maeve was always lavish with "the friendship of her upper thighs." Her requirements in a husband were that he be a generous man, without jealousy or fear. If he were not, she would outshine him in liberality and courage. And jealousy would never do, for, as Maeve declared, "I have never been without one man in the shadow of another." King Ailill fit the bill, and Maeve had it all—except for the Brown Bull of Cuailnge; we'll get to that part later. Chief among her lovers was the great hero Fergus Mac Roth. According to the lore, it took seven women to satisfy Fergus, unless he were with Maeve. As for Maeve, she would go with thirty men a day or go with Fergus once.

Needless to say these statistics fascinated me.

Excuse me a moment, all of you who just want me to get on with the story, while I speak with the fulminating scholars. You will argue that my mothers can't have known the Tales of the Red Branch, starring Maeve of Connacht, Cuchulain, et al. The stories are assumed to date from the 4th and 5th century C.E., recounting events that may—or may not—have taken place in my time. They were not written down until the first millenium when some randy Irish monks decided they really ought to be preserved. For the sake of posterity, you understand. Picture them bending over their manuscripts in their cold, damp scriptoriums, warming themselves with Maeve's exploits. (Thirty men a day! Begorra!)

I suppose you think time runs in a straight line, even though nothing else in the world around you does any such thing. But if you must think in linear terms, think along the lines of a tree. Say the branches are the tales that got written down, and the trunk is some event that you might call the historical basis for the stories. Now don't forget the roots, my dears, as vast and intricate a complex as the branches, as essential to the life of the tree as the new light-drinking leaves, though they are hidden from human sight under the ground. The stories of Maeve have such roots, like the stories of Macha, the great mare goddess, and the shape-shifting Mórrígán with her harsh cry and her raven wings.

Note the proliferation of M's—a sure sign of an ancient female force.

Because that's what Maeve is: a female force, and she cannot be pinned down or tidily contained. She is called The Intoxicated One Who Intoxicates. Her name means mead. She is Maeve of Connacht and Maeve of Leinster, kingmaker, whose husbands numbered nine. She is Mab, Queen of Faery. She is old as the hills where she lives still. You can't kill a female force. You can drive her underground, but those roots are alive, and she'll rise again in a new form. Especially if she's one of the M's. Just try to flatten the swells of the sea or to tamp down the Grand Tetons.

My mothers had been telling me these tales, and they'd taken root in my imagination. You will probably say that these stories lodged in my subconscious and caused what happened next. Fine. Interpretation is your job. I'm just the storyteller. All right, listen.

It was the eve of the full moon (the eve of anything being the magic time). Now that I had begun to bleed with my mothers, usually at the dark of the moon, I also experienced the other side of the hormonal rollercoaster ride: ovulation. Note the O for the microscopic moon drifting down the fallopian rivers, mirroring the full moon in the sky, the river of moonlight on the sea. O for the opening of the vaginal folds. O for orgasm, which I did not yet know a thing about. I only knew that my body was flooded with the strangest mixture of languor and restlessness.

My mothers did not say much to me directly that first cycle. But for the first time in my life, I was not left at the hut with whichever mother had drawn the short straw. They took me with them to the magic orchard, with its impossible heady scent of blossom and fruit, where the flowers opened to moon as well as sunlight, and the bees gathered nectar at midnight. There I entered the ecstatic dance.

We danced and danced for hours and hours, one mother or another drumming. We danced from moonrise—the moon appearing huge and hazy over the mysterious lands to the East—till the moon was high and small in the sky and somehow harder looking, like a smooth white pebble you could grip in the palm of your hand. We danced and danced, and then a silence fell. I could hear the waves on the beach and the drunken buzzing of the lunatic bees in the apple blossoms. I looked around the circle at the mothers who seemed wrapped in the silence. Or should I say rapt? Though I could see their faces, they were somehow obscured, as if they'd taken the moonlight as a veil.

Did you ever sneak out of bed and glimpse your mother in the arms of a lover (never mind if it was only your father)? Or maybe she was just sitting alone and staring at nothing. In either case, her apartness from you, her separate, secret existence was awesome, aweful. It was like that for me in that moment: my mothers were lovely and remote, belonging not to me, but to themselves. By ones and sometimes twos, they slipped into the tangled shadows of the orchard and disappeared. Grainne was the last to go. She looked at me and almost looked like the mother I knew. Then the night wind blew away the tatters of her baffled tenderness, and her face was bright and empty as the moon's. Suddenly, she too was gone.

There I was, left to my own devices. You might imagine that I'd be pleased, but in fact I did not know what to do with myself. I did not even know what I was feeling, though now I'd say it was my first taste of loneliness. I wanted an Other, not a mother but an Other. I wanted the Appended One. All the mystery and beauty surrounding me, the tantalizing secret of my own destiny would remain impenetrable—or unpenetrated—without him. He was the missing piece of the puzzle. I began to walk inland toward the Valley between Bride's Breasts, never mind it would take me the rest of the night to get there. I didn't have a clue where else to look, although I sensed, even then, that magic seldom repeats itself—which is why there has been no so-called scientific proof of its existence.

Maybe it was the moonlight or the midnight hour—one of the times doorways open between the worlds—but very soon I was lost among hills I did not recognize. For a time, I tried to force the strange landscape to conform to some familiar place, but when I came upon a lake, I had to give it up. There is no lake on Tir na mBan—pools, springs, streams, yes, but no inland body of water this size, with several branches disappearing among the hills. I'd hardly registered this shock when the lake shrank to a puddle.

Straddling it were a pair of muscular legs, swirling with woad up to full thighs and beyond to belly, breasts, and a broad face, with a snub nose. The woad couldn't completely hide the freckles. And the lime—twisting the hair into fantastical spikes that would put a punk rocker or the statue of liberty to shame—could not hide the fierce orange of the hair. Whoever she was, she wore nothing but a gold torque and a belt that held her sword. I spied her *laigen* and shield on the ground beside her. She was much too substantial to dismiss as a trick of moonlight, but in case you were inclined to, let me tell you the night was now dissolving into chilly, pre-dawn grey.

"There," said Herself, giving her bush—as orange as mine!—a shake and stepping aside to survey her puddle with pride. "That's better. Fergus is impatient, but I always say: Never go into full battle with a full bladder. It's so distracting, not to mention you might piss yourself in front of the enemy. And this will be a famous place of a famous battle, because I'm gonna whip that Little Hound Dog son-of-a-bitch Cuchulain's ass once and for all, so I am. And to mark this place, my stream, noble and mighty, will become a great lake with many channels. And from this time forward in all the worlds this place will be called 'Queen-Maeve-takes-a-leak.'"

"Queen Maeve of Connacht!" I gasped, recognizing one of Boann's stories come to life.

She turned to regard me, without a trace of the embarrassment most people would feel if taken by surprise while pissing and talking to themselves.

"The same," she said, obviously pleased with her identity. She picked up her spear and stood at ease, one hip thrust out. "And who might you be? No!" She held up a hand before I could speak. "Don't tell me you've come with another of those ridiculous, repetitive foretellings of doom." She rolled up her eyes. "'Red, red, I see very red!'" Maeve intoned in a high-pitched whine, her imitation, I gathered, of Fedelm the prophetess. "'Honey,' I finally said to her, 'Go get your eyes checked.' It's all propaganda." She waved it away. "But you, now! You're a fine, strapping young colleen. You don't want to end up some whey-faced, mealy-mouthed prophetess."

I shook my head vehemently.

"Then state your name, lineage, and business."

"I am the only daughter of the warrior witches of Tir na mBan. My father is Manannán Mac Lir. I don't know what I'm doing here, and—er—I'm between names at the moment." I frowned trying to think if I'd answered all the questions.

"The warrior witches of Tir na mBan!" Her eyes narrowed. "Aren't those the bitches that trained that Little Hound Dog?"

"Oh, no," I assured her, though undoubtedly my mothers would have loved to get their hands on a hero like Cuchulain. "That was Scathach and her daughter."

"Well, then, these mothers of yours, whose side are they on?"

"Oh, yours, of course!" I said hastily. They'd never said so explicitly, but that seemed to be the bias of their narratives. "They want you to win the Brown Bull."

At the mention of the Brown her eyes lost their focus, and I sensed she was not seeing me anymore.

"The Brown, the Brown. I must have the Brown. There are those who don't understand. They think this is just another cattle war, and I'm just a greedy, bloodthirsty bitch. Who knows what the bards will sing in times to come or how people will misunderstand my story? But you—" She fixed her eyes on me again. "Hear me now and understand. The White Horned bull was mine, born into my own herds. And when it left my herds to join Ailill's—in pursuit of a certain young heifer, I'll vow—people said it was because the White Horned did not want to be ruled by a woman! Now, do you think I can let a slur like that stand? My sovereignty is at stake." Queen Maeve stepped closer to me. "Your sovereignty is at stake and the sovereignty of every woman. There's only one way to restore the balance between Ailill and me, between all women and men. There's only one bull of worth equal to the White Horned Bull of Connacht."

"The Brown Bull of Cuailgne!" I cried, stirred by her speech.

"Exactly!" She beamed at me. "Now what was it you came to tell me? Have your mothers foreseen my victory?"

I was uncharacteristically speechless. In all likelihood the Ulstermen, temporarily recovered from the curse of Macha (five nights and four days of labor contractions), were massing against Maeve even now. And I didn't know if she'd consider it *her* victory when the two bulls fought to the death. Think about it: would you want to tell someone the end of the story when she was in the middle? I didn't, especially not after what she'd said about prophetesses.

"Speak up, girl!"

"Actually," I said, "I started out on Tir na mBan seeking a vision of the Appended One."

"The Appended One?" she puzzled.

"I wanted to see one of the people who piss standing up," I explained. "We don't have them on Tir na mBan."

"Oh!" She laughed a deep, throaty laugh. "A man, you mean! One of the ones with the cock-a-doodle-doos, the joy sticks, the magic wands."

It occurred to me that I had come to a veritable fount of information.

"Is it true," I ventured, "that you go with thirty men a day or go with Fergus once?"

"Thirty men a day!" Her breasts and belly shook with laughter. With the motion the patterns of woad became positively psychedelic. "Is that how my fame is sung? Well, I won't deny it, then."

"What is it like, to go with a man?"

"Colleen," she said, "I don't need prophecy to know that you're not long for Tir na mBan. What's it like? Think of having a flame-tipped spear rushing inside you. No, no, dear, it doesn't hurt. I don't mean that. It's flash after flash of lightning and the dark, weighty roll of thunder. Sparks fly upward. Stars burst in your breasts. The darkness blazes. And if it's really good, the fire comes right up out through the top of your head. It beats a cattle war all hollow. Believe me, I'd rather fuck than fight any day. But you can't have great sex without sovereignty. Never forget that!"

"Maeve? Maeve!" Just then a voice called. A dark sounding voice with a timbre I'd never heard. It gave me goose flesh. "Hurry up. The hosts are massing. You said you only had to pee."

"That's Ailill. I've got a battle to fight. Wish me luck." She turned away.

"Let me go with you!" I called. "My mothers haven't trained any male heroes lately, but they've raised me to be a hero."

On the brink of her famous battle, Queen Maeve of Connacht turned back for a moment.

"I thank you for that, colleen, but you're not armed and—" She broke off and a strange look came over her face. Under the woad she looked a little green. "A great warrior queen will spring from your line, whose fame will be equal only to my own." Then she shook herself like a dog who's just come out of the water. "I hate it when I have second sightings. I'm a warrior, not a prophetess. No, don't tell me what I said. I don't want to know. Just tell me your name again before you return to Tir na mBan."

"I've outgrown my childhood name, and I haven't found a new one yet."

"Ah," she cried. "Then it will be my pleasure to name you for myself. I can tell you are a colleen after my own heart, more like to me than my own daughter Findbhair. So I bestow on you the brave name of Maeve until such time as another name shall claim you."

And she re-traced her steps and gave me a loud smacking kiss on both cheeks, and then on the mouth.

"Oh, Queen Maeve, how can I thank you?"

"Keep fighting for our sovereignty. Without it, there can be no balance between men and women. Without balance, no blessings, only battles."

"I will be a warrior then, like you."

"One small disclaimer, honey. Bearing my name doesn't make you me any more than wearing my torque would. You'll make the name your own. No, I don't know your fate beyond whatever it was I just told you. But I'll wager it will make a tale worth telling. Farewell then, Maeve of Tir na mBan, daughter of the Shining Isles."

With that Queen Maeve of Connacht walked off towards the rise, growing larger with each step until the wild, limed hair, and massive woad-blue limbs took up the whole sky. Then she disappeared, and I was alone again, watching the morning mist rise from Lake Queen-Maeve-Takes-a-Leak.

"Little Bright One. Little Bright One." I recognized my mothers' voices, though I could not see them, the mist had grown so thick.

"My name." I moved my lips and sounded my voice with effort. "My name is Maeve."

As soon as I said the word, I found myself looking up into the anxious faces of my mothers. Beyond them, I saw the fruit-laden, blossoming branches of the orchard.

"What did you say?"

For a moment I could not remember anything.

"What's that blue smudge on your cheek?" Fand fingered it. "It looks like woad."

Then it all came back. "My name is Maeve," I told them again. "Queen Maeve of Connacht herself has named me."

Maeve. Maeve is my name. How do you say it? Only remember: it rhymes with wave. It rhymes with cave. It rhymes with brave.

5

THE FIRE OF THE STARS

Curiously, the coming of my name** affected my mothers more than the advent of my menarche had. I was no longer their Little Bright One but a brazen young hussy named Maeve after a hot-headed, not to mention hot-to-trot, warrior queen. They must have sensed I would soon be completely beyond control. I suppose they viewed it as their responsibility to see to it that I could conduct a cattle war of my own should the need arise. So they set about getting in their last licks, and maternal indulgence became a thing of the past. From dawn to dusk it was drill, drill, drill.

"Hep, two, three, four! Haul that lazy carcass off the heather!" Imagine a sergeant-private ratio of eight to one. I didn't stand a chance. "What do you think this is? A beauty spa? It's time for target practice."

Target practice meant spear casting. My mothers took turns providing a moving target, carefully shielding themselves, of course. None of the exercises was new to me, but before, each was just another game that I could quit when I was bored or tired. Now I constantly had to stretch the limits of my endurance. When I had been Little Bright One, I could do no wrong. All my efforts had met with a stream of praise from a seemingly endless source. Now my mothers hurled insults with more vigor than I hurled the *laigen*.

"Come on, Maeve! A pig that's been turning on the spit all day has more life in its limbs than that!"

"Och, lass! You bring shame on your mothers' heads. For who could believe that the daughter of Manannán Mac Lir would have such lousy aim!"

"I swear, girl, if I didn't know better, I'd think you were turtle spawn."

Their taunts had the desired effect. I was furious, and I learned to direct that fury through my arms into a lightning strike. Not only did I become adept at hitting a moving target, I could also cast a spear with some degree of accuracy while standing in a careening battle chariot. Swordplay was even more complicated, involving not only good hand-eye coordination but an encounter with another intelligence. There's a great deal of thought involved in single combat, but the trick is to think with the whole body. The beginning swordswoman, like someone learning a language, is hindered by a tendency to translate. My mothers kept at it, pushing and pushing till the barrier between my mind and muscles broke down.

And I persisted, partly because my mothers gave me no choice, and partly because I wanted to be like Queen Maeve, despite her proviso that I might not necessarily become a warrior. She was an older woman who was not my mother, and I'd encountered her magically. Ergo, I hero-worshipped her. How could I not? And that intense identification prevented me from noticing that, though I became proficient in all of the warrior arts, I was not gifted. Which is another way of saying the practice of these arts gave me nothing back. No joy. No enjoyment.

The only exercises I really relished were the ones that involved my voice. My battle cries were not only blood-curdling, they curdled the goats' milk. What's more, the hens stopped laying. Soon I was not allowed to practice any more. I also excelled at the pre-combat verbal challenge and insult. I could go for an hour without stopping, while the mother I challenged stood snorting and puffing, trying to catch me pausing for breath so that she could jump in. These sessions were deeply satisfying to me, and I wonder if all mothers and adolescent daughters might not benefit from a ritual expression of aggression. We were all passionately angry during that time. But there was nothing cold or corrosive about this anger. It was fiery, the fire of the forge, of which Bride is also goddess. My mothers were sure enough testing my mettle.

Although the ground rules were clear, and no serious injuries were sustained, there were plenty of cuts, bruises, and sprains. Here perhaps is a crucial difference between my mothers' warrior tradition and others: they practiced the healing arts as well. If my days were spent in combat, my evenings passed in learning to clean and bandage wounds, make poultices and slings, mix salves and tonics. Except for words of instruction, there was little talk at night. We were all tired, especially me. Though I was young and resilient, I was always engaged in combat, while they took turns to fight me.

And so I also learned, during those evenings, the power of silence and touch in healing deep hurt. Words had become part of our arsenal. At night we dispensed with them and rubbed liniments into each other's sore muscles. Our hands remembered the bonds between us. As we tended each other, it was not uncommon for one or more of us to weep. No one needed to ask why. The tears were there to wash the wounds, visible and invisible, and to make the hard places soft again.

It was on such a night that I learned the purpose of the heat in my hands. I had more or less gotten used to its coming and going, accepting it as one more mysterious manifestation of puberty. Then, one evening, Fand was in a great deal of pain. Reeling from a blow from my sword, she'd fallen hard and landed on a sharp rock. Likely she'd cracked some ribs. Various ointments had been rubbed in as gently as possible, compresses had been applied, and everyone had a different opinion about which position would give her the most ease. Meanwhile, Fand was moaning and threatening to keep us awake all night.

The mothers were beginning a debate about the most effective sedative to brew for her, when I felt the fire pouring through my crown and roaring into my hands. They burned so hot I could hardly believe they didn't glow like the peat coals. I felt as though sparks, random and dangerous, were shooting into the room. Then, in a flash, it came to me: I needed to direct that fire. It wanted to go somewhere. It had a purpose.

I approached Fand, and the other mothers, instantly alert, moved aside. Silently, I placed both hands on Fand's rib cage. She gave a cry of surprise, then drew a deeper breath than she'd been able to take till then. Soon her breathing eased to a long, slow rhythm, and she rested somewhere between sleep and trance. As for me, eyes closed, I could see a river of brightness flowing into her, melting the hard crystals of pain, mending the bruised and broken place. As the fire found its rightful release, the agitation of excess energy turned to a sense of peace I'd never known before. All I had to do was remain open and allow this force to move through me. I held my hands still until the heat ebbed, and my hands cooled.

When I let go of Fand, I opened my eyes, feeling a little bewildered. Though I had never been more present, I also felt as though I had been very, very far away, past familiar boundaries, beyond the confines of myself. Yet here I was again, just me, nothing more. My mothers eyed me intently as they might a wild horse whose measure they were taking. Would they try to put a bridle on me? Or would they give it up and let me go. They seemed to be waiting for some sign from me: flared nostrils and a rearing on hind legs? Or a quieting that indicated they might approach. I did not know what to do or say.

"The pain's gone." Fand spoke at last.

I nodded. Then the edges of my vision got blurry. Everything looked as though it were underwater. I stood up and moved through the thick air, heavy-limbed. At last, I dropped onto my heather bed and plummeted into sleep.

When I woke again it was deep night, but my mothers were still awake. They sat in a circle around the fire, some leaning against each other, their cloaks pooling, the boundaries between them indistinct.

"Who opened her to the Fire of the Stars?" one of them asked.

"The Cailleach, maybe," said another.

"That day in Bride's Valley, they were alone together for some time before we arrived," said a third.

I could tell you who each speaker was. Of course I knew each mother's voice as well as I knew her face. But understand: these mothers at their midnight council were more like one great mind probing itself, divided at times as great minds may be, but one entity. Their forms around the fire looked like the roots of a glowing tree that rose from their darkness. The silences between words had the quality of rich, black loam.

"Maybe it was Bride herself who gave her the fire. Didn't we name her Bride's flame?"

Their recollection of the day at the pool, their invocation of my old name brought back the moment when I saw my reflection in the water, the rich, honey light caught in my hair, igniting it. I remembered the fire in my head, how it felt like bees swarming in my skull. My mothers' minds seemed to catch the image.

"Now her name is Maeve. Her veins run with mead, and honey fire pours from her hands."

"Can it be right for such hands to hold a weapon? Maybe we're teaching her all wrong. Maybe she's not meant for a warrior."

"Why can't a warrior be a healer, too? Aren't we? Don't we all know how to summon the heat into our hands? Anyone can be taught to do that."

"That may be, but what came through her hands was not just heat. It was the Fire itself. She didn't summon it. It summoned her, and there's the difference. I tell you she's one of those who has the Fire in her head."

"Fire or no fire, how does that change anything? She's our daughter. She was born a warrior-witch. And what's more she's taken the name of the greatest warrior queen of all. Doesn't that confirm her vocation?"

I had not told them what Queen Maeve had said about how I must make the name my own.

"But Queen Maeve was not just a famous warrior, she was a famous lover."

"Which only goes to show that our Maeve can be both warrior and healer."

"Does it follow that because Queen Maeve both fought and fucked that our Maeve can use her hands to harm and heal?"

"Listen, as long as she's here on Tir na mBan, these questions are immaterial."

A silence followed. I could almost hear the muscles tensing.

"What do you mean." Someone spoke slowly without inflection.

"Only this: who is there here for her to fight or heal or love—besides us?"

Good point. I listened intently for an answer.

"We need a new hero to train."

That old saw.

"This time he won't escape so easily."

My ears pricked up. Here was a story I hadn't heard. Who had escaped? When?

"We need a whole shipload of heroes. We'll ask the Cailleach. Surely she's had at least a premonition concerning the next shipment. It's long overdue."

"And when the heroes come, Maeve could have a baby."

A baby! I was aghast. I was the child around here.

"Then she'd be content, and life would go on. Our lineage would continue."

Then I remembered: the blood, my new name. I was a child no longer. Was that what it meant to cease to be a child? You simply replace yourself? Was that what my womb mother had done? But no, it hadn't been like that. My mother was the beloved of a god. It was special. I was special. Not just generic hero spawn.

"But is she meant to stay?" someone sighed heavily. "We have to face the possibility that she isn't. We've raised her to be a hero-woman herself. We've taught her everything we know."

"Just so she can teach it in her turn."

"Yes, in her turn. We never meant her to go. She's ours."

"Listen, sisters, she's no more ours than the wild horses or the lost heroes or the waves of the sea. We have more control over the weather than we have over her destiny."

A tremor of fear and excitement shook me. I might chafe at my mothers' control, but it had not occurred to me that I might already be beyond it.

"Do you think the Cailleach knows what is to come?"

"It's almost *Samhain*. A good time for seeing."

It was also the time I was to go to her. I could tell by the weight of the silence that they were all thinking the same thought.

"There's so little time left," a voice quavered.

"We've done our best."

"But is it good enough? We've taught her how to handle a weapon, but not how to handle herself. Out there. With them. "

Them! They must mean the appended ones. My ears strained for more. But for the moment, my mothers seemed to have worn out their words and their worry. The next sounds I heard were a mixture of sighs, snores, and settlings as they curled into each other and the comfort of sleep.

I receded into myself, calling up the image of the dark eyes I had seen in the pool the day the fire came into my head. On the whole, it pleased me that my mothers did not know what was to become of me. My destiny must be so strange and wonderful it was beyond their collective powers of imagination. My thoughts slowly turned to dreams. In them, someone I'd never seen narrated the wonder tale of Maeve of Tir na mBan. The words, instead of hanging invisible in air, took strange forms, becoming not illustrations of the story but rising flames, diving birds, leaping salmon, falling stars.

∽

After that night my mothers were not so single-minded about my military training. It's hard to say if they slackened the pace because they'd lost their certainty of my vocation or because it was harvest time. Even warrior witches have to eat, and unlike warriors elsewhere, my mothers had no peasant class to labor for them. What I liked best at this time of year was to gather berries and nuts—a traditional child's occupation involving a race against time. After *Samhain* all the unplucked fruits of the earth belonged by rights to the *Fomorii*, a fierce misshapen tribe of beings, only partially subdued, who dwelt under the wave. Since I supposed my father had them in hand, tales of the ferocious *Fomorii* merely lent a pleasurable *frisson* to the season.

When all the grain was harvested, Fand enjoyed a free hand with fogs and mists. My memory of that time is full of beaded spider webs and bramble thorns. Now and then, Grainne slipped in a few days of perfect calm, warm at the center and crisp at the edges, like something good to eat. Then I'd see snakes on the move to holes leading deep underground; or sometimes a snake would just sun on a rock, storing the warmth in its body as if it were food. On the last of those days I remember sitting with Grainne overlooking the sea. The surf was a hardly a whisper and everything—the sea, the sky, Grainne, me—seemed to hold its breath.

Then one morning we woke to billowing black clouds, and a powerful wind, gusting from the North. (Boann couldn't help grinning). Oak leaves from the grove miles inland soared out to sea. No one said much, but everyone knew: it was the morning of *Samhain.* After we ate our stirabout, my mothers ganged up on me, ignoring my protests, and bundled me into many more layers than I wanted to wear. Outside, we corralled a couple of goats to pull a cart laden with gifts of food and cloth for the Cailleach. Then wordlessly—for our words would only have blown away with the leaves— we bent to the wind and made our way to the Valley between Bride's Breasts.

6

BENEATH BRIDE'S BREAST

"Drink," the Cailleach commanded me.

We were standing by the Well of Wisdom at what you might call the witching hour. My mothers had left hours ago, driving the herds from the far pastures to winter in the byres. I would not be there when they lit the bonfires. I would not stay up all night roasting hazelnuts and apples and listening to my mothers' stories. I was here in the Valley that was anything but golden now. The wind had blown itself away or perhaps never entered the Valley at all. The air was still and cold like something dead. The waning moon rose over the east breast. Now it was high enough for the pool to catch its reflection. The white curve in the water reminded me of the skull hidden beneath the pool's surface.

"You must drink."

"There's a skull in that water." I attempted to keep my tone light and conversational. The truth is, though I was thirsty, I did not want to drink. I was hungry, too; we'd eaten none of the feast my mothers had laid out on the rocks nearby.

"Drink," she said.

"I want to know how the skull got there first."

"This pool is one of the gateways," the Cailleach said. "Whoever clothed that bone with flesh has long since passed through. Birth. Death. They're the same door. There's only going in and out. In and out. That's the rhythm of everything."

I was so surprised to receive any answer, I was silenced for a moment.

"Drink now."

"Just one more thing," I stalled. "Do you go through the gateway when you're ready or does someone give you a shove?"

"It all depends," she said. "Drink."

Finally I gave up, figuring I wasn't going to find out what happened next until I got this part out of the way. So I knelt and cupped my hands, the reflection scattering into bright fragments as I broke the water. Once I got started, I drank for a long time. The water was burning cold, sweet and fiery at the same time.

"Now," she said when I stood again. "Since you raised the question: are *you* ready?"

I stared at her, the gleam of her face within the hood like the gleam of moon in the night. Then I stared at the pool where the moon's reflection had cohered again. The hairs rose on the back of my neck. My stomach tried to bail out of my body. I wanted my mothers.

"No, Maeve Rhuad," she said. "This is not the way for you."

In my relief, I barely registered that she had added to my name.

"But it is time for you to go inside. Into the dark. Come. I'll show you."

Abruptly she turned and led me from the pool towards the great darkness of Bride's eastern breast. She moved so swiftly that more than once I almost lost sight of her. At times I had the impression that I was following, not an old woman, but a grey wolf or a black bear. We hadn't climbed very far when she stopped, and I came alongside her human self.

"Here," she said.

First I didn't see anything but a cluster of rocks. Who knows? If I'd gone there another day or another time of day, maybe that's all I ever would have seen. That's how it is with the ways between the worlds. Then, as I gazed, I began to discern in the midst of the boulders a narrow sliver of pitch darkness. Slowly it dawned (or should I say darkened) on me what she had in mind.

"Are you ready, Maeve Rhuad?"

"Why do you call me that?" I demanded. "Maeve Rhuad."

"Because you are the Red Maeve."

"Queen Maeve of Connacht has red hair, too," I pointed out.

"Nevertheless, you are the Rhuad. Are you ready?"

"How can I know if I'm ready when I don't know what's going to happen?"

"Readiness isn't a matter of knowing what's going to happen. It's a matter of daring to find out."

The Cailleach had hit upon my secret weakness—or strength. It's a good thing I wasn't raised with other children. My life would have been driven by dares and double dares. Now here was this old witch daring me to go through a narrow chasm into the ground—on the night you'd call Hallowe'en. If you're wondering where all those fairytales of murderous, child imprisoning/ roasting/eating old women come from, consider: they might have had some basis in fact. And here I wasn't even being offered a last meal, though, in fact, since I'd drunk from the well, hunger and thirst had disappeared.

"All right," I heard myself saying. "Show me the dark."

She took my hand and led me closer to the opening. It narrowed at the top and the bottom, just wide enough at the middle for a pair of shoulders to squeeze through. Its shape reminded me of something, but at the time I couldn't think what. I peered in and saw only more and deeper darkness.

"This is your gate," she said pleasantly, as if she were some sort of stewardess. "Are you afraid?"

"Yes," I said, well past denial.

"Good. Always know when you're afraid, even if you choose not to show it to your enemies. Never deceive yourself. I'm not going to tell you not to be afraid, but I will tell you this: if you walk straight down into your fear, you will find everything you need. I will call you back when it's time, but I won't tell you when that will be. There is no time where you're going, and if you try to cling to it, you will waste your strength."

None of what she said was even remotely reassuring and hardly more comprehensible.

"So, Maeve Rhuad, are you ready?"

Are you crazy? I wanted to say. Ready to go through a dark hole that, for all I knew, might close over me? Is that where you'd want to spend your first night away from your mothers?

"Ready," was all I said.

"Take off your clothes. To pass through this gate, you need to leave everything behind."

I unknotted the bramble that fastened my outer cloak, and let the garment fall from my shoulders. The Cailleach picked it up. Then I began peeling the layers my mother had piled on, handing each item to the Cailleach. At last I stood naked to the night. The cold air touched my skin with its thousand invisible hands. I was close to tears. Then the Cailleach laid all my clothes, neatly folded, on the ground.

"O my daughter. O my daughter of daughters."

She wrapped me in her arms, enfolding me in her grey cloak. Over her shoulder I saw the moon. But there was nothing cold or distant about the Cailleach's embrace. I closed my eyes, and the darkness turned golden as the light when I'd first seen the Valley. I breathed the scent of apples that clung to the folds of her cloak, as if she carried the magic orchard with her. When she released me, I felt as warm as if I'd been lying in full sun for hours.

"Now," she said.

And I turned to the darkness.

∞

That night I went through the gateway all alone. Now I can take you with me. You're feeling claustrophobic? Don't worry, we all have a touch of claustrophobia. It's our body's memory of what we can't remember. Camel or not, we've all passed through the needle's eye. In and out, in and out, the silver needle flashes, the bright red thread of life blood turning to stitches on the black cloth: spirals, flowers, bursts of stars. We've all passed through the narrow gate, thrust our huge heads through our mothers' cruel and suffering bones.

Lead with your head again, squeeze your shoulders through. Now you're inside. There's just room enough to stand with a slight stoop. You can breathe this time. It's easier than that other passage. But it doesn't do to be too literal with metaphors. They fall apart easily, like the petals of a blown rose. Besides, this time you're going in, not out. Just keep moving. Feel the snake-belly curve of the earth under your feet. The walls are only just wide enough to allow you to pass. The rocks' sweat mingles with your own. You keep moving, around and down, around and down. For a while you wonder how long you can go on. But with each turn, time uncoils. You stop thinking of ending, because you no longer remember beginning. You no longer know your motion from the passage that shapes it. In the heart of gravity, in the gravid earth, you lose all sense of your separate weight. You are floating, sinking, whirling back to the place of no distinctions, no-thing, no you.

So when you come to the place of stillness, where your feet stop, it is not so different. The earth is still spinning and circling, and you can feel it, because you are not separate anymore. Curl into her. Her warm blood is all around you, welling up in a hot spring. It's not so different from before. Remember? Hear the muffled sounds of her inner workings. Listen, that's her heart beat. Or maybe it's yours. There's no difference anymore. You are made of earth. You are earth. There's no difference now. No difference between opening your eyes and closing them, between waking and dreaming. You are in the shape-shifting mother dark. You are blind. You will see.

(It's not all pretty. The earth knows terrible things. She receives all deaths, gentle and brutal. She bears the pain of every birth. She turns all things back into herself; she worries the bones to dust. She is changing, always changing. Layers sift. Her own bones crash and break. Tides heave. Rock erupts into fire. It's not all pretty. Beauty never is.)

∽

Here is some of what I saw:

The roots of a great tree, burning like stars, reaching deep into the earth. Into me. I can feel the roots eating me, drinking me, nourished by me. Then my eyes, or vision, travel up the roots to the world above. How strange. Such vast roots support only a stripped trunk with two branches, all the twigs lopped off. It hardly seems like a tree at all, so stark, so small against a huge, empty sky smooth and curved like the shell of an egg, if you could see an egg from the inside. Then the sky cracks, a jagged fissure. No, it's not the sky but a pair of cracked bleeding lips. I feel myself straining, still bound to the root, wanting to bring water to those lips, leaves to that tree.

At once I see a huge oak, groaning in a damp, night wind. For an instant the clouds part, and an almost full moon reveals a figure leaning against the tree, tied to the tree. I can't see the face, but I hear the sound of weeping. Before I can see any more, torrents of rain fall from my eyes, and everything is dark again.

That was the first wave of vision. Wave on wave followed. I soon learned to relax in the dark troughs between the waves as a laboring woman rests between contractions. Some of the visions were lovely, many troubling, most incomprehensible, even when I recognized something or someone. Once I saw Grainne with her face contorted, head thrown back, nostrils flaring and eyes rolling like a frightened mare's. In another seeing, I glimpsed a red-haired warrior woman I first mistook for Queen Maeve. She looked so familiar. The woman drove a chariot between two hills, leading a torrent of warriors like a spring flood into the narrow pass. The fury of her battle cry coursed in my blood long after the vision faded.

The sweetest wave was not sight but sound and sensation. A warm hand, with a light touch almost indistinguishable from sunlight, stroking my breast. A voice to match the touch spoke rhythmically in a language I did not know, a beautiful language, tender as the speech of doves. I wanted this vision to go on forever, but it rolled away, and the next one, the most terrible of all, hit me with double force.

It began with a woman, old as the Cailleach, with long, white hair and a blood-red tunic. One of her eyes was clear, the other one cloudy. She pointed the way to a pool among the rocks. Two eels surfaced, swished, and dived again. When the water stilled, I saw my reflection. As I gazed, the image of my face began to change, subtly at first, a hardening, a squaring. Then lines, deep and grim, slashed the smoothness of my skin. The green went out of my eyes, leaving them red-brown like a fox's. Finally, coarse, red hair bristled around my mouth and chin. But far more horrible than the strange harshness or the (to me) unnatural hair was the look in the eyes. I didn't even have a word for it then, but I registered its meaning, and it felt like a swift, hard blow hitting dead center: hatred.

I began to scream then, though I hardly knew my own voice. This wave of vision did not roll away. It broke over me or I felt broken, dashed on the rocks. Then I was staring up at a wide, dusky sky, my eyes following a flight of cranes, their wings beating together in perfect time. At a slower rhythm, I felt the rise and fall of waves beneath me. I was somehow floating on the sea. A new moon drifted down the sky. Then, reaching out over the water, came the sound of many voices singing: "*Hail to thee, thou new moon, jewel of guidance in the night.*" The sky turned black, and the stars sent down their burning roots.

⚭

I don't know how long the visions went on. The Cailleach hardly needed to caution me about clinging to time. There was no way to reckon time here, unless I'd wanted to keep count of the rhythms: the waves, the heart-beat, the breath. In and out. In and out. No time and all time. Though I must tell you the story in time—first this happened, then this—think of time as a snake shedding skin after skin, revealing layer on layer of one primal pattern.

After the visions, I went into what might better be described as quiescence rather than ordinary sleep: the state of trees when the sap slows; animals in hibernation. I came to consciousness again when something touched my foot. It had an almost watery quality, yet, at the same time, it was hard, muscular, sinuous. It coiled round my ankle and all at once I knew: it was a snake, a real snake, not a metaphorical one, and it was moving steadily up my leg. I stiffened and held my breath.

My mothers had taught me to revere snakes as beings wise in the secrets of the earth. I had handled snakes more than once. But it's one thing to stroke a snake in the sunlight surrounded by eight mothers eagerly offering lore and instruction; it's another to be underground, in the snake's turf, so to speak, naked and at its mercy. So I was faced with another of those subtle choices life offers in profusion. I could surrender to fear or I could just...surrender. The snake, perhaps sensing my alarm, had stopped mid-slither halfway up my calf. I let out my breath and relaxed.

The snake began to move again, and I began to enjoy the feel of living snake skin sliding against my own skin. I gasped when I realized another snake was moving over my hand up my arm. But after a moment that felt delightful, too. Do you begin to get my drift? The two snakes coiled closer and closer to the quick of me. The one winding up my arms moved to my breasts, gliding over, around, and between them. The other snake, yes, slid back and forth between my thighs, along the opening petals of my vulva. I could feel myself moistening, flooding as if some underground spring had suddenly gushed to the surface. When the pleasure became unbearable, I found myself shuddering, quivering, blossoming. Yes, that's how I saw it, how it felt, as if I was some huge, hot, trumpeting flower erupting from the quaking earth.

Afterwards the snakes and I rested, both of them coiled together on my belly. I was drowsing when I heard a voice. "The snakes are within you: the male and the female, the right and the left, the bright and the dark, the sky and the earth. Never forget." Then the snakes slipped from my belly and were gone.

After that, whether delirious from hunger or from being too long in the timeless dark, I let go completely. When I felt my moon blood beginning, I overflowed the boundaries of my separate self. Distinctions between who I was and what I saw dissolved in a red tide. Vision literally flowed from me as I fingerpainted all over the cave. Though I could not see with my eyes, I retain an image of glowing walls, bright with birds and snakes, spiral mazes, dripping breasts, and long-tailed stars. When the pictures faded, I rolled around on the ground. I licked the rocks. They tasted of honey and milk mixed with the faint, salt tang of blood. At last, I immersed myself in the hot spring, bathing and drinking at once.

It was then that I heard a sound, muffled and far away, coming through layers of earth, barely audible above the sound of the spring. I crawled out of the water and curled into a ball on the ground. I heard the sound more clearly.

"Maeve! Maeve Rhuad!"

I listened, but I did not connect the sound with myself or even recognize it as words.

"Maeve Rhuad!"

Mead. Meaning came to me. Red mead. I ran a finger over the cave wall, then tasted it. My mouth, I remembered, my finger, my tongue.

Me.

Still not fully comprehending, I got to my feet.

"Maeve Rhuad. I call you from the depths of the earth."

I began to move and soon found myself in the passage, spiraling up, just as the snake had climbed my leg.

"Come forth, Maeve Rhuad. Rise. Live."

I walked up and up. The darkness began to tatter and fray. The air changed, too, no longer close and still. It came to meet me, wild, sweet, insistent, plunging into my lungs, pouring over my skin like water. Then, in the thinning shell of earth, I saw a crack of brightness. I shielded my eyes.

"Come forth. Be born. Live."

It felt as though the passage was narrowing. I squeezed forward.

"Now!" the voice cried. "Head first! "

I bent my head to the brightness and butted.

" 'Atta, girl. You can do it. Push!"

My head eased through; the rest of me followed, and I was out, gasping and blinking, in the bare air. Then the earth tipped crazily over the sky and came smack down on my face.

7

COCOON

"**A**nd?" the Cailleach prompted.

Imagine that I am in her office, say six stories high, so that the noise of traffic is at a remove. There's a real, if threadbare, oriental carpet on the floor. The walls bristle with masks and other artifacts from exotic vacations. Her bookcases have glass doors to protect rare volumes from dust or mold. Oblique light comes through the blinds. I'm reclining on the analysand's couch. She sits behind me in a high-backed chair, her gold bird eyes darting from my head to her notebook where she makes jottings about my dreams.

Okay, but it's the first century. Neither psychoanalysis nor the Park Avenue practice has been invented yet. We are in the Cailleach's earth shelter, built into the side of a hill. The light comes from the fire, and I am lying on fur-covered heather. Also, we are not probing my repressed, traumatic memories of the past but of the future. Instead of scribbling in her notebook, the Cailleach wields a drop spindle. You know about the Fates, don't you? They show up in lots of mythologies. Whatever their names, there are always three of them, messing around with the threads of our lives: spinning, weaving, snipping, catching us like fat foolish flies in their beautiful web. They are often, though not always, pictured as old women. If you pay attention you will find not just one but three know-it-all old women in this story.

"That's about it," I sighed. We'd been at it for days. The fifty-minute hour hadn't been invented, either.

"There is something you haven't told me." She made this remark as an observation, not an accusation, as if she could care less. If I wanted to withhold vital information, that was my business—and my problem.

"I can't think what."

"The Well. What did you see in the Well, I wonder?"

"I told you. That horrible face. My face turned into that face with bristles like a boar."

"No," she said. "Not the pool in your vision. Your vision in the pool here in the Valley. Before I found you. On the day of your first blood. I wonder what you saw then?"

She fell silent again. I could hear the almost soundless sound of the thread she twirled, the peat-fire hissing. No, I hadn't told her about the One I'd seen, the One with the dark eyes and the bright stream. For all her knowing, I knew

49

something she did not. I did not want to give away my secret, but I was also bursting with it. I wanted more from her: hows, wheres, and whens.

"I saw my destiny," I announced.

"Did you?" She was maddeningly calm.

"Yes." I wanted it to be true. "What I saw in the other pool, the bristled face, that was just a nightmare."

"The great grey mare that gallops through our dreams never shows us anything true?"

"It can't be true," I insisted, afraid that it could be. "My face won't change into that face even if I live a thousand years. Even if I live to be as old as you."

You may think I was being rude, but neither the Cailleach nor I thought there was any shame in great age. That's an equation your century has invented.

"Change into a man's face?" she mused.

"A man's face? How do you know I saw a man's face?"

"Because the hair you describe grows on men's faces when they are no longer boys."

"But I don't want to be a man! I only want to see one!" I protested, as if men were some alarming species akin to purple cows.

"Maeve, Maeve," she laughed, not unkindly. "Set your mind at rest. You are not destined for manhood. No, not in this lifetime. You are about as female as they come. Terribly female."

"Then that proves it." I was triumphant with relief.

"Proves what?"

"That what I saw in that nasty vision is not true."

"No, dear. I'm afraid it doesn't prove anything. You are being too literal. A common failing among the young. How things appear is only the thin, papery outer skin of the onion. Of course, when you cut the onion open, your eyes sting and water, and then you can't see at all. You're lucky if you don't slice your finger."

"It helps to hold it under cold water before you cut it."

"Hold what?" said the Cailleach.

"The onion. Boann always does. Liban doesn't. She likes to cry."

"That was a metaphorical onion, Maeve," she said severely, as if she had not just followed her extended metaphor into a literal thicket. "Now as to your vision. You might have seen your what-ya-ma-call-it." She searched her mind for the first century Q-Celtic equivalent of animus. "Or you might have seen someone you are going to encounter. Now suppose you tell me more about your destiny, hmm?"

"I thought you were supposed to tell me," I said crossly.

I heard her sigh. Then she paused in her spinning.

"You are going to go on a long journey. A very, very long journey. You will meet a dark, handsome stranger."

This was more like it. "Go on!" I urged.

"Crap," she said.

"What!"

"Generic fortuneteller's crap. Want to hear the rest of it? You will have trouble. Trouble with your love luck. In your case I might add, you will be trouble. Trouble to that boy with the dark eyes. The boy you saw in the pool. And he will be trouble for you."

"You know about him!" I sat bolt upright and turned around to stare at her.

"It's my job to listen as carefully to what you don't say as to what you do say. When you hold such a strong image in your mind, I can catch an echo of it. He seems to be standing in an alley of a city I once knew well. I can't make out what he's doing there."

At least some things were still secret, and, to me, sacred.

"So," I fumed, "whether I choose to tell you things or not, you pick my mind." I began pulling out tufts of sheepskin. "But you! You don't tell me anything!"

"If you want to yank at wool, there's a whole basketful that needs carding."

She set down her spindle and brought me the wool and some carding combs. For lack of an alternative, I began to drag the combs through the tangled mass.

"Consider this wool, Maeve Rhuad." She sat down with her spindle again. "Let's say I have a vision of a beautiful cloak I want to weave. In my mind's eye, I can see the colors, the patterns. The wool I sheared from the sheep was all tangled with thorns and thistles, matted with mud, the hindquarters hung with dingleberries. I can understand women's lust for horses," she offered as an aside, "but I've never understood the proclivity of some men for sheep. Anyway," she resumed, "this wool was boiled in a cauldron, dried in the sun, carded, dyed, and spun. Only then do I begin to weave. It's the same way with a life story. However the cloak shimmers in your mind, you have to start with the sheep. Do you understand? I'm speaking metaphorically, of course."

Of course. Metaphorically speaking, my life story was still running around some little island on a sheep's ass. I dragged so hard at the wool, I could feel the fibres breaking.

"Knowing too much is as dangerous as knowing too little," she went on dispensing wisdom. "It can more easily mislead you. You may not know this, because you have not yet traveled beyond Tir na mBan. You will, don't worry. Or perhaps I should say: do worry. Believe me, when you come to a place where roads meet, if you strain too hard to remember what someone else has told you—right? left? where's that landmark?—you won't hear the road calling to you. You'll be deaf to the sound of your own sixth sense. If you look too hard for signs and portents, you'll see them everywhere, and you'll miss the real thing."

"Then what's the point?" I demanded.

"The point of what?"

"The point of my going down into the earth, into the dark, seeing those visions. What's the point of my telling you anything?"

"I will answer those questions one at a time," she said unruffled by my rudeness. "But first, remember: not everything that has a purpose is pointed, as you and every woman should know. As to going down: now a gateway has opened between you and the deep places. Most of the time you will be on this side of the gate, but you can come and go at need or at will."

"What? In and out of that passageway in the hill?"

"Watch it, Maeve, you're being literal again. There are many ways between the worlds. There are worlds within worlds within worlds. You contain the spiral passage and the deep chamber just as it contained you. And you contain the snakes. Oh, yes, I know about the snakes."

She laughed a rich, throaty laugh, and I felt that shock of embarrassed indignation that comes to adolescents when they are first confronted with adult sensuality.

"We're all made of earth, Maeve Rhuad. You got that much, didn't you?"

I nodded.

"Now you will never forget what many never know. Now you are initiate to the mystery."

"Oh." I felt somewhat mollified to be acknowledged an initiate.

"As to your second question—or was it your third? I've lost count. Never mind. To answer: you don't have to tell me anything at all, but giving words to your visions accomplishes two things. One, the visions you speak will travel with you between the worlds instead of sinking back into the earth. Then when you encounter them in another time or place, even in another form, you will be alert. Second, the more I know, the better I can prepare you."

"Prepare me?"

"For whatever is to come. Surely you understand that's why you're here with me."

"Yes, but what I still don't know is do you or don't you know what's going to happen to me?"

"There's knowing and knowing," she said unhelpfully. "I may catch glimpses of the cloak—the metaphorical cloak, remember?—but I don't know the exact pattern or how it will look when it's not just wafting in the air but flowing from your shoulders. Still, with my experience, there may be things I recognize, even at a distance. Places, languages."

"How did you recognize the place with all the walls? I thought you had always lived on Tir na mBan."

"No, not always. For a long, long time, but not always. For an even longer time, I wandered. I spun a very long tale before I wound it back into this Valley."

Her voice changed its tone. It was no longer the voice of admonition or instruction or wry observation. I don't know how to describe it, except to say that it was no longer her voice alone. It seemed to come right up through the earth floor. It resounded in my head, as if the voice were also mine.

"I have lived for ages and ages on this earth. I have been a queen. I have been a warrior. I have been a renegade. My life has been full of endings. Full of last battles and bitter retreats. Now I am a spinner of cocoons, a weaver of shrouds, a keeper of one of the secret places of refuge. There are others like me. We stir the cauldron of changes. We gaze on the moon's dark face. We know that what seems dead and gone forever will one day return, throw off the shroud, burst from the cocoon.

"O Maeve Rhuad!" She suddenly wailed my name.

The hair rose on my neck. Inside my head bees woke and swarmed. She stared, the thread suspended in the air. She wasn't seeing me, there before her in the earth shelter. She was seeing. And a true seeing is a wild, alive thing.

"O Maeve Rhuad, *thou new moon, jewel of guidance in the night.*" She chanted the words I'd heard in my last vision. Then she added new ones:

> O Maeve Rhuad, bright butterfly
> how bright your flame
> how bright your pulsing wings
> spread to the strong wind
> spread to the fierce light.

She cried out and stretched out her hand as if to stop someone or something.

"Is it too soon?" she muttered to herself. "Is it too soon?"

I could not see what she saw then, or know what she knew: how fragile those wings, how easily torn.

When the Cailleach came out of her trance, she was tired and cranky. She scowled at me. Never mind she had just called me jewel of the night, bright butterfly, and so forth. She didn't seem to remember any of that.

"No more late hours on a school night," she snapped. "Class begins tomorrow at dawn."

∽

And it did. That morning, and every morning for the almost year and a half I stayed with the Cailleach. It's not easy to learn three and a half languages in that amount of time. (In case you're wondering, I am counting as half the P-Celtic more commonly spoken in Britain and Gaul.) The other three languages I acquired were Greek, Latin, and, yes, Aramaic. I also learned the rudiments of their alphabets, including the Celtic Ogham alphabet.

It was a hell of an immersion course. I was awash in a roiling sea of languages. I'd no sooner master one vocabulary and grammar when another loomed, broke over my head, and took me under again. This crashing course might have been cruel if it had not been so necessary—the Cailleach insisted it was—and if I had not been so apt a pupil. I love words. I love to play with them. To me they are real and substantial. Forget the pen is mightier than the sword. Who needs a pen or a penis or a sword when we all have tongues. Don't you love it that another word for language is tongue? We speak of our mother tongues. Say it: mother tongue. Taste it.

Even with my aptitude, I might not have attained such fluency if the Cailleach had not employed some unconventional techniques. Using what you might call hypnosis, she regressed me, at least once a day, to the age of eighteen months or so when the mind is most receptive to learning language. She'd give me clay or sand to play with and chatter away in whatever language I was learning that day. Also, I suspect she sacrificed many a night's sleep to speak to me as I dreamed. So, you see, long before my foster brother's disciples got zapped by the Holy Spirit, I received the gift of tongues from the Old Woman Who Lived Under the Hill.

My other course of study was geography, the lessons conducted in the language of whatever region we were studying. She would draw maps in chalk on a big, flat rock near the shelter. When the rain washed the maps away, it became my task to draw them from memory. My understanding of the world's shape traveled back and forth through my hand and arm. As I scratched on the stone, I also traced the outlines of coasts and mountains and borders in my brain.

The Cailleach's maps not only delineated what scholars call the known world, she also made maps of the secret world, the mythic world, so called because it was retreating from consciousness. Disappearing under the waves, into caves. Wherever there were far-flung isles like ours or dense forests or sheer mountains with hidden valleys, there were people, often women alone, living in secret, the Cailleach said. Though she also drew these maps on the rock, I fancied I could see a map more clearly and indelibly in the lines of her face.

I was so engrossed in my studies that I hardly noticed the seasons changing, except when my mothers, who seemed much smaller than I'd remembered, came to visit on festival days. The moon waxed and waned. I paid scant attention with my waking mind. Relentless study is almost as effective as running laps and taking cold showers for keeping the hormones in check. But now and then, perhaps when the moon drew closest to the earth, I'd be so restless I'd wake and walk. Usually I'd climb one or the other of Bride's Breasts. I'd stand at the top and try to make out the shape of the distant lands in the dark, bringing to bear the full force of my imagination to try to flesh those maps into masses of land, rivers, mountain ranges, cities, peopled places. More than once I went to the Well of Wisdom at just the right time to catch the reflection of the moon's face. But that was all I saw: the moon round and ripe and self-contained. I never saw the face I longed to see.

It was after one of these moonlit wanderings that I returned to the shelter to sleep and had what you may believe is a dream. To me it was more real than much of what passes for reality. There are times when the rules of the universe are bent out of shape. I believe I passed through—perhaps not a gateway between the worlds—but a gap in the fence or a minute tear in a tightly woven cocoon.

8

THE DESCENT OF THE DOVE

For the sake of convenience, we'll call it a dream. Maybe you remember dreams of your own that took you to places you have never been, showed you things completely outside the realm of your experience. As you know, I had lived all of my life in a wattle and daub hut on an isolated island.

∞

Now I see a huge space, open to the sky, but enclosed by massive columns that look to me like impossibly straight tree trunks stripped of branches. This vast wall of what you would call colonnades surrounds latticed inner walls. Through various doorways more people than I've ever imagined come and go in an unceasing flow. Within the inner walls, I glimpse a roof made of solid gold, vying with the sun for glory.

But it's the people that amaze me most. They crowd closer together than trees in a forest; they cluster like stars. But stars and trees are still. The courtyard is more like an amplified anthill, full of motion and commotion, the rumble, murmur, and shrill of many voices, male voices, issuing from lips obscured by the alarming facial hair. (I keep a sharp eye out for a fox-colored beard.) Some of the people have animals in tow: sheep, goats, birds in cages. Now and then, over the human roar, I hear an animal scream. When the hot wind blows across the outer courtyard from the inner one, it carries the scent of blood and offal.

Where am I in all this? I do not seem to have a visible presence in this world. I see from atop one of the columns. Now my vision, which has been sweeping the courtyard, narrows. Below me in a shaded portico something is about to happen. Two men with astonishing beards almost to their chests, the hair on their head covered with round caps, sit on chairs facing one another. A crowd gathers, and the men begin to speak, not only to each other but to their audience.

At first I am too fascinated by the rhythm and tone of their voices to pay any attention to content. I know nothing of formal discourse or public speech. In contrast to what I'm used to—my mothers' free-for-all fights with everyone talking at once—what I hear now sounds ponderous, an argument, yes, but in slow motion, with more weight given to each point. It is some time before it dawns on me: the men are speaking Aramaic. Then I give all my

56

attention to understanding. But even as I catch more and more words, much of the meaning escapes me completely. Here, listen for yourself. And please excuse my crude—in every sense of the word—translation.

"If three women were sleeping together and blood was found beneath the middle one, all are considered unclean." The man with more grey in his beard and a slightly rounder belly is holding forth, his forefinger dancing in the air, keeping time with his speech, as if it's a second tongue. "But, if blood were found under the one sleeping next to the wall, the two on the inner side are considered unclean, and the outer one is clean. If blood be found under the outer one farthest from the wall, the two on the outer side are deemed unclean, but the one next to the wall is clean." He furls away his forefinger and folds his arms.

In case you are wondering, this is not an obscure math word problem we're hearing. (If you have three women and one blood stain, how many are menstruating?) It's a *Mishnah*, an oral teaching on the law of Moses. These disputations on the fine points of the Torah have since been written down. If you don't believe me that debates like this actually took place, go read *The Mishnayoth*. You'll find this very discussion in the volume called *Taharoth*, in the tractate *Niddah*, chapter 9, *Mishnah* 5.

"As always, Rabbi Meir, your sound wisdom resounds in this holy place and the very stones rejoice to hear you, but—" The second speaker, a leaner man with a sparser beard, perhaps because he tugs at it so impatiently while waiting his turn to speak, brings his forefinger into play. "This proposed ruling of yours can only apply if," he pauses dramatically, almost caressing the air that will receive his words, "and only if the three women came into bed by way of the foot of the bed. For if blood be found under the outer one, and all had passed into the bed across it, then all of them, I say all—dispute me who will—all are unclean."

From the audience there is a murmur of assent and acclaim for this speaker's cleverness, his attention to the all-important detail. But his opponent is neither daunted nor done with what he has to say.

"I congratulate you, Rabbi Judah, from whose mouth wisdom burbles like pure water from a deep spring, on the fine point you have made. But are we not both overlooking the matter of test rags? Consider: if one of them made examination and found herself clean, she alone is clean but the other two are considered unclean. If two examined themselves and found they were clean, then they are clean but the third one is unclean."

"Now wait just a minute, Rabbi Meir," the other one interrupts, leaning closer to his opponent. The tips of their beards brush each other and threaten to tangle. "You are blatantly contradicting what we just agreed. Didn't we just agree?" He appeals to the crowd. "If the outer one is unclean, and they crossed over the bed instead of coming in by way of the foot of the bed, they are all, therefore, unclean."

"But that, Rabbi Judah, was before they used their test rags."

"Test rags," Rabbi Judah fulminates. "Who said anything about test rags? How do we even know they had their test rags with them, seeing as they were sleeping together and not, clearly not, with their husbands?"

Perhaps you are not following this discussion any better than I am. I do not even know that they're talking about menstrual blood (or, as it's called in English translation of *The Mishnayoth*, menstruous: a combination of menstrual and monstrous.) Let me explain. Nice Jewish women test themselves with a rag before they fuck their husbands to make sure they're clean (i.e. not menstruous). Otherwise, God forbid, contact with her blood would make him unclean, too. For seven days.

"Of course they had their test rags. Or they got some when they discovered there was a stain on the bed. It goes without saying. We're not talking about those dirty Samaritan women, who think nothing of bleeding in public. Rabbi Judah, please! Be gracious enough to let me finish my point. I think you'll like it. If, I say if," he resumes, "if they all examine themselves, and all find themselves clean, then all three of them are unclean!"

Rabbi Meir sits back, immensely pleased with himself. Even his opponent looks impressed, nodding thoughtfully and tugging at his beard.

"Dispute me who will!" says Rabbi Meir, opening his arms and gesturing magnanimously to the audience.

Suddenly, the crowd stirs as someone pushes his way forward. The two rabbis shift in their seats and confer together. Perhaps because I have been magically transported here, I can hear their off-the-record remarks.

"Look! It's that smart-ass kid from Galilee again," says Rabbi Judah. "I can't think why his parents give him such a free rein."

"I doubt he has his two hairs yet." Rabbi Meir is referring to the two pubic hairs requisite to prove a man or woman of marriageable age. "Shall we put him to the test before we let him speak?" he chuckles.

"His virgin ears should not even be attending this debate. It's unseemly. Besides, educational standards are so poor in the countryside. It's not clear to me that he's even literate. The way he mangles the scriptures! He makes a fool of himself."

"Untutored he may be, but he has a quick mind. Admit it, Rabbi Judah. What really worries you is that he might make fools of us. Let the boy have his say."

Then I see him, surfacing from the crowd like the salmon of wisdom leaping from the water: my own Appended One. His body is longer than when I saw him last but still without a grown man's height or girth. On his

face, a few hairs straggle awkwardly in twos or threes like guests who have
arrived too early at a party. Despite his gangling youth, he carries with him
an air of authoritative, energetic calm that makes him the instant eye of
this and every storm. His eyes are just as I remember them: dark, curious,
intent. They are trained now on Rabbi Meir.

"Worthy Rabbi, I don't understand," he begins, speaking Aramaic with an
accent. A twang. A sort of cowboy Aramaic. Though I detect the difference
in pronunciation, it's the voice I hear. I know this voice. I have heard it before,
in the dark, in the chamber beneath Bride's Breast. Then the words were
rounder, more rhythmic, the deep source of this flatter, more prosaic tongue.
But the voice, even with the comic breaks in range that mark the change from
boy to man, is the same.

"What don't you understand, my son?" From his tone, he might as well
have said sonny boy.

"If they have all examined themselves and all found themselves clean, why
then are they not all accounted clean, no matter which way they got into
bed?"

"Why, the answer is obvious, boy," says Rabbi Judah. "They must all be
accounted unclean by reason of doubt."

"Quite so." Rabbi Meir isn't about to let Rabbi Judah expand on his point.
"Now, to what may we liken this matter? It is like to an unclean heap that was
confused with two clean heaps. And they examined one of them and found
it clean, but the other two are deemed unclean. If two were examined and
found clean, they are clean, and the third one is unclean. But if all three of
them were examined, and they were found clean, all of them are unclean. For
as I always say: Whatsoever is under the presumption of uncleanness continues in uncleanness until it becomes known unto thee where the uncleanness is.
And so you are answered. Be satisfied."

This was such a broad hint that even I understood it: You've had your
moment. Get lost, kid. But my foster brother just stood there, brows knit,
chewing his cheek. Adorable.

"Esteemed Rabbi, we are not talking about three heaps," he objected. "We
are talking about three women, who have examined themselves and found
themselves clean. How can it be right that they should be deemed unclean and
bear all the extra work and care and shame of uncleanness?"

"My son, you are young and unschooled. Clearly you do not understand
the use of metaphor in illustrating a point. Also, whether we are talking
about heaps or women, the important thing to remember is that you can't
be too careful when it comes to determining cleanness or uncleanness. If
you err, err on the side of caution. Remember that, and you will prosper
and live a long life."

"But how do you know," my foster brother presses on in pursuit of justice, undeterred by the wisdom of his elders, "that the stain was menstruous? If they have all examined themselves and found themselves clean, isn't it more likely that the stain was caused by spilled wine? Or perhaps it was an old stain that had set, even though the bed clothes had been washed?"

There is a great shaking of beards; four hands are thrown up.

"Show a little respect, youngster," scolds Rabbi Judah. "Learn the rules before you presume to interrupt. You cannot change the premise of a debate. Of course the stain is menstruous! This is not a question. Besides, how could there be an old stain in the bedclothes? The sages teach and everybody knows, there are seven kinds of material used for treating blood stains. Now pay attention and maybe you'll learn something here: tasteless saliva, water from chewed grits," he begins reeling them off, "urine, natron, lye, Cimbolian earth, and wood ash. If the cloth—"

"Worthy Rabbis, forgive my ignorance and my ill-manners," my foster brother interrupts again, "but even if the stain is menstruous, as you say, if all have examined themselves and found themselves clean, must not all yet be accounted clean? For is it not true—metaphorically speaking, of course—that search must be made until hard rocky ground or virgin soil is reached?"

This, to me, obscure turn of phrase causes a ripple of wonderment in the crowd and frowns to crease the faces of the rabbis. If you read *The Mishnayoth*, you will find that my foster brother's words were eventually approved by the Sages. At the time, his point escapes me completely. I only know that he is my twin. We are two of one kind. I yearn for him with all my might, and—

Suddenly I am hurtling towards him, flashes of brilliant white on the edges of my vision. Then I am settling on his head, folding my wings and fluffing out my feathers. My feathers? Yes, it takes me a while to notice that I'm a bird—a white dove to be exact—because when you're a bird it seems perfectly natural to plump your feathers when you alight and fold your wings.

But everyone else notices immediately, and my choice of a perch causes quite a stir. Rabbi Meir smothers a smile, while Rabbi Judah is further incensed.

"You make a mockery of this Holy Place," he hisses.

The crowd is going wild. I catch a few words here and there: "A sign. It's a sign. Shekinah. Sophia. The Dove of Asherah."

Through it all my foster brother stands still, as still as a tree in the middle of a dense forest where no breeze stirs. I, on the other hand, trapped in an unfamiliar form, the sudden focus of a huge crowd of male beings, am becoming increasingly flustered. I struggle to muster my command of Aramaic, thinking to speak a few words on my own behalf. But from my throat come only a few panicked coos.

Perhaps sensing my distress, my foster brother begins slowly raising his hand. I can feel its heat as it nears my breast. Ah yes, this is what I want: to be cupped in that hand. Yes. But the surrounding chaos, the tension of anticipation overwhelm me. (And I am, after all, a bird. I really can't help it.) As they say in the *Song of Songs*, my bowels are moved for him. That's right, I shit on his head. Well, anyway, his yarmulka.

There is something about shit. (In this case, guano.) No one really outgrows scatological humor. Now there is no more ooh-ing and ah-ing over the descent of the dove and its possible significance as a sign. Everyone simply cracks up, even Rabbi Judah. They're all laughing, laughing at him whom my soul loves. I can feel his head growing hot, and I cannot bear it that I have humiliated him. I am mortified. I can't think what to do.

My wings think for me. Soon I am flapping (none too gracefully, I fear; I'm new at this) over the assembled who make a great show of ducking and shielding their heads. Believe me, if I had control over the matter, which clearly I do not, I would spatter as many of them as I could.

I am flying randomly about wondering where to go when a whole flock of my kind swoops down from some high place and swallows me in its numbers. I find myself soaring willy nilly over the wall of colonnades. I catch a dizzying glimpse of the city sprawling on hill after hill. Then we are diving again, half falling, half floating to a garden set in the hillside that climbs to what I now know is the Temple of Jerusalem. The garden smells sweet and spicy. I hear the sound of running water as a stream spills into a pool. Amidst a white storm of wings, I hit the ground with too much momentum and turn a couple of complete somersaults before I stagger to a stop.

Someone is laughing, a woman. When the world stops reeling, I see her, looming over me, so much larger than human beings look when you are one yourself. (I am still a small bird, remember.) At first I think she's the Cailleach; the lines of her face seem so familiar. Then I see the differences: her skin is darker, her eyes almost black. She wears a black tunic and a cloak that covers her head. The only touch of color is a purple shawl draped on her shoulders. There are teeth missing from the smile she gives me. She's singled me out from the other doves feeding on crumbs around her. I wonder does she know each one and recognize me as a newcomer? She beckons to me.

"Come, little dove. Come to Anna," she croons in Aramaic. "You're all in a tremble. Don't be afraid. Come. I have matzo for you. I know all about what happened. They don't know how I watch and listen. Women are not supposed to know anything. But I know everything. Well, almost. Can I help it if Sophia herself has blessed me with wisdom? Or should I say cursed, maybe. Come, little one. Don't grieve. Not yet. There is time enough for that."

It is such a relief to hear a woman's voice. Soon I am tottering towards her on spindly bird's legs and fluttering into her hands. She feeds me crumbs of some bread I've never tasted before, but it's just what I want. In a woman's hands, however bizarre it is to be a bird, I feel safe. Then I sense a shift in her attention. Her fingers stop stroking my breast. Her body tenses with alertness.

"Yeshua!" she calls. "Yeshua ben Miriam."

I don't know yet how unusual it is to call someone the son of his mother, how it can imply illegitimacy and be taken as an insult—even though a child must be born of a Jewish mother to belong to the tribe of Israel.

"Yeshua, stay your steps and listen to the words of Anna the Prophetess. I alone can speak the words you must hear."

No one could disobey this voice, and he doesn't. From Anna's lap I gaze up at my foster brother with my doves' eyes, drinking him in. From where I sit, I can't see the splat I made. I wonder if he recognizes me as the dove who shamed him before all the hairy men. Right now his attention is fixed on Anna.

"You do not know me, but I know you," she tells him. "You don't remember when your mother came to this Temple forty days after your birth to be purified. I saw her walking across the Court of Gentiles to the Court of Women. In one arm she carried you, the tiny daystar, whose light my eyes alone could see. In the other, she carried a wicker cage with two turtledoves and two young pigeons, all she could afford as a thank offering for the male child that opened her womb. (Never scorn the birds, Yeshua. They've shed their blood for you and for many.)

"I followed behind your mother. And when Simeon the priest raised you on high, I spoke a prophecy over you. Of course, I have to admit, Simeon beat me to the punch and said his piece first, but still I had my say. Shortly after that, Simeon departed in peace, just as he said he would (though he was a good twenty years younger than I am.) So he'll never be held accountable for his utterances. The Eternal One often gives a sweeter deal to men, I've noticed. No doubt you still think life is sweeter than death. Well, maybe it is, but it doesn't do to forget the bitter herbs. That's why we make you taste them when you're young, even though you don't understand what they mean.

"Stay, Yeshua. I know—though you don't say so; Miriam's brought you up too well—that you think I'm a raving old woman who runs on at the mouth, because she's more used to talking to birds than men. (At least the birds listen.) But I'm coming to the point. No, don't even ask. I'm not going to tell you the prophecies. I've learned a thing or two since those rash days that you would do well to remember: prophecy always loses in the translation and gains in the interpretation. But gain can be as dangerous as loss. Remember that, if you remember nothing else I say. This is the voice of wisdom speaking here. Now, listen. I'm going to give you some instructions. It's up to you whether you follow them or not.

"Leave. I don't just mean the Temple. I don't just mean Jerusalem. I don't just mean Judea and Galilee. Leave all you know. Step outside your world."

"Why would I want to do that?" My foster brother is wary. "And even if I wanted to, how could I? You call yourself a prophetess. How do I know you are not a sorceress?"

"Sorcery's beside the point. Listen. When you come back, you will see your people with new eyes. You will love them with a new love. You will find beauty in the despised; you will find secrets in the cracks between the stones."

I watch him listening to her. He is not used to the windings of old women's speech. He resists being drawn into the labyrinth. Yet something holds him there at wisdom's gate. At the river's rise.

"The world is a big place, Yeshua. And it's small. Small as a mustard seed, small as a hazelnut."

A hazelnut? Did they grow in this world?

"You need to know this. Trust me. Don't waste time asking questions. The questions you need to ask, you don't even know yet. But the people need those questions, the way the earth needs rain to plump the grain. Go find them. Go."

"Go where?" he asks, reasonably enough.

"Go to Egypt. To Alexandria," she instructs. "Your parents have friends there. Tell your mother: 'Anna says,' and she'll help you set out. She won't like it, but liking it is not what her life is about. Her name means bitterness, sweet Yeshua. Surely you know that.

"When you get to the seaport, find the people the Greeks call the *Keltoi.* You speak Greek, don't you? Take ship with the *Keltoi.* They'll take you where you need to go. Now go with my blessing. Go!"

Suddenly she is speaking not just to him, but to me. She is tossing me into the air, and I am forced to remember my wings.

"And don't despise this shitty little dove when you meet her again, though you may not recognize her. You may not think so, but she did you a favor today by disgracing you in the Temple and driving you out to me. And someday you may need her again."

He is looking perplexed as I balance my wings and rise into the air. Then the tense lines in his young face ease. He relents and holds out his beautiful brown hands to me.

⁂

That was my last glimpse of him in that dream or vision or whatever it was. Nothing fluttered but my heart, back in my human body in the earth shelter in the Valley between Bride's Breasts on Tir na mBan. You might think I'd be relieved not to be a bird anymore. But I didn't care who or what I was. I'd been so close, so close to his touch, I could hardly bear the loss.

9

TEN TAKE AWAY ONE

Do you remember what I told you about the number nine? The magical three times three? The Greeks named nine muses. The Hebrews revered nine for its pleasing quality of returning to itself whenever multiplied by adding the digits in the answer: 9 x 9 = 81; 8 + 1 = 9 and so forth. Try it yourself, if you haven't already. You'll like it. As you know, there are nine hazelnut trees growing around the Well of Wisdom. As well there might be. Nine is the number of wisdom. Nine is the number of completion. Nine is the number of this chapter, the last chapter of my childhood. Soon there will once again be nine women on Tir na mBan.

I didn't know it then, but I know now: I had a great childhood. I wonder if people whose childhoods are tragic or just plain miserable know it at the time. Maybe childhood, happy or sad, is simply something you survive—if you're lucky. If you do, it survives, too, becoming an entity in itself. In a sense, you own it. You get to add the adjectives to it. But it also owns you. As Anna says of prophecy: memory gains in the interpretation. After awhile it gets a little heavy, that old battered suitcase you drag around with you. Maybe you'd like to leave it somewhere, accidentally on purpose. The bathroom of a bus station. Or perhaps you should bury it under a thorn bush like the pot of gold it is. Good or bad, it's your source material. Buried or discarded, you still take it with you. You have no choice.

The gift of my childhood, the lasting impact of being adored by eight warrior witch mothers, both imperiled me and stood me in good stead in the years to come. To put it bluntly, I exited my childhood cunt-sure of myself. Well, why shouldn't I say cunt-sure instead of cock-sure? Does assurance require a protrusion; or a proclivity for crowing at dawn, if you insist that cock in this context refers to a rooster? Did a rooster ever lay an egg? Now, there's something to brag about. As far as my mothers were concerned, I was the egg, the golden egg, the golden apple of all their eyes. I was one of the wonders of the world—though the world didn't know it yet and wasn't exactly prepared.

But we are concerned here with my preparation for the world. Early in the month of Shoots-Show, what you would call April, the Cailleach held a Commencement Day for me, never mind that she'd told me zilch about what I was commencing next. In the morning, my mothers arrived in the Valley Between Bride's Breasts. They listened gravely and without comprehension as I addressed them formally in Greek, Latin, and Aramaic. They exclaimed over the ogham inscription I had carved on the flat edge of one of the menhirs that littered the island.

I would like to tell you that I made some profound remark on this stone, some pithy expression of the meaning of life in this cosmos. Carving in stone is not easy, so I was brief and to the point: "Maeve was here." At least I asserted my presence in a more durable medium than spray paint.

In the afternoon, we played games and had contests of strength and skill usually reserved for our celebration of *Beltaine*—which made me wonder where I would be then. In the evening, we feasted on roast pig. Afterwards we lolled outside around the fire, listening to each other's digestion and watching the stars come out. In my memory of that night, the stars look as tender as new grass, soft as the fleece of new lambs, impossibly young in an ancient sky.

"We have built the boat," Fand spoke from the silence.

"It might even be seaworthy," Boann added.

"What boat?" I demanded. I had been curled with my head in Grainne's lap while she stroked my hair. Now I sat up. Though our shoulders barely touched, I could feel her arm go rigid.

"Have you told her nothing?" wondered Liban.

Within the shadows of her grey cloak the Cailleach might have passed as a menhir herself. Still, all eyes turned toward her.

"I find it advisable to keep the very young firmly rooted in the present for as long as possible. Nor has the next step of Maeve's journey been entirely clear to me or to any of us. Until now. Now I believe we are agreed."

"Or resigned," sighed Etaine.

"Wait a minute," I objected. "Don't I have any say in this?"

"No," said the Cailleach without apology. "The time is coming when you will confront terrible choices. For now we will make them for you. Enjoy it while it lasts."

I attempted to sulk, but I was bursting with excitement. Something was going to happen at last. It didn't much matter what. I knew I was going to find *him*. Anna had as good as said so.

"Maeve Rhuad, I have taught you all the tongues I know," the Cailleach continued. "With them, you can travel across lands more vast than you can imagine. You are now equipped to talk yourself into and out of trouble in several languages. But there is more to language than talk, and more to learn than I can teach you. We are sending you to the forge of language, where you may learn to be a wordsmith. You will have a chance to become one of the *Aos Dana*, the gifted people."

"What do you mean?" Surely I was gifted already.

"We are going to present you as a candidate for admission to the Druid College on the Isle of Mona. If you are admitted, you will begin training as a bard. If you work hard and stay the course, you will learn by heart three hundred and fifty stories, becoming a poet of the Golden Branch. That is what it means to be one of the *Aos Dana*. You give yourself to the people. Your mind becomes a treasure house, a storage chamber for stories."

"Then I am not to be a warrior?" Despite what Queen Maeve had said about finding my own way, despite my mothers' doubts that the warrior's life was right for me, I still found it hard to comprehend that I would not grow up to be like my mothers. "I am to be a...bard?" I tried out the concept.

"If you stay the course. A bard's training, which is the first part of a druid's training, is longer and more stringent than a warrior's. But then, it's the stories of a people that give the warrior something worthy to defend. It can take twelve years to attain the Golden Branch. And to become a full-fledged druid takes almost twenty years."

Holy shit! Do you know how long that sounds to a fourteen-year-old? Still, the idea of being a druid held some allure. In the stories I'd heard, the druids were the ones who called all the shots. They could start or stop battles. Kings and heroes had to heed them—or else!

But there was one thing that puzzled me. Just who were "the people?" The Cailleach kept repeating this phrase. Anna had used that expression, too, and my foster brother seemed to know what she meant by it. But I didn't. And I wasn't sure I wanted to give my mind to anyone for any purpose.

"Who are the people?" I asked.

"Don't you remember anything of your lessons, Maeve? The tribes spread out from the Holy Isles through Gaul, parts of Iberia, all the way to Galatia. There are many tribes, each with its own name, and each one warring with another. It's the stories and druidic law that make them a people. Where you're going, they call themselves the *Combrogos*, the companions."

"But am I one of them?" I still wasn't satisfied. "Are we?"

"That's a matter for debate!" snorted Boann.

"Don't let's start again, sisters!" warned Liban.

"We've been arguing for months," Dahut explained to me.

"All while trying to build that damn boat," put it Etain. "More than one finger has gotten mashed in the process, I can tell you."

"Enough!" The Cailleach knew the signs of my mothers warming up for an argument as well as I did. "Let me put it this way, Maeve Rhuad. If we are not precisely one of the *Combrogos*, we are, without question, one of the stories they tell themselves."

The profundity of this remark silenced everyone for a time. I wasn't so sure I wanted to trade in being a story for memorizing another three hundred and forty-nine. But I was eager to start my journey, and I had other more pressing questions.

"Are there men on the Isle of Mona?" I ventured

"Are there!" exclaimed Fand. Then she clamped her mouth shut.

"There are," said the Cailleach.

"Do they speak Aramaic on the Isle of Mona?"

"No, child." The Cailleach gave me a penetrating look. "Don't you remember your geography at all? The Isle of Mona is just off the coast of Albion looking out to the Hibernian Sea. The people there speak one of our languages."

"Then I don't get it." I threw up my hands. "Why did you teach me all those languages, if I'm going to be stuck on one of the Holy Isles for twenty years memorizing stories in a language hardly different from the one I've spoken all my life!"

"I thought it best to prepare you for any eventuality."

That might be true. But there was more she wasn't telling me. More that everyone knew except me. I could practically smell it.

"A ship can be blown off course. I'm speaking metaphorically here. Because, of course, the boat that's taking you to the Isle of Mona won't be diverted."

She didn't need to add: and that's an order. You could hear it in her tone. I looked around the circle at my mothers, who all seemed particularly intent on star-gazing. All except Grainne, who looked down the length of her arm to where our fingers just touched.

"You might end up anywhere," the Cailleach went on. "The world is a big place, Maeve Rhuad. And small, small as a mustard seed, small as a hazelnut."

Anna. That's what Anna had said. And Anna had said something else, too. "Take ship with the *Keltoi*." Suddenly everything snapped into place.

"On the Isle of Mona, the people there, the *Combrogos*, are they...are they what the Greeks call the *Keltoi*?"

"Yes," said the Cailleach.

Our eyes met across the fire. She looked straight at me, into me and beyond. Her eyes glimmered gold. Then in their depths I caught a glimpse of a dark grove of trees with leaves so thick there was no sky.

The Cailleach had not told me the Isle of Mona's other name: Ynys Dewyll, the Island of Dark Shadows.

BOOK II

THE WRITING IN THE SKY

10

EMBARKING

My mothers have built a brave little boat, a coracle made of wicker and skins and dense, packed seaweed. The boat sits low to the wave and slides up and down the swells like a child's saucer sled. Its oak mast and leather sail, lowered and raised by an iron chain, look heavier than the boat itself. For steering it has only a set of oars. Anyone else might have been alarmed at the prospect of embarking on the high seas in a small craft of such dubious design, but I've never seen another sea-going vessel, and I am still child enough to trust that my mothers know what they're doing. Besides, what they lack in nautical expertise, they can make up with their prowess in weather magic. We can count on smooth sailing—at least for awhile.

It is a clear spring dawn. A steady wind blows from the West. The sky brightens in the East. At the tattered edge of night, the morning star shines huge and bright. It's time to say goodbye to my mothers—or anyway to the six remaining on Tir na mBan. After heated debate, the mothers finally decided that Fand and Boann would be the ones to escort me to Mona and see me through the admissions process. Fand staked a claim to the greatest knowledge of worldly (as distinct from Otherworldly) etiquette. Boann was chosen for her physical strength and for the calm that descends on her ordinarily excitable nature the moment calamity actually strikes. Now Fand and Boann wait by the boat, a gentle surf swirling around their ankles. The other six mothers stand on the shore, facing me. The Cailleach has not left Bride's Valley to see me off, but I am certain she is watching us in the Well of Wisdom.

No doubt you and my mothers both know better than I do what this parting might mean. To me, finality is not yet real. I only know that after all the bustle and fuss, loading the boat, the absurd combing and re-combing of my hair, the bedecking of me with bracelets and brooches, and a torque I can't wait to take off (jewelry being the 1st century woman's equivalent of a credit card), we are suddenly still. It is a single moment, suspended between night and day, between breath indrawn and released. It is timeless. It is instant. It is over.

Then I am being passed from one pair of arms to another, pressed against all those breasts. It is hardest to let go of Grainne. Not only is she my womb mother, bearer of the inner sea where I began, but I can sense

71

there's something she wants to tell me, but she won't or can't. She clings to me, and I cling back. At last we let go—or the others gently part us. I turn blindly and climb into the boat that will bear me over the second ocean.

Boann begins to row us out of the harbor between the sloping thighs of Tir na mBan. The scent of the magic orchard follows us on the wind. For days there will be hints of its blossom and fruit on the breeze, all the stronger for the orchard's being lost to our other senses. Now the sun is fully born on the eastern horizon. My mothers' voices rise with it, singing a song I've loved since my cradle days:

> Hail to thee, thou sun of the seasons,
> As thou traversest the skies aloft.
> Thy steps are strong on the wing of the heavens
> Thou art the glorious mother of stars.

Boann, Fand, and I take up the song.

> Thou liest down in the deepest ocean
> Without impairment and without fear.
> Thou risest up on the peaceful wavecrest
> like a queenly maiden.

I peer round Boann to look back at the shore just as the sun catches Grainne's hair. O my mother, my own mother sun, bobbing up and down in and out of my sight as we ride the bigger and bigger swells. The island wobbles, shot through with blinking rainbows. When my vision clears again, we are well beyond the harbor. Tir na mBan is a shining darkness, rising from the sea, her proud breasts thrust against the sky.

♒

This is the story of a journey (maybe all stories are) but it's not a travelogue, so I won't point out the sights or detail our stops as we sail past the Hebrides through the North Channel into the Hibernian Sea. Just hear the slap of waves, the endless whoosh of wind over water, the occasional cry of seabirds. Add Fand's admonitions to me, the running exchange of insults between Boann and Fand, our words punctuated with silences of increasing length as the immensity of sea and sky impresses us with our insignificance.

Our last stop before Mona was Man (an island sacred to my father, my mothers told me, though he failed to greet us in person). We refreshed ourselves before taking ship in the small hours of the morning to cross our longest stretch of open sea. By late afternoon, we came in sight of Holy Island, an island's island, separated from Mona by a ribbon of water, rising to cave-riddled cliffs where thousands of seabirds nest.

No wonder islands are held to be magical. You can't reach them by pedestrian means. You have to float or fly. And there they are, with the seas surging around them, waves caressing or crashing their shores, sending up spray. All those infinitesimal drops catch and intensify the light, making the air around islands brighter. When the light slants, even the grayest rocks turn gold.

"Are we almost there?" I asked, like any kid from any time in any conveyance.

"I hope so," declared Boann. "I don't want to be anywhere near those cliffs after nightfall. Fand, are you sure there's no place to land on the North side? It looks like there might be sands over there." She gestured with her head toward the northeastern coast of Mona, flat and shimmering in the distance.

"The Cailleach expressly said we were to sail around Holy Island and land on the southern coast of Mona at a place called Rhosneigr. That's where everyone coming from Hibernia lands for the *Beltaine* festival. So do boats coming from the South. The Cailleach was quite definite about it."

"Look!" I pointed, rising suddenly to my knees.

"Maeve! How many times must I tell you not to make violent motions. You'll pitch us into the drink yet."

"In the distance!" I ignored her. "You can see other boats heading in south of Holy Island, just as the Cailleach said."

"That might be some comfort if we had a better wind behind us. It's practically dead now," grumbled Boann. "We must be getting out of Deirdru and Etain's range."

"Why don't you revive it?" said Fand. "Aren't you a weather witch, too?"

"I am and I would," huffed Boann. "But in case you've forgotten, you all made me swear by every sacred thing you could think of not to do any wind calling. As if I had no subtlety or precision. As if I couldn't control the velocity. But if you want me forsworn—"

"Oh, all right, all right," snapped Fand. I knew she was embarrassed, because, gifted as she was in calling up fog (not exactly what was wanted at the moment), she'd never mastered whistling and could only manage a gusty blowing damp with spittle.

"I'll do it," I said.

"You?" For once they spoke in accord.

"I'm not a child anymore." I straightened my spine, puffed out my ripe breasts, pursed my lips, and before either could say another word, I turned to the Northwest and let out three perfectly pitched notes—not too loud, not too soft—of exactly the right length.

The response was instant. The bellying sail and the quickened pace lifted our spirits and broke the tension. Boann laughed out loud as she gripped the chain, and Fand looked at me with something approaching approval.

"She'll do us credit," Fand murmured to herself, just loud enough for me to hear.

We sailed on in silence for some time. As we drew nearer to the cliffs, I confess I felt some disappointment. They were not so different from the ones on the western shore of Tir na mBan. I wanted everything to be new and startling. Then, all at once, as if on some invisible cue, the cliffs came to life with an unfolding of wings and long fabulous shadows cast over their rugged surface by the slanting light. A flock of cranes rose into the deep sky over our heads.

None of us needed to cry out to the others: Look! The flight of all birds is oracular, especially cranes'. From the pattern of their wings in flight came the sacred ogham alphabet, as who should know better than I, the daughter of Manannán Mac Lir, the god who carries the secrets of the ogham in his magical crane bag. That's what his strange treasures really are, the Cailleach had told me.

"What do the crane wings say, Maeve?" asked Fand

Not that writing on the wing is easy to read, mind you. The letters flash and disappear a lot more quickly than subtitles. But here the pattern repeated and repeated.

"M-A-E-V-E," I spelled. "Maeve!" I cried with delight, but not as much surprise as you might suppose. I was the daughter of a god. Why shouldn't my father arrange skywriting for me? "The cranes are announcing my arrival."

As soon as I spoke, the pattern shifted, again repeating and repeating until I spelled out the letters E-S-U-S, which at that time meant nothing to me.

"E-sus," I tried the word aloud, and the cranes, apparently satisfied that I'd received the message, rose higher. Turning in an arc, they flew over the cliffs of Holyhead in the direction of Mona.

It was then that I saw the others: three black forms on the cliff's edge. At first I took them for ravens, but their wings were too loose and wind-blown. Also, I realized after a time, the figures were too large to be birds. Whatever they were, I sensed that their eyes were trained on our small boat. Fand and Boann had seen them, too. I caught them exchanging a speaking glance over my head.

"Who are they?" I asked.

"Priestesses, I believe," said Fand a little stiffly. "The priestesses of Holy Island."

I did not have time to give Fand's manner or the trio's scrutiny much thought. Running with the wind, we rounded the head, and a whole new vista opened up. Now I could see miles of Mona's lush body, stretching languidly towards a whole range of mountains. The effect was wondrously different from the two pert breasts of Tir na mBan. Here was a huge, unbreaking tidal wave of mountains, shimmering and blue, with white caps of cloud. I had never seen so much land massed against the sky.

Then the foreground claimed my attention once more as we came closer to the other boats. We weren't near enough yet for me to make out the passengers, but, even at a distance, I could tell that the boats were bigger than ours, longer, with a prow and a stern (not that I knew those terms at the time) raised high out of the water. We moved towards them and away from Mona at a diagonal.

"Aren't you going the wrong way?" I asked in alarm.

"I'm going out so I can head straight in. Grab an oar and help me steer, Maeve," instructed Boann. "When we come about, switch sides."

While I held the oar and Boann the sail, Fand went into a tizzy.

"Where's that comb! Sit still, Maeve," she shrilled as she nearly capsized us with her frantic rummaging. "And your gold. You must have it on when we land. Here's your torque." She nearly choked me as she yoked me. "And your head piece. I know you're holding the oar. Just give me your other arm. There. Where is that comb? Oh, here!" She began yanking at the snarls. "You're the daughter of a god," she reminded me. "You've been raised by queens, yes, queens. Do you hear? We can't have you looking like some captive taken in a raid. You must show your lineage, Maeve!"

I did not understand the fuss Fand was making over my appearance. I had no concept of rank. All I knew was that Fand, in her hovering, was blocking my view of the other boats. I tried to peer around her.

"Maeve!" shrieked Fand. "For the love of Bride, don't lean. We don't want to swim the rest of the way!"

"Coming about!" shouted Boann.

Our coracle joined the bobbing procession of boats and headed straight for the shore.

11

One of the Crowd

eltaine, the feast of Bel, the Shining One, was one of the two greatest of the four yearly festivals. It marked the beginning of the bright half of the year just as *Samhain*, across the great round of nights and days, ushered in the dark. All through the dark time, the Pleiades rode the night. Now, at *Beltaine*, the seven sisters set, as if melting into the brimming light.

Of the festivals, *Beltaine*, later known as May Eve, was a particularly exuberant one. Oak, beech, ash, and larch were all on the verge of exploding into leaf. You could practically live on the air alone, rich as it was with the fragrance of flowering gorse, thorn, may, apple, and plum. The crops, already sown, sliced through the soil with their brave green blades as if the earth were a cake. After wintering in the byres, the cattle were about to rampage between two purifying fires out to their lush summer pastures. With the fair weather, the *Combrogos*, too, would be on the move: poets, traders, bands of roving warriors, and just plain folks getting together to have a good time.

As everyone knows to this day (and remembers with secret longing), for centuries the eve of May was a socially sanctioned orgy. Running off into the woods with someone who wasn't your spouse was practically your civic duty. You were obeying the oldest law. You were multiplying the orgasms of the sexy, fecund earth. Hey, it could only help the crops—and hence the tribes. So just this once, go ahead. Surrender. Let go and let god/dess. That was the mood of *Beltaine*.

Of course, on Tir na mBan we celebrated all the festivals with our own peculiar panache. But consider the difference between a glass of champagne with a few old friends on New Year's Eve and joining the screaming crowds in Times Square. Despite a dearth of neon lights and peep shows, the Isle of Mona was a gathering place of equal popularity and more importance. Not only was it the site of one of the most prestigious druid colleges in the Celtic world, it was also the grain basket that fed the warrior kings and fueled their resistance to Rome. If that weren't enough, Mona was the first major pit stop for traders on the gold route from Hibernia's Wicklow Hills. Here the tribes congregated, not only to revel, but to wheel and deal, to make and mend quarrels, and to debate politics and policy.

As soon as I set foot on the sand at Rhosneigr, I found myself in the midst of throngs. Can you imagine the impact on me of that concentration of human energy? For a time after I stepped out of the boat, I just stood still, feeling it rush in around me, or break over my head like a wave. A less brazen temperament than mine might have been bowled over by this first contact with the human crowd. For me it was as if something hot and pulsing had been pumped straight into my bloodstream. My every pore was open and drinking.

"Maeve!" Fand's commanding voice cut through the roaring in my ears. "Come help unload the boat."

Compared to the other stores being unloaded on the shore, ours were meagre. We had no caskets of raw gold or other metals. We had no huge smoked haunches. Warriors though my mothers were, they had not brought their horses, nor were they assembling their battle chariots on the beach. With less than half a mind, I lifted from the boat our jugs of mead and water, our baskets of oatcakes and fruit from the magical orchard. Apart from food, there was only my spare summer tunic, two warmer ones for winter, my cloak and sandals, which Fand insisted I put on, and a few heavy plaids for sleep and shelter. As Fand and Boann fashioned our belongings into separate bundles for each of us, I minded my P and Q Celtic, trying to catch phrases as they flew past me. In particular, I thrilled to the timbre of male voices and stared as openly as I dared at the bodies that issued those robust tones.

I soon observed that there was no generic model among the Appended Ones. Some had more facial hair than face. Others had naked chins with hair overhanging the upper lip. Sometimes the hair drooped down the side of the mouth, reminding me of walrus tusks. Still other men had no hair on their faces but their skins were rough and bristly like a pig's. As a rule, they were quite large, though many of the women were almost as tall. (Fand and even muscular Boann stood out as small in this crowd). The women shouted commands with as much authority as men. I offer this detail for your benefit. Women in authority were nothing new to me.

But I did notice that some people gave commands while others carried them out. The ones in command—male and female—had tunics of brighter colors, often striped or plaid, bordered with gold or silver braid. Their cloaks flashed with brooches and their arms clanked with gold. The people fetching and carrying had a dimmed quality, as if a layer of dust had settled permanently. Even their hair was duller, and not from lime wash.

Lime was used to heighten appearance, not diminish it. Some of the warriors had fantastically sculpted hair, spikes and manes so stiff with lime that even the sea wind could not disarrange a single hair.

Speaking of hair, as you may have gathered, my hair—convention calls its color red, but fiery orange is more exact—is important to me, important to the story. Remember how it caught the light in Bride's Valley and served as a conduit for the fire of the stars? In case you've forgotten, my mothers, except for the golden-haired Grainne and the grey Cailleach, were all dark. Only in my dream-vision had I ever seen another redhead—until this day.

Here, in the festival crowd, bobbed head after head of flame, an erratic congregation of torches. Sometimes they swarmed in clusters, if the gene for red hair had flared in the four generations of extended family that comprise a *tuath*. At first I felt a jolt of alarm every time I saw a red-haired man, but none had the chilling features of the face in my vision. Then a subtler feeling began to surface.

You may recognize the feeling more quickly than I did. Very likely you have suffered the affront of a sibling's birth. Even if you didn't, you went to school and sat in a classroom full of gap-toothed six-year-olds. Possibly there was even another child in the class with the same first name as yours, and you were called Susie Q. to distinguish you from Susie P. One way or another, you got the gist: you're one of many.

So here I am, at fourteen years of age, in a flash no longer unique. Or only unique as in "everyone is unique," which just doesn't cut it as far as the ego is concerned. All right, so no two people are alike, no two stars, snowflakes, or, for that matter, no two sheep, warthogs, or mayflies. Listen! There were other redheaded fourteen-year-old-girls in the world. This is the stuff of identity crisis.

Little did I know my troubles with fellow redheads were only beginning. But that's getting ahead of the story. In that moment on the beach, I didn't have time to ruminate on an unsettling sensation that takes much longer to describe than it did to experience.

Twilight at that time of year goes on and on, but there was a touch of chill in the air. The shadow of Holyhead stretched towards Rhosneigr. I turned from my gawking to see what my mothers were doing. Boann was still fussing with the boat, though it was well secured, its sail neatly folded, and Fand was tying and retying the bundles. I wonder: does every child know this dizzying moment? My all-powerful mothers appeared at a loss. They did not know how to proceed. And, most important, they no longer stood between me and the ripe, juicy world. As if on cue, someone just out of sight struck up a jaunty rhythm on a drum. A pipe shrilled. The crowd, still milling at the edges, was becoming an impromptu procession inland over the marshy dunes. The party was beginning, and I intended to be at the heart of it.

"Come on!" I commanded, picking up one of the bundles and starting to walk. With unprecedented meekness, my mothers followed.

Now that I was part of the general movement, my sense of personal displacement gave way to the pleasure of belonging to a larger body. A good beat and a common direction can bond you to strangers—or at least give you the illusion of unity. Since then I have known many human crowds, but this was my very first. A crowd is a living organism. It can easily turn into a monster, baying for human flesh, tearing to pieces any victim tossed into its maw. But the holiday crowd on Mona was, for the moment, benign, a happy creature like a big, friendly dog wanting to lick everyone's face. The air rang with snatches of song, cries of greeting between people who hadn't met since the last festival, guffaws at the revival of old jokes. As I walked along with everyone else, I did not feel excluded. I laughed, too, whether I got the jokes or not, for the pleasure of it.

I was laughing out loud when I tripped. I was not used to wearing a long tunic—as Fand had insisted women did, in contrast to men—and I hadn't yet grasped the necessity of lifting it on an uphill grade. We'd just begun to climb from the shore. Moreover, my bundle blocked my view of my feet. So down I tumbled, knocking Boann and Fand off-balance so that they staggered back a few feet. Fortunately, the crowd was moving at a leisurely pace, and we were in no danger of being trampled. Before we could sort ourselves out, we were surrounded.

I can still remember that sudden sensation of anti-gravity as a good portion of my weight was taken from me. Even more vividly I retain the image of arms thicker than any I'd ever seen, as thick as a young tree trunk, covered with black hair almost as coarse as a beast's. And gigantic hands! But the most pungent memory of that moment is of the scent. As those hands and arms drew me up to chest level, I got my first strong whiff of *man*. Maybe it's all that excess hair everywhere. Scent clings to it, not just the man's sweat, but whatever is in the air—in this case salt from the sea, the sweet pollen scent of the trees, and the man's own particular musk. I closed my eyes and inhaled it.

"The maiden is swooning." I not only heard but felt the vibrations of that voice. The strong arms held me secure. Small wonder Victorian ladies went in for vapors.

"Maeve!" squawked Fand. "Stop this at once!"

Of course I hadn't fainted at all, and I was much too curious to keep my eyes closed. The visual effect of staring up into a large, male face, complete with nose hairs and five o' clock shadow—(the man was one of those with a walrus mustache)—was not as appealing as the other sensations. I righted myself and drew apart.

"I thank you, kind stranger," I said in my slightly accented P-Celtic, assuming the role of spokeswoman. Boann and Fand spoke Q only and appeared to be tongue-tied. "For your timely aid."

I was young and mistook stilted speech for grandeur. The man hid a smile.

"My kindness was a small thing and as for my strangeness, you shall know me better."

At a word from him, other men from his party shouldered our bundles. We fell into step together.

"Allow me to introduce myself. I am Bran Fendigaid, ab Llyr Lleidiaith, ab Baran, ab Ceri Hirlyn Gwyn, ab Caid, ab Arch, ab Meirion..."

Welcome to the oral culture, folks. At this convention you will find no registration table, no little stick-on "Hello, my name is" tags where you scrawl one or two paltry words.

"...ab Ceiraint, ab Greidiol, ab Dingad, ab Anyn, ab Alafon..."

Never having received a formal introduction before, I confess I was somewhat taken aback myself. Fand and Boann, meanwhile, were exchanging furtive looks of deep disapproval. Despite their unfamiliarity with the P dialect, they understood enough to know that Bran Fendigaid ab infinitum was introducing himself through the paternal line. Shocking!

"...ab Brywlais, ab Cerraint Feddw, ab Berwyn, ab Morgan, ab Bleddyn..."

For my part, I was wondering how long this list could go on. We were now marching to its rhythm.

"...ab Rhun, ab Idwal, ab Llywarch, ab Calchwynydd, ab Enir Fardd..."

I was also worried about what to say when it came my turn—if it ever did.

"...ab Ithel, ab Llarian, ab Teuged, ab Llyfeinydd, ab Peredur..."

And was *everyone* going to make introductions of such length or was it just a man thing?

"...ab Gweyrydd, ab Ithon, ab Cymryw, ab Brwt, ab Selys Hen..."

We'd probably covered a good half mile of ground by now.

"...ab Annyn Tro, ab Brydain, ab Aedd Mawr."

It took me a moment to realize he was finished. We were all a bit breathless. And come to think of it, what had stopped him? Run out of fathers, presumably. Somewhere or another, you had to start with a mother. Everyone knew that. It was only common sense. The silence lengthened, and I realized some response was expected of me.

"Yes, well." I cleared my throat, trying in vain to remember Fand's last minute lessons in etiquette. Why wasn't she prompting me? Why couldn't she at least manage a polite greeting? "I am honored to meet you, er—"

Have you ever forgotten someone's name as soon as they said it? Try remembering someone's lineage.

"You can call me Bran." And we were back to where we started a half an hour ago. "To the tribe of the Silures, I am king. But I don't stand on ceremony. I leave all that folderol to the bards. A king earns his fame on the battlefield and through fair dealings. If he takes care of business, others will take care of his name."

Taking care of King Bran's name would be no small task, I considered. I had heard of the Silures. The Cailleach's geography lessons were coming in handy. I was able to call up a map from memory and place his tribe to the south of Mona on the mainland. I was not as awed as you might be to find myself ambling with a king. I was barely socialized, even to the Celtic culture of my time. Besides, there were lots of kings then, warring with other kings, raiding each other's cattle, competing for wealthy clients. They were more like your congressmen—here today, gone tomorrow, running amuck in corruption and scandal. Whereas the druids were always there, an overwhelming, overbearing supreme court. But I didn't know any of that then. Nor did I know that under King Bran's fiery leadership, the Silures had become controversial players in the debate over traffic with Rome.

"And now," said Bran, "unless you've sworn a vow of secrecy or must of necessity cloak your identity, may I know the names of the beauteous women who walk beside me, whose loveliness calls to mind the first stars blooming in the twilit sky?"

He addressed this question to my mothers in deference to their age. I hoped they'd answer, because I was choking on what can only be called a fit of giggles. You must remember this was my first exposure to male charm and flattery. It acted on me like laughing gas.

"Our daughter will speak for us." Fand said slowly in an approximation of P-Celtic.

"Ah," said Bran. "Do I detect the accents of Hibernia?"

"The accents, perhaps." I recovered myself. "But we do not come from that large island." I paused, took a deep breath, and plunged in. "I am Maeve Rhuad. Daughter of, er, Queens Fand and Boann." I nodded toward each of them. They began to beam. I was doing it right. "Liban, Deirdru, Dahut, Emer, Etain, and Grainne of the golden hair...."

Now what, I wondered? Bran was looking politely confused by this time. That made two of us. Then inspiration struck.

"And by their...um...queenhood and sacred sisterhood my mothers are daughters of the Cailleach who is, let's see, the daughter of Bride."

"Daughter of Dugall the Brown," King Bran chimed in, "ab Aodh, ab Conn, ab Criara, ab Cairbre, ab Cas, ab Cormach, ab Cartach, ab Conn. Each day and each night that I say the descent of Bride, I shall not be slain, I shall not be sworded, I shall not be put in a cell, I shall not be hewn, I shall not be riven..."

I stared at Bran, not understanding, as doubtless you don't either, that I had prompted him to recite the geneology of Bride, a charm known to every Celt from the time he could speak the way you know "Twinkle, Twinkle, Little Star" or "Now I Lay me Down to Sleep."

"...I shall not be anguished, I shall not be wounded, I shall not be ravaged, I shall not be blinded, I shall not be made naked, I shall not be left bare, nor fire shall burn me, nor sun shall burn me, nor moon shall blanch me—Oh, excuse me." He suddenly remembered me. "You were saying?"

What had I been saying? Oh yes, I had just claimed descent from Bride. Need I say more?

"And your father?" he prompted.

"Oh. Him. My father is Manannán Mac Lir." There. That ought to do it. If your father is Son of the Wave, you shouldn't have to trace his lineage any further. "That's Manawyddan ab Llyr to you," I translated helpfully.

"Yes, well," King Bran said in his turn.

You can hardly blame him for being somewhat at a loss, having just been introduced to someone whose descent was divine on both sides. Even my foster brother's chroniclers stopped short of that claim—if only just.

"You can call me Maeve. And the two queen mothers traveling with me are Fand and Boann," I refreshed his memory.

"It is a privilege to walk with queens."

He bowed his head in their direction. They nodded stiffly in return. But I could tell they were beginning to thaw. I could practically hear the drip, drip, drip of icy reserve melting.

"Where did you say you came from?" Bran asked.

"We didn't, but I can tell you. I think."

I glanced at Fand and Boann to see if they had understood the question. They conferred together in low tones. Then nodded to me.

"We have sailed here from Tir na mBan."

"The Land of Women," he repeated in P-Celtic.

A dreamy look came over his face, a look I was to see time and again on men's faces when I spoke that name. The rapturous response was not the only one I was to encounter, however. I soon learned that if I wanted to know something about a man's nature, at least a Celtic man's, all I had to do was pronounce those syllables: Tir na mBan.

"I've heard about such islands." His voice was full of longing. "It has never been my good fortune to find one."

"Well, they're not always easy to find." Fand had clearly followed the gist of the conversation. "But if you want directions...."

Boann started to giggle. There is no other word for it. I was shocked. What had gotten into my mothers? They were acting, well, not like *mothers*.

"I've often wondered what it might be like..." Bran went on dreamily, focused not on Fand and Boann (at least not as I knew them) but on some rich fantasy unfolding before his inner eye "...to slip out of time and into all those waiting arms and perfumed—"

Boann, I must report, gave a loud, ribald snort. And Bran came to.

"But when you're a king," he sighed, "not to mention the head of a large *tuath*, it's all work and no play. Still, I've a good mind to turn it all over to Caradoc—he's my eldest—while I'm still hale enough to have a mythic adventure or two before I go West permanently."

A euphemism for dying that may have originated with the Celts.

"But what brings you happy queens and your lovely daughter from one of the Shining Isles to a place like Mona?"

What did he mean by that, a place like Mona? I was about to ask when he went on, answering his own question.

"Looking for a match for the maiden? Not much traffic on Tir na mBan these days, I should imagine," he went on. "Young men are not what they used to be. I put it down to the Roman influence."

"Heroes have been scarce on Tir na mBan." Boann bellowed in Q-Celtic, as if volume would translate for her.

As it turned out, Bran readily comprehended Q-Celtic. In the days to come, I was to hear many conversations like this one, each person speaking in his own dialect.

"But we are not here to look for men." Fand felt obliged to remind us all. "We are presenting Maeve Rhuad as a candidate to the college. She is to become a poet."

"To be sure!" Bran answered heartily. "That should have been plain to me at once. After all, that's one of the chief reasons I'm here myself with my own daughter, Branwen. I lay odds the two of you are the same age. Fourteen, am I right? She's here somewhere. Branwen!" he bellowed. "Probably gone ahead with the women to set up camp. She'll be glad to meet a classmate. She's a bit shy, what with losing her mother a few years back."

Losing her mother! The concept of motherlessness was almost beyond my grasp.

"Branwen's got her mother's talent and memory," he continued. "She was an educated woman, my Gwynefere. Could have been one of the *Aos Dana*. Me now, I'm no great intellect. Same with my sons. I could never get them interested in anything but fighting. But I promised Branwen's mother before she died that if ever they opened the college to women I'd give Branwen a crack at getting a Silver Branch at least. But a twelve year course of study!" He shook his head. "It's not easy for a young girl to last that long, if you get my drift."

Personally, I didn't see how anyone could.

"Well, then, here's our camp now." Bran gestured to the left. "Would I be too bold and presuming, O queens from the Shining Isles of the Blest, if I invited you to join our company?"

Too bold! Here we were with our plaids and our sodden oatcakes. Down a small slope, in a grove of large, sheltering beeches not far from a small river gleaming silver with the last light, I could see cook fires with meat already roasting on the spit. Someone was playing a harp. Other people were setting up shelters and making beds with evergreen boughs.

"That would be most acceptable," said Fand.

"She means we accept," Boann hastened to add.

Bran got the gist. "I'm honored," he said, offering a massive, muscled arm to each of my mothers. To my amazement, Fand and Boann looped their arms through his without a murmur. "And there's Branwen," he said, leading us down the slope. "That little shadow there in the gloaming. She's been to the *Beltaine* festival many a time. She'll show you around, Maeve Rhuad. Branwen. Ho! Branwen! Come meet your new classmate!"

Through the green-smelling dusk, I saw a slight young girl running towards us, her bare feet gleaming. She fit her father's description of her as a shadow. Her dark braids seemed thicker than her narrow face. The largest thing about her were her eyes. They were enormous, and with the pupils dilated they looked bottomless, mysterious like a scrying pool. I was relieved that she wasn't one of those strapping redheads.

In fact, Branwen and I could not have looked more different from one another in face or figure. Our breasts could have been used to illustrate the extremes of size and shape in human mammaries. Mine threatened to split the seams of my tunic; hers were barely visible. Thrust at each other by her father, we stared for a few moments as if we were both much younger children. I don't know who smiled first. I suspect it was simultaneous. Branwen's smile was as sudden and bright as a shooting star. It made me think of Grainne's.

That one smile was all it took. We were friends.

12

THE LAKE OF LITTLE STONES

They are waiting for us on the shore of Llyn Cerrig Bach, the druids of Mona. They are standing, white robed, row on row, in a semi-circle. If you were a night-hunting bird looking down from above, their ranks might have resembled a crescent moon. And don't forget the moon's shadowed side. Though tonight they are not present, remember the black robed priestesses of Holy Island.

The druids are waiting to meet us, the *Beltaine* crowds: the traders, the warriors, the wandering poets, the members of respectable *tuaths* who will present sons and daughters as candidates to the College. Tonight, on the shore of the Lake of Little Stones, the druids preside over the opening rite of the five day festival. They will mediate for us with the Otherworld; they will receive, appraise, and offer to the lake our jewels, our weapons, our prized possessions.

Think of layers and layers of gold, iron, and bone sinking, settling, shifting through water, mud, earth, and deeper. And the little stones—the tips, perhaps, of huge megaliths—rise and stand, ambassadors from the world under the water. Minnow stars swim around their stillness, distracting from the secrets beneath the surface.

You can see better than I could then. I only glimpsed the druids from a distance as we climbed over the dunes to the meadows by a lake, which could more properly be called a marsh. On the northern shore there was enough dry, level ground for a gathering. When we halted, I found myself in the middle of the crowd, and I could not see well enough to suit me. Though I was taller than Fand and Boann, there were plenty of taller people surrounding me, especially men. Fascinated as I was by the appended ones in general, I didn't find staring between their shoulder blades all that interesting. Soon people began spreading plaids and sitting down. (Branwen had warned us this rite went on forever.) But still I fretted at being so far from the main stage.

"I want to go closer to the front," I whispered to my new friend.

We had walked with Branwen from the camp grounds. It was she who explained to us about the votive offerings. Fand and Boann had dropped behind us to confer anxiously. Later I understood that they were worried, like many parents, about the cost of my education. They hadn't reckoned on having to make a non-returnable deposit, so to speak, before I was even admitted. As for me, I was blissful in my ignorance. I did not know the value of gold or the meaning of sacrifice. I only hoped I'd be allowed to toss my onerous torque into the bog.

"We have to stay with our *tuaths*," Branwen explained. "That's how we're called when we go to make our offerings."

"I don't have a *tuath*," I pointed out.

"You and your mothers are our guests." Branwen laid a gentle hand on my arm. "You'll come with us."

"You're kind," I had the grace to say. "But let's just go to the front for a little while. I can't see anything from here."

"There's things I'd rather not see."

Branwen was close enough so that I could feel her shudder. Of course, that hint made me all the more determined to get a front row seat.

"I might not want to see them either," I tried to be agreeable, "once I'd seen them already, that is. But you see, Branwen, I've never seen anything. I've lived my whole life 'til now on an island so small you could eat it for breakfast and be hungry again by noon. I never saw anyone, and nothing ever happened," I said with the callow exaggeration and sublime ingratitude of youth. "I'll only be a minute. Don't tell my mothers!"

For the first but not the last time, I left Branwen holding the bag. Before she could say a word, I ducked under an arm, darted around a massive warrior, and began worming my way to the front.

I secured a seat some fifty feet away from the phalanx of druids just as a rather unimpressive looking specimen came forward to address the crowd. He had a moth-eaten beard of indeterminate color and a concave chest. His gold torque looked too heavy for his neck. I couldn't imagine that the far reaches of the gathering could hear his high-pitched voice, but no one was paying much attention anyway.

And what was he saying? What were the first words of esoteric wisdom to fall from druid lips into my tender, untutored ear?

"And we remind you that bathing in the Menai Straits is inadvisable when the tides are turning. Drink from non-votive wells only, and you should not drink from Afon Crignu until you are several miles inland, because of the high saline content...."

Some things haven't changed as much as you might think. Wherever two or three are gathered together, there will be announcements. The druid continued with a run-through of the festival schedule, the time and location of various rites and events. I tuned out. It was my mothers' job to remember such details. Instead I turned my attention to the druids standing behind the speaker. I'd never seen so many beards gathered in one place since the dream I'd had of my Appended One. They came in all shapes and sizes and assorted colors—

All at once my heart stopped. I know that's a hackneyed phrase, but no other will do. That's what it feels like. You're the mouse hidden in the grass when suddenly you see the glow of the cat's eyes. It hasn't seen you yet, but any moment it might. Your heart stops, as if you could will yourself into the safety of non-existence.

He was there at the far edge of the front row of druids: the man from my vision, the man who stole my face.

I had an overwhelming urge to run in two directions at once: back to a mother's arms, back to Tir na mBan, back to before. The other impulse was worse: to dart into the open, to draw danger to me. The two instincts cancelled each other out and kept me still. My heart went back to its job, and as it calmed, I reasoned with myself. With such a large crowd, and red hair everywhere, there was no reason he or anyone should notice me. For the moment, I was willing to relinquish all claims to uniqueness.

I took advantage of my anonymity to study the man of my nightmare. The more I looked, the more his face seemed only his own, whoever he was, and not a distortion of mine. In fact, I could hardly see any resemblance between us beyond the red hair. His eyes were smaller than mine and his nose larger and more defined. From what I could see of it under the hood, his hair was straight. Mine was springy and wild as heather. Silver glinted in a beard that was neatly trimmed and glossy as a fox's coat. He was broad-shouldered and had a fine, straight bearing. From this safe distance, I could see that his looks were pleasing.

I barely noticed when the lightweight druid's droning ceased, and he melted back into his place. Then the drums began, and the whole mood changed. Even the wandering breeze shifted and came to attention. Another druid emerged from the crescent formation, positioning himself just beyond its curve as if he were the evening star in relation to the new moon. With the light playing on his impossibly long, white beard, he had the commanding brilliance of the brightest star. To say that he was a very old man would give the wrong impression. There was nothing frail or diminished about his presence. He was ancient, rather, as a tree is ancient: massive, thick, complex with gnarls and knots of root and branch, the lines in his face like the cryptic inscriptions insects make under the bark. An old tree is host to a plethora of life: nesting birds and squirrels, burrowing creatures among the roots. This man was a human center; a whole people grew or withered in his shade.

He stood before us, his gaze steady. Have you ever noticed how the eyes of a statue or painting seem to follow you, even though you know they are motionless? His eyes were like that. No one escaped. He looked for a long time, until you felt he had not only seen you but seen through you to a place beyond, visible to him alone. Then he raised his staff. The drums ceased, and he began to chant and pace a circle. At first the sound was barely human, more like wind in branches or waves rolling over stones. Then, from this elemental song, words rose.

> I am the wind of the sea,
> I am the wave of the sea,
> I am the sound of the sea,
> I am a stag of seven tines,
> I am a hawk on a cliff,
> I am a tear of the sun,
> I am fair among flowers,
> I am a ruthless boar,
> I am a salmon in a pool,
> I am a hill of poetry,
> I am a flood on a wide plain,
> I am a god who sets the head afire with smoke,
> Who but I knows the secrets
> of the unhewn dolmen?

On and on he chanted, pausing in his steps to mark the four quarters. Soon voices all around me answered his. Words sang themselves through me. Not just words but images. The air teemed with the forms he invoked. I could see the flash of the salmon's scales and the gleam of the stag's tines.

Silence fell again. The old druid made his way to the center. There he raised his staff over his head, then he plunged it into the earth that opened magically to receive it.

"Here now is the center of the world."

For an instant I glimpsed the Tree.

It was so tall, I couldn't see its highest branches. Its roots reached as deep. I could feel the pull of them. The leaves were gold. I don't mean yellow or even the rich-yellow brown you see in autumn. I mean hot, fresh gold drawn up from the molten places in the earth, exploding into leaves.

Then the vision passed. I saw only the staff, but now I knew what it was.

The center of the world established, the druid turned and walked towards the lake. At that moment it would not have surprised me to see him walk on the water's surface or disappear beneath it into the Otherworld, but he stopped at the edge. As the druid stood by the lake muttering and motioning with his arms, my willing suspension of disbelief suddenly snapped. I shifted into technical appraisal.

He was doing weather magic. I was sure of it. Subtly, he was changing the temperature of the air and water. Soon the surface of the lake came alive with eddying mist. He called forth marsh lights, turning the mist a rather lurid green. (Believe me, special effects are nothing new.) The ancient druid was a master. I hoped Fand had a good view, though she was probably green as the marsh gas with envy and itching to get her hand in. Now the druid gathered all the little mists and shaped them into one huge form, both gorgeous and terrifying.

The Lady of the Lake reached out with long phosphorescent fingers. You'd have to be braver than most to hold out on this dame.

13

CONSPICUOUS DISPOSAL

So this isn't your idea of how you'd dispose of your disposable income? Down votive wells, earth shafts, into sacred springs and lakes? And if you are thinking that the druids helped themselves to these soggy sacrifices on the quiet, you're wrong. What went down did not come up. There was no equivalent to your Savings and Loan scandals. The Celts were banking with and on the gods. Before you shake your head over the waste of all that wealth, think about the votive well where you deposit your own waste.

That's right. You flush it down the toilet. It's carried away in torrents of once clean water to pollute rivers and seas instead of replenishing the soil. (Soil and dirt; they are practically dirty words in your language.) You literally don't give a shit, do you? At least the Celts and other so-called primitive peoples returned some of their wealth to the source of all wealth. They grasped the real meaning of "no deposit, no return."

There may have been a worldly as well as Otherworldly aspect to this ritual, not so different from your own practice of conspicuous consumption. You buy a Mercedes Benz at least in part so that other people know you can. Therefore, murmurs of awe and envy followed a Brigante chieftain as he drove a bronze-fitted war chariot along the crowd's edge towards the waiting druids. The chariot was drawn by a beautiful mare, so sleek and black that she looked like a horse-shaped piece of night. Behind the chariot processed tribesmen and women, some wearing helmets plated with gold. One strikingly handsome woman was cloaked in a mantle of her own heavy, black hair, one white streak running through the length of it. She carried a huge, bronze-backed mirror swirling with delicate, asymmetrical designs. I could imagine her placing it in the Lady's fingers.

The drum beats built in intensity as the procession of Brigantes drew nearer the druids, then ceased abruptly when they finally came to a halt. The ancient druid stood still with his arms spread in a gesture of receiving, but his eyes seemed unfocused on the foreground.

Three other druids stepped forward to make an appraisal of the offerings and, no doubt, to file in their archival memories precisely who had given what. Flanked by two others, one grizzled, one the skinny druid who'd made announcements, stood the druid with the fox-red beard. Foxface, I named him. His fellow appraisers made their assessments of the chariot and other offerings quickly, as if the examination was a mere formality. But Foxface refused to be rushed. With his eyes narrowed, the loose flesh beneath them puckered into folds. He looked older and more severe. It unnerved me to think of him turning the full force of his critical attention on my bracelets and torque. At last, he nodded. The whole crowd let out its breath. I felt flooded with vicarious relief.

But wait! There seemed to be some dispute about the horse. After she'd made her offering, the woman with the streaked hair had slipped through the ranks to the chariot. While the druids were busy appraising the mirror, she had apparently undone the horse's harness. Now she held the horse's reins while her kinsmen exhorted her, and the druids conferred in a triple knot. One large man made a lunge for the reins. The horse reared and screamed, and everyone backed out of range—except the woman. When the horse's hooves plunged back to the earth, she flung herself on its back. Her voice rose above everyone else's, ringing through the air that had suddenly stilled as if it, too, wanted to hear.

"I told you, assholes!" She spoke in P-Celtic but with a strong Hibernian accent, which meant she was not a Brigante by birth. "This mare belongs to the goddess Macha! And when Macha wants her, she'll whistle. Till then she's in my keeping. No fucking way am I going to see her throat slit to make the Brigantes look good. Or to please Our Lady of the Bog. What do you know about the Lady anyway, you druids. You *men*."

She spat the words. Then, without warning, she charged the druid trio, grabbing the bronze mirror out of Foxface's hands. She held it over her head and brandished it, scattering shards of refracted light through the crowd.

"See? I am giving her my grandmother's mirror, who had it from her grandmother, who had it from Goibnu, Brigid's own smith. If that's not good enough for the Bog Lady, then fuck her. And she'll receive it from my own hand or not at all."

With that, she turned her horse and galloped towards the water's edge. A moment later, we heard a smacking splash as the mirror went in broadside. I waited for her to ride back to her kinsfolk. Instead, she urged her horse forward into the water. All around me people began to exclaim and speculate until the white-bearded druid raised his arms and spoke.

"The Lady has taken the mare and the mirror and the woman into the bargain. She will not be cheated of her due."

Not yet under the full sway of druid authority, I thought differently. Surely the woman with the comet streak in her hair belonged to the Otherworld and could come and go through veils of water at will. In the silence that followed, I thought I heard a horse whinny in the distance. It dawned on me that there might be a simpler explanation.

Before any of us could give the matter much thought, the archdruid (for so he was) lowered his arms, now with palms down—a gesture I was to witness again and again that night—signaling that a sacrificial offering was complete.

I'm afraid I must tell you that, after this dramatic beginning, the rite became as routine as passing the collection plate in church or standing in line for a communion wafer. *Tuath* after *tuath* came forward to offer riches. Once they were pronounced satisfactory, the druids carried them to the lake, then—*splash*! The drums followed the same pattern: escalating beat for the procession, silence for judgment, then something like a circus drum roll for a high-dive act as the goods were given the old heave-ho. Over and over: the same motions, the same gorgeous junk presented, the same conclusion. Even Foxface's eyes glazed over after a while.

I was not used to sitting passively through long rituals. I was also exhausted after the day's sail and the excitement of arrival, but, of course, I could not possibly admit that to myself. I just stared and stared, widening my eyes to keep them from closing. Do you know how it is when a repeated word loses its meaning and becomes mere sound? It was like that with the scene before me. The torches became blurs of light; the faces and figures, not human, just arbitrary arrangements of meaningless motion; the gleam of jewels and weapons, erratic flashes of brightness. Light, dark, mass, space: I had stumbled upon the principle of abstraction. In another moment, I slumped to the ground, fast asleep.

I don't know how long I slept. It could have been ten minutes or two hours. When I opened my eyes—

He is there, my brother, my other. He is standing beneath the tree of golden leaves. His eyes are dark as the earth is dark. His skin is dark with the brightness of gold shining through. But something is wrong. His mouth, his beautiful, tender mouth is frowning in a way that closes the rest of his face. Suddenly I know. He is missing me. I am meant to be standing with him under the tree of golden leaves, with the snakes—I see them now—twining in the branches above us. The male and the female. Trembling, I rise to my feet and take a step towards him.

Then someone yanked my cloak, and I came all the way awake—or what the world calls awake. Who is to say that what I had just seen was any less real than what I saw now?

He was indeed standing in the center beside the staff, my own Appended One. At last, it seemed, we were in the same place at the same time. I could barely contain my joy and might have rushed forward, except that now I could also see the four druids, the three appraisers and the ancient one, standing behind him debating with another man. The newcomer was wearing a tunic in a shade of hot blue—that you might call neon—trimmed with gold braid. He didn't look like a warrior. If he were, he would have been fined for his overflowing belly. His arms and neck could not have supported one more ounce of gold. He was so bedecked that I swear if there was an ornament for the asshole he would have been the first to sport it.

"Maeve!" someone hissed, yanking so hard at my cloak that I had to bend my knees or lose my balance. "What on earth do you mean by running off without telling us where you were going!"

Fand and Boann had found me. Each latched on to one of my arms.

"Ssh! Please!" I pleaded. "I've got to hear this!"

The argument surrounding my foster brother escalated. Their voices rose; my hearing sharpened. Foxface, I later learned, spent much of his time addressing large crowds. His were the first words I caught.

"It is not customary to make the Great Sacrifice except at dire need, and then only in a Quinquennial year, which this is not. Nor can such sacrifice be made on the spur of the moment. There are procedures that must be followed."

"The burnt piece of barley cake and what not," put in the concave druid helpfully.

"Not that we don't appreciate your generous offer of this fine young man as the supreme sacrifice," the grey-bearded druid hastened to add.

Sacrifice! What sacrifice? But I knew, and so do you. So here we are. My cosmic other and me. The first time we manage to get ourselves on the same patch of earth and he's a candidate for human sacrifice. Should that have been a warning to me? Unbidden, the image rose of the pool in Bride's valley; I remembered the skull I'd held between my hands and fought a wave of nausea. I had to keep my wits about me.

I searched my foster brother's face to see if he understood what—and who—was at stake. Either he was holding himself aloof or he didn't know the language. Then again, maybe he was drugged. I waited, crouched and ready to spring to his defense.

Now the archdruid began to make slow, ruminative noises, as if he were bringing something up from the deep, digestive recesses of himself, rolling it around in his brain, chewing it with his teeth to activate its juices. Before he could make whatever profound pronouncement he was readying, the man in hot blue lost his temper.

"I say that's what's wrong with druidism today!" He appealed to the crowd, making the most of center stage while he had it. And whether or not his sacrifice was accepted, he'd gone the Brigantes, with their war chariot and escaped mare, one better. "It's gone all wishy-washy and namby-pamby. All form and no substance. All gloss and no guts. All bluster and no blood. All sauce and no sacrifice."

Foxface was getting seriously annoyed, but he didn't interrupt the man. No doubt, like everyone else, he was curious to see how long Hot Blue could sustain the alliteration.

"All dithering and no death. All bondage and no bodies. All chopped liver and no chopped heads."

He hesitated, confused by his own conclusion. Anachronism has that effect.

"But can you present a reason," demanded Foxface, "other than the satisfaction of your own blood lust, why this sacrifice should take place now?"

"Why? I should think you could tell me why. That's your department, you druids. Me? I'm just a humble merchant. You don't think things have gone from bad to worse? Who am I to tell you? Maybe it's okay with you that we have to pay toll to the Romans on all our goods going to Gaul and beyond."

Now Hot Blue had everyone's attention, especially Foxface's. I didn't know it then, but Foxface was considered the foremost expert on the Roman question.

"Maybe you don't mind that there are spies everywhere trying to find out the secret locations of our gold and tin mines. Here in the Holy Isles we pride ourselves on our independence. Oh, how much fiercer and cleverer we are than the conquered tribes of Gaul. But I tell you, the Romans don't have to send armies to invade us. They've already bought us. Even now, in the South, there are whole settlements of Roman merchants. Not only do we tolerate them, we mimic them! Some of us are so worried about not looking like savages and headhunters, we're getting downright Romanized. As if the Romans didn't hunt heads, just like everyone else, before they got so sissified with their cities and their swanky sewer systems. Why, the Romans don't know how to take a good honest shit in the woods anymore. And pretty soon we won't either. Is that what you want, you druids!"

Hot Blue had the crowd eating out of his hand. Shouts of "Hear! Hear! Tell it like it is!" erupted when he paused for breath.

"I say we're neglecting our gods, that's what. Now our gods may not know much about so-called civilization, but they know what they like. Time was when it was routine to offer a dozen slaves at a time to the Old Girl. How do you think our grandfathers and great grandfathers beat back Julius Caesar? If the gods are gonna fight on our side, I say we gotta feed 'em.

"And as for oracles, sure you've got your raven croaks and your crane wings, your scattered bread crumbs and your magpies. But when was the last time you plunged a bright blade into a man's flesh and marked how he fell? When was the last time you read the entrails? These are our traditions, and we're losing them. Mark my words, the gods notice. And they're getting hungry."

To my amazed horror, the man's argument did not sound as absurd to everyone else as it did to me. I mean, I may not know much about sacrifice, but even I could see that Hot Blue was wearing his weight in gold. None of his wealth appeared to be on offer. Just someone else's life. What a bargain. But the crowd, the big, jolly holiday crowd I earlier joined so happily, was now striking up a Celtic rendition of "Gimme that Old Time Religion."

I had to do something. I shook myself free of my mothers and got to my feet. Over a deafening chorus—"If it's good enough for grandpa it's good enough for me!"—I shouted at the top of my lungs in Aramaic:

"Yeshua ben Miriam! Get the hell out of here! Now!"

He heard me. I called again as he looked around for the Aramaic-hollering voice. Our eyes met. For a moment everything else disappeared, all sight, all sound. There was only him, me, the bright air between us.

Then—

> Give 'em stabbing, hanging, drowning,
> And them gods'll quit their frowning,
> 'Cause they'll know that we're not clowning,
> And that's good enough for me!

I repeated my warning with accompanying gestures. First he looked merely bewildered. But when my mothers yanked my tunic again, and I lost my balance, he almost burst out laughing. As I recovered myself, I felt a prickle at the back of my neck; something singed my peripheral vision. I knew, without looking, that Foxface had seen me.

Fortunately, at that moment, someone far more effective than me intervened. A great, roaring bull of a man charged into the circle, placed a protective arm around my foster brother, and began to bellow at Hot Blue:

"You thrice-cursed son of a mud eel, you slippery spawn of pond sludge, you weasel-whelp of a mangy stoat!" Celts *do* love triptychs. "I should have known you were up to no good. Thought you could drug my wine, did ye? Thought to leave me snoring under those great blood-innocent trees. Well, it didn't work. The gods wouldn't have it. They sent a great dripping, thundering, black mare with Macha herself astride its back to rouse me. And here I am, so!"

The man, who also had a Hibernian accent, had made a great entrance, demonstrating his verbal prowess. For the moment, the crowd was his. The druids, masters of the esoteric art of licking a finger and sticking it into the wind to see which way it was blowing, nodded for him to continue.

"This young candidate—"

"No way!" spluttered Hot Blue, oblivious of Foxface's restraining hand.

"No way can he be a candidate. He is not one of the *Combrogos*. He has no lineage. He's no better than a slave—"

At a signal from Foxface, two other druids stepped forward to enforce the restraint.

"This young candidate," the Hibernian man continued, "yes, I said candidate—for I myself am presenting him for admission to the College—this young candidate is named Esus."

A ripple of excitement spread through the crowd. They recognized the name as one of the gods'. At that time I knew nothing of the god Esus or of the tree and the cranes and the bull associated with him. I knew nothing of sacrificial kingship. Nor did I know, as you doubtless do, the Greek form of his name so close to the Celtic name the man had given him. But as I heard the name Esus, I saw the crane wings forming and re-forming: Maeve and Esus. "That's the name," I whispered to my mothers.

"What name?" asked Boann.

"The name in the sky."

"She's delirious with exhaustion," said Fand. "Keep a firm grip on her. I do wish they'd get on with it, and get it over."

"Ah, I see that name means something to ye," the man went on. "Let that teach you to show kindness to strangers."

He was no stranger. Not to me. But the Hibernian had touched a nerve in the crowd. Our gods were not safely elsewhere. Past and future, human and divine had a way of getting all mixed up. A god could turn up anytime, like a troublesome relation. In fact, they were our relations. It did not do to offend them.

"I met him at the docks in Alexandria. That's in Egypt, in case you don't know. We were preparing to take ship. Some of us prefer to sail through the treacherous narrows and risk the open sea rather than to travel on Roman roads through Gaul. The young man approached me. He addressed me in Greek and said he was seeking the *Keltoi*. That's what we're called in the Greek tongue, for those of you who are linguistically limited. Upon questioning him, I found him to be a young scholar, fluent in Aramaic and Greek, with a smattering of Latin. His people don't like to use that barbarian tongue. A very proper sentiment, I say. But he was lacking the knowledge and training he could only find here among the *Combrogos*. He asked me if the *Keltoi* had any great teachers. Well, I ask you!" He made a deferential gesture towards the druids' ranks. "I'd taken a liking to the young man, so I offered him passage—"

"Now there you're right!" Hot Blue burst in. "*You* offered him passage, even though *I* own more shares. And could he pay for his passage? No! Not a single coin, not a torque, not so much as a dagger. Nothing. He owned nothing but the clothes on his back—and those were none too clean, I might add."

"What are you talking about? He paid with his labor. If anything, we owe him, and I intend to make good my debt by standing surety for him."

"Bilgewater! He's a land lubber. He'd never set foot on a ship before. What's more he drew bad luck like a dead fish draws sharks. First there were pirates and him with no weapon. Then mermaids—"

"Now, really. You can't blame him for the sailor who lost his head and dived overboard."

"And dense fog at the straits. Whoever heard of fog there before?"

"And who stood by the helmsman and helped guide the ship?"

"And then bowel sickness. Everyone had it but him."

"That's because he was the only one who didn't eat the spoiled meat."

"So you say. And what about ten days of the doldrums?"

"He rowed with the best."

"And then that storm! The worst I've ever seen."

"Yes, and who calmed the waves?"

"The same one who caused the storm in the first place! Just to show off."

As they debated, you could almost feel the rocking of the ship, the pull of one force against the other. All the while, Esus stood, more compelling in his stillness than either man. The faintest trace of a smile played at his lips. He probably couldn't follow the rapid-fire P-Celtic, but no doubt he'd heard it all before. As for the druids, they were no longer heeding either merchant. All eyes were trained on Esus. Without saying anything, he had captured the attention of the entire druid body.

Then the archdruid stepped forward. With one impatient gesture, he swept aside the arguing pair and all their verbiage as a horse sweeps flies from his back with one casual swish of his tail. He walked towards Esus and planted himself in front of him. Even today I wish I knew what each had seen in the other's eyes, but I could only see the druid's back, and he blocked my view of Esus's face. The look that passed between them seemed to go on forever and ever. Whole forests grew up and mountains wore away to sand. At last the druid turned from Esus to address the crowd.

"There will be no blood sacrifice tonight. Gold will suffice." Here he fixed a stern eye on Hot Blue's arms. "As for the candidate, there is no law saying that he cannot be presented. But this is not the time or place. If he is found acceptable, so be it. If not...." He allowed a moment of enigmatic silence. "Now. Come forward with your offerings, any who have not made them by *tuath*."

"He means us." Fand and Boann got to their feet. "Come on, Maeve."

"I can't go up there!" I whispered in panic.

"You have to! What's wrong with you? It isn't like you to hold back."

"I just can't," I repeated, unable to explain my dread of Foxface.

"Come on, Maeve." They hauled me to my feet and dragged me forward.

Then I forgot about Foxface. I forgot the offering. I shook off my mothers' grip and walked straight towards Esus. I stopped before him, mere inches between us. No more veils of water. Just sheer, shimmering air. He returned my gaze, his own a little quizzical. Then he said in his slow P-Celtic:

"Haven't I seen you somewhere before?"

Yep. Those were his first words to me: his sister, his other, the one destined to stand with him beneath the Tree of Life. And my first words?

"Remember when that dove shit on your head?" I blurted in Aramaic. "Oh, no, you probably wouldn't have recognized me then. Well, do you remember a time, when you were, um, relieving yourself in an alley. Did you maybe see a—"

He looked so completely disoriented, I found myself unable to go on. And why wouldn't he be? Here he is far away from home among the *Keltoi* and this red-headed broad comes up to him and starts talking about crude bodily functions like a Galilean home girl—except that no nice girl of his acquaintance would ever have spoken of any such thing.

Before I could try another tack, maybe make a better impression, my mothers seized me and hustled me away. Suddenly I was face to face with the red-bearded druid. For someone so much in command of himself and everything else, he looked startled—no, more than that: as if he'd had an unwelcome seeing, the sort Queen Maeve of Connacht deplored. I half-expected him to ask me the same question Esus had.

"No," I wanted to answer. "No. You're mistaking me for someone else."

The look was gone in an instant. He began to examine our bracelets and brooches, a dagger Boann had decided to toss in at the last minute. Maybe he was tired. After the most perfunctory of inspections, he signaled his acceptance and waved us away without looking at us again. I noticed that he had not asked our names or lineage. Only one druid was needed to carry our gifts to the lake where the mist Lady sagged, losing her shape, as if she, too, was weary of the proceedings. Our offerings made a small, unimpressive splash.

It was over—for now.

When we turned to go back to the crowd, Esus was already gone.

14

WHAT YOUR MOTHERS
NEVER TOLD YOU

I am sure you understand—even though my mothers refused to—that I was wild to find him again. My Appended One, Yeshua, or, as I now thought of him, Esus. My mothers understood me well enough to lock their arms through mine. It was two against one. When we rejoined King Bran and his company, I was even more outnumbered. King Bran, though sympathetic to my high spirits, was firm. I was not to wander off on my own again. As for the young foreigner I'd approached so rashly in the sight of all, King Bran assured me I'd see him soon enough when the candidates were presented for admission.

Of course, that was not soon enough for me. I fully intended to disobey again as soon as everyone was asleep. All I had to do was to search every campsite and probe every sleeping body—a very foolish thing to do considering that most warriors slept with their weapons at the ready. What might have happened if I'd made good my plan, I'll never know, because Fand and Boann took turns guarding me all night long. If you are assuming that one slept while the other watched, let me set you straight.

"Where's Fand?" I asked, trying to get comfortable, which was not easy with Boann sitting on me. With her added weight, the pine boughs prickled me through the plaid.

"Gone to pee at the trenches?" Boann suggested.

"She's been gone an awfully long time just for that."

"Go to sleep, Maeve," Boann ordered. "You'll need your rest for tomorrow."

"Just tell me where she is."

"Go to sleep."

Mothers always say go to sleep, as if it were a matter of will. But it's almost impossible to sleep when someone's sitting on your diaphragm, immobilizing you, while your mind races. Think of the day I'd had. Arriving on Mona; practically swooning in the arms of the first man I met; attending the votive sacrifices; seeing a horse goddess plunge into a sacred bog; and to top it all off: a hot debate over whether or not my cosmic twin should be sacrificed. I had enough on my mind to give me insomnia for a century. Now Fand had disappeared, probably off to investigate Esus for herself. And I was supposed to sleep? Meanwhile, Boann had decided to stretch out on me full length, fully relaxed.

"Boann!" I poked her in the ribs. "I know Fand is not at the trenches. Just tell me where she is, and I promise I'll go to sleep."

"Taking a damn long time about it," grumbled Boann. "It's not fair. When I let her have first go."

A loud caterwauling rent the night.

"She could at least have the decency not to make so much noise. She sounds like a whole pack of hyenas in heat."

Don't ask me how Boann knew anything about hyenas. Put it down to racial memory, our African mother of mothers. A little while later Fand returned, not from the direction of the trenches but from King Bran's bower.

"Took you long enough," said Boann crossly as she rolled off. "Is there any left for me?"

Fand, amazingly mellow, merely murmured, "I'm sure you'll manage, dear. After all, you're a witch."

Then Fand stretched out on me, as if I were the most comfortable of couches and had the effrontery to go to sleep. Despite Fand's snores, I could still hear throaty laughter followed by moans. Boann working magic, presumably. Finally sheer exhaustion claimed me, and I slept after a fashion, only half-waking as Fand and Boann changed places again—and again.

∽

I've always found that morning is a hopeful time after a restless night. You can give up the exhausting business of trying to get enough sleep. The full force of fatigue won't hit till later. We didn't have caffeine in those days, but if you're waking outside in springtime, the rush of morning energy can have just as stimulating an effect. Birds, insects, flowers, all cued to the light and the shifting temperature of the air as the dew evaporates. Everything rising, opening, flying. Even the water flowing in the river sounded louder that morning.

We broke fast with the Silures. My mothers sat on either side of King Bran in a benign stupor. They sipped the morning slowly, sensuously. Weary of holding my leash, so to speak, they allowed me the run of the Silures' camp as long as I agreed to stay with Branwen.

"Did you get *any* sleep last night?" I asked her as we skipped away from the parental triumvirate.

She knew exactly what I meant, and we convulsed ourselves with laughter. The pleasures of friendship were new to me, and sweet. Without any effort on her part, Branwen restrained me that morning more effectively than my mothers could have. She held no grudge against me for giving her the slip last night. I was glad, and I didn't want to get her into trouble again. At least not so soon.

We'd hardly begun to enjoy our relative freedom before our parents called us back to break camp. We had a ten mile journey to make that day to the site of the College. Most of the teaching groves and the clusters of round huts where students and faculty lived ranged along Afon Braint from Bryn Celli Ddu (The Mound of the Dark Grove) to two enormous standing stones that marked the way between the world of the college and the rest of Mona.

Our few bundles were soon loaded into one of the Silures' wagons. While we waited for the rest of our party, my mothers drew me apart for a mothers-to-daughter heart-to-heart. I suspect they had suddenly realized that today might be our last full day together. They had to wring themselves of their last drops of wisdom. As my brace of mothers bore me off, I turned and waved to Branwen, catching a look of wistfulness on her face. I remembered she had no mother. That moment stays with me, perhaps because it was the first time I clearly saw through someone else's eyes. When I came back to myself, I found I was missing Grainne very much.

"Well, Little Bright One," said Fand as we strolled towards a large copper beech and sat down in its shade. "We don't have much time left together."

All right, then, I thought. I'll let the baby name pass.

"We think there are things you haven't told us that, as your mothers, we ought to know about," Fand announced.

"Like what?" Put it down to sleep deprivation or to the automatic response of a daughter when any mother pries. I honestly drew a blank.

"Oh, just little things," said Boann. "Like the 'name in the sky' you babbled about last night. And just what you meant by standing and shouting in an unknown tongue."

"Aramaic is not unknown to me," I pointed out.

"Don't get smart with us, Maeve," said Fand. "And why did you walk so brazenly right up to that young stranger? Is that how we've raised you to behave?"

I thought it best not to answer that question.

"Here's the long and the short of it," Boann summed up. "We're worried about you."

"Yes," agreed Fand. "How can we leave you here when you show such poor judgment?"

"I didn't show poor judgment at all," I protested. "To meet the one you call stranger is the very reason I've come here."

"It is not," declared Fand. "You have come to the Druid Isle to train as a bard, not to meet boys."

"Oh?" I decided to get really smart. "And why did you come here?"

"Why did we come here?" they both echoed. "To see that you get admitted to college."

"No other reason?"

"No, absolutely not."

"Then what were you doing last night?"

Fand and Boann exchanged a look across me and smirked. There is no other word for it. I smiled to myself. My mothers were so easy to distract.

"What do you think, Boann?" said Fand. "Given our Maeve's impetuous nature, perhaps we ought have a little talk with her about that. It occurs to me that her knowledge of relations between the sexes may be more theoretical than practical."

Now, there was an understatement.

"Maybe we'd better start by finding out how much she does know," suggested Boann. "Maeve, do you know what Fand and I were doing last night?"

"You were offering King Bran the friendship of your thighs," I answered, proving that their tales of Queen Maeve of Connacht had not been lost on me.

"Well, yes." They smirked again, embarrassed but clearly enjoying themselves. "Now, do you know exactly what that means?"

"I've seen pigs and sheep." I did my best to sound bored. "I know which parts go together."

"Er, quite," said Fand, a little nonplused. "But did you know that people often—not always, mind you, but often—do it face to face? It adds a certain... *je ne sais quoi.* "

(No, Fand did not suddenly start speaking modern French, but that's the best translation I can make of what she did say in Q-Celtic.)

"Most animals can't do it face to face," said Boann thoughtfully. "Comes of having four legs, I suppose. Think of trying to do it frontally with hooves."

"Well now, Boann, I have to say, I don't think it's just the number of legs." Fand gave her agile mind to the conundrum. "It's just that other animals don't walk upright. Therefore, the head in relation to the legs makes it difficult to embrace frontally. Don't you see?"

I knew from experience that any two or more of my mothers were capable of pursuing a bizarre tangent indefinitely. Now that we were on the subject—you might say *the* subject—I realized there might be more I *did* want to know.

"Okay. So people do it face to face," I broke in.

"With either partner on top," added Fand.

"Or both on their sides, don't forget," said Boann.

"Or standing. And remember the rear entry position is an option."

"Fand, I just thought of a great one." Boann was getting into to it. "Hanging upside down from a tree branch. Have you ever tried that?"

"I have, but I don't recommend it for beginners or for people with back problems."

"I disagree. I think it's an excellent position for people with back problems. It puts all the strain on the thighs—"

"How old do you have to be?" I got right to the point, the one that mattered most to me. "When can I do it?"

Fand and Boann stared at each other, looking pretty dumb for a couple of shrewd witches. They had stumbled right into the pitfall especially reserved for enlightened parents. They prided themselves on their ability to impart information, but they couldn't make the leap to application. Talk about a gap between the theoretical and the practical.

"Well, Maeve, that all depends."

"On what?"

"Why, on whether or not you're ready." Boann sounded vague.

"And we don't think you are," Fand hastened to add. "You have to be mature, responsible...."

"Fand, I think we better get down to brass tacks. We don't have much time left. We can't have her getting pregnant."

Pregnant? On Tir na mBan, my mothers had seemed to think my having a baby might be a solution of sorts. Now they seemed to regard it as a problem. I still found the very idea almost unthinkable. I was a *daughter*, not a mother.

"She can always say no. Abstinence is the better part of valor."

Valor?

"Ha!" snorted Boann. "Believe it! Listen, Maeve, let's get one thing straight. If you get pregnant—you *do* know how that happens, don't you? That's what we've been talking about—you might have to leave college. King Bran told us that the druids are admitting women to College for the first time this year. It's being regarded as an experiment by the druids and by the priestesses of Holy Isle."

(I know that some people in your century like to believe that the Equal Rights Amendment is of ancient Celtic origin. It is true that Celtic law, taking its cue perhaps from the traditions of the pre-Celtic native traditions, recognized and respected rights of women that were later trampled upon by Romans, Angles, Saxons, Jutes, Normans, not to mention the 104th Congress of the United States. Women could inherit and own land and herds, marry and divorce as freely as men, and rule in their own right. There were priestesses, and all manner of -esses who had training equivalent to druids. But despite inroads matriarchy had made into an essentially patriarchal conquering horde, there remained male bastions. The Druid College of Mona was about to be infiltrated. And if you are wondering why it took close to two thousand years for the British Groves of Academe to open again to women, well, read on.)

"What happens if I do get pregnant?" I was careful to keep my voice neutral. I didn't want them to guess that I might not mind having twenty years of drill cut short.

"That's just it. We don't know. Boann, we must have a conference with the priestesses before we go. They must have some sort of contingency plan. And surely they're planning to teach them how to protect themselves."

"Yes, but we can't leave sex education to the schools, Fand!"

"So educate me, already!"

I wasn't interested in the druid's open admission policy and the repercussions of pregnancy. I wanted something I could apply to myself—and Esus.

"All right. Now, Maeve, you know about the moon?"

"The moon?" It took me a moment to sort out this apparent *non sequitur.*

"Yes. The moon goes through phases like a woman. Or a woman goes through phases like the moon. At the dark we bleed, and at the full—"

"We're horny as hell," broke in Boann. "Here's the catch, Maeve. At the full moon, you're most likely to get pregnant. But it's also the time you're most likely to get laid. Or to want to, anyway. So before you—"

"Don't mislead her, Boann. Unfortunately, it's not that simple. You see, Maeve, on Tir na mBan we're eight witches cycling together. Just us and the animals, and the moon and the tides. Very low stress. Nothing to break the rhythm. But you are young, away from home for the first time, and you're excitable—to put it mildly. Anything could throw off your courses. You can't count on counting."

"Still," Boann insisted, "she ought to understand the theory. Even when she's out of sync with the sky, she ought to learn to know when her own moon is full. Do you know the signs, Maeve?"

I nodded. "It's as if you're an egg cracked open. You're all runny with egg white."

"You have to admit, our Maeve can turn a phrase." Boann beamed at me.

"If you know that much, then you better know not to go frying any cracked eggs in the bushes," admonished Fand freely mixing metaphors and euphemisms.

"But, Fand, that's just when she's most likely to lose her head."

"And her maidenhead."

"We should have thought of this." Boann was rueful. "We could have given her a supply of those seeds. You know, what-do-ya-call-ems. But it's not seed time now, even if we could find them. Still, maybe the priestesses have a store of them."

"There's stones," suggested Fand. "Listen, Maeve, as soon as you can, find a smooth flat stone, preferably from the beach. Before you do anything—and as I said I really don't think you ought to—put it inside you as far up as you can."

I stared at her unbelieving. I could not connect stone with the glimmering I had of "it" as something hot, live, melting.

"It blocks the seed from reaching fertile ground," Boann explained. "Which is to say, your womb. Certain kinds of dried seaweed also work."

"Oh, I wish we had time to show you," fretted Fand. "I wish we had thought of this on Tir na mBan. We could have given you lessons, demonstrations. When I think of all the time we wasted on sword play and spear casting."

"Well, not wasted entirely," put in Boann. "It did improve her hand-eye coordination."

"But if she becomes a druid, she'll never so much as touch a weapon. Druids aren't allowed to bear arms," Fand lamented. "Why didn't the Cailleach tell us sooner? Why didn't any of us know? What's the use of our being witches if our second sight only works in reverse like everyone else's?"

Mothers are made to worry. But as I've noted, I was very much a daughter. I felt detached from their concerns. Nothing would happen to me that was not meant to. I had a destiny, and it was unfolding. Too bad they couldn't see that.

"It's no use moaning over missed opportunity," said Boann. "We've got to tell her as much as we can right now. There's one thing we haven't mentioned yet, and it's the most important of all."

"I can't think what we haven't thought of."

"Sovereignty," said Boann solemnly.

"Oh, yes, of course, sovereignty."

Sovereignty! I pricked up my ears. For the sake of her sovereignty, Queen Maeve of Connacht had fought to win the brown bull. "Fight for our sovereignty," she had urged me.

"Pay attention, Maeve," said Fand. "Never go with a man—or a woman, come to that—unless you want to."

"Not to please. Not to placate," Boann chimed in.

"Never on any terms but your own."

It had never occurred to me to do *anything* on any terms but my own.

"And what, exactly, were your terms with King Bran?" I decided to put them on the spot.

Fand and Boann exchanged a glance and actually blushed.

"They were extremely cordial," said Fand.

"Pleasure. Mutual pleasure," added Boann.

That sounded simple enough. "Are there any other terms you'd consider?" I wanted all the information I could get. I intended to come to terms with Esus as soon as possible.

Fand and Boann looked uncertain.

"Should we tell her about love?" wondered Fand.

"Doesn't love complicate matters unnecessarily?" Boann was dubious. "I've heard it sometimes results in temporary insanity."

"And what about marriage?" persisted Fand. "I confess I've never fully understood its purpose, but Queen Maeve of Connacht seems to have managed to have one on her own terms, though there was that unfortunate mix-up over the bulls. I believe marriage often leads to cattle wars."

"And then there's babies," Boann reminded her. "Don't forget babies. That's sometimes one of the terms."

Babies. I kept forgetting about them, and no wonder. I had never seen a human baby in my life. Then a disturbing thought struck me. The moon was close to full.

"About last night." I tried to sound offhand. "Did you use stones or seaweed?"

Their answer was silence; you might even say a pregnant silence.

"You did it to get babies!" I accused. "You did it on *purpose!*"

"Now that is not strictly true," objected Fand.

"We did it for fun," Boann insisted. "King Bran is a jolly old soul and a good sport."

"Simple, too," added Fand. "A virtue in a man. But as for babies...."

"Yes, as for babies...." repeated Boann.

They both looked far away and dreamy.

"As for babies!" I prompted loudly.

"To tell you the truth, Maeve, we didn't do it on purpose, but we wouldn't mind if that's what happened. We haven't had a baby since you, Maeve."

"Parthenogenesis isn't all it's cracked up to be," Boann observed.

"What about Manannán Mac Lir?" I demanded. "Why did he only come once?"

"Oh, gods are like that," said Fand vaguely. "Fickle, unpredictable. You can't leave everything to gods."

"So it's not quite the full moon, but we can hope," said Boann.

"You want to replace me."

"Replace you?" They both looked genuinely startled. "Replace you! Darling Maeve! As if we could. It's just that we'd like to go on being mothers for a little while, if we can. You can understand that, can't you?"

I couldn't, really. Not then.

"I don't get it," I said. "If thigh friendship is so much fun, and if it can get you the babies you seem to want so much, why are you living on Tir na mBan? Why haven't I ever seen a man in my life till yesterday? What's the big deal?"

"It's not always as simple as that," sighed Fand.

"The way it was with King Bran, she means," explained Boann. "A good time had by all. No fuss. No muss."

"Yes, when women don't have their sovereignty, it can be very messy indeed. Now, we are queens and witches from our own sovereign isle."

"Sovereignty, Maeve. Belonging to yourself. Your own terms," Boann got in as much drill as she could.

"Tir na mBan stands for the sovereignty of women," continued Fand. "If it exists nowhere else in the world, it exists there. Remember that, Maeve. Sovereignty is your birthright and your inheritance. Next to sovereignty, gold torques and brooches are mere trinkets. Never surrender your sovereignty, Maeve. Carry it with you wherever you go."

Their words were stirring but abstract. Then an image rose in my mind of myself as a sort of floating island, shining, a sovereign vessel on a vast and dangerous sea.

15

ADMISSIONS

Did you go to college? Do you remember your interview with the admissions officer? Of course you were nervous. But maybe you had other things going for you: SAT scores off the curve, straight A's, great recommendations? Interesting hobbies, at least. None of these mattered to the druids. No one had a manila folder in hand, fat with your accomplishments. The interview, so to speak, was it. And this was no cozy affair in some well-appointed little office, tendrils of ivy curling outside the window, with the interviewer doing his or her best to put you at your ease. No.

Picture this: The candidate stands before twelve druids, seated cross-legged and straight-backed on the ground. Behind him waits a crowd of competing candidates and their families. Although it is still daylight, and the huge oaks are not yet in full leaf, the grove has a hushed, dimmed quality, as solemn as any court or cathedral. On most islands—and certainly on Mona with its lush, flat expanse—the wind is ceaseless. But the druids, being druids, can command a hollow of stillness, an eye of attentive silence. If it had been the right season, you could have heard an acorn drop.

The candidate is flanked by his sponsors, who might be parents, the head of his *fine*, or even the King of the *tuath*. To have arrived at this moment, the candidate has to have the support of his people, not only for his maintenance in college (twelve to twenty years) but for his lifetime as a druid. And druids were apt to be longer-lived, being forbidden to bear arms on the one hand and, on the other, being expert practitioners of the healing arts. "Declaim your lineage!" The druids command the candidate.

If you falter, forget it. Never mind if the preferred ancestors really did exist and have done the necessary begetting. You're going into the memory business. Reciting nine generations of direct ancestry is kindergarten stuff. There are druids on the admissions board who specialize in lineage. You're not telling them anything they don't already know. You're just meeting the first of three requirements. If the druids are satisfied with your recital of nine generations of freeborn forefathers (that's right, fathers) then they ask:

"Who stands surety for this candidate?"

No less than twelve people will do.

To pass the third test—remember I told you how the Celts love threes?— the candidate must recite a longish piece of poetry. Not long by bardic standards, but long enough to show you have a capacity for memory and enough potential flair and style to be worth training.

You'll agree, these three tests would be bad enough even if you knew about them ahead of time and were amply prepared. I didn't, and I wasn't. What's more, one of the twelve druids on the panel, the one furthest to my left, lurking in my peripheral vision, had a sleek, red beard and watchful eyes, focused (for now) not on me but on the victim of the moment.

"Was your great grandfather or was he not Kulhwch ab Kilydd etc....," the grey-bearded spokesdruid interrupted the candidate's recital, "a notorious cattle thief taken captive during a raid, stripped of his lands and herds and reduced to the status of a slave?"

"Well, yes, but his daughter bought his freedom when she married King Lludd, and after that all his descendants were freeborn."

"But his son, your grandfather, was not."

"Not exactly, but later he—"

"Case dismissed." The grey-bearded druid waved the candidate away.

As he turned, I caught a glimpse of his face distorted with the sobs he was trying to strangle.

"I can't go through with this," I hissed to my mothers, who had me literally in hand or under arms, so that I would not go crawling through the crowd looking for you-know-who.

"Of course you can, Maeve!" they insisted. But I could tell they were nervous, too.

"What about my lineage?" I demanded.

"There's nothing wrong with your lineage," said Fand huffily.

"But who's going to stand surety for me?"

"Never you mind. That's all taken care of."

It took me a moment to figure out what that meant. But I'm not dumb. Neither were my mothers. Cordial terms. Mutual pleasure. I reckoned something else had been thrown into the bargain.

"What about the poetry? Why didn't you warn me about the poetry?" It's not that I didn't know stories, but I was fairly certain my mothers' stories had not been imparted to me in the proper prosodic form. "What am I going to recite?"

"Wing it," said Boann unhelpfully.

I looked again at the druid panel listening gravely to a young woman this time. She was very tall and slender, with smooth, red hair to her waist, and she seemed excessively sure of herself. I took an instant, unreasoning dislike of her. When she finished declaiming her lineage in proud, ringing tones, the druids nodded, then signed to each other in nose ogham. That's right, nose ogham. You can use the nose as well as a seam in a rock to form the stem of ogham. Foxface's nose, being long and straight, was particularly well suited to this form of communication.

"Fand," I whispered, "do you see that druid on the far left with the red beard?"

"What about him?"

"He was there at the sacrifices. Don't you remember him?"

"Really, Maeve, they all look alike to me. How can you tell them apart?"

"There's something about him. He makes me nervous."

"Don't be silly, Maeve. Now hush. I want to hear the young woman recite. She's telling the story of Goewin rather prettily." The tall redhead had passed the second test in a flash. "I don't want to miss the part where Gwydion and Gilfaethwy have to mate as swine. Such an ingenious way for King Math to avenge Goewin's honor, I always think."

The druids approved her story, too. When she finished, she was promptly admitted to college (with scarcely a finger to the nose on the part of the druids.) Her kinfolk cheered wildly, and the rest of the crowd joined in. And it was that much closer to being my turn. My mothers' talon-like grip on me notwithstanding, I remained in that darkening grove for one reason, and one reason only.

The sun began to set, shooting its last rays to the highest tree branches. I leaned my head back and gazed at the sky beyond. Small birds, so high I couldn't tell what kind they were, flew across my range of vision. From right to left, I noted. Not a good sign. I wondered if anyone else had noticed. Then, off-setting that omen, an owl woke and cried loudly from my left side. Relieved, I lowered my eyes and looked towards the druids, reflecting that for them the cry came from the right. It struck me then that our luck was opposed.

There was a lull in the proceedings as the druids ordered some torches lit. Then the grey-bearded druid gestured for the next candidate to come forward.

It was Esus.

He stood with the merchant who had championed him, wearing a clean, plaid tunic of Celtic design. Unlike the Celts, he was not bare-headed but wore a round hat like the one I'd perched on (so to speak) in my dream. I couldn't help wondering if it was the same one, and if he had managed to get the stain out. But now was hardly the moment to inquire.

"Declaim your lineage!" the druid commanded as he had every candidate.

But Esus was not just another candidate, and everyone knew it. The crowd murmured and stirred, all of us craning our necks to get a better view, straining our ears for the first syllables to fall from his lips.

"Do you understand what you are to do?" the druid inquired.

"I do," he answered in heavily accented P-Celtic. "I am Esus ab Joseph ab Jacob ab Mathan ab Eleazar ab....."

Do you really want to hear the whole thing? He did not stop at nine. His lineage was far, far longer than King Bran's. After awhile, the druids (who had been counting on their fingers, thrown off, perhaps by the Hebrew names) held up their hands and gestured frantically for him to stop. But he kept right on going back through Solomon and David all the way to Abraham. Why he stopped there, don't ask me. Maybe he sensed he was losing his audience.

"Er, quite," said the spokesdruid when it became apparent that he had finally finished. "And are all these forebears freeborn men?"

"That," he answered in his charmingly accented P-Celtic, "is a long story."

Without waiting to discover whether or not the druids were inclined to hear him, given that his answer was not a straightforward yes, he turned his back on the panel and faced us with that extraordinarily sweet smile of his. (Sweet? Think of wild strawberries warm from the noonday sun bursting on your tongue.) He smiled that smile blindly into the crowd. And then he asked:

"Is there an Aramaic speaker in the Grove?"

Is there!

"Maeve! What are you doing?" my mothers demanded as I struggled to free myself from their hold and get to my feet.

"The Aramaic speaker. That's me."

"You!?!"

"Yes, me! The Cailleach taught me Aramaic. Don't you remember? And this is why. Now let me go!"

"Well, if it was the Cailleach's idea," Fand and Boann conferred, "well, all right. But we're going with you."

Like the prow of a boat, I plowed through the crowd, with Fand and Boann a trailing wake.

"I speak Aramaic," I kept explaining to people as I stepped over or on them.

At last I stood before Esus, ignoring the heat on my left side where Foxface's gaze grazed my cheek. Now Esus's smile was for me alone. I answered with my own.

"I want to tell the story of my people." He got right to the point. "But my Celtic isn't up to it." He paused, then added, "I knew you'd come forward if I asked."

Rather sure of himself for a foreigner who might be turned into a human sacrifice at any moment.

"Will you translate for me?"

"Sure," I said, attempting nonchalance. "I'll give it a try."

While we were speaking together as if only the two of us were of any consequence, there was a murmur rising to a roar from the waiting crowd. Urgent ogham signals, both of hand and nose, passed from one end of the druid panel to the other and back again.

Then Esus turned from me and stepped back, standing sideways, so that the druid panel and the people could see him. When he spoke, everyone fell silent. He could command a crowd even then.

"You have asked me a question, and I will answer it. But since the answer is long, I prefer to speak in my own language—"

"And I will translate," I jumped in. I didn't need anyone to speak for me.

"Who is this maiden?"

Even before I looked, I knew it was Foxface who had spoken. Although I was trembling, I turned to face him.

"I am Maeve. Called by the Cailleach Maeve Rhuad. My name means red mead, and the fire of the stars flows in my veins."

Don't ask me why I said that.

"She's a candidate," Fand hastened to add.

A look passed along the druid line, then a barely perceptible nod, which I took to mean: We'll deal with her later.

"Proceed," said the grey-bearded druid.

"Wait a minute!" A man in the crowd rose to his feet shouting. "If his ancestors aren't all freeborn, then what's the point of going further? He's automatically disqualified. We've been waiting here all day. This is a waste—"

"We wish to hear this case." The druid cut him off. "Anyone who cannot wait may leave now. There will be no heckling. You all know the penalty for such disturbances. You, there. You've had your first of three warnings."

The druid nodded to Esus. Until then he had been standing. Now he sat down cross-legged on the ground and motioned for me to sit facing him. Fand and Boann plunked themselves down on either side of me, eyeing Esus with suspicion. Esus waited for a moment, becoming very still.

Then he took a deep breath and began to speak.

16

LOST IN TRANSLATION

"These are the names of the Israelites** who went with Jacob to Egypt, each of them with his family: Reuben, Simeon, Levi and Judah, Issachar, Zebulon and Benjamin, Dan and Naphtali, Gad and Asher. In all, the descendants of Jacob numbered seventy people. Joseph was in Egypt already. Then Joseph died, and his brothers, and all that generation. But the Israelites were fruitful and prolific; they became so numerous and powerful that eventually the whole land was full of them."

Esus paused, and I translated, somewhat haltingly at first. As you doubtless recognize, he'd picked up the story at the beginning of Exodus. None of us had any context. On the other hand, in those days we had much longer attention spans and much higher tolerance for long, detailed narratives full of hard-to-remember names and complicated relationships.

"Now there came to power in Egypt a new king, who had never heard of Joseph." (Never mind that we hadn't either.) "'Look,' he said to his people, 'the Israelites are now stronger than we are. We must take precautions to stop them from increasing any further, or if war should break out, they might join the ranks of our enemies. They might take arms against us and flee the country.' Accordingly, they put taskmasters over the Israelites to wear them down by forced labor."

He paused again. Soon we established a rhythm. As I grew more accustomed to his narrative style, my translations became fluid, almost seamless. Have you ever translated for someone? If you have, you know it creates an intimacy. The speaker is trusting you with his words, his meaning. You take those words inside yourself, your own mind. Then they are reborn from your lungs and throat, rolled about on your tongue, issued from your lips. What could be sexier? He poured Aramaic into me and out of me flowed P-Celtic, though, sensitive to nuance, for songs and poetry, I shifted to Q.

When you imagine this feat of storytelling and translation, don't just think of the linguistics. Remember, words are not just things-in-themselves, though they are that, too, each one a story. Words are magic. An invisible power. With his words a whole world passed through me and shimmered in the air of the Druid isle. Picture them, these forest dwellers, leaning against each other for warmth as they listen. Soon they forget the chill of the grove. They can feel the harshness of Egyptian noon, the dry dust coating their

113

skins, parching their throats. They suffer with the Israelites the pain and indignity of the lash.

And in this exotic tale of a faraway place, the *Combrogos* also hear their own favorite stories: the life-giving waters of the sacred river, the divine child borne there. Though the narrative omits the details of his training, Moses is clearly a druid, with his snake staff, his conversation with the burning bush, his power to command the elements. We are past worrying about Esus's lineage now. We want to know what happens next.

I must admit some things may have been lost—or altered—in translation. Neither I nor any of the listeners grasped the gulf between Moses and the Great I-Am. We had no concept of monotheism. Clearly YHWH was an elemental force that Moses mediated. We didn't worry too much about YHWH's— or anyone else's—motivation. It was enough that wonders were occurring. Rivers turning to blood, day to night, plagues of frogs and locusts all held plenty of interest. The parting of the Red Sea was more of the right stuff. But the subsequent drowning of the Egyptians in their chariots caused a bit of consternation. Chariots were a key feature in Celtic battle, and audience identification suddenly swung from the fleeing Hebrews to their pursuers.

"What does it matter if they escaped?" The same man who'd objected before piped up again. "They were slaves. And did they buy their freedom with gold? Did they fight like honest warriors?"

"Strike two!" warned the grey-bearded druid. Then he turned to Esus. "Well? Is there more? How many generations between these escaped slaves and yours?"

"Quite a few." Now Esus began counting on his fingers.

"More than nine?"

"About thirty-six, I would say."

"Oy gevalt!" The druid threw up his hands.

(No, he didn't suddenly break into Yiddish, but that is the best translation I can render.)

The druids, to put it bluntly, were floored. Maybe for the first time in their professional lives, they did not know what to do. Standard operating procedure was stalled, and they had a grove full of candidates yet to examine. Still, they were curious and impressed. The foreigner appeared to have a tribal memory that stretched back—according to some swift mathematical calculations—at least 2,000 years, far longer than the *Combrogos* had been in the Holy Isles. The stranger's memory was as old as the hills where the *Sidhe* dwelled.

"Look here, Esus ab Joseph, these subsequent generations, were they all freeborn?"

"Well, that's a long story."

"Why don't you just ask him about the last nine, for the love of Don. We haven't got all night!" shouted the same man.

"Strike three!"

At a nod from the druids two armed guards—bouncers, you might call them—advanced on the outspoken man.

"Hey, no fair," he protested. "That wasn't heckling. That was just a suggestion."

"When we want suggestions, we'll ask for them," snapped the druid. "You were warned."

"Hey, leave off!" The man struggled to get at his sword, but his neighbors grabbed him and held him fast, while the two warriors sliced his cloak off at the waist. A standard penalty, I later learned. Druid crowd control, and perhaps (though I know I'm on shaky linguistic and historic ground) the origin of the word embare-ass-ment. In any case, that was the effect, literally and figuratively.

"Remove him from the Grove," ordered the druid.

"Hear me, you druids," the man shouted, putting up an impressive resistance. "I have as much right to be here as anyone. I've paid the penalty. My best *sago* ruined and the ground hard and cold beneath my bare ass. But no way am I leaving until the proceedings are over. It's my right, I tell you. And besides, I want to hear the rest of the story."

At that the tension broke. Laughter rose and roared like surf. Even the druids laughed, including, to my obscure relief, Foxface. Maybe it would be all right, I thought vaguely, not at all sure what I meant.

"Well, then," said the Greybeard, "it seems we do have all night, if need be. Make yourselves comfortable. If anyone has a flagon of wine, let him be free with it. And whoever has an oaten cake, let him share it with his neighbor."

(Yes, a sneak preview of the feeding of the five thousand. Esus did pick up a trick or two from the druids.)

"Now." The druid once more turned to Esus. "Tell on. But—er—leave out the boring bits."

Now you all know how interminably long the Hebrew Bible is. In writing down what began as an oral tradition, people have tried to make some order of it by dividing it into various sections and genres: the Torah (and we were only halfway through that!) the historical books, the wisdom books, the prophets frothing at the mouth for pages and pages with scarcely a pause for breath. A wintering bard could have plucked tales from the Hebrew store of stories every night from *Samhain* to *Beltaine* and still have plenty left over for next season.

I didn't know that then. But I did know that his confidence, so crucial to his success, not to mention his survival, was wavering.

"What's the problem?" I whispered in Aramaic.

"There are so many stories." He held out his hands helplessly, as if rushing cataracts of words tumbled willy-nilly through his fingers. He didn't know how to contain them, how to fashion a vessel that could hold a manageable portion.

"Just pick a few of the most exciting ones. Did your people have any cattle wars?"

"But I can't separate one story from the others. It would be like separating one thread from a garment. All the stories are one story. Just as the God of Abraham, Isaac, and Jacob is one God."

I stared into those deep brown eyes, hoping for a salmon-flash of illumination. I didn't have a clue as to what he was talking about. Sure, there were stories of gods, lots of them. Our gods literally littered the landscape, inhabiting trees, rivers, wells. You could hardly take a step without tripping over one of them. And if there were lots of gods, there were even more stories. But there was no time for literary or theological debate. The crowd was getting restless. Out of the corner of my eye, I glimpsed a flurry of frantic nose ogham.

"All right," I said, "so there's one story. Listen, don't think of each story as a separate thread. Think of each story as containing all the rest, the way each piece of an oaten cake contains all the ingredients."

Light dawned, as they say, in those dark eyes. I had obviously said something very profound. I pressed my advantage.

"And remember, what they care about most right now is your lineage, that you come of freeborn people, nine generations. They're the ones that count. You understand that much, don't you?"

"But what is freedom? Is it only a matter of whether we labor for ourselves or for another?"

Perhaps you begin to understand why the elders in the Temple were so exasperated with him. He couldn't take anything at face value, couldn't let conventional wisdom go unchallenged.

"Esus."

(It was the first time I had spoken his name. It was sweet in my mouth. Have you ever noticed that? How your mouth loves to say the beloved's name? How even the most ordinary names—Sam or Susie—become ambrosia when you love? But I didn't have time to savor those syllables now.)

"Esus, stop thinking and start talking. Fast. If there's another slavery part, tell about that."

"I can't just start there. I have to say something about what led up to it."

"Okay, but make it snappy."

He's right, of course. You can't understand Jewish history without knowing something about Mosaic Law. Or rather you can't understand how the people understood their story: their sacred (and often onerous) covenant with an invisible, rule-making god, whose name could not be pronounced, who mooned Moses but would not show his face.

One thing was certain: if he was invisible most of time, he certainly wasn't inaudible. In fact, you could say he was a compulsive talker. Not one detail of his people's lives had escaped his attention—or comment. As Esus's self-appointed editor, I did not let him get that deeply into Leviticus. Most of what I learned about the Law I learned later from Esus and from the years I spent living among the Jews. To the listeners in the oak grove on Mona the distinction between things clean and unclean was an alien concept, prohibitions against eating pig positively incomprehensible. Also YHWH seemed to have something against the *Combrogos*, since he not only forbade worship under spreading trees or among sacred stones but ordered his people to destroy such places.

Esus didn't go into fine detail, but I got the gist. If YHWH had punishing powers as advertised, Esus was in trouble, but at the moment, it wasn't YHWH that worried me on his behalf, it was the druids. I signaled to Esus: Enough already! Then I translated simply:

"The Hebrew god laid a whole lot of *geasa* on the people."

A *geis*, you may remember, is a cross between a taboo and a curse. "I lay upon you a *geis* of death and destruction, if you...." Fill in the blank. I admit my translation was not exact, since a *geis* was generally laid on one person. That a god should lay upwards of six hundred *geasa* on a whole people required a great stretch of the imagination, but the audience seemed capable of it. As a consequence of breaking *geasa*, the Babylonian captivity made sense.

Way before we got to Babylon, Esus told the story of David. Here was a hero after a Celt's heart: a boy-wonder who starts his career by killing a giant, and goes on to become not only a warrior King but a legendary lover and a bard to boot. Esus obliged with a few of David's compositions. The audience was won over, not to YHWH, who remained incomprehensible, but to a heroic people and their dramatic reversals of fortune. When Esus finally told the story of the Fall of Jerusalem and raised his voice in lamentation: "How deserted she sits, the city once thronged with people!" there was not a dry eye in the house (at least of the eyes that were still open).

There are some great stories from the Babylonian exile—Esther's, Daniel's—but it was getting on for midnight. Despite Esus's gift for narrative—and my sensitive, not to mention poetic, translations—there were a few snores floating on the still air of the Grove. Boann had her head in my lap. The grey-bearded druid, who should have had more self-control, was nodding. Just before he keeled over, he jerked awake. After taking a moment to focus, he asked yet again:

"How many more generations?"

"Fourteen," Esus answered, certain this time. "From the rebuilding of the Temple in Jerusalem to my birth."

"So your people did return from exile?"

"Yes." Esus was speaking Celtic now. "When King Cyrus of Persia captured Babylon, he set my people free, because he knew it was our God, the God of Abraham, Isaac, and Jacob, who had given him his victory."

"So, from that time forward, your forebears were all free?"

"Well—"

"I know, I know," said the druid. "It's a long story. Listen, you're coming down to the wire. That is, the last nine generations. Are you or are you not the son of slaves?"

"To serve the living God, that is freedom."

"You must answer the question."

For the first time I sensed shame in Esus.

"The Jews of Palestine are no longer a sovereign people."

He could not confine his concern to nine generations of direct ancestry.

"First the Greeks conquered. They defiled our holy places and persecuted us for obeying the *geasa* of Moses." He'd caught on to the word I'd used. "Then came the Syrians. Great leaders rose up from the people and waged war for forty years."

He was still speaking for himself. I'm sure he would have liked to tell the heroic exploits of the Maccabees. But he sensed the druids had extended tolerance and suspended judgment for as long as they could. Just because his god was long-winded, you must not get the idea that Esus was a bore. Nothing could be farther from the truth.

"For a time, Israel and Judea were free, paying no tribute to any foreign power. Then—"

"Then?"

"Just over forty years ago, Jerusalem fell to Rome."

At the name of Rome there was a collective hiss and some hearty spitting.

"Our Temple still crowns Jerusalem, and we still worship the God of our forefathers," he said defiantly. "But Judea is occupied by Roman troops and groans under heavy taxes. In Galilee, where I come from, we have a so-called King, but he is no more than a Roman puppet."

"But that doesn't make you a slave, boy!" It was the same man who'd had his cloak cut. He was irrepressible. "Hark, you druids, if Roman rule disqualifies a candidate, then you can't admit any candidates from Gaul."

There was a murmur, generally of assent. Rome did not look upon the druids with favor. In the not-too-distant future, the Roman Senate would outlaw the practice of druidry in all of Gaul. Esus's probing for a definition of freedom was hitting home. The grey druid addressed Esus again.

"Discounting Roman military occupation or rule, direct or indirect, is your father freeborn?"

"Yes."

"And his father?"

"Yes."

"His?"

And on to the ninth generation. The druids nodded, satisfied at last on the first count. As to who would stand surety, his friend in the gold trade had made arrangements. And, in fact, more than twelve men stood up. Esus had captured the imagination of his audience. Not only could he tell a good story, he *was* a good story. I glanced at the druid panel. It was clear that they had taken note of the popular response to Esus. But the silent tap of nose ogham suggested that they still had reservations.

"You are not of the *Combrogos*," the druid stated. "Why do you come to us? Are there no wise men among the Jews? Why do you seek to know our stories and our secrets? Why should we impart them to you?"

I could have answered that! My mind flew back to the sweet, spicy garden on the hillside below his temple. I could still see his half-awed, half-wary expression as Anna the prophetess gave him his marching orders. I could still feel her brown, ancient hands on my dove's breast.

Once again Esus seemed at a loss. It was a tense moment.

"Anna told him to come here!" I blurted out.

"Anu!"

The exclamation swept through the crowd. All attention—the druid's, the people's, my mothers', his—suddenly focused on me.

You must understand, the name I had uttered meant something different to the *Combrogos* than it did to Esus. They had immediately translated Anna as Anu, another form of Don or Danu, mother of all heroes, the very ground of the Holy Isles.

For Esus, I had called up a memory he might well have wanted to forget. He had been humiliated that day of the dove. He might not want to admit that he had been spooked enough to heed an old woman. Perhaps he had even persuaded himself that his little excursion with the *Keltoi* had been YHWH's idea.

"Is it true that Anu called you here?" asked the druid.

Esus looked at me in utter bewilderment, in need of translation of something way beyond words.

"Just say yes," I encouraged him in Aramaic.

And do you think it was a lie? She had told him to find the *Keltoi*. She had told him to step outside his world. *The world is a big place, Yeshua, and small, small as a mustard seed, small as a hazelnut.* Maybe old Anna was Anu herself. How else would she know about those hazelnuts? Suddenly I saw the well of wisdom again, the hazelnuts dropping into the depths where I had first glimpsed Esus. Before I knew what was happening I heard myself shout:

"He is the salmon in the pool!"

Esus looked more alarmed than enlightened. Who could blame him?

"By what authority do you speak, Maiden?"

Maiden? So he hadn't troubled to remember my name.

"She can't help it," Fand intervened. "She—er—has the sight."

"Not to mention a big mouth," muttered Boann.

"Let the stranger speak for himself." The druid turned to Esus again. "The maiden would have us believe that you have been called here by divine powers for some divine purpose. What do you say?"

That was just the beginning of the awkward questions that would dog him all his life.

"I am here," he said simply. "I do not know why or what it is I may learn from the druids that the rabbis, the wise men of the Jews, cannot teach me. Only you can answer that."

That clinched it. Here was this mysterious stranger, bearing the name of a Celtic god, possibly called to Mona by a Celtic goddess, daring to give the druids this cryptic non-answer. They had attempted to place the burden of persuasion on him, and he had gracefully, casually, lightly, tossed it back into their collective laps. Teach me—or not. Take this cosmic dare—or not. Find out why I'm here—or not. It was irresistible. He was irresistible.

There was a wild flurry of ogham hand signals that made me think of the flight of cranes, and then —

"Dear Candidate, we are delighted to inform you that you have been accepted for admission to the College of Druids on the sacred Isle of Mona."

The crowd roared approval. The gold merchant pounded Esus on the back. Esus and I exchanged a glance.

"Wait a minute!" The obstreperous man objected. "He hasn't recited his piece of poetry yet!"

The druids sighed as one.

"I think we can waive any further demonstration of the candidate's ability to meet that requirement."

At a signal from the druids, two students from orientation came forward.

"You will wish to rest now," the druid informed Esus.

Everything happened too fast. Esus was on his feet, bowing his head courteously to the druids as I struggled none too gracefully (my left leg was all pins and needles) to stand.

Then Esus gave me (*me*! his cosmic twin, his tireless translator, his goddamn prophetess, for Anu's sake!) the briefest smile before he turned and went with his escorts out of the grove, leaving me to face the druids alone.

17

WHO STANDS SURETY
FOR THIS CANDIDATE?

I had to pee.

There is no other way to say it. Well, come to that, I suppose there is: Take a piss; take a leak; urinate; void water; relieve my bladder. Euphemisms such as "visit the little girls room" or "powder my nose" or even the all-purpose "go to the bathroom" did not exist. Celts were not mealy-mouthed or prim about bodily functions. You may have noticed that I am not exactly shy. Still, if you were facing a panel of twelve druids (you could have found menhirs with more expressive faces) how would you put it?

"Excuse me," I said. "I'll be right back. Save my place."

And I bolted, crashing through the undergrowth till I deemed myself a respectful distance from the Grove proper. I count that exit as one of my minor heroic deeds. Soon everyone, druids included, followed suit. For a brief span of time, all you could hear was the hiss of hot piss hitting the ground. If we had been gods and goddesses, no doubt we could have altered the geography of Mona. Drowning a host of Egyptian chariots would have been a cinch. As it was, a collective steam rose up, a creeping yellow ground mist

(Do you think there is too much pissing in this story? I don't. Just think of it as a belated release for all the characters who held it for the duration in 19th century novels.)

My own release was all too brief. Soon I was facing the druids again, with Boann and Fand on either side of me cutting off the circulation in my arms with their tight, anxious, grips.

"Declaim your lineage!"

I was glad I'd had a chance to practice with King Bran. When I got to Bride the same thing happened. The crowd behind me and the druids before me all began to recite the genealogy of Bride complete with all its protections:

"I shall not be hewn; I shall not be riven...." I lip-synched along with the rest, taking advantage of the moment to prepare myself for the inevitable next question.

"And your father? It is customary for candidates to trace their lineage through the father's line. Nine generations."

"This is a female child," Fand objected. "Why shouldn't she declaim her matrilineage? You don't ask male candidates to recite the mother's line."

Although what she said made sense, Fand's interruption surprised me. My descent from Manannán Mac Lir had always been a point of pride with my mothers.

The grey-bearded druid turned a mild and courteous gaze on Fand.

"Be that as it may, the candidate must declaim her paternal line. You may begin," he instructed me.

"I am Maeve Rhuad," I stated once more, "daughter of Manawyddan ab Llyr or, as we call him, Manannán Mac Lir."

This declaration caused a ripple in the druid ranks; eyebrows rose in a domino effect all along the line of druids. Seeing all those pairs of eyebrows rise and fall made me think again of the crane wings.

"I don't know who Lir's father is, do you?"

"Maeve, don't get smart," warned Boann.

"But no one can say Manannán and his father are not freeborn," I blithered on. "Unless you choose to argue that the tides are slave to the moon."

"That's enough, Maeve!" admonished Fand.

"Anyway. That's who I am. I don't know any more than that."

There followed another heated exchange in nose ogham. Curiously, I did not feel nervous anymore. My lineage was the druid's problem now.

"Have you ever seen your father, Maiden?" the grey-bearded druid wanted to know.

"He lives in the Land under the Wave." Surely the druids ought to know that! "It's not easy to visit."

The druid sighed, sensing that this line of questioning would lead nowhere.

"Why do you name eight mothers instead of one?"

"I'll answer that if I may," Fand jumped in before I could make any more wise-ass remarks. "Naturally," she said, as if there were nothing supernatural about the circumstances of my birth, "naturally, one woman gave birth to her, but all eight of us nursed her. Think of us as foster mothers, if you like."

The druid nodded. Fosterage and wet-nursing were common enough among all Celts, though granted, fourteen extra breasts might be considered excessive by any count.

"To what *tuath* do you belong?" The grey druid persisted in his attempts to place me in the conventional scheme of things.

"Surely," said Fand, standing precariously on her dignity, "we have answered that question already."

"Can't you see!"

I swear not only my balance but the balance of the whole grove shifted as Foxface rose, in one fluid motion, to his feet.

"They are the *Bean Sidhe*."

Have you seen the way the wind, just before a storm, lifts the leaves, exposing their silvery undersides? It was like that as the crowd registered the presence of the Otherworld in its midst.

"Maiden," said the Greybeard, "where do you come from?"

"I come from the Shining Isle of Tir na mBan."

It was as if I had unstopped a vial of some pungent scent. The air in the Grove became heavy with fragrance. You know how smell calls up memory more powerfully than any other sense? That's what happened. People were remembering, remembering things they had forgotten for a long time, things that may never have happened, except in dreams. Only for some, the dreams were not sweet. Grief was unleashed with the name Tir na mBan, and yearning and anguish, even terror. All the passions hung in the air, thicker than the smoke from the torches. It was becoming difficult to breathe.

Foxface was still standing and staring, wild-eyed. The grey-bearded druid, looking lost in thought, came to first. He clapped his hands twice in the four directions. Then the air was ordinary again, though perhaps a little stale. People stretched and yawned, unaware, I sensed, of the Otherworldy interlude. Foxface resumed his seat. I stole a glance at his face. His expression now was closed, neutral, as if he had never lost his composure.

"Maiden," Greybeard resumed. "Why do you seek entrance to this college?"

Good question, I thought, though no other candidate, except Esus, had been asked to answer it. More evidence that he and I were cosmically paired.

"Destiny," I said.

"Excuse me?"

Before I could elaborate, Fand jumped in.

"You see, we have taught Maeve all we can of our arts, and the girl's not bad with a sword, although she's a bit lazy with her shield arm. Actually, her strong suit is the slingshot, and when it comes to casting the *laigen* she's got pretty good hand-eye coordination—"

"Fand," hissed Boann, "get to the point!"

"But it became apparent to us that Maeve's greatest gift is her tongue. She's good with languages, you see. We believe she'll make a fine bard. When I look back, I realize that ever since she was a tiny babe, guzzling from her mothers' breasts—"

"Fand!" Boann and I both moaned.

"—in the air around her there's been a faint tinkle, tinkle of the bells on the poet's branch. The reputation of your college here on Mona has reached us even on—"

"Quite." The druid cut her off before she could pronounce those dangerous syllables and trigger another mass psychotic episode. "You do understand that the full course of study is nineteen years, as long as it takes for the sun and the moon to complete a balanced cycle. To become a competent bard can require as much as twelve years." He spoke slowly and with exaggerated care in Q-Celtic, as if Fand not only spoke a rustic dialect but was not very bright. "Due to the rather obvious seasons and cycles of a woman's life, we must be very sure of a candidate's suitability before we take him, or rather her, into training. I am going to ask you a blunt question. Have you considered arranging a marriage for your daughter?"

"We have not." Fand was affronted.

"Many a chieftain would welcome a wife trained so thoroughly in the warrior's arts."

"We just told you." Boann took over as spokesmother. "She's got the poet's gift. Do not insult us with condescending suggestions. We have thought long and hard about what is best for Maeve Rhuad, eight times as hard as most mothers, and nine, counting the Cailleach." (Obviously my opinion still didn't count.) "We have made a long journey to come here and present her as a candidate. Will you have her or not!"

"Hear! Hear!" A small chorus rose from the waiting crowd.

"We must determine if she meets all the requirements," said the druid.

"The last one didn't!" called the man with the sawed-off *sago*. "Not really. But you let him in. Don't try to fool us. You druids always do what you bloody well please, and we all know it. So get on with it."

"If you don't want to lose your tunic, too, keep quiet, man," snapped the druid. "Now if we accept your lineage as stated, you are, at least, freeborn."

"Why shouldn't you accept it?" The man was not so easily quenched. "Everyone knows the gods are even hornier than we are. She wouldn't be the first god-begotten brat the world has seen. And as long as there are meddling gods, not the last."

"Strike two!" warned the druid. "Now then, who stands surety for this candidate?"

"We do. Obviously," said Fand.

"And I stand for her."

I looked over my shoulder and saw King Bran on his feet fulfilling his part of the "extremely cordial terms."

There followed an unnerving silence. The druids let it lengthen.

18

TRIPLE GODDESS MOTHERS

"**I thought you had this all arranged!**" I whispered to Fand and Boann.
"So did we."

The three of us turned around halfway and peered into the crowd. There was King Bran, still standing alone, looking perplexed and aggrieved.

"Come on, lads. Speak up! You gave me your word."

Silence.

"So that's what your word is worth. You'd let me down. In a sacred Oak Grove. In front of the druids. Have you no shame? You'll be selling your scummy hides to the Romans next."

"Ah, Bran," one man whined. "Don't hold us to it. We didn't know. You didn't tell us that they were *them*."

That may sound impossibly obscure, not to mention ungrammatical. I believe they were objecting to the Otherworldliness of my mothers and me. I don't know if 20th century minds, overlaid with celluloid conventions (the good guys vs. the bad guys), can grasp what the Otherworld meant to my contemporaries. It was in no way seen as demonic. It was simply Other: shining, beautiful, dangerous. Most Celts had a healthy respect for the Otherworld that included a wholesome fear. By wholesome, I mean a fear untainted with hatred, judgment, or moral revulsion. Of course, heroes tended to be fatally attracted to perilous adventure in magical realms. (It's their job description.) But your average Joe Celt would just as soon leave well enough alone. So you can't really blame these men, who would walk cheerfully into battle or fight to the death over a cut of meat, for being afraid of faery women from an enchanted isle.

But of course I did blame them. I was furious. And (I have to admit) my fury had a competitive edge. Half the crowd had stood up for *Esus*.

"It appears then," began the grey druid, "that the case is—"

Suddenly I rounded on the crowd.

"Are you men or are you fishbait!" I roared.

It was the first thing that came into my mind. I'm not sure what prompted that image. Maybe it's that appendages flaccid (and I had not seen one in any other state) reminded me of the juicy worms Boann would set me to gathering when we turned the earth for planting. At dusk we'd all go fishing from the rocks. As soon as I spoke, I could just picture those worms, dangling from a jagged hook, dancing in the current. So, apparently, could the men I'd challenged. More than one placed a protective hand over that tenderest of parts. I'd evoked, too, those treacherous, watery realms from which dangerous women rose to lure unwary men. Fishbait! I could hardly have touched off more masculine fear if I'd tried. Nice going, Maeve.

"By Anu!" It was Big Mouth again. "This red-headed hussy has balls."

This was the first time I'd received this form of masculine approbation. I assumed he was referring to the spherical perfection of my breasts.

"I'd stand up for her," he declared, getting to his feet.

"I'll just bet you would!" someone whooped.

Everyone snickered and guffawed. I didn't get it.

"If I could, that is," the man amended. "But I've got a nephew to stand for. Sister's son. Know what I mean?"

And it was the first time, but certainly not the last, that a man declared his admiration for me, but scuttled sideways when it came to backing it with something hard—cash or other.

I looked at the druids again. It was easy to read the nose ogham this time: "Does that count as strike three?"

Greybeard sighed wearily. "If you're not standing for her, then sit down. And don't open your mouth again or I'll have it sewn shut. It remains clear that there is inadequate support for this candidate."

"But you are forgetting," said Fand. "There are nine of us on...where we come from, that is. We two stand for the Nine."

"Nine and one makes ten," observed the druid.

You see, numbers were important to us. They were not just abstractions drifting unmoored in empty space till you needed them to balance your checkbook or figure out your taxes. They were the unseen substance of relationship. You ignored them at your peril. As I've noted before, ten either takes you over the top or back to square one. In this instance, ten didn't cut it. We needed twelve. Four threes. Three fours. The solidity of four combined with the magic of three. Far more than twelve had stood for Esus. But apparently that was acceptable. His support entered the infinite category (stars in the sky, grains of sand) while mine—

Suddenly, Foxface rose to his feet. Was he standing for me? He opened his mouth.

I never found out what he would have said. At just that moment, a wind sprang up in the still Grove. A seeking, circling wind, with a low, sobbing note in it. Think of a sea monster mourning. Full of damp, the wind went for the bone, reminding you that flesh was flimsy stuff, temporary shelter at best. Yes, that wind made us all feel like fishbait. Foxface sank down again, huddled within his cloak, staring into the crowd.

Following his gaze, I turned and saw *them* walking towards the druids. The crowd parted to let them pass. I say them, but until they were almost in

front of me, they appeared to be one entity, not exactly human. It was as if
a piece of the blackest night sky had fallen into our midst, or the darkness
of sea, fathoms deep, had risen and taken form. As they neared us, I saw
that the great black shape had three heads.

"What an entrance!" murmured Fand, impressed.

"And how!" said Boann.

The wind subsided as suddenly as it had begun. Three women in flowing
cloaks stood beside us. In my mind's eye, I saw the golden cliffs of Holy
Island and the black bird-women keeping watch. I was certain that they now
stood beside me. They carried with them the smell of the sea, the hint of
secret places hollowed out of rock.

"What business have you with us, Sisters of the Night, Wings of the Raven?"
The grey druid's tone was respectful but not exactly welcoming.

"If you had been watching the signs, Brothers of the Sun, Wings of the
Crane," answered the priestess in the middle, "then you would not need to
ask that question, nor need us to answer it."

Both spoke in the solemn tones of high seriousness. For all that, the druid
and the priestess were ranking each other as nastily as any sibling rivals.

"There are signs and there are signs, and there is watching and there is
watching," said Greybeard. "There is knowing and there is asking and there is
speaking so that you may be understood."

Translation: Of course *I* know. *I* know even better than *you* know. But
you're the one who barged in here, so get to the point.

"Brother, if you have observed the signs, then declare what the cranes'
wings have spoken in the sky."

Translation: I bet you don't know diddly squat.

The druid took a deep breath, stretched out his arms, and rolled his eyes,
stalling for time as he shifted into oracular mode. It wouldn't do to admit that
he had missed a major augury. Before he'd managed to compose a message
cryptic enough to cover his ass, I beat him to the punch.

"Maeve and Esus!"

The druids and the priestesses and my mothers united in scowling at me. I
guess it's bad form to read your own portents.

"Say then," said the druid, ignoring my gaffe, "that there have been signs.
And say that these signs have been noted. Say, too, that there is as yet no
saying what these signs may portend." (Translation: Just because you think
you saw her name in the sky doesn't mean we have to admit her to our
college.) "And finally, since you are here, say why. Is it your intention,
perhaps, to take this over-mothered, strangely-fathered maiden into your
own keeping and to your own place?" he concluded hopefully.

Oh no, I thought. Anything but that. However impressive these priestesses were, hadn't the druid himself just said that I was over-mothered? If I

was going to be packed off to a tiny island with the priestesses I might just as well have stayed on Tir na mBan.

"Listen, you druids," said the priestess, "before you came to the Holy Isles, we were here. We sang the stones into standing and brought the dance of the sky to earth. We conversed with the green world and received the secrets of the serpents. The bones of these isles are our bones, and we know the way between the worlds. You've drunk from our holy wells. You've sucked at our tits and grown fat with knowledge, forgetting its source. You have stood up proud against the sky and cast us into your shadow, naming us Sisters of the Night. Remember, night births the day, and flame shoots from our wombs. Day does not belong to you, nor can night contain us. You have taken our wisdom to enrich yourselves. You have claimed the power to counsel kings. Your words are stronger than weapons. It is time for you to offer your teaching to us and ours. And so you have agreed. Do you renege so quickly? Are your mighty words meaningless?"

"We agreed that all candidates who meet the requirements regardless of, er—"

"Gender," supplied the priestess to the right of the central one.

"Not that all of us think coeducation is wise," added the one on the left.

"—would be eligible for admission," continued the druid. "But this candidate before us, to begin with, her lineage—"

"Is as ancient as the earth and sea," interrupted the central priestess.

"Yes, well, we've already more or less agreed to make an exception on that requirement. But she still lacks the necessary support. Only ten people stand for her."

"Have you not understood what is plainly before you, O Wise Ones?" A little sarcasm here.

"And what might that be?" More than a little weariness.

"We stand for her." All three priestesses spoke, and then again. "We stand for her. We stand for her."

A slight pause for counting.

"Thirteen."

A little shiver ran through the crowd. The wind that had accompanied the three stirred just a little, as if it were a dog at their feet, quiet now but ready to spring at their command. Thirteen is the number of the last moon of the year, the moon of *Samhain,* where end and beginning meet. Thirteen is a powerful, Otherworldly number; it skews everything, throws it off balance. Yet it is unwise to despise thirteen. The druids at least had more savvy than Sleeping Beauty's parents who did not invite the thirteenth fairy because they had only twelve gold plates.

"Very well." The grey druid bowed to my triple goddess mothers. "The second requirement is met. And now for the third requirement—"

Oh, shit.

The crowd shared my dismay. A collective groan arose. The sky began to pale towards dawn.

"You have our permission to keep it very brief," the druid instructed me.

Since I had prepared nothing, I did the next best thing: I went with the first idea that came into my head, and the crowd was treated to my own special rendition of "Queen-Maeve-of-Connacht-Takes-a-Leak." The druids, including Foxface, listened with an unnerving lack of expression. But when I'd finished, my pal with the ruined cloak huzzahed and whistled, and I received a modest round of applause.

"Dear Candidate," the Grey druid yawned, "you're in."

Did you notice the absence of "delighted to inform you?" I did. Where was the rejoicing? Fand and Boann beside me seemed stunned. My triple goddess mothers gave me an inscrutable look, then turned away, billowing out of the Grove as if they were a cloud formation on the move.

I turned back to the druids. The Grey one signaled for the orientation crew, then began conferring with the other druids in nose ogham, probably about whether or not to call a breakfast recess. Only Foxface was still intent on me. I could feel it. I risked a direct look at him. Our eyes met for the briefest moment. Then he looked away abruptly.

One of the students tapped me on the shoulder. As I turned, both Fand and Boann cried out.

"Little Bright One. O Maeve!" They sounded as forlorn as I felt. Strong arms and salty kisses. Then I was led away blind into one of the bleakest dawns I've ever met.

BOOK III

UNDER THE STONE

19

THE TIME OF BRIGHTNESS

My first term at the College on Mona began in the Time of Brightness. That's what May and June are called on the Coligny Calendar, which the druids invented. Whatever their faults, in their own time of brightness the druids held time and space in the palm of their hands. The ogham, the key to all stories, all lore, all law, are encoded on the hand. Free from the need to grasp weapons or common tools, the druids could contemplate the wonder of the hand. They found the whole cosmos dancing there in that warm, cupped space. (Don't your hands naturally curve when you let them?) Look at your own hands now. Maybe you'll glimpse what they saw: a sacred geography, plains and promontories, swirls and whorls echoed in Celtic metalwork, roads and riverbeds, and blue rivers under the thin crust of skin. See how the empty hand holds the shimmering air.

Everyday the sun lingers longer, drinking the mist and clouds, till the sky is a soft, naked blue. Look at the light-charged air; breathe the heady sweetness of hedgerows blossoming with whitethorn and wild rose. Feel the touch of sun and sea wind on bare legs and arms. And then, picture this:

I am lying in a dark hut. Here the Time of Brightness never arrives, and the warmth of summer lags a month behind. I mean it's cold in here. I am lying on the earth floor instead of on skins because I am not supposed to be comfortable enough to fall asleep. Only my head and face are warm, and they itch because they're swaddled in a thick wool plaid. To top it all off, I have a large stone on my stomach, an oversized paperweight, you might say, though I hardly feel light enough to scatter on the nonexistent breeze. In fact, the air in here is stuffy, since heavy blankets cover the door.

Have I been very bad, you are wondering? Is this some proto-Dickensian druidical punishment? No. Although I cannot claim to be a model student, my present circumstances are shared by all my classmates. Believe it or not: this is study hall.

Why do people assume that only pleasure distracts? You see, the idea of the darkened room and the swaddled head is sensory deprivation, which is supposed to help you memorize—and, in time, compose—poetry. But my senses are not in the least quiescent. They are aggrieved, and I can scarcely concentrate because of their complaints. I can't even heave a sigh, because it's impossible to take a deep breath with a study stone smack dab on your solar plexus. Why the stone? I suppose it could have a centering effect. Literally. As for me, I have an irresistible urge to wriggle.

"Settle down, Maeve Rhuad." The voice of Nissyen, the druid on duty, penetrates the layers of plaid. "Remember: memory is the mother of all poetry, so latch onto that tit and give it a good suck."

For some reason that image works, helping me to focus as the swaddling plaid and the study stone have not. I picture a huge breast, blue veins branching like tree limbs. Another apt image. Poets carry a silver or golden branch, depending on their degree of accomplishment. Each cluster of stories is the branch of a great tree. The branch itself divides into smaller branches and twigs. The tree keeps growing, and the poet grows with it, learning one branch after another, and perhaps extending the branch, however infinitesimally, with a new song or story.

Right now we are learning the ogham alphabet, which I already know. That is, I know how to read ogham carved on stone or stick or winging across the sky. But ogham are not just letters. Each one corresponds to a tree, a bird, an animal, the string of a harp, a color, a branch of stories. Look at your hand again and see it as that great, deep-rooted, sky-touching tree. With all the ogham and their complex, multiple meanings stored there, your hand becomes a living Library of Congress.

For a time I forget my discomfort and silently sing over my lessons as earlier that day our ogham instructor sang them aloud over us. The word for teach in the old Celtic languages translates as to sing over. And so I sing the series of questions and answers which lie at the root of the tree.

Q: How many divisions of ogham are there, and what are they?

A: Not hard. Four: B, five; H, five; M, five, besides diphthongs.

But I don't suppose you want to do my homework with me. No doubt there are other things you want to know, such as what has become of Esus. Was he, too, laboring alongside me under the stone?

He was not.

To my dismay (and outrage) the druids had placed him in the second form with those studying to attain the status of ovate. Ovates presided over that branch of druid learning that had to do with divination and healing, ritual and sacrifice. You might have supposed that the druids would instead have required remedial studies, considering that Esus did not have full command of even conversational Celtic. But no. Esus had amply demonstrated that he had the equivalent of a bard's training in his own people's literature and law. In their wisdom, the druids had decided that Anu had not called Esus to the Holy Isles to be a Comp Lit major. At his own request, Esus had an ogham tutor, but for all intents and purposes, he was majoring in magic.

To add insult to injury, not only did Esus and I attend separate classes, but the second form students were housed at Caer Idris more than a mile away from the bardic students at Caer Leb. Since we had been admitted to college, I'd seen Esus only in passing. I didn't get it. The signs that our fates were linked were so clear to me. How *could* there be more barriers between us?

The one Appended One I wanted was still out of my reach. But ironically, there was no dearth of appendages in my daily life. I was surrounded by them. All seven of us were. (Yes, seven. If you want to know the numerical significance, I believe the druids chose to admit seven female candidates, because seven is the number of stars in the Pleiades. A pleasing number, magical enough, but not as formidable as nine.) The seven female first form students were an experiment in coeducation, and the druids had decided to make it a radical one. We were not given any special treatment. We lived in the same hut with the rest of the first-year students. We ate, slept, studied, and played with our male classmates. We even used the same latrines. And so we seven were stripped of any mystery or allure seclusion might have lent us. Such familiarity between the sexes bred not contempt but a sort of brother-sister incest taboo. But no, taboo suggests forbiddenness and restraint. The atmosphere of our hut was anything but restrained.

To our delight, the druids had not been so wise in their choice of our dormhead, or, as he called himself, our nursemaid or even our foster mother. Nissyen was very old with lovely white hair as soft as thistledown. Sometimes he would allow us to comb it or to sculpt it with lime. I would liken him to a benign dog surrounded by impertinent kittens, except that most of us, with the exception of Branwen, far outweighed him. He was little and brittle and joked that he had to carry stones in his pocket to keep the wind from blowing him to the Cambrian mountains. It was plain, even to us, that the other druids considered him a lightweight. We loved him.

In his haler years, Nissyen had been a wandering bard. About whether or not he had completed the full course of nineteen years of study, he was evasive. When his feet wore out, he returned to Mona and charmed his way into a job "by not threatening anyone's importance," he explained. Because he was not a player in the intrigue and politics that riddle every institution, the V.I.D. s (Very Important Druids) tended to underestimate him. He delighted in knowing the inside story and had formidable powers of observation. You have heard people wish they could be a fly on the wall? Nissyen did more than wish. When he needed to bring us into line, he would dangle tidbits of information in front of our noses the way someone training a dog offers a biscuit as a reward.

"Three Crows blew in last night," he hinted one evening.

We were in the midst of our post study hall roughhousing, playing a no-holds-barred game of something resembling blindman's bluff. When Nissyen spoke, we tumbled to a halt at his feet.

"Yes, three great flapping black Crows."

Nissyen liked to speak in code. "Crows" was his term for the black-robed priestesses of Holy Isle. Cranes stood for druids.

"Why are *they* here?" I was perturbed. I had not forgotten my triple sponsors. Were they keeping tabs on me?

"Getting on for the dark of the moon," Nissyen observed. "The Cranes are in a flap. There'll be some feathers flying, black and white, before the moon is fat again."

"Does anyone know what he's talking about?" complained Bryan.

Seven of us had a fair idea, but we weren't saying.

"Not that it's just a black and white matter. There are plenty of both feathers on each side. There's them that say boys will be boys and girls had better be boys, too. And there's them that say seeing as how women's mysteries are mysteries, they ought to be kept separate and secret."

"Mysteries?" scoffed Lleu. "There's no mystery about these young, wet-nosed—"

"Now, now, Lleu." Nissyen wagged a finger at him. "Your own mother was a woman, I'm thinking. Show some respect. And then there's some Crows with suspicious minds as believe this women's mystery business is a Cranish plot. Keep women out of class for a few days every cycle of the moon, and they'll soon fall behind. Then someone will say as how the great experiment has failed. Women are unsuited to be full-feathered druids. Now I have a solution to this dilemma, but does anyone ask old Nissyen? They do not."

"We do. Tell us!" we clamored.

"I say make women's mysteries a requirement for everyone. Hang the bloody rags from the trees and augur from 'em."

By now the boys had caught on and were protesting that Nissyen was a dirty old druid and their *tuaths* hadn't pledged good gold for them to study bloody rags. The girls were blushing, except for me. I didn't quite get it. No one on Tir na mBan had ever used a rag.

"I'm serious," Nissyen insisted. "Don't you think it's a shame to waste good, fresh blood? Why, if my idea caught on, we could do away with all that nasty stabbing and disemboweling." He scraped his throat, and we all moved out of range. Nissyen had been known to spit for emphasis. "Myself I never did have the stomach for entrail reading. Catch me playing ovate! I'll stick to prosody, which I'm sure you'll agree is bloody enough. Now everyone into bed, and I'll sing you to sleep."

The Crows and Cranes alike assumed that the seven of us would bleed on schedule. Just as my mothers had predicted, our cycles that first month were skewed. We staggered our bleeding like some wounded she-elk lurching through the forest. I went first, and I blazed quite a trail.

I had never before bled alone, and I was blue. The homesickness I'd fought off more or less successfully swamped me when my flow began. Nissyen saw how it was with me, and obligingly dozed off—or pretended to—when I slipped out from under my study stone one afternoon and went off to be alone. After wandering aimlessly for awhile, I came to an outcropping of sun-drenched rock in a sheltered glade. Without a second thought, I cast off my tunic and tossed aside the moss I'd used to staunch the flow. (I hadn't wanted to borrow someone else's cloths.) Now I thought of my mothers romping on the beach with red thighs and fingers, rock painting and face painting, and I had a good cry. When I was done, I stretched out on my stomach, and, lulled by the mothering warmth of the rock, I went to sleep.

The first thing I saw when I opened my eyes was a long, straight seam of darker rock running through the large, flat, lighter stone. I knew at once that it was perfect, just perfect, for forming the stem of ogham. Naturally, I pulled myself to a crouch and dipped my fingers in the original inkwell. You don't need to be told what I wrote, do you? As I carefully made the lines of the ogham along the stem, I was absorbed and content, feeling linked in this act both to my mothers and to the one whose name I inscribed with my own. I scarcely noticed the approach and retreat of several sets of footsteps. I was just completing a second coat when a shadow fell across my handiwork.

"Maeve!"

It was Viviane, the other redhead among the seven, the one who had gained admission to the college so effortlessly. The way she pronounced my name, she might as well have greeted me with a dagger's thrust. I looked up at her rabbit-blue eyes. (Yes, I know rabbits don't have blue eyes, but if they did, they'd look like Viviane's.) You could argue that her blue eyes with that russet hair (hers was a shade more decorous than mine and smooth as water) resembled blue sky paired with autumn leaves. Okay, she was beautiful. Usually. But at that moment, her face was mottled with fury and shame. We were on trial, the seven of us. We'd been warned that anything one of us did would reflect on all the others. Viviane did not like what she saw.

"No wonder the Romans think we're savages," she hissed. "Do you know how many people have seen you? Except, of course, they were too embarrassed to look. What's wrong with you! How can you—"

"How can I what?" I turned back to my inscription, attempting to treat her presence as an annoying but insignificant interruption.

"Are you shameless or are you just stupid!" Her voice rose. "Look at you! Naked, with your thighs all bloody!"

I put a final dab on the last letter and turned to look at her again. She really did look like a rabbit, the way her nose was twitching.

"And your fingers!" Viviane's lip curled in disgust. "You're no better than a baby, playing in its own, its own—"

She could not bring herself to say it.

"Shit!" I roared, hurtling to my feet. I'd had enough. "Shit! Is that the word you want? Shit! You're calling the sacred blood of the womb *shit?*"

The memory of my first blood surged back to me. I could hear the Cailleach commanding: *Anoint me.* In a flash it came to me what I must do. Viviane wasn't exactly worthy, but—

I dipped my fingers into the source and got a generous coating. Before Viviane knew what was happening, she had my bloody fingerprints smeared across her cheek.

Viviane gaped at me, stunned. But only for a moment. Then she let out a shriek that betrayed our common *bean sidhe* ancestry and lunged for me.

Apparently the druid code of nonviolence had made no impression on either of us. You can lay down your sword and shield and still have fists at your disposal, not to mention teeth, nails, knees, and feet, none of which we hesitated to use. Viviane was stronger than I'd imagined from her willowy build and the languorous poses she affected. I was heavier and better trained, but I'd never before fought with anyone who was livid with me.

Stand aside with me for a moment and watch these two redheads wrestle each other to the ground, rolling from the rock into the gorse and bracken. I am streaked with menstrual blood and scratches, both from the gorse and Viviane's fingernails. Her green tunic is torn and dirty. It's getting harder for either of us to use our hands, because our fingers are so tangled in each other's hair.

I'm sorry. Did you want to think that women have no aggression? Should Viviane and I have displayed more sisterly solidarity? Just consider. In her own self-interested, self-righteous way, Viviane was doing just that. No tip-toeing away with averted eyes for her. Though I wouldn't admit it for a long time, I respected the way Viviane cast aside her civilized pretensions in a robust rage. But then, Celtic notions of femininity did not require denial of will or temper. Womanliness included the capacity to fight fiercely on provocation. So when our ruckus attracted the attention of others, there was not the same degree of shocked censure or titillated fascination that a "cat fight" provokes in your time.

Okay. Before we break it up, let's jump back in. Now we're both on our feet again. Breasts heaving against each other. (Hers were no match for mine.) Eyes stinging with sweat. Mouths full of hair. The fury of locked muscles. Distorted glimpses of cheekbone and eyeball. The two of us one hot, straining mass of flesh. Yet for all the intensity, I have a strange, peripheral awareness of the sweetness of cooling earth, the enveloping brightness of sky.

Then someone grabbed me under the arms from behind. The earth pitched for a moment, and the edges of my vision blurred. When the ground settled and my sight cleared, I found myself staring at Viviane from a distance of several feet. Panting and bloody, Viviane was also being restrained by a pair of strong, male arms. Together we formed the center of the attention of some half a dozen second form students. I knew their status, because they wore the blue tunics of novice ovates.

I almost (not quite) felt sorry for Viviane, who was nothing if not vain, appearing before second formers at such a disadvantage. We were not in a movie where the heroine (I'll grant Viviane that status for a second) looks fetching in her dishevelment. Viviane was a mess. Hair bedraggled, skin blotchy, eyelashes not bedewed with tears but caked with dust and sweat and separated into clumps. The student holding her was one of those ridiculously handsome Celts with blue-black hair, eyes to match, and flawless skin. They would have made a handsome couple under other circumstances.

"This is a piece of luck," said Viviane's restrainer. "The closest I've gotten yet to this delightful experiment."

He meant us?

"Doesn't seem to be working out too well, does it?" another laughed.

"Oh, I don't know. It all depends on your perspective." The one with the blue-black hair grinned at me over Viviane's head. "Looks like you've had the worst of it, though." His eyes raked my naked length.

"I have not!" I said hotly.

"I did not remove her tunic, if that's what you mean." Viviane was blushing from head to toe. "She was already naked when she accosted me."

"I accosted *you*!" I struggled to get at her again. The grip on me tightened.

"You did! I didn't lay a finger on you, until—"

"I anointed you." I cut her off. "That's all I did. You don't know an honor when you receive one."

"Maeve!" she snapped at me. "We will not discuss your disgusting behavior in public."

"Oh, public. That means us," said a plump second form student.

"Well now," said the blue-black one. "If we let you discuss your differences in private, how can we be sure that you will not mar your loveliness further, which would be a shame and a pity?"

"I have nothing further to say to this...this maiden." From her tone, Viviane might as well have said "slut."

"Let's have your word on it then, both of you. Any more displays like this one and the druids'll pack you off to the priestesses on Holy Isle."

Viviane and I both shuddered.

"You have my word." Viviane glared at me.

"And mine," I said through gritted teeth.

Viviane's young man released her. She gave a toss of her head worthy of Macha, the mare goddess. Of course, the light caught her hair. Unkempt as it was, it glowed richly as Viviane strode away, in so far as someone switching her hips like that can stride.

"Wait," called Blue-hair. "I'll give you safe escort."

The rest of the company began to move on. My captor released me. As the heat of that unknown body receded, it occurred to me to turn and see who it was.

Oh, shit.

Just like the Eve I hadn't yet heard of, I saw that I was naked. Shame I hadn't quite grasped. But it was a hell of an awkward moment.

"Esus!" My voice came out a whisper.

His eyes averted, he turned and began to walk away.

"No, Esus. Wait! I can explain."

You probably understand better than I did at the time what he must have felt. Here he was, a pious Jew. He'd just grabbed hold of someone who could hardly have been more unclean. A bleeding, gentile woman, for godssake. Now he was unclean, too. Yet when I called to him, he paused, turned around, and had the courage to look me in the eye. He was a mensch.

"Esus."

I didn't know what to say, but I think all my hurt and longing came through in those two syllables.

"Maeve."

It was the first time he had spoken my name. The sound of my name from his lips broke my heart. No dagger's thrust this, but a different kind of penetration. Deeper. No less painful for the sweetness.

"Maeve, I'm sorry. I can't handle it. It's all too much. The pork-eating, the idolatry, and now...this." He looked down at himself in dismay. "I should never have come here. It's all a mistake."

Again he turned away.

"Esus," I implored. "It's not a mistake. By Bride's Breasts, I swear it's not."

He paused for a moment by the rock where my inscription glistened in the slanting light. Did he know enough ogham to recognize his name? Over his shoulder, he shot me a swift glance that I couldn't read. Then he walked on over the rise, his body dark against the brightness.

20

I Take Action

There was no way a bloody brawl between two female first formers could be kept quiet. It made too good a story, and we were, after
all, enrolled in a college for storytellers. The tale spread, each teller em-
bellishing it, adding a snatch of dialogue here, a visual detail there. The druids
took no direct disciplinary action, but Nissyen assured us the incident had
been on the agenda of more than one faculty meeting.

In the end, the druids decided to wash their hands of Women's Mysteries.
They first invited, then begged the priestesses of Holy Isle to send three of
their number to be resident at the college on Mona and to take charge of our
hormonal excesses. Finding themselves in a position of strength, the priestesses refused until the druids agreed to accord their representatives the status
of full faculty members. The priestesses also insisted that the druids develop
a corresponding course in Men's Mysteries. When the druids blustered that
there had never been such a course and that to institute one now would be
highly irregular, the priestesses suggested the druids could do a lot with the
Boar and Stag cycle. And if all else failed, the druids might assign the male
students to run laps around standing stones and take bracing dips in the Menai
Straits. Finally all parties agreed to the arrangements, however grudgingly. The
priestesses were due to be installed at the next full moon.

Before the Crows arrived to crimp our style, I was determined to find a
way to speak with Esus alone. Whenever I saw him during the day, he was in
the midst of a group, often with a druid or two in attendance. He would
amble along with his claque, debating some point or another, the whole party
oblivious to their surroundings. Then late one afternoon I spied him walking
apart from the other students with Foxface. Since admissions, I had learned
that the red-bearded druid's name was Lovernios, which means the fox. He
was a V.I.D. par excellence, but not one of the druids who spent a lot of time
teaching small classes or tutoring individuals. He was a military strategist
and was often on the road as consultant to kings. That he should single out
my foster brother for special notice was unusual, and, I was sure, significant.

Esus and Foxface began moving away from the teaching groves where
afternoon classes had just broken up. Because the afternoon was warm, they
kept to the shade of a row of huge beech trees, which stretched out from the
groves between two barley fields. The massive tree trunks gave me some

cover as I followed them. (Of course I did.) Because of the sound of the wind blowing unimpeded across the flat fields, I could catch only snatches of their conversation. I knew they were speaking Greek, probably because Esus wasn't fluent enough in Celtic for a complex discussion. The word Roman came up repeatedly. That made sense. Foxface was giving a series of lectures to the entire college on the Gallic wars, with detailed analysis of the Roman campaign, how and why it had succeeded in conquering the Gallic tribes. Esus came from the other fringe of Rome's expanding empire. No doubt Lovernios was broadening his knowledge of Roman methods.

Then, suddenly, just as I had come out from behind one tree, Foxface, stopped, half-turned, and gestured for Esus to sit with him beneath the tree before them. There were several seconds when either one of them could have seen me as I back-tracked as silently as I could to the shelter of the tree next to theirs. Fortunately, they were deeply engrossed in their conversation, and neither looked in my direction. I could hear much better, now that they did not have their backs to me.

"Tell me about these Zealots," Foxface was saying.

"They are a remnant of patriots who refuse to recognize Roman rule. In order to survive and go on resisting, they live in wild places in the hills, of Galilee mostly. They don't even begin to have numbers comparable to the Romans, but they make governing more difficult for the Romans by stirring up trouble, causing riots and rebellions. They attack by stealth, and sometimes single out individual collaborators for assassination."

While my foster brother spoke, commanding Foxface's full attention, I climbed up into the crux of the beech. The long, sweeping branches veiled me, but I could see through them.

"A lot of people," Esus was saying, "even those, like the Pharisees, who decry Roman rule, think the Zealots are too extreme, misguided in their methods. They don't like the violence, the anarchy. Other people dismiss them as fools for a lost cause. But Israel has a long history of prevailing against the odds, like David against the Philistine giant Goliath."

"And you?" Foxface probed, seeking for something more than general information. "What do you think of the Zealots?"

Esus did not answer right away. I could imagine him chewing his cheek, his brows almost meeting in a straight line as he drew them together.

"At one time I thought I would join the Zealots."

"I do not understand," said Foxface. "How could you be a warrior, destined, as you clearly are, for the path of knowledge?"

"My people don't make exactly the same distinctions as yours do. King David, after all, was both a poet and a warrior."

"I had wondered about that." Foxface looked thoughtful and stroked his beard. "Then what did decide you against joining the Zealots?"

Again, Esus did not respond right away. I wondered if he was thinking of Anna, and debating whether or not to tell that story.

"I cannot answer that," was all he said.

Foxface hesitated for a moment, then shrugged. "Very well," he said. "You mentioned collaborators. Are they merely individuals or are they an organized body?"

There followed a long and complicated discussion about the Sadducees, the distinctions between them and the Pharisees. I confess I did not pay close attention. Foxface did. I watched him listen. I could almost feel the keenness of his trained druid mind. He would remember every word. Later he would retrieve this conversation from his memory and examine each new piece of information. Then he would find the right compartment of his brain in which to store his new knowledge, so that he could tap it instantly.

Perhaps because I was seeing Foxface now without reference to myself or my strange, inexplicable fears, I was able to notice how well-proportioned his features were, how bright and intelligent his eyes. Of course, I had attended his lectures, but this glimpse of him was more intimate.

"And so," Foxface spoke again, "your wise men, the Pharisees and the Sadducees, are divided against each other, and there is no unified resistance to Roman rule among the Jews."

"The Sadducees are only a small part of the whole people," objected Esus.

"But as you have said, they have disproportionate wealth and power. Naturally they want to protect it. The Romans understand their position and make use of them."

"Yes," agreed Esus. "It's not only wealth and power the Sadducees abuse, it's the Law of Moses itself. They observe only the letter of the Law, what is written down. We have an expression: 'They put the Torah in a corner.' They refuse to let it live and breathe. As long as they keep clean, and fast, and make sacrifice on the appointed days, they count themselves as righteous. Since the Law says nothing specifically about whether or not to cooperate with Roman rule, they believe they are justified in doing as they please. They forget the spirit of the Law, which is justice and truth."

"That is what comes of the written word," observed Foxface. "If you write the law in stone, it becomes as stone. That is why we druids are sparing with inscription. It is not that we can't write, as those Roman barbarians suppose, thinking us primitive and backward. It is that we choose not to. We have too great a respect for the power of the word. And perhaps because the law is alive within us, given new birth on our tongues each time it is spoken, the wise men of the *Combrogos* have greater unity in their understanding of their law than your wise men, your priests and rabbis, your Sadducees and Pharisees."

"But what is it worth, this unified understanding of druid law, when the tribes of the *Keltoi* are constantly warring with each other, as the tribes of Israel have long since ceased to do?" countered Esus. "And how can the druids hope to bring the tribes into unity when they worship so many different gods?"

I held my breath, anxiously searching Foxface's expression to see if he would take offense at my foster brother's brashness.

"Ah, I see you have paid attention to my lectures on the Gallic wars." Foxface was smooth. "It is perfectly true that the Romans took advantage of our tradition of tribal warfare. This is a problem the druids must address in the Holy Isles. But if you suppose that our gods are the cause of conflict, there you are mistaken. Tribes fight over cattle and land, and sometimes out of restlessness and boredom, but not over gods.

"You say your Sadducees don't acknowledge the law of Moses as a living, changing force. Our gods and the stories our bards sing celebrate the shifting forces of life, in all forms and aspects. We do not seek unity as an end in itself. Unity," he shook his head. "Listen, Esus, son of a strange people, brother to the *Combrogos* in resistance to Rome, listen well. Roman rule is unity. If the Romans have their way, the whole world will live in unity—and slavery. The Romans, with all their gods, have only one god, the Emperor. Tell me, how is that different from your one god, and the one immutable law to which your Sadducees cling?"

As much as I adored my foster brother, I found myself stirred by Foxface's eloquence. Perhaps the trees were, too. (There is a deep connection between druids and trees.) In any case, the wind, which had lulled for a time, suddenly picked up and tossed the sheltering branches of my tree. Just at that moment, Foxface looked in my direction.

He saw me. I am sure of it. That's why I didn't duck or try to run away. He was looking straight at me. Even after the veil of branches fell again, he peered through the leaves. I waited for him to call out and demand to know what I was doing there. I would not have been surprised if he had stood up and hauled me from my perch. But he did neither of these things. Instead he turned pale and wild-eyed and looked as though he might, at any moment, be violently ill.

"Rabbi, Rabbi!" Esus cried out in alarm. "What's wrong!"

Then the look passed.

"Nothing is wrong. Why do you ask?" He recovered himself instantly. "Are you afraid you have offended me with argument? Debate has its place in a druid education. You are young, gifted, and a little arrogant." Foxface almost cracked a smile. "But not too stubborn to learn, I trust. I have enjoyed our conversation. We will speak again. But now other duties await me."

Foxface rose to his feet and turned to walk back past my tree. Surely now he would expose me. But he didn't. He walked with his eyes on the ground. Esus followed, brows knit, chewing his cheek. I knew he was considering how he would answer Foxface's last argument when next he had the chance. I wanted to attract his attention, throw something, call out to him. But he was too close on Foxface's heels for me to risk it. In a moment, the opportunity was past.

∞

Have you ever dreamed that you were writing a story? Then, as the words take form, you find yourself in the story. You keep writing, but the story leaks through the lines, bleeds through the page. You lose control of it. Well, we have dreams like that in the oral tradition, too.

That night I dreamed I was telling a tale of Queen Maeve of Connacht to a huge crowd of listeners. It is not a tale I've ever heard before, but it has some of the classic elements. Queen Maeve is off to some battle in the company of King Ailill and her chief lover Fergus. Only there are no massing hosts behind them or ahead of them. The three ride alone in Maeve's war chariot. (She holds the reins. Who else?) Then suddenly, she draws them in, and the chariot comes to a screeching halt.

"The hell with the Brown Bull of Cuailgne!" she cries, and she hops out of the chariot.

I watch her stride away, beckoning the two men to follow her. Then, although I can still see the upturned faces of the listeners, still hear my own voice narrating, I *am* Queen Maeve. A green hill swells into view, seemingly out of nowhere. Instead of climbing it, I lean forward and rap on it with my knuckles. I can hear its hollowness. The two men draw alongside me, only they are no longer Ailill and Fergus. Or if they are, they are also Esus and Foxface. I rap on the hillside again. The hollowness rings. I rap a third time, and the ringing sound surrounds us. The delicate bones of our inner ears vibrate at an almost intolerable frequency. I glimpse the listeners holding their hands over their ears, trying to escape the sound, which, instead of dying away, grows stronger and stronger until, all at once, the hill gapes, glowing inside, all pinks and reds, as if someone lit a huge cavern of a mouth with a torch.

Then we are swallowed, the three of us, and everything is dark and wet, hot and slippery. Naked limbs slide and twine into intricate knots. I have no idea now who is who, where I or anyone else begins or ends. Whatever remnant of me there is, I surrender, as I surrendered in the cave between Bride's breasts to the snakes. This time the pleasure is even more intense. As I swim the churning darkness, I see the green mound again, I am the mound, and my hollowness is filled to overflowing.

∞

All the next day the dream stayed with me, more vivid than than my surroundings. I went through the motions of the daily round, attended classes, sang over my lessons, but all the while the dream worked on me, making me restless to the point of desperation. I wanted to fly out my skin into the sheer sky. At the same time, I wanted to wallow in my senses, roll naked in heather, coat myself with hot mud. Clearly, I had to *do* something. When the seemingly interminable day drew near its end, and a plump moon rose, three days shy of the full, I knew I had to act now. If I could not reach Esus during the day, I resolved I would go to him at night, this night. I would creep into his hut at Caer Idris and haul him out to face me by the light of the moon and stars.

So I plotted, as I sat silent during our evening meal (something resembling haggis: various obscure animal parts ground to anonymity, and remember we had no ketchup then, or salsa). The usual repartee went on around me, but I paid no attention, letting friendly and not-so-friendly insults pass without a retort. As soon as I'd finished eating, I wandered off in a cloud of preoccupation to sit on the embankment overlooking the mountains beyond the straits. There I watched the changing light and rising moon as impatiently as you might watch a clock.

"Is something wrong, Maeve?"

I started and turned to find Branwen sitting next to me. Her eyes were so large and liquid, I could glimpse myself in them, a salmon flash in dark pools. Branwen was not only my first friend but my closest. We slept beside each other in the hut, often snuggled together for warmth and comfort. But at the moment her concern irritated me. I didn't want anyone, even Branwen, observing me too closely.

"Nothing's wrong," I said a little sharply.

Branwen turned her face towards the straits and kept silent. That was one thing I appreciated about Branwen. She never pushed or probed. If my mothers thought I was holding out on them, they'd hunt my secret down like a pack of ruthless bloodhounds. It was little short of a miracle that I'd kept from them my vision of Esus. They doubtless would have had the whole story out of me if I hadn't been hustled away so abruptly after being admitted to college.

But Branwen was different, I reminded myself. She'd never force a secret, and I was certain she could keep one. Did I want to tell her about Esus? I considered for a time and discovered that I was afraid, not of telling Branwen, but of exposing my life's secret, so deeply embedded in me, to the uncertainties of air.

"Shall I go away?" asked Branwen presently.

"No," I said, putting my hand over hers. "No, please don't."

The truth was, I had almost forgotten she was there. She was one of those rare people who know how to be quiet. With Branwen, it was possible to be both solitary and companionable at the same time.

"I've got a lot on my mind," I explained. "It's not that I don't want to tell you, it's more that I can't. Do you know how it is when you begin to make a poem? There's maybe a picture in your mind, a few lines. But you don't know how they fit together or where they're going. You can't say it to anyone yet."

"Oh, yes," said Branwen. Though we both still looked out at the straits, I could feel her growing animated. Poetry was her passion. She was far and away the most promising first-year student. "Yes, I call it the Dark Time. It's like the seed underground or the child in the womb. If you speak a poem too soon, the light and air kill it."

"How well you put it," I said.

And how peaceful the kinship between us, unlike as we were. But with my twin, my Other, I sensed the potential for cataclysm. Think of tectonic plates colliding, volcanoes erupting, tidal waves rising. Forces that change landscapes, make and mar worlds.

∽

At last the day ended. The hut was filled with the soft, surf sound of rising and falling breath. I waited until I heard Nissyen's signature rattle and wheeze, then slowly, so as not to disturb Branwen next to me, I eased out from under my blankets. Just then, I heard someone else moving about the hut. When whoever it was lifted the flap over the door, I recognized Viviane by her cloak of hair, the red faintly visible in the moonlight. I waited for a moment after she let the flap fall behind her, then I followed just in time to see her tiptoe to meet someone in the shadow of the eastern embankment. Ciaran of the blue-black hair, no doubt. I had seen them together several times since "the incident." He did not seem to hold her brawling against her. No doubt he just thought she was high-spirited.

You have to hand it to the Celts. They appreciated savagery in a woman. Just look at the goddesses. They all have animal forms: mare, sow, crow. So why didn't I find a nice Celtic boy, with antlers sprouting from his head, who would appreciate my finer qualities? Because Esus was my destiny, damn it.

Bother Viviane. Not only did she have the effrontery to have red hair—I couldn't help feeling that she was trespassing on my territory—but she appeared to be way ahead in a game I hadn't even begun. Now she and her little friend were scrambling over the embankment, which meant I could not take the direct route to Caer Idris, without the risk of running into them.

I stood for a moment feeling peeved. Then I decided to head for the straits instead. By walking along the shore, I could find the path from the water's edge to Caer Idris. It would take me more than a mile out of my way, but the route had several advantages. Anyone who chanced to see me would not suspect my final destination. It would be that much later by the time I arrived, and that much more likely that the inhabitants of Caer Idris would be sound asleep. And since I'd be walking for awhile along the shore, it occurred to me that I just might pick up one of those round flat stones my mothers had mentioned....

Casting one glance around the Caer to make sure no one was lurking in the shadows, I made for the southern embankment. Soon I was running barefoot as fast as I could across the fields to the shelter of the hedgerow and the woods beyond. After keeping still all day and containing the turbulent feelings the dream had churned up, movement exhilarated me. I took in lungsful of moonlit air, rich with the scent of damp night earth. As I ran through the thick woods near the straits, the sweetness of the new leaves mingled with the salt tang of the tidal marsh.

When I reached the straits, the tide was turning. I caught my breath and watched the moonlight catch the intricate patterns, swirls, webs, and crosshatch, where the conflicting currents met. After a time, I waded into the gravelly shallows and bent over feeling for stones. Almost at once my hand closed on one that was smooth and round and fit perfectly in my palm. Well pleased with myself, I turned back to the shore. And then I got one of the shocks of my life.

Standing before me was Esus.

21

INCARNATION

It was a good thing I was standing at the edge of the water instead of the edge of a cliff. I was thrown so off balance that I might have pitched over it. As it was, I lost my footing on the slippery rocks. Esus put out his hand and gripped my arm to steady me, a swift, spontaneous gesture. As soon as I regained my balance, he withdrew his hand, but the warmth of it lingered. It was the second time he'd touched me, the first being when he'd hauled me off Viviane, unless you count—(but who's counting? Well, okay, I am)—the time he'd almost placed his hands on my dove's breast in our dream encounter.

Now my human breasts were within inches of his chest. Neither of us moved or spoke for a time. Just looked. There was something almost resigned about his expression, as if he'd fought it but finally accepted that he had to face me. I managed not to smile. Perhaps I even scowled a little. Still, I could not help noticing that the moonlight on his face brought out a hidden tint of gold in the brown.

"Orange," he said out of the blue.

I did not know why he said it, but it struck me that he'd been standing there, searching his P-Celtic vocabulary list to come up with the word.

"Orange?" I repeated.

"Even in the moonlight, I can see the orange."

He reached out his hand and lightly touched my hair, just barely grazed it. I might as well have been struck by lightning. That touch sent a shock from my crown right through my toes. Speaking of toes, my hand opened and I dropped the stone I'd been holding onto his foot. He bent to retrieve it and held it out to look at it in the moonlight.

"A good skipping stone," he pronounced. "I don't know if you can skip stones on the straits with all these cross currents. May I?"

Speechlessness is not one of my afflictions, but I felt unequal to explaining the use I'd intended for this stone. I made a vague ambiguous gesture, which he took to mean: go ahead.

He moved a couple of steps away from me in order to take unobstructed aim at the straits. It was a pleasure to watch him curving his arm and body, his energy concentrated in the strong, supple movement of his wrist. There it went: the perfect round stone, a miniature moon, spinning out over the

149

straits, skimming the water, skipping once, twice, six times altogether before it disappeared with hardly a splash beneath the surface.

So much for contraception.

"Not too bad," he said. "Though sometimes I've skipped a stone as much as twelve times. I always think, if only I knew how, if I could put the right spin on each step, I could walk on water."

"You mean, they haven't taught you that yet?" I said, as if water walking was elementary—which I suppose, literally, it is.

He glanced at me curiously, as if not sure what to make of me. Then he gestured with his head, "Let's go," and he started to walk. Awfully damn sure of himself. Instead of following—let's get one thing straight right now, I am not and never was his or anyone's follower—I stood gazing, coolly I hoped, at the moon. In a few moments, he turned around and came back.

"Will you walk with me?" he asked. "We have things to talk about."

"All right," I said, and I fell into step with him.

Despite or maybe because of all there was to say, neither of us spoke. The silence lengthened as we walked the shore well past the path that led to Caer Idris. The shore rose to a small cliff crowned with a grove of yews. Just at the edge of these, Esus sat down abruptly. I stumbled and landed in his lap.

Which was pretty much where I wanted to be, except that now that I was there I did not know what to do. Neither did he. So we sat, his arms tentatively around me, our faces close, but mine a little higher. I could see the top of his head, so dark and curly I couldn't help thinking of black fleece, but his hair was shinier, glinting with moonlight. Though I was scarcely breathing, I took in the scent of his hair. How to describe it? It was a concentration of sun, sea, salt and some kind of earthy sweetness. I wanted to bury my nose in it, get that scent all over my face. But I didn't move, just stared at his head as he stared past me at the mountains beyond the straits. His lap was so different from a mother's lap, no comfy layer of fat, just bone girt with muscle, ribs barely contained in skin. But I liked the hardness, the tautness, even if it was not quite comfortable.

"Um," he said after a time, "my leg...."

I probably weighed almost as much as he did. I shifted myself from his lap and sat cross-legged next to him, my right knee and his left almost touching.

"Why did you come out tonight?" I asked.

"I couldn't sleep, so I came out to walk. Don't you think it's strange that we both chanced to be walking the shore at the same time?"

"Maybe strange, maybe not so strange," I hinted.

When was he going to get it? Chance, destiny. What did it matter what you called it? Did the moon intend to draw the tides or did it just happen to be passing by?

"Everything looks so different in moonlight. I like to watch it on the water. Do you?"

"Yes," I said, at a loss for more words.

He sounded like a foreigner, making polite conversation from memorized lessons, which I suppose he was, being new to P-Celtic. Still, I wondered why this conversation was not more momentous. I did not understand then how difficult it can be to close the gap between the mystical vision and the mundane, what a hell of a job it is to make anything fully incarnate. I could hardly have imagined a more romantic scene, being alone with Esus, an almost full moon beaming on a swelling tide. But fancy leaves out the pins and needles in a cramped foot; midges feasting on exposed flesh; the awkwardness of knowing someone's soul—or believing you do—but almost nothing else about him.

"When I was a child," I found myself saying, wanting to shape the air between us into words, "I used to sneak out when the moon was full and the tide was high and wait for my father on the cliffs."

"But why would you sneak out to see him?" Esus was puzzled. "Was he an outlaw or in some way unclean?"

"Of course not!" I said. And I remembered that though I had heard almost the entire story of Esus's people on the night of admissions, he knew nothing about my lineage, having waltzed off before it was my turn to be examined. "My father is a god."

"I'm afraid my Celtic still isn't very good. I didn't get what you just said. I thought you said your father was a god," he laughed.

"I did," I assured him. Then I remembered that Esus had some bizarre notion about there being only one god. "And my father is not just any old god," I went on. "He is Manannán Mac Lir, son of the wave, god of the sea."

Esus was silent for a moment. I stole a glance at him. He was pondering. I knew the look: the sucked in cheek. Though I couldn't see them in profile, I knew he'd drawn his brows together so that they made a continuous line.

"When he came to the cliffs where you waited in the moonlight...."

"At high tide," I added.

"It had to be high tide?"

"Details like that are important."

"Well, how did he come? How did you know he was there?"

How, indeed? I had only told Esus I'd waited. He had jumped to conclusions.

"By the way," he said, "I think your Aramaic is better than my Celtic. If you don't mind, could we speak in Aramaic? I want to understand exactly what you're saying."

I certainly did not mind at all having his full, probing attention. So in the language of the Jews, of whom at the time I knew almost nothing, I told Esus the story of Manannán Mac Lir and his magical crane bag where he kept his treasures (to refresh your memory: the king of Caledonia's shears, the king of Lochlainn's helmet, Goibne's smithhook, the bones of Assail's swine, Manannán's own shirt, and a strip from the great whale's back). All these treasures were visible only when the moon was full and the tide, high.

Now you must remember that I was not only at druid school for the express purpose of studying the art of storytelling, I was the daughter of eight mothers who raised me on their own homespun stories. My standards of truth were quite different from Esus's and perhaps from your own. Facts were nothing in themselves. You used them or discarded them according to whether or not they served your narrative of the moment.

So I did not tell Esus that I waited until the moon set, or until I fell asleep and some mother found me and carried me home in her arms. I told him what I wanted to have happened: how my father would rise, splendid and gigantic, from the sea in his green cloak with a finely wrought circlet of gold on his head. With the help of Goibne's hook, he would scale the cliffs. Then he'd sit down, take me onto his lap, and empty his bag of the treasures, spreading them out in the moonlight for me to see.

The more I elaborated, the more I believed my own story. As I spoke, I could see the gleaming bones of the swine. I knew that Manannán's shirt was the color of moonlight and softer than the feathers of new-hatched birds. In contrast, I could feel the bristled roughness of his cheek against mine. I could breathe the seaweed scent of him.

"Then he is just a man," Esus interrupted, almost rudely.

"Why do you say so?" I demanded.

"Because you saw him and touched him. You said he had whiskers."

"Well, why shouldn't a god have whiskers?" I demanded.

"God is not a man." Esus had not yet grasped the concept of incarnation. "What I mean to say is that God does not take form. He certainly doesn't smell, and you can't sit on his lap."

"Well, maybe *your* god can't take form—"

"I didn't say *can't.* I said *does not.* Form is too finite, too limited—"

"But your god sure has a big mouth."

"What do you mean?"

"Well, in your stories he talks all the time."

"That's different," argued Esus. "A voice can be, well, a voice can speak in many ways. The voice of God can speak inside your mind so that nobody else can hear it—which can be awkward at times. But these days the Most High doesn't speak as plainly as he did in the days of Moses, or even of the great prophets, like Isaiah and Jeremiah."

"Does your god talk to you?"

Esus didn't answer for a moment.

"He does." Esus spoke so quietly that I leaned closer. "But I'm not sure what he wants. It's hard to understand him sometimes."

"That's the trouble with gods," I said sympathetically, but insisting on the plural. "I guess that's why you have to study divination."

"I am studying divination." He sounded pensive. "I just hope I'm not breaking any commandments."

I sensed he was speaking to himself now. I thought of the 600 *geasa*. I could practically hear him ticking them off in his mind. But then I remembered I had concerns of my own.

"It's not fair!" I burst out. "It's not fair, the druids promoting you to ovate studies while I have to memorize endless poems about cattle raids and not even get to fight any battles the way Queen Maeve of Connacht did. The druids ought to know, your *god* ought to know: we were meant to be together, you and me. We're the same!"

Until now, except for the occasional glance, we'd mostly been looking towards the straits. I don't know who turned first but suddenly we were eye-locked. His eyes were so dark, so deep. To stare into them was like gazing into the pool between Bride's breasts. I swear, once again, I saw the salmon leap.

"Tell me what you mean." His voice was almost angry in its intensity.

"You *know* what I mean. This time you tell me."

"I only know that I feel as if I know you." The blaze went out of his eyes and voice and he looked away again. "From the moment I saw you at Llyn Cerrig Bach and you shouted to me in Aramaic. And by the way, how do you come to know Aramaic? Now that I've been here awhile I see how strange it is that you do. Lots of druids and even some of the students know Greek, but no one else knows Aramaic. Who taught you?"

"The Cailleach taught me, the same as she taught me Greek, Latin, and P-Celtic."

"Who's the Cailleach?"

"The old wise one. A goddess, I suppose. She lives between Bride's Breasts on Tir na mBan where I come from."

"The Land of Women?" he translated, sounding puzzled, though clearly the name did not have the same effect on him as it did on the *Combrogos*. "Only women?"

"Unless you count the male animals. You can't rely on gods for everything."

"You were born there?"

"Yes."

"And there are no men? Are you sure your father doesn't live there, in hiding, maybe?"

"I told you. He's the god of the sea. He has his own place."

"So how did the Cailleach come to know Aramaic?" He abandoned the subject of my paternity once again.

"Before she came to Tir na mBan, she had a long life, full of strange adventures and places and tongues. She taught me some geography, too."

"But why did she teach you these things?" he probed. "For what purpose?"

"What do you mean for what purpose!" I was indignant. "Haven't I already helped you by translating? If it hadn't been for me, you probably never would have gotten into college. You would have been lucky not to be a human sacrifice!"

"Jews do not believe in human sacrifice," said Esus almost primly. "We have not practiced it since before the time of Abraham. I refuse to believe such enlightened and knowledgeable teachers as the druids would allow such barbaric practices. Even the Romans have outlawed it."

"Yeah, right." I'd attended Foxface's lectures, too. "Romans don't practice human sacrifice. What about those, what do you call them, crucifixions? What about those gory, gladiatorial games?"

I felt a shudder go through Esus. He knew a lot more about the Roman executions and entertainments than I did.

"True enough," he said. "Far be it from me to defend the Romans. But just because they are cruel and depraved and hypocritical into the bargain doesn't justify human sacrifice for other peoples. Have you ever seen a human sacrifice?"

"We didn't do things like that on Tir na mBan," I said hastily.

Then it was my turn to shudder as I remembered the skull in the well. That was one tale my storytelling mothers had never told.

"But don't your people have some kind of blood sacrifice?" I asked, remembering the smell of blood in the Temple.

"Burnt offerings and sin offerings. Of animals." He made the distinction, a little defensively, perhaps. "People used to bring their own animals or their own grains, from their own land, from their own hands, from Israel herself. Now, more often than not, the priests find some reason to reject any animals people haven't bought from the Temple marketplace. Most people find it more convenient to buy their offerings on the spot. But then, if they are rich, what have they sacrificed but coins? And the poorer peasants from the countryside can't afford to buy costly sacrifices."

I sensed his mind was far away from Mona now, back in that world where I had first glimpsed him, brooding over things I had no way of understanding. How could I? I had no concept of commerce. I had never seen a coin. I did not know what poverty meant. But it puzzled me that people had to go to such lengths to shed blood. If blood was an important element in sacrifice, why not go to the source, the fount that renewed itself with every turning of the moon?

"Do you know what Nissyen said? That's our druid, us first-year students. He said if we augured with women's blood, maybe we wouldn't have to have stabbings and disembowelings. It would solve a lot of problems. When we bleed on Tir na mBan, we have parties on the beach and paint the rocks. Maybe that doesn't seem like blood sacrifice to you. But as Nissyen says, why waste good blood?"

A squeamish silence followed.

"Is that what you were doing....that day?"

He had a problem. I didn't understand it, but I suspected it had something to do with the 600 geasa. And suddenly it dawned on me that the argument I'd overheard in the Temple about the stain on the bed and whether or not the women were clean or unclean was about blood, women's blood. Menstrual, monstrous, menstruous blood.

"Well, sort of," I said. "But Viviane didn't approve. She thought I was being *primitive*." I mimicked her voice. "Listen, Esus," I touched his arm. "There's something you don't seem to understand. I am as much a stranger here as you. I left my people behind, too. I tell you we're the same."

He smiled at me and shook his head. "Maeve, whatever else we are, the same we're not. Maybe we're both strangers. Maybe we both stand out from the crowd a little—"

A little?

"But you come from a place I can hardly imagine where only women live. You inscribe names with your....your *menstruous* blood!"

(So he had recognized his name that day!)

"While I come from a place where men thank God every day they were not born a woman, and women with their blood on them are considered unclean. Men don't even come near them then. By the way, you're not...."

What, can't you count? I wanted to say. But I didn't want to staunch this flow of information. I merely shook my head.

"What's more, you tell these strange stories of gods and goddesses, as if they were as familiar as your next door neighbor. What am I saying? You said your *father* was a god. Whereas we do not even pronounce the name of the Most High. Sometimes I think God is punishing me, exiling me among idol-worshipping, pig-eating gentiles, gentiles so gentile they don't even know they're gentiles."

He was right about that. I didn't know what he was talking about.

"Then other times," he went on, "I think there are things I was meant to learn here, powers I was born with that need to be harnessed and disciplined. Maybe the druids do know something the rabbis can't teach me. Besides, to be honest, I've been thrown out of most of the Hebrew schools in Galilee at least once."

"For what?" I was intensely curious.

"At the time, I refused to understand the reasons. But while I was on shipboard, I had some time to think things over. We were at sea for a long time. On board ship, everyone has to pull his weight. You have to accept the captain's authority. If someone's a troublemaker, first time there's a storm, he's overboard, especially if he's a stranger in strange circumstances."

"But what did you use to do that got you into trouble?"

"I always had a smart remark at the ready. It was hard not to. I learned things more quickly than other people. A lot of the time, I thought I knew more than my teachers did. I used to dispute just for the sake of disputing, just to waste time. Also I have to admit, I used to enjoy scaring people. I knew how to make storms on a clear day. I don't know how I knew, I just did. I liked tornadoes especially. Once I tore up an orchard of old olive trees. I'm sorry about that now. Also, I learned how to put people into trances, so that they would lie down and scarcely breathe. Rumor had it that I was striking people dead, then raising them. The truth is, I was showing off. They weren't really dead. But the whole performance was pretty dramatic. And, well, you know how people are."

In fact, I didn't. I'd never had a large population to terrorize.

"All kinds of wild stories spread about me. Crazy stories. Like the one about how I turned some children who wouldn't play with me into a herd of goats. I am supposed to have changed them back again, of course, but a lot of people were a little afraid of me, including my brothers and sisters, even my half-brothers who are older than I am."

I was beginning to think Esus was right about how different we were. He came from a crowded world where he was evidently accustomed to throwing his weight around. You could even make a case that he was—or had been—a spoiled brat. I may have been the adored only child of eight mothers, but it had never been within my power to overwhelm them with a little weather magic.

"On Tir na mBan goats were my playmates," I told him. "And pigs and horses and other animals. It didn't occur to me to change them into children. I'd never seen another human child, until the day I saw you in the pool."

"What do you mean you *saw* me?"

"Just what I said."

"Maeve! Come on. Tell."

"How badly do you want to know?" I gazed nonchalantly at the straits.

He was nonplused. I bet no one had dared treat him that way before. Just let him try to impress me with his little tricks. Then I felt his hand on my cheek. With a gesture that was somewhere between a caress and a command, he turned my face toward his. There were those eyes again.

"You cannot entrance me," I informed him, not at all sure that he couldn't.

"I wouldn't even try," he said. "Please, tell me what you know. You seem to know more than I do."

From his own account, he had quite possibly never made such a statement before.

"All right," I said. Just to look at his eyes brought back that day at the pool so clearly. "I ran away to a secret place on Tir na mBan where I was not supposed to go till I was initiated."

"Initiated?"

"Until I had my first blood."

This time he didn't blanch at the mention. Clearly, I was a good influence on him.

"Only I didn't know that then," I continued. "I just wanted to find out what my mothers were keeping secret from me."

"Mothers?"

"Yes, I have eight. That's another story. Do you want to hear this one or not?"

"Go on. I promise I won't interrupt again."

And so I told him, as best I could, about the valley between Bride's Breasts, the sacred pool with the hazelnut trees surrounding it. I spared him no detail, trying to make him see what I had seen, feel what I had felt. When I came to my vision of him, he interrupted again.

"Are you sure it was me?"

"Of course I'm sure."

"You saw my face?"

"More." I admit it, I started to giggle, like the teenaged girl I was.

"Where was I? What was I doing?" He sounded skeptical.

I laughed harder, leaning against him for support.

"You were in some dry, hot-looking place with lots of buildings," I gasped between bursts of laughter.

"Hilarious," he said dryly. "Sounds like Jerusalem. We go there for the feast of Pesach."

"And you...." I was laughing too hard to speak. "And you were....taking a piss."

"This is a joke?"

"No. No, I'm serious." I finally got a grip on myself and took a deep breath. "You have no idea how amazing it was. I'd never seen one before, you know. Not on a human being."

I didn't need to look at his face. Embarrassment was emanating from him in hot waves.

"Don't you remember anything about it?" I asked. "I could swear that for a moment you saw me, too. You looked straight at me."

"I have lots of visions," he said crushingly. "I couldn't possibly keep track of every single one."

We were both silent for a time, seething companionably.

"There's something else I've been wondering about," he said. "When the druids asked me why I was here, you said: 'Anna sent him.' How did you know about Anna the prophetess? Did you see that in the pool, too?"

Now it was my turn to be embarrassed.

"No. I have dreams sometimes...." I said vaguely.

He nodded. He knew all about clairvoyant dreams. They figured prominently in the stories his people told.

"So you dreamed what Anna said to me."

"I'm not exactly sure." I decided to come clean. "I tried to tell you about it that first night at Llyn Cerrig Bach. Listen, Esus, if it wasn't just a dream, I'm really sorry. I didn't mean to shit on your head."

"What are you talking about?"

"If you were ever a bird, you'd find out. Birds have no control over their bowels. None. I just got flustered, and...."

I trailed off, aware that he still wasn't following me. I'd left out something vital.

"I was the dove," I confessed. "You know, the dove that shit on your head and embarrassed you in front of all those people. Unless....Maybe it was only a dream?" I added hopefully.

"It was not a dream," he said slowly.

I turned to look at him. He was staring at me, not exactly with horror but maybe with horror's next of kin.

"And believe me," he added. "It was way beyond embarrassing."

"I'm sorry," I said again. "I swear I didn't do it on purpose."

"You know, it's a good thing you don't live in my country. You'd be accused of sorcery. Some people believe it's unlawful to allow a sorceress to live."

A shiver went through me.

"Well, what about you?" I countered. "With your tornadoes and striking people dead and changing children into goats."

"Thank God I was not born a woman."

"What's that got to do with anything?" I demanded.

"You see, I was born a man," he explained. "I might grow up to be a prophet or a healer. I might become a great leader who will free the people from Roman rule. I might be...." His tone changed and he spoke with mock seriousness. "I might be the Messiah. Who knows? People take a wait-and-see line with a boy."

"Why not with a girl?" I honestly didn't get it.

"It's just different," he said.

"Now I know why Anna sent you here," I said. "You've got a lot to learn."

"From you, I suppose." I could hear his smile.

"Could be."

Then we were silent again. It was a different silence from the first one, when we walked beside the shore carried along by a dark, wordless current towards inexorable, treacherous whitewater. Now we'd ridden our first rapids together, and we rested in a sweet flow of silence. The moon drifted west to set in the Shining Isles of the Otherworld.

Esus did not know about the Otherworld. A different land had fed him; different stories formed him. All right, Esus. I spoke to him silently as I turned West to look at him. So we are different, as different as day and night. But listen, don't day and night meet again and again, one turning into the other? Isn't that how the world is made and made new? Face it, Esus. Face me.

Then he turned to me.

Do you want to know why people laid aside their fishing nets to follow him? Left husbands and wives, mothers and fathers? Think of looking into a sky full of stars on a clear night. You wonder at that unknowable vastness. With Esus, it's as if that gorgeous mystery is looking back at you, wanting to fathom you.

"We'd better go, Maeve" was all he said.

He took my hand and we scrambled down the cliff, back along the greying shore where low mists swirled over mud and rocks, exposed by the ebbing tide. When we came to the turning for Caer Idris, he dropped my hand.

"I go to the Yews in the afternoon sometimes. To study," he said.

He seemed about to say something more, then he changed his mind. Before I could think of what to say, he took the path and soon disappeared among the thick trees.

I stared after him for a moment, then walked on alone. Night and its magic went out with the tide, leaving me stranded in the light of day, like a jellyfish on the rocks.

There was something I hadn't told Esus about the treasures in my father's crane bag. They form the last five ogham in the alphabet. When the moon is full and the tide is high, you can read the ogham in the waves. So really, my father did spread out his treasures on full moon nights. But I wanted more than ogham.

I wanted words made flesh.

22

GEIS

So. **What do you think should happen next?** No, this isn't one of those adventures stories or CD ROMs where you get to choose. I'm the storyteller here. We are apt to be adamant about that, those of us brought up in the oral tradition. As I've explained before, we couldn't write something down, then forget it, trusting to the page to preserve our knowledge. We had no back-up disks. We had only memory with all its tricks of time and change. What we forgot was forgotten. So we were strict about stories, singing them over and over, learning not with mind alone but by heart.

Not that I am telling you this story in the don't-change-one-word-or-inflection style I learned at druid school. This story is not that refined, although it's old, ancient as earth, the ground you stand on, the substance you're made of. It is also new, molten. No one has told this story quite this way before. That's because they've left *me* out, the hot lava flow that changes the shape of everything you thought was permanent, immutable.

No, I'm just asking because I'm curious. Do you picture us meeting again and again? Dating, so to speak. Going steady. People begin to recognize us as a couple. Maybe we exchange tokens of some kind. We progress from holding hands to kissing, and more. Or do you want to go on thinking of him as utterly singular, physically and psychically unable to couple? (Except with the Church, of course, his mystical bride. Only at the time, remember, the Church wasn't even a gleam in anyone's eye.) Does it upset you to think of him having something so sweet—even silly—as a highschool sweetheart?

Relax. (But not too much.) Things were never so simple.

The Crows arrived on schedule, three of them: Morgaine, Morgause, and Moira. Crows tended to travel in threes. They liked that triple-headed effect. It made them more formidable and Otherworldly. All of us found it difficult to distinguish between them. Unlike my mothers, who kept their edges (and tongues) sharp, the Crows' boundaries blurred. Not that they were together every second. But when you saw a Crow without her sisters, she looked strange and incomplete, like someone without her glasses or some essential item of dress.

Our dormitory arrangements remained unchanged. The Crows had their own hut, as far from the others as it could be within the confines of Caer Leb. The Crows added herbcraft—or what might more accurately be called psycho-botany—to our course load. I did not mind the extra work, because they were teaching the same course to the ovates, which made me feel more on a par with Esus. Their teaching methods differed from the druids. They relied less on memorization and more on trance. We learned not only to identify plants but to identify with them. The Crows believed that only by entering the plant's state of mind (or matter) could you know its properties and inclinations.

Of course, as agreed, they took charge of Women's Mysteries. The blood mysteries were in fact an extension of our herbcraft course. They had many botanical uses for our blood, and they threw lots of ceremony into the bargain. Their rites weren't as freewheeling or as much fun as fingerpainting with my mothers, but they were preferable to bleeding discreetly and doing your best to pretend you weren't. To my satisfaction, the Crows had no patience with Viviane's disdain of "savagery." Insofar as they were capable of displaying anything as human as approval or disapproval, the Crows looked upon me with favor—at least in the beginning.

The Crows also took us into custody at the full moon when our hormones rose to flood tide levels. Though there was something nun-like about the Crows, you would be mistaken if you imagine them as guardians of our chastity in any conventional sense. On our first full moon with them, the Crows took the seven of us on a seven mile hike to the sand dunes of Caernarfon Bay where the Menai Straits widen to embrace the Hibernian Sea. We walked along the shore till we came in sight of a small tidal island, a dark swell of land against the moon-bright sky and sea. I was struck at once by how the island's form resembled a woman's, not a woman lying on her back, gazing skyward as Tir na mBan did, but a woman lolling on her side, sensuous, enticing, with full curves and hidden folds. I assumed the island was our destination and skipped ahead eagerly.

"Maeve Rhuad!" a Crow called after me.

I turned and saw that our company had come to a halt. One of the Crows struck up an irresistible beat on her drum.

"But aren't we going to the island?" I asked one of them, Morgause, it may have been. It was so close to the shore, I didn't see why we couldn't have waded out.

Morgause shook her head. "That is Dwynwyn's Isle."

"Who's Dwynwyn?" I asked.

But Morgause didn't hear me. She had begun an eerie wailing song that sounded not like a human voice but like a pipe, not the high bird cry of a bagpipe, but something low, earthy, sultry, more like an animal in heat. For you, that music, the wild, wordless songs and those rich, complex rhythms, would have conjured images of bellydancers, navels flashing with jewels, tits hung with tassels. And, indeed, the small, dark ancient peoples that settled the Holy Isles long before the Celts might have come from the Mediterranean. As if we could feel that southern heat, we shed our tunics. The Crows drummed and sang, and the seven of us circled and spiraled, hips rotating, bare feet slapping wet sand, bare breasts swinging in the breeze. Several times, as I turned round and round in the dance, I glimpsed someone in the distance dancing alone, long, white hair floating on the wind, above a black cloak and—even in the moonlight you could see it—a blood-red tunic.

That night I felt the snakes—remember the snakes?—stir and uncoil from sleep, spiraling up my spine, until my crown burst and blossomed, a fiery rose. It was like the time when the fire of the stars came into my head, only in reverse. Though we didn't talk much about our full moon ecstasies, I know I was not the only one who felt the snakes rise. At the time, I had no awareness that the Crows had given us a great gift. I did not know then how rare it is for a young woman to experience sexual power as inherently her own, not just a response to some man's need. I can't claim that this knowledge saved us from grief or foolishness with men. But at some level, we always knew who and what we were.

If the Crows made any mistake, it was that they remained, despite their intimate knowledge of our hormonal cycles, inscrutable and impersonal in their bearing towards us and, indeed, towards everyone. Yes, impersonal is the word. They regarded themselves as voices of the earth, mediums of wind and water and soil. Insofar as they were able, they spoke earth's truths and pronounced earth's judgment. They had deliberately sacrificed personality. In exchange for this death, they became something other than, more than, human. They taught us to see the world from the point of view of a gooseberry bush, say, or a swamp cabbage. We understood the sentiments of the lapwing as she dived into the air and drew her enemies' attention from her hidden nest, but we knew nothing of what the Crows thought or felt.

And so we did not go to them with our sexual or emotional quandaries or even, very often, with our minor physical complaints. It's not that they couldn't have advised us; it's just that it didn't occur to us to seek their advice in the first place. It would be far easier to talk to a tree; most rocks seemed softer and more comforting than the Crows. Their inner life was a mystery. We knew only what we could observe. For example, though they taught some classes during the day, they tended to be nocturnal creatures. You could not wander abroad at night without risking a disconcerting encounter with one or all three of them.

∽

The Time of Brightness came and went, followed by the Time of Horses, so named because people traveled then, when the planting was done and the herds out to pasture and winter still far away. Esus and I managed no more moonlit meetings, but the late, luxuriant afternoons were ours. The Crows, at that time of day, were pretty well out of it, like the owls and the possums. Nissyen had a sweet habit of nodding off then, too. So off I'd go, trying to make up for the loss of study time by singing over my lessons in time with my running footsteps.

We met in the grove of yew trees where we'd sat that first night overlooking the straits. Yews are one of the sacred Ogham trees. Their thick, down-sweeping branches root and rise as new trees. When the inside of an old yew dies, a seedling springs to life from its decay. That's why the yew ogham carries the meaning of life and death. You still find yew groves sheltering old graveyards. Since death and sex are so deeply linked—(Think about it, you wouldn't have one without the other; and Eve as everywoman is blamed for both)—maybe it's fitting that the yews sheltered Esus and me as we teetered at the brink of death's tandem mystery.

Yes, teetered, because, for some reason that made no sense to me, Esus, the rabbi's bane, the scourge of Hebrew school, had become a serious student. When I arrived at the yews, flushed and breathless from my run, I would often find him scratching ogham in the dirt with a stick. He was fascinated by ogham, the web of meaning woven from each one. We once spent a whole afternoon debating whether or not the ogham that made up a person's name could predict destiny.

Esus was skittish about divination. YHWH apparently didn't approve of it. The Most High had withdrawn his favor forever from King Saul, because Saul had consulted the Witch of Endor, a well-known diviner. By then I'd garnered a working knowledge of the Hebrew Bible from listening to Esus. So I pointed out that YHWH's own priests were in the habit of using ephods—a divining instrument consisting of twelve stones for the twelve tribes of Israel—and I demanded to know why ephods were approved by YHWH and other methods of divination weren't. Esus both loved it and hated it when I pointed out YHWH's inconsistencies, which I did every chance I got. I relished the perturbed look on his face. He would pace and chew his cheek and then suddenly let forth a loud burst of laughter that was invariably followed by more argumentation on YHWH's behalf.

Esus's theological quandaries and what you might call his spiritual identity crisis took up an inordinate amount of our time together. I have to admit that I had rivalrous feelings towards the Unpronounceable One. Not very pretty of me, you say? A good woman does not come between a man and his god.

A good woman is willing to sit quietly in the back seat of the chariot (with its flaming wheels) murmuring encouragement, a demure cheerleader (please, no short skirts and thighs here, no pom poms). A bad woman is like Delilah or Eve or any other self-centered, demanding bitch who wants her man to love her more than God or Truth or the Good, or whatever abstraction he holds dearest.

So, yes. While he was pacing or sitting cross-legged examining his conscience and conducting his exhaustive (and exhausting) independent study in comparative religion, I *was* lolling on my side, displaying my hips and breasts to their best advantage—(I'd learned a few things from Viviane)—except when I became so irate that I, too, had to stand and expostulate. But I am here to tell you that categories labeled "good girl" and "bad girl" cannot contain me. And if you think you can make a clear distinction between virgin and whore, read on. You cannot cast me as a mindless slut attempting to seduce him from his lofty purpose, because, as you ought to know by now, our purposes were linked. And if YHWH thought otherwise, then maybe *he* was the tempter, the seducer.

Did Esus notice the feast stretched out beside him? Yes, but he didn't know what to do with it. It was like his being hungry but unable to eat pork, very like that. Then, one day, he touched my breasts—or at least the considerable portion of them that overflowed the deep V-neck I'd made in my tunic. He was sitting for once, and a silence came over him as the slanting light and the shifting breeze caused a shaft of light to spill over my breasts. In the green dusk under the yews, they shone like twin moons. Esus reached out with one finger and lightly—so lightly—touched one of the blue-green veins that flowed over the roundness.

"They are like the rivers," he said, "the rivers flowing from Eden."

Then he began to speak slowly, rhythmically, in a language I did not understand but which I knew from the depths of my soul, a language a little like Aramaic but rounded and liquid, tender as the speech of doves. I closed my eyes and drank in the voice of my beloved. His hand played over my breast, warm and subtle as sunlight. There are not many times in a life when you can simply weep, without your face contorting, without a sob rising in your chest. But this was one of those times for me. My tears were warm as his touch; they tasted like the sea. My vision had been true. The vision I'd had beneath Bride's breasts had come true.

His voice stopped, and his hand rested on my breast. I could feel him bending over me. The light slid from behind my closed lids as his head blocked the sun, but the heat intensified. The air was on fire. I could feel his breath on my lips, and then—

Suddenly he drew back. The sun struck my face again, but all the warmth was gone. It was as if the sun had retracted its rays, turning into a bright, cold ball. Esus was speaking, muttering to himself in harsh, hurried tones. With a sickening jolt, I recognized the rhythms of YHWH's *geasa*.

> I am YHWH, your God: You must not behave as they do in Egypt where you used to live; you must not behave as they do in Canaan where I am taking you, nor must you follow their laws.
> I am YHWH.
> None of you will approach a woman who is closely related to you and have intercourse with her. I am YHWH.

Could that mean me, I wondered? Then YHWH got more specific, beginning each injunction with: "You will not have intercourse with." Let me see if I got it all straight. You will not have intercourse with your mother, your father, your sister, aunt, granddaughter or son; or a man if you're a man; or a woman and her sister; or a woman and her daughter. (Oddly, there didn't seem to be any prohibition against a man having intercourse with his own daughter.) Oh, yes, and you must not have intercourse with any kind of animal.

"Why not?" I interrupted, remembering the snakes and some of the animal forms my father had taken in my mothers' conception tales. Besides which, I'd had enough of YHWH and his stupid list.

I had the momentary pleasure of seeing Esus completely nonplused. But I'm afraid I undermined my own cause. My moral obtuseness put me completely beyond the pale, outside of YHWH's jurisdiction altogether, though doubtless if YHWH had known about me he would have added to the list: redheaded hussies from the Pretannic Isles. But he didn't know about me. I was none of his business.

"Because," Esus continued citing YHWH, "you would become unclean by doing so. Nor," he added, still quoting, "will a woman offer herself to an animal to have intercourse with it. This would be a violation of nature."

This struck me as splitting hairs, something YHWH spent a lot of time doing.

"Is that all?" I asked.

Esus frowned and considered. Imagine having to hold all those prohibitions in your brain. It's a wonder he had any room for his own thoughts. It's a wonder his skull didn't split.

"I think so," he said slowly.

My heart beat and breath quickened. A wave of heat washed over my body. Why would he be considering who he could and could not "have intercourse with" unless he wanted to have it with me? Yet he made no move. He sat with his face turned away from me, staring through the branches towards the straits. I sat up and moved closer to him.

"He didn't say anything about not having intercourse with girls your own age who aren't your father's wife's daughter," I mimicked YHWH's awkward phrasing.

He turned his gaze on me. It was so tender, my eyes welled again.

"Aren't you my sister, Maeve?"

"Is your father Manannán Mac Lir? Is your mother Grainne of the golden hair?"

He didn't answer. He just kept looking at me, his expression a disconcerting mix of sweetness and sadness.

"Why do you supposed Anu sent you here anyway?" I snapped, fighting back tears.

"Anna," he corrected. "To learn what I could learn in the poorest quarter of Jerusalem or at the gates of any heathen temple? I don't think so."

One day I would know both the slums of Jerusalem and heathen temples well. At the time I knew only that I had been insulted past bearing.

"Moreover, it is written—"

"Listen, Esus, I've had enough of your god and his *geasa*. Moreover, the reason all his *geasa* got written down is because they're too ridiculous to remember."

"They are not really *geasa*," he quibbled. "They are divine laws that the Most High gave to his chosen people through his prophet Moses, so that we should remember him and honor him in all we do."

"Well, he didn't choose me or my people. So we don't have to obey his silly rules. *I* don't have to obey him. What's more, I don't see why anyone should. He's overbearing and bossy. *Our* gods mind their own business. Around here, gods don't have the corner on pronouncing *geasa*. Anyone can do it."

"Anyone?" he queried. "I thought that was the prerogative of the druids. I thought that was one of the things that made the druids so powerful among the *Keltoi*, that they control all forms of sacred speech, the *geis* as well as the *glam dicin*."

He was certainly paying attention to his lessons at druid school, heathen or not. What he needed to learn was to pay attention to *me*.

"Ha!" I said. "They'd like you to think so. They'd like us all to think so. But they ought to be more careful about the stories they make us memorize. Ever hear of Grainne and Diarmuid?"

"There's a story about your mother?"

That threw me off for a second. It was hard to connect my quiet womb mother, sweetly submitting to the goodnatured bullying of her seven sister-mothers, with the willful Grainne of the story who had forced Diarmuid to become her lover.

"No. That is, I don't know. I don't think she's the same Grainne."

"You know, Maeve," he shook his head, "it just doesn't make any sense to me: the things you do know and the things you don't know. You know Aramaic. You claim to have seen me in an alley in Jerusalem...." Here he cleared his throat. "You also claim to have seen the Temple of Jerusalem from a birdseye point of view. You claim to have a divine father, but you have never seen where he lives. Now you're not sure whether or not your mother is the same as a character in one of your interminable Celtic stories, which, thank the Eternal One, I've been spared from committing to memory, and which could not possibly be true anyway, judging from the ones I've heard."

"Oh, right! And your stories are, I suppose." I was furious. "Burning bushes that talk. Angels, which you deny are gods, interfering with human sacrifice at the last minute. If I was your Isaac, I'd never let my father near me again. I'd rather have Manannán Mac Lir for a father any day. Let's see, what else? Oh yes, the sun standing still at Jericho. A women turning to a pillar of salt just for looking over her shoulder. Our stories couldn't possibly be more far-fetched than those.

"I know what's really eating you," I pressed on. "In *our* stories, women get to do something besides giggle when they conceive after their blood has stopped. In our stories, women get to lay down the *geasa* from time to time. Do you know what Grainne said to Diarmuid? Do you? Well, do you!"

"Obviously, I don't."

We were both testy. (Note: testy has the same root as testosterone.) Sexual frustration doesn't lead automatically to sublimation. It's more likely to make you very cranky.

"She said—"

Suddenly, I was on my feet. I was towering as befitted my rage. Esus wasn't about to take anything lying down, so he stood, too. We were face to face, within spitting distance.

"She said: 'I place on you a *geis* of danger and destruction, O Diarmuid, unless you take me with you out of this house tonight before Fionn and the chiefs of Hibernia wake from their slumbers.' And I say unto you, O Esus," (I borrowed YHWH's syntax; I was speaking Aramaic), "I say unto you that I place on you a *geis* of danger and destruction unless....unless you take me as your lover!"

We stared at each other, the color draining from his face and flooding mine, both of us scared out of our wits. For a long time, neither of us spoke. We just stood, breathing the *geis*-charged air.

Maybe you think I should have taken back my words, laughed, and said: Sorry, just kidding. That's because in your time the spoken word has no power, hence, your obsession with tapes and paper trails. To us the spoken word was not only real; it created reality. I could not unsay what I had said, any more than I could have closed a fissure in the earth or put back the spilled contents of a cauldron. I was appalled at the potential horror I'd invoked.

Despite clay tablets and scrolls, Esus, too, knew the power of the spoken word. His god had called the world into being with words. Esus lived by "every word that proceeded from the mouth of God." You have to understand that to know how brave he was, and stubborn, too, when he finally answered me:

"You cannot force me with word magic, Maeve."

Of course, now that I had tried to do just that, I knew that I did not want him to be my lover because of threats or tricks. I wanted him to want me. It was supposed to happen, our lovemaking, just happen by itself, because it was inevitable. But Esus wasn't allowing it to. Or YHWH wasn't. So I was furious—or had been until I scared myself so badly.

"I am not one of the superstitious gentiles, like the *Keltoi*," he added, taking refuge from fear in rank arrogance.

I was terribly relieved. Now I could be angry again.

"I am a Jew. My people have a covenant with the One True God. 'The Lord is my protection...'"

With protection like that, you could argue, who needs a *geis* of danger and destruction?

"Let's just leave your god out of it," I said instead. "That's how this fight got started."

I brightened momentarily at the idea that it was all YHWH's fault that I'd laid a *geis* on Esus.

"Listen, Esus, I have an idea. Couldn't you just choose to, well, I mean, *choose* to love me. Then I wouldn't have forced you, and we wouldn't have to worry about danger and destruction. We could forget all about that silly old *geis*."

"But I do love you, Maeve."

For an instant everything changed. The green air warmed to a throbbing gold, and we stood beneath the Tree of Life.

"But I can't, well, you know, be your lover now."

"Why not?" The gold seeped away. I felt cold all over.

"Don't you see? We'd never know. We'd never be sure whether I was doing it freely or because I was afraid of the *geis*. The *geis* would always be between us."

Here you get a glimpse of the mind, schooled by the Pharisees, that drove the Pharisees crazy. Pharisees scrutinized behavior, but Esus went after motive, the secrets of the heart, the adultery thereof. Only, whoever heard of an unadulterated heart?

I suppose I could have pointed out to Esus that since he claimed not to believe in the power of the *geis*—or anyway believed that YHWH's power superseded it—he could not, therefore, act under its compulsion. But I lacked Pharisaic training and was, moreover, beyond reason, quite a bit beyond it. I was stunned. The gates of paradise (and I use the Biblical imagery deliberately) had just slammed in my face. And like Eve I'd been told (more or less politely) that I was to blame. I was not capable of conjuring clever arguments on my behalf, and so I went straight to the unadulterated heart of the matter.

"You know what, Esus?" I said. "Sometimes you are really full of shit."

Seizing the consolation prize of the last word, I turned and stalked away from the yew grove without a backward glance. If YHWH wanted to turn me into a pillar of salt, he'd have to find another excuse.

But I hadn't gone more than thirty paces before plenty of salt came pouring from my eyes.

23

WARNINGS

Have you lost all sympathy and patience with me? Are you thinking: If she's so damned sure of destiny why'd she have to go and try to force the hand of fate? Consider this. Maybe Grainne (of Grainne and Diarmuid) and I were fated to pronounce those *geasa*. The druid Cathbad prophesied over Deirdre of the Sorrows at birth, declaring that she would bring ruin on the land and disaster to her lover Naiose and his two brothers. What choice did she have?

Listen, some people are born to cause trouble. No doubt I was one of them, but so, for that matter, was Esus. Don't get me wrong. I'm not asking you to excuse me for laying a *geis* on Jesus Christ. No one told me to take Grainne as a role model. I suppose you could argue that Grainne's story is a cautionary tale—except the Celts were never big on caution, and their stories had no morals in any conventional sense.

Anyway, whether it was fated or whether I was jumping the gun, as usual, I did it. I uttered those words. Now you know about the *geis*. Certainly throws a curve into the story, doesn't it? (The curve is a major component of Celtic design. Look at the Celtic cross.) His life story, as told in the official canon and elaborated over the centuries, is already a mishmash of the Hebraic tradition and the Greco-Roman. So why not add a Celtic twist? I'll leave it to you now, to dismiss the *geis* factor as preposterous or to incorporate it into your theology (supposing you have one). I'm just telling you the story.

For awhile, pride prevented me from so much as looking for Esus. It is not that I felt no remorse, but I was still angry and very confused, as people are when they invoke more power than they can handle. One afternoon, thick, glaring haze blotted the mountains from view. The air was uncannily still. Even when it stirred, it was so hot it brought no relief. It felt like the breath of some poor, panting animal. Everyone was on edge. I could stand it no longer. In the late afternoon, I high-tailed it to the yew grove. The air was so saturated with moisture, it couldn't absorb one drop more. My sweat streamed and spattered the ground as if I was a walking rainstorm, or an ocean uneasily contained in human bounds.

The grove was empty of him. It was eerie standing alone among the death-life trees, and I fought off a sense of foreboding. I told myself it was just the threat of rain that kept him away. The damp, dense air brought out the midges, and they feasted fiercely. I tried to summon anger, but fear was too strong. Fear and something more: an underlying grief, the premonition of some intolerable loss. Then the wind picked up and the rain started. I ran back to Caer Leb, dodging the lightning bolts that dogged my heels.

By dusk the storm had passed. The first stars shone, bright and sharp-edged. It was impossible not to feel better. After our evening labors under the stone, I asked Nissyen if I could speak alone with him. Both he and Branwen had been eyeing me anxiously for the past few days, but I hadn't wanted to tell anyone what I had done—not even Branwen—for fear of making it more real. Now Nissyen and I left the confines of Caer Leb and walked towards the field of the two great standing stones. They are not a matched pair in size or shape, one is squatter than the other. They appear to incline towards each other as if in deep, brooding conversation. If you stand and look through them towards the caers and groves of the college, the stones echo the shapes of the mountains, the gap between them corresponding to a dip in the range. I was relieved when Nissyen stopped at a distance I judged—however absurdly and anthropomorphically—to be out of their hearing range. I did not want the stones standing in judgment on me.

"Now then, Maeve Rhuad," said Nissyen, spreading out his cloak and settling himself cross-legged on the grass. "Tell old Nissyen all about it."

"I wanted to ask your advice," I began tentatively. "On a literary matter."

"Ah, to be sure," he said, his tone both kindly and skeptical.

"It's just this." I took a deep breath. "Are there...well, do you know of any stories about someone removing a *geis*?"

"And why would you be wanting to know that, if I may ask?"

"I need to know, um, for a poem I'm composing. I mean, are there precedents or would I be breaking a literary convention?"

"Maeve, what have you done?"

"Please, Nissyen, just tell me."

He obliged, pondering for a time, no doubt cross-referencing *geasa* in the vast library of his mind. I bit my lip and waited.

"I cannot recall any accounts of *geis* removal," he said at last.

"But does that mean it can't be done or just that no one ever tried it, as a plot device, that is?"

"Well now, as a plot device *geis* removal would present problems," Nissyen considered. "You don't want to set up conditions and consequences, then unmake them. The listener would rightfully feel that you're cheating. Take the *geis* laid on Cuchulain against eating dog meat. (Though why he'd want to I never did understand unless there were no pigs left in Hibernia.) You don't want to further point up the absurdity of a *geis* by removing it. I mean, imagine someone announcing to Cuchulain: 'It's okay. I've removed the *geis*. From now on you can eat dog meat three times a day.'"

"But what if, say, Grainne wanted to remove the *geis* she'd laid on Diarmuid?"

"Why would she want to do that?" demanded Nissyen. "The poor girl had a hard enough time even with the *geis* getting that high-minded booby into bed. Even after they ran off together, he wouldn't lie with her for the longest time, remember. She had to taunt him and tell him how the mud that spattered her thighs was bolder than he was."

"But then he found out that he really did love her," I said. "And that's the whole point."

"Is it?" queried Nissyen. "I'm not sure it's wise to assume that a story has a point, per se, Maeve. After all, Grainne and Diarmuid were still in a mess. Fionn never forgave Diarmuid his treachery, *geis* or no *geis*, and in the end Fionn tricked Diarmuid to his death."

"So he met danger and destruction even though he honored the *geis*!"

"Well now that's difficult to say. Remember that Diarmuid broke his word to the one-eyed guardian of the magic rowan berries. He took those berries at Grainne's urging. Then there were all those *geasa* laid on him in childhood, such as never refusing a companion's request. Without all those *geasa*, Fionn never could have snared Diarmuid.

"You see, Maeve, when you're a hero, *geasa* come with the territory." Nissyen warmed to his subject. "They're essential, really. You don't want a hero growing old, garrulous, and flatulent. That's the druid's fate, alas. A hero has to be too skilled a warrior to die in ordinary battle. He's got to have *geasa* to trip him up so that doom can befall him in a suitably poetic and memorable fashion. That's why the *geis*, as a plot device, is so terribly useful—"

"But what do you think would have happened if Grainne hadn't pronounced the *geis*?" I persisted.

"Hadn't pronounced the *geis*?" Nissyen was incredulous. "Why, there would have been no story. Grainne would have married Fionn—and marriage without adultery is inherently boring, Maeve—Diarmuid would have remained a loyal member of the Fianna. And we never would have heard of either of them."

"Oh." I was downcast. "You mean you don't think they could have fallen in love on their own?"

I was staring out at the mountains, which looked, more than ever, in the dusky sky, like a huge, black wave about to break on Mona. I felt Nissyen's scrutiny and kept my face turned away.

"This is all rather hypothetical, Maeve. Suppose you tell me about this poem you are composing. Though it is my duty to tell you that I don't think it's wise for you to be so involved in original composition when you've by no means memorized the basics. Kindly remember that we are doing *Tales of Unlikely Conceptions* and *Marvelous Births* this semester. I can't imagine why you are so obsessed with *Treacherous Elopements*, although, to stretch a point, you could argue that elopements do sometimes lead to conception and births...."

Nissyen was off and rambling again. I took a moment to consider how to describe to Nissyen my putative work-in-progress.

"In this poem I'm making," I began, "the woman—I haven't quite decided on her name yet—pronounces the *geis* in a fit of passion."

"Hmm. In a fit of passion or a fit of pique?"

"Don't interrupt," I said crossly. "Then the man—"

"You haven't decided his name either, I suppose. Now why is that?"

"Then the man," I repeated loudly, "says that he can never be her lover because he would never know if he was acting freely or under compulsion. And of course she wants him to love her freely, and she doesn't really want doom befalling him on her account. And well, as a plot device, I think doom's been done to death, don't you? I thought I'd try something a little different. Something fresh and original. Any suggestions?"

"Hmm. She's certainly gotten herself into a pickle," Nissyen observed.

"Perhaps if I had her seeking counsel from a very wise druid, he could tell her what to do?" I prompted.

"I don't know that he could now. You see, Maeve, she's unleashed certain powers, this nameless young ninny of yours. She's set certain events in motion. That sort of thing gathers its own momentum, like a boulder rolling down hill. I must say the young man sounds unnecessarily scrupulous, but heroes often suffer from an *ideé fixe* and are notoriously inflexible. Let's see...."

"What if—" An idea had suddenly come to me. I saw myself outstripping that rolling boulder, placing myself in its path, perhaps to be crushed or to tumble down with it, but surely, surely I could change its course. "What if she took his doom, the danger and destruction and all that, what if she took it on herself?"

I could feel Nissyen frowning. It was almost dark. Star after star appeared, focused and intent.

"It seems to me," Nissyen said, "that she is already well out of her depth. Given her inexperience and general recklessness, I would discourage her from attempting anything of the sort, even if it was within her power to do so, and it is not clear to me that it is. Offhand, I can't think of any precedent—at least not in our tradition. You might find that sort of thing among the Greeks—one person taking on another's fate."

"But what if their fates are entwined?"

"As I remarked, she's in a mess. She's *made* a mess. I strongly advise her to leave fate alone. Remember, sometimes things have a way of righting themselves, especially when those things are young and full of sap. A wave crashes on the shore, but then it recedes. Lightning splits the oak, but, often as not, it grows around its wound. Let your headstrong young woman—and why you need to invent another one when our stories are already full of them, I don't know—let her trust to nature. Nature likes nothing better than to see young limbs entwined, never mind fates. Leave fate to the Mórrígán, bloody old bitch that she is. She's trouble enough. She doesn't need young girls meddling in her business."

"Yes, but will it work as a plot device?" I teased, feeling much relieved. "Aren't people who mind their own business inherently boring?"

"Maeve, if I asked you to recite the *Conception of Lugh Lamfada* right now, could you do it word perfect? The truth, now."

"No," I admitted.

"Then as your nurse maid and academic adviser, I suggest you set aside all other concerns and give your undivided attention to your studies. *Lughnasad* is less than one change of the moon away, and you will be called upon to recite not only for your teachers but for the *Combrogos.*"

∽

In the days to come I made an honest effort to do as Nissyen said, and to my surprise, I succeeded. Esus had distracted me from my studies; now my studies distracted me from him—or from his absence. He continued not to be at the yew grove, and after a time I stopped looking for him. I was willful, yes, but not stupid. I got the message. I had tried to force the hand of fate and gotten my own hands slapped instead. It was fate's move now. I was tired of having secondhand arguments with YHWH, while Esus tried to second guess him. I was going to leave YHWH to the Mórrígán. Let them duke it out.

Still, I did not take Nissyen's advice in entirety. In what little spare time I did have, I began to compose the poem I'd sketched for Nissyen, the story that I am telling you now. I discovered that I loved words. I loved something besides him, and I loved that love in myself. So although I could not admit it at the time, Esus's thwarting of my will (as much as my desire) had a bracing effect on me.

Then one fine morning while our form was outside eating stirabout, Viviane sat down next to me, without greeting me by word or look. Nor did I acknowledge her. We were not exactly on cordial terms. Branwen had just left my side to go to the trenches, so I assumed Viviane had something nasty to say to me alone. I could have ignored her and flounced off, but I was curious.

She had not approached me for any reason since the day of our brawl.

"He wants to see you. The Stranger."

"Esus?"

"Who else?"

"Did he say why? When did you speak to him?"

In spite of myself, I turned to look at her. She did not look back, just shrugged with supreme indifference.

"Ciaran asked me to give you the message."

That explained it. She certainly wouldn't do me any favors. Ciaran of the blue-black hair was in Esus's form. Viviane still managed her trysts with him, despite the omnipresence of the Crows.

"Is that the whole message?" I pressed.

"That's it. He didn't say where. He didn't say when."

He didn't need to, and I was glad he hadn't. I didn't want anyone, certainly not Viviane, to know about our meeting place under the yews. I waited for Viviane to stalk off so that I could give myself over to exultation, but she continued to sit next to me, eyes still fixed straight ahead. It occurred to me that perhaps I was supposed to say something.

"Thanks for bringing me the message," I managed.

She gave a curt nod of acknowledgment and remained where she was. I considered getting up and going off to look for Branwen, but I decided against it. Viviane was the one who had parked her carcass here. It was up to her to move, not me.

"I'd be careful if I were you," she said at last.

"Careful of what?"

"Of having anything to do with the Stranger."

"Why do you keep calling him the Stranger?" I demanded. "You know his name is Esus."

"So he says. Or so everyone has chosen to call him. It's dangerous to be named for a god."

"Well, lots of people are," I pointed out. "It's hard not to be. There's so many of them, almost as many gods as there are people."

Did I detect the hint of a smile at the corner of her mouth?

"And it's not always so easy to tell the difference between them," I added.

"That's more or less my point," Viviane said, getting to her feet just as the conversation was getting interesting.

Well, I wasn't going to feed her self-importance by pressing her further.

"Whatever," I shrugged.

My show of indifference goaded her. Besides, like all human beings, she had an overpowering instinct to mind other people's business.

"Ciaran says he talks too much. He argues with the druids constantly.

And when he listens, he listens too intently. No one really knows who he is or what he might do with our secrets. The druids took a big risk letting him in, and they know it. Count on it, the Cranes are watching his every move. And if you get up to anything with him, the Cranes and the Crows will be watching yours. Oh, well." Viviane tossed her head. The ends of her hair flicked my face. I hoped she'd wrench her neck someday showing off that showy hair. "Don't say I never warned you."

"Oh, go sit on a sea urchin," I said.

But Viviane was already walking away. It's debatable whether the last word of this charming exchange was hers or mine. In fact, I did not doubt what she said about the Cranes and Crows watching Esus, and probably me as well. But it did not particularly disturb me. Notoriety, special status, these were to be expected, no more or less than Esus and I deserved.

Then suddenly the full import of her message hit me. Esus wanted me! A sudden rush of energy brought me to my feet. I bounded toward Branwen, who was on her way back from the latrines, and nearly knocked her down with the exuberance of my embrace.

24

Bryn Celli Ddu

W hen I arrived at the yews that afternoon, Esus was already there, sitting under the trees, gazing out towards the straits. A strong wind soughed through the thick branches, and he did not hear my approach. Instead of rushing towards him, I found myself hesitating, not out of shyness, exactly, but a kind of awe. It is not often that you glimpse someone in solitude. He was waiting for me, yes, but he was alone, not battling wits with druid or rabbi, not sparring with me. He was simply there, with himself. Or maybe he was not alone. Maybe his invisible god was visiting him, hissing commandments in his ear. Maybe that's why the lines around his mouth, the set of his jaw looked so tense.

Quietly, the sound of my movements covered by the wind, I stole towards him and sat down beside him. He turned and looked at me for just an instant, a look I couldn't read. Neither of us spoke. Then, without warning, he laid his head in my lap. His yarmulke slipped off.

At last I had license to touch his hair, and I was lost in the wonderment of it. I cupped both hands over his head and felt the hardness of bone beneath his thick, springy hair. Though I had never seen a human birth, somewhere within me I heard the words: he's crowning; the head is crowning. Then, for the first time since leaving Tir na mBan, I felt the fire of the stars burning in my own crown, streaming down through my hands into him. He stiffened and sat up, drawing apart from me.

"What are you doing?"

"Nothing," I said in confusion, not knowing how to explain.

And it was true. I was not doing anything; something was happening, using me, willy-nilly, to accomplish its purpose.

"Your hands are like fire. You put fire in my veins," he accused, his eyes smoldering, not with anger but intensity.

"It's just something that happens to me sometimes. Usually when I touch someone. One time I eased the pain of Fand's broken ribs. Are you in pain, Esus?"

He ignored my question.

"Did the old woman, the Cailleach, teach you to do that?"

"No one taught me. I told you about the first time, that day I ran away from my mothers to the secret valley. Remember? I was looking at my reflection in the pool. My hair looked on fire. Then I could feel it, the fire starting in my head, flowing through my whole body, especially my hands. It felt as though rivers of fire were streaming from my fingers. I held my hands over the pool. The water rippled and changed. That's when I saw you."

"You are a witch." He stared at me, with those eyes, black and bottomless as the sacred well.

I did not understand what the word witch conjured for him. For me it was more or less synonymous with the word woman, with my mothers. Esus was regarding me as though I were something utterly alien to him, even dangerous. "Oh, come off it," I snapped. "Whatever it is—my mothers called it 'the fire of the stars'—it's only natural. I mean it happens naturally. It's like wiping someone's tears or staunching the bleeding from a cut."

"Natural," he considered. "Natural. Like a storm or a flood or a bolt of lightning."

"Or like sunlight," I countered, "or soft, soaking rain. Not everything natural is destructive."

I was on the verge of citing YHWH's fondness for floods and plagues, but I thought better of it. Something was troubling Esus. He had laid his head in my lap. I didn't want to fight with him now.

"Viviane said you wanted to see me," I prompted.

Talk to me, I pleaded silently. Talk about the *geis*, that invisible boulder inching its way towards some awful edge, some irreversible fall.

But he was still staring at his hands, palms cupped, his alarm changing to curiosity.

"The fire is flowing through my hands now, just the way you described it. Feel."

He held his hand out towards my cheek. I closed my eyes. Even before his skin connected with mine currents of hot, swirling gold washed over my face. Strangely his touch left me feeling calmed, cooled, as if I had just bathed in a clear spring.

"Will my hands feel like this all the time?" he wondered.

For the moment, his tension was gone. He leaned back against the trunk of a tree. He looked tired.

"With me it comes and goes," I said. "I haven't felt the fire for a long time, until just now. You still haven't answered my question. Are you in pain? Are you hurt in some way?"

He looked at me for a long time without speaking. I sensed some inner argument was going on. It troubled me that he didn't trust me enough to confide in me without hesitation. I tried to rouse my indignation, but I couldn't. His gaze had the effect of making me look at myself through his eyes. Right now, what I saw didn't look so good. I'd laid a *geis* on him, because he wouldn't do what I wanted him to when I wanted it. Before that, he'd found me brawling and smeared with 'menstruous' blood. Then there were our Otherworldy contacts. I'd shit on his head in public, and, in one of his more private moments, I'd spied on him, however unintentionally. A case could be made that I was a walking natural disaster.

"Esus, about the other day," I began. It was not easy. Fluent as I was in several languages, I could count on one hand the number of times I'd apologized. "About the *geis*. I'm sorry. I'm sorry I did that to you."

"Oh, that's all right."

We both knew it wasn't, but 'that's all right' seems to be a universal response to 'I'm sorry.' Somehow it sounds so much more forgiving than 'I forgive you.'

"I'm sorry, too," he added.

He didn't say for what, but I nodded and we sat in silence for a while, the comforting, comfortable silence that comes when both people let go of the need to be in the right.

"But something's bothering you," I said. "Has any disaster befallen you?"

"I don't think it has anything to do with the *geis*, Maeve, if that's what you're worried about."

"Then, what is it, Esus? I know something's wrong."

"I am afraid, Maeve."

He spoke so softly. It seemed to me that everything—the air, the trees, even the shifting currents in the straits—stilled to hear him. I did not know then how hard it is for any man or boy—Celt, Hebrew, or other—to say those words: I am afraid. But I knew he was choosing to trust me.

"There's going to be an initiation rite at the festival called *Lughnasad*," he continued. "While everyone else is playing games, singing, feasting, hearing stories—"

"Or telling them," I interjected. "Our form has to perform. If we're not up to scratch, we fail the first term and have to begin all over again."

"Well, our form, along with some of the chief druids, is going to be performing a three-day rite. It starts right after the opening session of arbitrations, which we're all required to attend so that we can observe druid law in action."

"Who is being initiated?"

"Me." The starkness of that solitary word was eloquent.

"Only you?"

"Only me. Remember, I've skipped almost a dozen years of preliminary training. Everyone else has already been initiated into the first degree of mysteries." He paused, and then he said again, "I'm afraid."

"Well," I hesitated, feeling my way as if I were walking in the dark trying not to stumble. "I think that's the idea. You're supposed to be afraid. An initiation is some kind of ordeal or test, but I know you'll pass."

"I know, I know," he gestured impatiently. "That's not what worries me. You don't understand."

Those three words could sting me like no others.

"I've had my initiation into manhood among my own people," he went on. "It's like what your form has to do on *Lughnasad*. You stand up and recite a whole section of the Torah from memory. You prove your knowledge and learning. The initiation rite at *Lughnasad* is nothing like that."

"What's going to happen?"

"I don't know," he shook his head and stared at the ground. "The druids don't exactly spell things out. With them everything's a mystery. Everything's a secret. How else could they keep a hold on so many squabbling tribes? People think the druids know something they don't know, control things that ordinary people can't control. I haven't been here long enough to figure out whether they really do possess secret knowledge or whether they're just masters of illusion. I have a feeling I'm about to find out."

"They haven't told you anything?"

"I don't even know where it's going to be. Not officially. Some of my friends have dropped hints. They're not supposed to say anything directly. It's against the rules. But I think I know."

Suddenly I knew, too. Bryn Celli Ddu. The Mound of the Dark Grove, the heart—or perhaps more accurately the bowels or womb—of the druid college. Of course it would happen there. The mound was reputed to be ancient. The trees surrounding it were as old—or maybe even older. No one knew. When the druids came to Mona, they had recognized the power of the place and had appropriated it for their own purposes. Bryn Celli Ddu was strictly forbidden to everyone but druids and initiates. Naturally, breaking that taboo was on my mental 'to do' list, but I'd been too busy sneaking off to the Jews—until now.

"I get the feeling that this initiation involves some sort of enactment of death," Esus went on.

The summer air suddenly felt cold on my skin. All my hairs stood up. Viviane's warning sounded again in my mind: It's dangerous to be named for a god. Did Esus realize that the *Keltoi* called him by a god's name? "Uncouth Esus of the barbarous altars," the Romans would write of this god. Esus's victims hung from trees, dying of ritual wounds.

"Death?" my lips form the words, but I could not summon enough breath to make a sound.

"Not actual death. I'm not afraid I'm going to be killed or anything like that. It's a symbolic death. You come back changed. You're reborn."

"Oh," I cried. "I know what's going to happen. I just realized. I've been through it. I've already been initiated."

"You have?" He sounded both relieved and disgruntled.

"Yep," I preened. Neither of us was above a little cosmic sibling rivalry. "Where? When?"

"On Tir na mBan when I first went to stay with the Cailleach. But I'm not sure I should tell you any more. It might be against the rules."

He made the sort of rude nonverbal response my smugness deserved.

"So don't tell me. I'm not worried about what's going to happen. That's not it at all."

"Esus," I said, remembering that he'd trusted me with his fear. "I was only teasing. I'll tell you anything you want to know."

He shook his head. "No, don't tell me now. The rule makes sense. Besides, even if you told me every detail of your initiation, it wouldn't tell me anything about mine. It's different for me."

I bit back my automatic response: No, it's not. We're the same. I asked gently, "What is it, then? What frightens you?"

"Maeve." He reached for my hand and gripped it hard. "I know you won't understand this, but I'm afraid....I'm afraid I may go so far away from the God of my forefathers that he won't be able to find me. Or I won't be able to find him."

He was right. I didn't understand, and I hated it that I didn't understand. I hated his god. I wished Esus *could* get away from him.

"The *Keltoi*, the druids, you, Maeve, you worship the earth as if it were...as if it were, well, a goddess. I find your people's stories very confusing. This *Lughnasad* festival seems to have something to do with your god Lugh dying, becoming a seed in the womb of the earth mother. It's death, marriage, and rebirth all at once."

I did not see what was so confusing about that. It told the story of the grain. The shining beauty of the god who made the strength of the sun into food. When the god was cut down, he became the seed falling into earth so the grain could rise again. What could be simpler?

"If I enact this rite, I will be breaking the First Commandment."

"The first commandment?" I repeated. Esus had recited the ten prime *geasa* for me, but I couldn't recall them. I had a much better memory for Hebrew stories.

"'I am YHWH your God who brought you out of Egypt where you lived as slaves. You shall have no other gods to rival me.'"

"But he didn't say anything about goddesses," I pointed out.

"It's implied, Maeve," he said impatiently. "Goddesses are even worse. They demand all sorts of abominations and fornications for their worship."

It sounded good to me. The mystery was that anyone worshipped YHWH.

"Until now on Mona I've been listening and learning and observing, but as a Jew, Maeve. I've been a stranger in a strange land, as many Jews have been before me, but I have kept his commandments. I have not abandoned the God of Abraham, Isaac, and Jacob, the God of Moses and Aaron, of David and Solomon. But if I perform this rite, surely the Most High will abandon me. And if I refuse—"

"He won't abandon you."

My voice sounded harsh, raw as an oracular raven's. I spoke against my will. Esus dropped my hand and turned to me with a startled look.

"He will not abandon you," something compelled me to go on, "any more than he abandoned Jonah in the belly of the whale. Do you think that there is anywhere that he is not?" Drat him, I added to myself.

Esus gazed at me in wonder, and no wonder: I wasn't myself. I was starting to feel cranky and a little queasy. I recalled how Queen Maeve of Connacht had turned green around the gills when she uttered her prophecy over me. She was right. It was extremely disagreeable.

"But if I break his commandments," Esus anguished.

"He still won't leave you alone," I said crossly. "Jonah was disobeying orders when he got swallowed. Your god could have just let him be digested and serve him right."

"That is true," said Esus slowly. "But I don't want to disobey his orders. The trouble is—" He lowered his voice and leaned closer to me, as if he could make an aside that YHWH wouldn't catch. "I don't know what he wants. Is he testing me? If he is, am I supposed to refuse the rite or go through with it? Maybe there is something I am meant to learn here that I can't learn any other way. I wish I knew why he called me here. If he did."

You came here to find me, you hopeless idiot, I wanted to scream. How can someone so smart be so stupid?

"Anu said," he began.

I smiled to myself and did not say: you mean Anna.

"'Leave all you know. Step outside your world. When you come back, you will see your people with new eyes. You will love them with a new love. You will find beauty in the despised. You will find secrets in the cracks between the stones.'"

"'The world is a big place, Yeshua,'" I continued. His Hebrew name felt so tender and sweet on my tongue, tears thickened my throat. "'And small, as small as a mustard seed, as small as a hazelnut.'"

"What do you think she meant by that?"

He looked at me hungrily, almost humbly, as if I were the source of all knowledge and wisdom.

"It's all right," I said slowly. "This rite is all right for you. You'll learn what the seed knows."

O plant yourself in me, Yeshua, Esus. Let me surround you.

I didn't speak those words. He had turned to me again and buried his head in my lap. Suddenly I felt calm and strong and certain. YHWH would not abandon him, more's the pity, but neither would I. I would be there with him, keeping watch by the Mound of the Dark Grove.

∽

Though I had never been there, I knew how to find the Dark Grove. All I had to do was follow Afon Braint, the river that runs all through the college like life's blood. As soon as I left Esus, I did just that. Picking up the thread of the river a mile and a half further in from Caer Leb, I walked east towards Bryn Celli Ddu, the late shadows lengthening before me. I wanted to case the joint, stake out some cover for myself, maybe explore the fabled mound where, rumor had it, human bones lay in a silent huddle. And I wanted to make sure of the way, so that I could find the Mound, night or day, when the time came.

For a while, the river ran through planted fields and grazing meadows, now and then a copse. Gradually, the trees and shrubs grew more dense, and the air around me was damp and green. Yet the moment I entered the Dark Grove itself, I knew it. The very air surrounding the wood, riddled with protective charms, gave resistance. As you know, I was an old hand at trespassing. I held my breath and wriggled through the invisible wall, just as you might squeeze through barbed wire, taking care not to let it catch your clothes.

Once inside the Grove, I stood still, waiting for my extra senses to waken and tell me which way to go. The wood was uncannily silent, as if the trees, almost all gigantic oaks, held their breath and suspended their judgment while they waited to see what I would do. The prevailing winds moaned in the distance. Everything and everyone seemed far away. I looked up at the forest roof, the leaves so thick I could not see the sky. The last light caught the highest branches, and they glowed green, high, high above me. Except that I could breathe, I might have been gazing up through fathoms of water at sunlight rippling on the surface.

No wonder I felt dizzy and disoriented. If I'd had any sense, I would have turned and run back to Caer Leb. Instead I turned to my left and began to walk slowly away from the river into the wood. I followed no path, but so little light found its way through the leaves, there was practically no undergrowth. Despite the growing darkness, I did not stumble, yet it seemed every soft, bare footfall reverberated. Then, through the spaces between the trees, I saw the mound rising in the midst of the dark grove, an earth swell, a fallen moon gleaming in the half-light, round and smooth and unmistakably secret. I stopped mid-step and stared.

At that moment, a murder of crows came screaming into the wood, racketing into the branches above me. You wouldn't have to be a superstitious Celt, reading omens or ogham in every flap of a bird's wing, to believe that these Crows were sounding the alarm. Imagine being a burglar in the middle of a heist hearing the wail of a siren. It was like that. My heart started to pound and my legs shook so badly it didn't matter that I couldn't decide whether to run or to hide. I couldn't move. Then as suddenly as they had come, the crows took off again, their cries fading into the distance. The dark grove was silent again, except for a faint stirring among the uppermost leaves—and the sound of footsteps behind me coming closer and closer.

Was it ordained from the beginning of time that I should be in this dark grove, turning, endlessly turning, to find Foxface walking towards me, closing the ground between us, as if he had been following me forever? His face gleamed white. Even in the half-light I could see the red of his hair and beard.

"You." He stopped within a few feet of me. "You."

The word was both accusation and identification, and in a horrible way it sounded more intimate than if he had spoken my name. He was more than angry. He had that haunted, almost hunted look that had fleetingly crossed his face during admissions and that I had seen again when he glimpsed me in the tree. Then he had not confronted me. It had seemed as though he'd persuaded himself that I was an apparition. Maybe if I kept still, he would delude himself again. After all, it was twilight, one of those dangerous times, when the Otherworld and the ordinary one get mixed up together. I could very well be a vision, except that I had seldom felt more fleshly. My cheeks burned, my palms sweated, my knees trembled, and there was a strange heat and swelling between my legs. I hoped I wouldn't piss myself in front of the enemy, as Queen Maeve put it. But was he my enemy? And if he was, why? Suddenly I wanted to know. So I blew the only cover I had.

"Yeah, it's me," I said brazenly. "What do you want?"

The sound of my voice snapped him out of his trance. I was no longer a dangerous being, strayed from the Otherworld, but a female first former breaking the rules big time. And he was no longer the dreaded figure from my nightmare vision, but a Very Important Druid, which, under the circumstances, was bad enough.

"What are you doing here, young woman?" He addressed me sternly, impersonally, masked now with authority.

"My name is Maeve Rhuad." For some reason I wanted him to know that. "I am exploring."

"This grove is forbidden to all but initiates. Surely that has been made clear to you."

"I am an initiate," I asserted.

"That is not possible," he informed me. "You are a female student. You are, therefore, in the first form. You have not completed one year of study. You are not even a candidate for initiation. Your presence violates this grove. You have committed a serious offense against the entire College."

His face and tone were grave, concerned, not for me, but for the College, its rules and standards. No doubt he was about to tell me he would be forced to report me. I had to make my case now.

"Lovernios."

"You know my name," he observed.

"Who doesn't know Lovernios? I have heard you speak about the Roman question. And...and I agree with you. A client king is no better than a slave!"

My blatant use of flattery and diversion embarrassed me, and I realized that I didn't want him to fall for it. I didn't understand it then, but I wanted him to be a great man, larger than life, worthy of my fear.

"How gratifying to know that first year students heed my warnings." His tone was as dry as last year's leaves. For a moment he looked bleak and abstracted. "But that is not the matter at hand." He focused on me again. "You claim to have been initiated. I know you have not been initiated by this College. Who initiated you? By what authority?"

"Is it the druids' power and authority that makes the initiate?" I challenged. "Or is it what the initiate sees and knows in the darkness?"

"When and where did you enter the darkness?"

"A fox should know that there is more than one passageway into the earth."

I knew I was provoking him. I couldn't seem to stop myself.

"Answer me," he spoke softly, watching me intently, as a fox might watch a rabbit's hole. "Answer me."

"A door opened in Bride's breast. I climbed down into the chamber beneath her heart." I felt like I was talking in my sleep, forcing sound through a silent barrier.

"Bride's breast. What do you mean by Bride's breast?"

"Mountains," I mumbled. "On Tir na mBan."

Without warning he lunged for me, seized my hair, and yanked back my head. He brought his face close to mine. His pupils dilated so wide, the red-brown rim almost disappeared. I could see my own face reflected in those empty pools, and suddenly I was back inside my nightmare vision: my face turning into his, his face turning into mine. I bit my lip to keep from screaming.

Then, just as suddenly, he released me. I stumbled backwards and almost fell.

"Run, Maeve Rhuad," he said.

He looked and sounded as terrified as me. You may think I'm crazy, but I felt a strange pity for him. He seemed so trapped, a fox caught in a cruel, biting snare. I reached out my hand toward him.

"Run!" he shouted. "Run!"

He was almost pleading with me. I cast him one questioning look. Then I turned and ran away from Bryn Celli Ddu as fast as I could.

25

THE WOMANLY ART OF CABER TOSSING

We haven't had a crowd scene in this story for a while. Just one after another of these intense, intimate encounters under the trees. If trees could talk, the tales they could tell. And who says they can't? Listen to the hiss and crackle of wood when it burns. The trees breathe our words and our songs, our cries, our curses and our softest whispers. When wood burns, our old secrets explode, come, literally, to light. Trees can talk, and you better believe, they listen.

The festival of *Lughnasad* is the perfect occasion for a good crowd scene. The weather is still fine for traveling, and the tribes gather to hold games of skill; to make or dissolve trial marriages, and to present claims to the druid court. Everyone honors Tailtu, Lugh's foster mother, who died of exhaustion after clearing the land for planting. (Come to think of it, there are a number of tales of exhausted goddesses. Some things never change.) Lugh and his foster mother are among the gods who are friendly to the human tribes and want to feed them. At *Lughnasad* the harvest begins. At *Samhain* it ends, and then everyone is under a collective *geis* not to pluck even one remaining berry. After *Samhain* the fruits of the earth belong to the Old Ones who are the earth itself.

The *Combrogos* took passionate delight in this balance of the human and Otherworld, dark and light, female and male, opposites, not opposed so much as matched, partners in a ceaseless circle dance. At *Lughnasad* the games were balanced by legal hearings; the riotous festivities, by the mysteries of initiation in the Dark Grove. And to bring it to a personal level, the first-form students were both having a holiday and facing our first real test as bards-in-the-making.

Branwen and I were a pair of opposites, too, she dark and quiet and studious, and me—well, you know about me. On the morning of *Lughnasad*, Branwen wanted to stay at Caer Leb and practice the performance she would give that evening, but with the blessing of King Bran, who had come to Mona for the festival, I prevailed and dragged Branwen off to the first century Celtic equivalent of a county fair.

Merchants and traders filled one huge field near the College with their wares, all manner of metalwork: weapons, jewelry, and torques so massive you'd have to have god-like strength to wear them. There were displays of weaving as well as raw wool for sale. One whole field was fenced off for cattle, mostly to be sold to traders from Gaul where meat was not so plentiful.

Now I must tell you an ugly truth. Not far from the cattle pens were captives. I did not even know what I was seeing at first when I looked at the chained groups of people, mostly women, Hibernian by their accents. Their hair looked tangled as bramble bushes. There was a fierceness about the women, especially the small, dark ones, that reminded me of my mothers. I tugged at Branwen's sleeve.

"Why are those people chained?"

"They were probably taken in a raid. Don't stare at them, Maeve," she whispered, pulling me along. "You'll shame them. They might have been free people once."

"But what's going to happen to them?" I still didn't get it.

"They are most likely for export. Or they might be traded here for cattle. One *cumal* is worth three cows."

Branwen's tone was flat and matter-of-fact. I could tell she did not like to talk about it. Branwen had grown up amidst cattle raids and wars that she was powerless to prevent and had learned to accept things that were unacceptable. I was shocked. Growing up on a mythic island in the care of Otherworldly mothers had not prepared me for human harshness.

But I was young and, if not callow, I have to confess I was easily distracted. We spent a few of King Bran's coins on barley cakes and a flask wine from Gaul. The transaction was a wonder to me, since, of course, we had no coins and no buying and selling on Tir na mBan. It seemed a dubious kind of magic. There were also vendors selling cheeses, pig knuckles, and fresh fish roasted over a fire. Our bellies full, we walked on towards the playing fields where there appeared to be several ballgames going on at once with enthusiastic onlookers shouting encouragement—and even detailed instruction, none of which made any sense to me. My mothers and I had played games on occasion with a ball made out of a stuffed pig's bladder. Their approach to sports, as to life in general, was anarchic, the competitive aspect being each one outdoing the others in inventing new arcane rules at the spur of the moment. I had my own sure-fire strategy. I'd wait until the inevitable arguments reached a certain pitch, then I'd grab the ball and run, with my mothers laughing and shrieking in hot pursuit. If I made it to a standing stone without being tagged, I won.

Now Branwen and I watched some two dozen or so players chasing a ball with long sticks. Most of the time, I could not see the ball, the players swarmed so thick around it, but I was terribly aware of the sticks, and I noticed that the players were all boys. So I concluded that the stick had something to do with their appendages, perhaps acted as an extension, but I could not figure out the object of the game. The players mostly seemed to be bashing each other's shins.

"They're playing hurley," Branwen explained. "There are two sets of players, and each one is trying to get the ball to go through one gate or the other."

She gestured and I saw, in essence, what you would recognize as prototypic goal posts. At that moment, the ball, flying clear of obstacles, sailed through one set of posts. The players and the crowd went wild, and several fist fights broke out. Not having any stake in the outcome of the game or the brawls, Branwen and I wandered on, pausing here and there to watch other displays of chance or skill. In addition to foot and chariot races, there were more stationary competitions: dice games and a tournament of *fidchell*—the Hibernian board game played by the heroes at Tara. The *fidchell* players were mostly older men; no doubt they'd had enough barked shins and sprained limbs to last a lifetime and now preferred to match wits instead.

In any space not taken up by some sport or game, there was music and dancing. More than once Branwen and I were grabbed indiscriminately and whirled into wild reels. The scent of male sweat, the dizzy spinning from one pair of male arms to another, made me drunker than the strong Gaulish wine. For most of the day, I wallowed in the moment, heedless of my own pending ordeal, almost—but not quite—forgetful of Esus's.

Part of me kept an eye out for him. I saw several from his form, including Ciaran of the blue-black hair who wandered aimlessly and alone through the crowds, his usual ease of manner missing. But I didn't give Ciaran much thought. Esus, I assumed, must be preparing for his initiation. I didn't give him much thought either. I wasn't thinking, on what turned out to be the last day of my innocence. I was having fun.

Just after midday, Branwen and I arrived at one of the farthest fields. A large space had been cleared for some event, and a crowd was gathering at the edge. A couple of burly-looking men, each the equivalent in mass to three slender students, were arranging logs on the ground in order of size.

"I know what this is!" I clapped my hands with pleasure.

"Step right up and get in line for the caber toss!" one of the men bellowed to the crowd. "Try your strength and skill. To the winner, a vat of the best Gaulish wine. Step right up!"

I didn't need the lure of a prize. I loved caber tossing.

"Maeve! What are you doing?" Branwen grabbed my arm.

"I'm getting in line for the toss."

"But, Maeve, caber tossing is only for men. Can't you see?"

"On Tir na mBan, caber tossing is only for women." I pulled free of Branwen's grip and joined the line.

"Maeve!" Branwen called after me. "You're not on Tir na mBan anymore. We're not supposed to make spectacles of ourselves. You can't afford to get into trouble today."

"Oh, I won't." I waved away her fears. "Stay and cheer for me, Branwen. I'm going to win. Just you watch."

Some of you may not know what caber tossing is in these decadent days of bridges. Bridges? By Bride's breasts, some of your bridges have eight lanes and four levels. You have bridges not only across rivers but across bays, bridges to what used to be remote islands. It takes the challenge out of travel. It used to be a great adventure crossing a gorge or ravine with sides so steep you could never hope to climb down, much less up. Faced with such a prospect, what did you do? No, you did not plant hemp, wait for the harvest, twist a rope, macramé a bridge, and take turns trying to lasso something solid on the other side. Not in the prehistoric Holy Isles. No, you'd find a good straight tree and, begging its pardon, cut it down and strip it clean of branches. That's a caber, what you call a telephone pole these days. You'd lift that great stick with the palms of your hands, balance it against your chest, and run. When the momentum is just right, you toss. The caber goes end over end and comes to rest right across the ravine—that is, if you're any good at caber tossing. Of course it's not every day you have to cross a treacherous gorge, so it pays to stay in practice. Besides there are few things as exhilarating as tossing a caber and watching it fly.

So I stood in line with the great, hulking men, some of them warriors with fantastic spikes of lime-sculpted hair. There was some exclaiming over my intention to compete and quite a few hairy, over-sized hands patted my back and tweaked my curls. When the official in charge saw that I was serious, he laughed and said, "Sure and let the colleen try her luck."

"Skill," I corrected him. I had never before encountered male condescension, and I was feeling a bit miffed and all the more determined to make a good showing.

I ignored the increasingly large and titillated crowd and gave my attention to appraising the technique and timing of those who went ahead of me. Each contestant was allowed three tosses, and each toss was judged on three counts: the size of the caber; the distance of the toss; and how straight the caber landed. The perfect toss would find the caber pointing straight ahead of you, at what you'd call twelve o'clock. Most of the men made good tosses, erring no further from the mark than one or eleven o'clock.

As my turn drew nearer, I began to feel nervous. I was so unaccustomed to the feeling that I hardly recognized it and dismissed the agitation in my stomach as the result of too many sweetcakes. Still, I could not help noticing what you no doubt realized from the beginning: their massive arms gave the appended ones an undeniable advantage over me in this sport. I could not hope to win on the first two counts, but I was determined to excel in timing and angle.

Now, my turn was next. With each breath, I narrowed my concentration. I don't mean that I shut out the crowd. I mean I concentrated, literally. Everything in my field of vision, the field itself, with all its roiling energies, I took and made into one tiny radiant point that I contained—and that contained me. As I stepped out before the crowd, the air around me was living gold, all sound, all motion and commotion melted into the silent pulsing of that light.

That's what it looked like from my point of view. If you were standing in the crowd, you would see a young woman with hot, orange hair and a short, green tunic, somewhat the worse for wear, slit way up the sides. Although she's got a husky build, she's a good head shorter than the shortest of the men, and her nicely fleshed upper arms are sticks in comparison to theirs. The only thing she's got that's bigger than what they've got are breasts. These are causing quite a stir among the men.

"Her paps are bigger than the paps of Anu!"

"Now I ask you, where's there room to rest a caber between those two luscious faery mounds."

"I wouldn't mind resting my caber between them, I tell you."

And maybe you would have joined in the laughter as the girl, waving away the officiant's offer of the smallest caber, chooses one two sizes larger— though not the largest. (Am I foolhardy? Yes. A fool? No. I know my strength.) But when the girl spreads her thighs and bends her knees, walking her hands down to the base of the caber, then balancing it as calmly and deftly as mother might lay a baby against her shoulder to burp it, you fall silent, amazed at how softly the huge caber seems to rest on the slopes of her breasts.

As a matter of fact, my breasts helped me balance the caber by keeping it centered. With caber tossing, as in many other arts, balance is the key. Slowly, I straightened my legs and came to a standing position, the caber leaning almost lightly against me. I paused for a moment, letting the caber become a part of my body, my very own enormous appendage, then I ran, gathering momentum with each step.

It's a strange thing, but carrying a weight can make the earth feel springier, as if you sink in more and bounce back accordingly. The earth gives you a gentle, little shove to get you off her back. As I ran, the caber felt lighter and lighter. It's at that moment of near weightlessness that you toss the caber. If you hit the moment just right, you feel as though you're flying with it, end over end through a spinning sky. Then, after that second of suspended gravity, comes a resounding thud and a bone knowledge that needs no eye: the caber has landed dead on.

I looked at my caber lying on the ground straight and true, and I let the sound of wild cheering penetrate the pulsing light around me. If crowds in general gave me a buzz, being the center of an admiring crowd hit my blood like a shot of neat whiskey. Remember one of the meanings of my name is "drunk woman." I was drunk that moment with all the pleasures of drunkenness and none of the hindrances. I could taste my triumph all the way to my toes, my world bright and liquid with melting boundaries. I was drunk as a honey bee deep in the heart of a trumpeting flower.

Now listen, all of you who think modesty is a virtue and that those of us who love the limelight are self-infatuated fools, give me a break. Give me this moment. I was a virgin. I didn't know then about the fickleness of the human herd, how quickly cheers can turn to curses, accolades to stones. All moments pass. That doesn't mean a moment can't be perfect while it lasts.

My next two tosses were as flawless as my first, and each succeeding time I managed to toss the caber further. I was making love to the crowd, as all the best performers do, and the caber, to borrow Queen Maeve's metaphors, was my joy stick, my magic wand.

Then my turn was over, and the crowd that had been eating out of my hand got completely out of hand. Or should I say the crowd began to handle me? Manhandle me, literally. A whole flock of huge, hairy hands lifted me, as if I weighed nothing, and began to parade me around the field. Those who could not touch me cried out to me.

"Marry me, you flame-tipped beauty."

"No, marry me, radiant spark, sun-borne, I'll make you a queen."

"Moon-breasted maiden, whose every breath brightens the night, marry me."

"Marry only me. I will give you a chariot made of pure gold and a pair of horses, black as night, with silver manes and tails."

Being Celts, they began with words, each one extolling my loveliness more extravagantly than the last; every unfounded offer of riches more fantastical than the one before it. Being Celts, their verbiage was a preliminary to battle; language was an exquisite, artful hors d'oeuvre before the main course: heads rolling on the grass. Hurley anyone?

"I'll tell you what," the contest official took charge. "You can toss the caber for her and may the best man win."

His suggestion met with cheers.

"I'll toss for her. She's finer than Gaulish wine any day."

"Sweeter to the tongue and hotter in the blood."

All this male ardor was very flattering, but in a moment it became frightening. Disputes broke out over whether to start the contest over or to count the tosses already made. The afternoon was hot, and most of the men had been drinking steadily since dawn. Even more than they professed to want me, these warriors wanted a fight. Fists were starting to swing; nose and jaw bones to splinter and crack. It was only a matter of moments before the swords came out. All the while, two men still held me aloft, with one hand each, the other being used to fight off the men who were grabbing for me.

Now in case you've been wondering what first century Celts wore under their tunics, the answer is: nothing. So I couldn't help it, any more than a rose can refuse its scent, that a strong whiff of estrogen wafted out over the heads of the crowd swirling through air already thick with testosterone. What is more, through no fault of my own, the moon was nearing the full. So I was wide open and glistening, if anyone cared to look, and clearly they did.

I shouted and shouted for the men to stop, to no effect, which probably comes as no surprise to you. To me it was a shock. Here I was being compared to any number of goddesses and pledged the riches of any number of kingdoms, while no one paid the slightest attention to my words or my wishes. Coveted prizes, I learned that day, have no authority and no control, not even—especially not—over their own persons. In fact, they are no longer persons. You might say I was having an object lesson—with myself as the object. And I objected to it. Strenuously.

I cast about for a way to escape. Only the sky presented itself, empty and blue and silent over the chaotic din on the ground. I closed my eyes for a moment and willed my body to remember its dove shape. If only I could tumble free into the sky, spattering those ridiculous warrior hairdos with guano. Nothing happened. But when I opened my eyes again I saw that something was about to.

A corridor opened in the crowd as warriors sprang apart. Striding down this corridor came Foxface in his spanking white druid robes, oak leaves crowning his head, his tunic gathered at the waist with a gold belt. He made an impressive sight. He was not looking at me as he parted the crowd, leaving silence in his wake, but I feared I was his object, too. The prospect of being handed over to his authority was more daunting than the danger of being carried off by some ham-fisted champion.

Shit. If this was rescue, who needed trouble?

As Foxface came to a halt before them, the two men who had hold of my haunches lowered me to my doom. Still Foxface did not look at me. I know, because although I had an unprecedented urge to hang my head, I resisted it and stared straight at him.

"Gentlemen," he said—or the P-Celtic equivalent. Gentlemen is a bit of an oxymoron, especially as a description of Celtic warriors. "I would not willingly interrupt your sport. But this rash maiden is under the jurisdiction of the College of druids at Mona, being a first year student and a dedicant.

Therefore I act *in loco parentis*"—(or the P-Celtic equivalent)—"when I inform you that she is not marriageable."

"Ergo," someone from the crowd volunteered, "there is no point in fighting to the death over her?"

"My point precisely," said Foxface.

"It's a bloody waste of fine woman flesh," someone muttered.

"How is that?" demanded Foxface. "Speak up, man."

"A woman like that," said the man who had offered me a golden chariot, "belongs in the bed and on the battlefield. She's not made for laboring under the stone and cramming her head full of verses. Meaning no disrespect to you, Lovernios," he added. I realized that as a military strategist Foxface must be well known among warriors.

"This young woman has secured admission to the College, which means she must have brains." Foxface sounded a little dubious. "Consider this, all of you. Her beauty—"

Beauty? Not that I had ever doubted that I was gorgeous, but that Foxface should note it interested me.

"Her beauty will last but a few seasons. Her strength in battle perhaps a few more. But if she submits her mind to the discipline of study—"

Big if.

"—her mind may be made a treasure house. Long after her breasts have shrivelled, and her thighs grown slack—"

Really, did he have to make me sound like an overcooked chicken?

"—the treasures of her mind may be poured out to benefit the *Combrogos* for generations to come."

"Oh sure," someone said. "We know you druids have it all over us warriors—long life, health, and wealth, while we spend our short lives fighting and fucking our brains out, such brains as we have. Now you're taking the best women, too. It's not fair."

"We are not taking them," said Foxface sharply. "They come to us seeking learning. If they are worthy enough—"

"Or wealthy enough," someone grumbled.

"—we accept them as students. As to the respective privileges and merits of druids and warriors, each calling is rewarding if it is our own and we answer it. Pardon this intrusion. Let the games continue." To me he said, "Come."

Without looking at me, he turned and began to walk. I came to heel, feeling like a bad little dog back in its master's control. I was somewhat heartened by the subdued cheers that followed me from the field. But the fear in my stomach was worse than any indigestion I'd ever had. I felt as though I'd swallowed a study stone. Whole. Still, I held my head high and smiled and waved as I went. I saw poor Branwen biting her nails down to the cuticles on my behalf. At the edge of the field, looking up and away from Foxface's rigid back and taut neck, I spied Esus in the branches of a silver fir where he must have had a fine view of the whole event. He caught my eye and winked. Clearly he did not share Branwen's concern for me. As a matter of fact, he was laughing. The whole tree shook with his laughter. And suddenly—after all the strain how could I possibly help it?—I burst into laughter myself.

Foxface rounded on me. "You dare to laugh!" he hissed. "Your brazen behavior put at risk the lives of some of the finest champions in the Holy Isles and Gaul."

I sobered right up. "I didn't mean to," was all I could think of to say.

Foxface took a step closer to me. I had all I could do to keep from backing away. His right hand closed on my left arm. The ferocity of his grip sent shock waves through my whole body.

"Come along," he growled.

Indeed I had little choice. He kept his grip on me and hustled me further from the crowds to a secluded spot under some beech trees. He released my arm abruptly. For a moment, all I could think was that it felt good to be out of the sun. My arm, though sore, felt light and springy now that he'd let it go. I put my right hand over the bruised spot; my arm sheltering my breasts. The V-neck I'd cut in my tunic had ripped. My breasts were all but exposed, not to mention streaked with dirt and sweat and reddened where the caber had rested. I could hardly have been more at a disadvantage, but I managed a defiant stare.

To my consternation, I found Foxface staring back at me in what appeared to be utter confusion. Beads of sweat broke out on his brow. He looked the way you feel when you wake from a nightmare and haven't yet realized you were dreaming. Then he recovered himself, as I had seen him do before, his face reordering itself into austere lines, his fox eyes sharp and watchful.

"Have you anything to say for yourself, young woman?" He was back in arch high school principal mode.

"What should I say?" At least *my* character is consistent.

"Do you care to explain your extraordinary behavior?"

"To me it was not extraordinary. At home I always toss the caber on *Lughnasad*."

"And where is home?"

Wait a minute. Hadn't we been through this before? Could he possibly not remember catching me out of bounds in the Dark Grove? I was a bit miffed to think that I might be so unmemorable, but I wasn't stupid enough to remind him of the incident. And I wasn't about to risk pronouncing the words Tir na mBan either.

"Oh, just a little island. You wouldn't know it."

It looked for a moment as though his strange panic might come back, but then it passed.

"And women there participate in caber tossing?"

"Yes," I said, not elaborating.

"Perhaps you may be excused on the grounds of naiveté. It is not, however, an excuse you can use for long. Personally, I am a proponent of absolute equality between the sexes. I don't approve of separate rites or schools or dwelling places. It may be that women ought to be included in all contests of skill and strength. You did not, however, see any other women waiting to toss the caber today."

"No," I conceded.

"In your naiveté you may not understand: warriors are simple men, rather like dogs, loyal and useful when well-trained, but easily distracted. Throw a bone into their midst, and they will forget discipline and fight. No rabbit would have been as stupid as you were today."

Stupid?

"In addition—"

There was more?

"You did not see any of your fellow students, male or female, participating."

"No," I had to admit.

"It is unseemly behavior for a dedicant. Everyone has a function. Bards, ovates, and druids are not the muscle of the tribes, they are the mind. We and our students must conduct ourselves accordingly. What you did today, young woman, was both thoughtless and mindless."

He was not angry anymore, I sensed. He was enjoying himself. I didn't like it. I preferred his rage, antagonism, that tonic edge of fear between us. Now he was being merely pompous. He might have been lecturing anyone. I had become generic student instead of myself, Maeve Rhuad, whose name he appeared to have forgotten.

"It was not mindless," I contradicted him boldly. "I thought very carefully, from choosing the caber to the moment of each toss. You've obviously never tossed a caber if you think it's just a matter of muscle. You have to think with your whole body. And my body—" Here I dropped my arm and displayed my breasts full force. "—happens to be very intelligent!"

I succeeded in throwing him off balance. For an instant his face was as naked as my breasts. My own daring excited me. I did not know what would happen next, and I did not care. I wanted to get to the heart of the matter.

Why did he frighten me so much? Why did I frighten him? With my whole body, I dared him to bare himself. It was a big mistake.

His face closed like a fist. With his eyes looking just past me, he spoke through clenched teeth.

"Go back to Caer Leb and stay there. Don't let me find you on the fields again."

I made no move.

"Go!"

"But I am to recite a tale tonight. And I want to go to arbitrations. King Bran is making a case."

"What do you know of King Bran's affairs?" he demanded.

"I am his foster daughter," I said proudly.

Foxface frowned. Bran was a wealthy, powerful king, active in the resistance to Roman incursions. Until that moment, I thought Bran had adopted me purely out of affection for my mothers and because I was Branwen's friend, as no doubt he had. Perhaps he also wanted to make sure I had a male protector, something it had never occurred to me I would need—until now.

"Go clean yourself up," Foxface said curtly.

This time he did not wait for me to comply. Without another word, he stalked past me back towards the playing fields, leaving me standing under the attentive trees.

∞

When I reached Caer Leb, the whole place seemed deserted. I ducked into our hut and hurriedly stripped off my torn tunic, groping for another before my eyes had had time to adjust to the dim light.

"That must be our Maeve," a voice from the other side of the hut made me jump. "Always making a racket. Always rampaging about like a brush fire out of control. I swear I can feel the heat all the way across the hut."

"What are you doing here, Nissyen?" I could see him now, lying on his pallet with a plaid wound around his head. No stone lay on his stomach, however, so I gathered he wasn't composing. He was napping, or had been until I interrupted. "Why aren't you at the games?"

"Why aren't you, is more to the point," he countered. "Me? I've been to the games five times as many years as you've been alive, lass. There's nothing new under the sun, so I'd just as soon stay out of the sun. Besides I keep better track of what's going on when I'm asleep than most people do when they're awake. So are you going to tell old Nissyen what you've been up to or am I going to tell you?"

Omniscience was a standard ploy of Nissyen's for eliciting confessions. Occasionally we tried to call his bluff, but he was a master bluffer, and we usually ended up spilling everything for the comfort of hearing him cackle.

"Do you think Owen would mind if I borrowed his plain tunic?" I said, still proccupied with what to wear.

"If he does, offer him a squeeze of those glorious titties he's been slathering after. That'll shut him up."

Though I was fond of them, my breasts were beginning to seem more trouble than they were worth. I didn't understand, having grown up with sixteen breasts at my disposal, just how hungry so many people were.

"So the neck of your tunic finally ripped," remarked Nissyen, his eyes still swaddled. "I told you, when you cut it, to hem it securely, but did you listen? Of course not. So who ripped it?"

"I thought you knew everything," I said crossly.

"Come on, Maeve. You know I like to hear the story."

"It ripped during the caber toss."

"You were tossing the caber?" He laughed with delight. "And did you win, colleen?"

"I didn't get to stay around to find out. After I tossed, I suddenly took the place of a wine vat as a prize."

"Ah, I can see it. I can see it now. Well, I'll miss you, Maeve, love. We all will. But it must be your destiny to be a queen like your namesake. For sure it was a king who won you. Oh, what a song it will make. It will be sung around every fire many a winter. It's enough to make me want to rhyme again. Maeve, fetch me a stone. Then tell me all."

"Nissyen, I am not a vat of wine to be won." I was angry, not with him exactly, but with everyone. "I am not a thing to be carried off. I am not going anywhere."

"Ah," he said. "Someone put a stop to it. No, don't tell me. I see it. A druid, not just any druid, but a v.i.d."

"Lovernios." I cut him short. I did not want to miss the arbitrations.

"Lovernios." The amusement vanished from his voice. "That's serious. Very serious. No wonder you're so testy. What did he say?"

"Not much. There wasn't much he could say when I told him I was King Bran's foster daughter."

"And a good thing, too," muttered Nissyen.

"He just said that I'd been naive, stupid, thoughtless, and mindless to join the caber toss, and I told him I wasn't mindless at all."

"Maeve." Nissyen was still alarmingly serious. "I hope you didn't show him any of your cheek."

"No, just most of my breasts."

"Maeve, Maeve!" Nissyen lamented. "You've got to be careful around that one. He's dangerous."

"What do you mean?" My pulse started to race with fear. "Come on, Nissyen. We tell you everything. And you just drop hints. Tell me what you know about him."

"I don't know much about him. Not really. That's why I say he's dangerous. He doesn't add up. There's some mystery there."

"How can you not know anything? I thought all druids knew everything about everyone. Didn't you have to study genealogy in order to become a full-feathered druid?"

"I'm not talking about lineage. I'm talking about character, Maeve. Lovernios is a brilliant man and an able druid. He's never been a great poet. You can tell by the set of his jaw. Too tight. But he excels at moral philosophy and *brehon* law. And of course as a military strategist no one can touch him. He maneuvers kings as if they were so many pieces on a *fidchell* board. It's no secret that he's a contender to succeed as archdruid. A dazzling career, you could say. But it wasn't what he wanted in the beginning.

"I remember him when he was young. Maybe not what you'd call young, but what I would. He started his training very early in life, so even after the full twenty years of study, he was only thirty or so, handsome, quick, virile, sleek, and glossy as a fox. He'd had enough of study. He wanted adventure. The *Combrogos* are not like the Romans—so lacking in imagination all they can think of is conquering people and stealing not just their land but their stories, their art, their gods. Lovernios wanted no ordinary conquest. He wanted to sail West, far West, beyond the Shining Isles of the Blest. He had heard stories of how way, way across the western sea there is an island so large our islands are little more than a cluster of rocks by comparison. Some call it Turtle Island. On its back rests a world.

"He started out in a *curragh* worthy of Manannán Mac Lir. He took no weapons. He was a druid. And no warriors either. He went alone, armed only with a keen mind and a strong will. He did not aspire to be a king. Myself, I think he wanted to be a god." Nissyen paused.

"Why did he come back?"

"That's what no one knows, and he will never tell. A year and a day after he sailed away, someone sighted him drifting past the Isle of Mannin. When he finally came ashore, he was wild-eyed and raving. No one could understand what he was saying. He was crazed with hunger and thirst, and it took a long time to nurse him back to health. When he had recovered, he refused to tell his tale. Some think he cannot remember; others believe he is under a *geis*. No one knows.

"He went on with his life and made good use of his druid training. I respect the man for that. But there's something hidden in him. Something that torments him. Whatever it is, he keeps a tight rein on it. Too tight. A man who lives in fear of himself is a dangerous man. You wouldn't want to draw his personal attention to you any more than a hare would ask for notice from a fox."

"I am no rabbit," I asserted. It was the second time today that I'd been compared to one. I didn't like it.

"No, you're more like a bird, a great, honking goose, maybe," Nissyen laughed. "But a fox doesn't scruple, Maeve. It will kill whatever it can catch. Be ready to fly. But better yet, learn to be quiet and blend into the scenery when the fox is on prowl."

"I'm afraid it's too late for that," I said. "Although he never seems to remember who I am."

"Eh? What's that?" Nissyen pushed the plaid up off his ears.

"Nothing," I said firmly. I had no intention of alarming Nissyen with an account of my encounter with Foxface in the Dark Grove. "I have to go now, Nissyen. I want to hear the arbitrations."

"Ah, yes, King Bran and the King of the Atrebates, what's-his-name, Borvo, will be going at it. It's almost enough to get me out of bed. But I have to save my strength for watching my poor lambs go to slaughter tonight."

"If you mean our recital, all I can say is your metaphors leave a lot to be desired."

"Tell me I may rest assured you're ready, Lambchop."

"As ready as I'll ever be," I answered with truth and ambiguity.

I bent to kiss Nissyen's cheek. It had that withered apple softness that reminded me of the Cailleach.

"Ah, Maeve," he murmured, pulling his plaid back over his ears. "You are intoxicating. The sweat of Macha, the great mare, and the scent of Emain Ablach all mingled. Breasts to die for. You'd better learn to guard such treasures. Do you understand that?"

But I was already slipping out the door, and I didn't understand, any more than I understood the strangeness that came over men when they heard the words Tir na mBan.

26

PROPHECY

Before we get to the arbitrations where the Roman question will be once more hotly debated, I want you to run with me over the lush earth of Mona Mam Cymru, Mona the mother of Wales, her wide lap full of ripe grain. If you could fly over Mona, you would see that the crops are planted in curves and swirls. There is not a straight line in sight. Feel in your body that love of roundness, of intricate loops and twining knots, and you may better understand why Rome with its legions of straight lines was anathema.

Arbitrations were held in—what else?—a grove. Think about it. The columns and arches of all imposing buildings, whether classic or gothic, are nothing but an imitation of the real thing: trees. The druids knew the connection between trees and justice. Between trees and everything. Who needed a courtroom? No courtroom column ever sheltered a singing bird or drank the dark waters under the earth.

The trees in this particular grove were primarily ash, a slender, graceful tree, with excellent posture and high branches. The delicate, five-leaf clusters let in more light than the oaks. Underneath the arching boughs, the grove was spacious and airy, easily accommodating the crowd that gathered around the central tree that was set apart not because of its girth or height, but because it topped a small rise. Beneath it twelve druids waited. One of them was Foxface.

With uncharacteristic restraint, I decided it would be better not to push my way to the front of the crowd. Instead I climbed into the branches of a lone willow. A small stream ran beside the tree, and from my perch, I noticed that it joined another at the edge of the grove. I climbed high enough to get a good view of the crowd, about a hundred men and women, heads of tribes and *tuaths*, I reckoned. They were dressed in rich colors, and their heads, arms, and necks flashed with gold in the dappled, moving light. At the front of the crowd, I saw King Bran, laughing and bantering with his companions. I recognized many of the women of his household. Branwen was among them, looking serious and keeping quiet, giving all her attention to worrying for him.

I looked around, trying to decide which man was King Borvo. He had sold out to Rome, Branwen said, and her father was reviving some old grievance against him in hopes that the druids would strip him of his authority. I decided he must be standing across from King Bran in the semi-circle gathered round the tree, because he kept fixing Bran with killing looks that Bran ignored. King Borvo wore a heavy torque and a crown as well. His cloak was bright red, but all his finery made his complexion appear more ashen.

King Bran was a massive man. He was not fat—no warrior could afford to be fat. Indeed, any warrior whose girth exceeded the standard length of the girdle had to pay a fine. But King Bran's appearance made you think of feasting, sinking your teeth into a juicy haunch, quaffing ale, reveling in all the pleasures of the flesh, including the ones my mothers had enjoyed with him.

King Borvo was nothing but bone and gristle. Even his mustache was sparse, and his hair, though thickened with lime, revealed patches of scaly scalp. In short, he looked unwholesome. If he were Jewish, YHWH would have considered him unclean. Still, he was surrounded by stout enough warriors, and he had a woman by his side who looked young enough to be his daughter, though his manner towards her suggested a different relationship. No one could doubt King Bran's devotion to Branwen, but he was not focused on her. In contrast, King Borvo kept touching the young woman, even as he spoke to others, drawing her close, repositioning her—now beside him, now in front—as if she was a shield to be used to the best advantage.

At one point I got a clear view of her profile, and I was astonished by her shape. Her belly extended far beyond her breasts. It was perfectly round, round as the full moon. I wondered if she had eaten something foul that had caused her to blow up with gas.

I forgot about the strangely shaped young woman as a hush fell over the crowd. At a gesture from the old archdruid, the wind stilled, and even the stream seemed to make an effort to quiet the sound of its flow. The archdruid sang to the quarters. Every note lingered till the air was thick with magic. This time the archdruid did not plant his staff. The ash tree rising behind him became the Tree and stood for a justice that was more than human.

Now the archdruid stepped back and sat down cross-legged beneath the tree. Everyone else sat, too, except for Foxface, who stepped forward, and the two kings, whom he called to stand before him. Foxface was the arbiter, the keeper of the rules, which he stated clearly before he allowed either king to make his opening statement. As the two kings spoke in turn, I paid as much attention to Foxface as to the arguments. He was at his best in this role: grave, attentive, and scrupulously fair. King Borvo was clearly on the lookout for any hint of anti-Roman bias, but Foxface showed King Bran no favor.

In fact, unschooled as I was in politics and law, I could tell that King Bran's line of attack was failing. A glance at Branwen's troubled face confirmed it. Bran argued that King Borvo was his *celsine*—his client. He based this claim on some old war between the Silures and the Atrebates. The Silures had taken hostages and for a time Bran forced King Borvo to pay tribute. Bran maintained that Borvo could not become a client to Rome, since he still owed tribute to the Silures, not to mention fines for nonpayment.

"The Atrebates owe tribute to the Silures?" snarled King Borvo. "In exchange for what? Tell me, Bran Fendigaid ab Llyr Lleidiaith, what have you done for me lately?"

"Oh, nothing much. Just offered your tribe the use of some prime grazing land. Not to mention putting at your disposal the strength of the Silures' arms."

"It's been a generation since any of my people grazed cattle on any land controlled by the Silures. Every time we did, we ended up getting raided. As for protection, the Atrebates have scant need of it, except against you and your friends the Ordovices. Savages. All of you. You, who claim to prize freedom above all else, who scorn relations with civilized foreign powers—"

"Rome? Civilized!" Bran restrained himself—barely—from spitting. Foxface would have penalized him. But there was quite a bit of hearty expectorating in the crowd.

"Understand, all you who have assembled here. I am no *celé*," King Brovo declared, "no commoner. Nor have I consented to be a client to any other king. I never paid tribute in some orderly, civilized exchange. I ransomed my people and bought back their freedom."

The child of my mothers, I felt no surprise that there should be two contradictory versions of the same events. What was new—and unnerving—to me was that here contradictions had consequences. One account would be accepted; the other, rejected. That may seem self-evident to you. To me, it was a seismic revelation. I was on the edge of my branch.

"No *celé*, you say. You boast of buying your people's freedom even as you sell them to Rome. Hear me, everyone. He didn't buy their freedom from me! I granted it as part of an agreement. I am no slave holder or dealer—"

"No, you've never needed to deal in slaves with the stranglehold you Silures have on the gold trade. And how did you get that stranglehold? By raiding. You control the Cambrian Mountain passes. No one can get through unless they've paid—and paid dearly—for safe conduct. And you dare to talk of freedom!

"And now you seek to strip me of my sovereignty by exhuming an old war that no one admits to losing. For I will never admit it. And if you can't best me with your specious arguments, I know you plan to stoop to lower tactics to discredit me before the *Combrogos.* Hear me, all of you, and behold. I am a sovereign, a potent sovereign. Here is the proof." He thrust the blown-up woman towards the crowd. To the druids he said, "I have witnesses to attest to my prowess."

There was a moment's silence as everyone registered the turn the case was taking. Then someone snickered, and one of the Silures called out rudely, "Yeah. He needs a cheering squad to get it up."

Suddenly I got it. The young woman wasn't bilious. She had a baby in there! Now you must understand I had never seen a pregnant woman before, much less a baby. (Seeing a pregnant sheep or goat is not the same.) Now I remembered Branwen explaining to me that morning that a king had to have the power to get a woman pregnant. If he was impotent, the crops would wither and the cattle sicken and die. Apparently there were rumors that King Borvo's appendage no longer rose to the occasion. Or, as King Bran might have put it, he'd sold his nuts to Rome.

"You anticipate an argument that has not been put forward." Foxface's voice was not loud. It didn't need to be. Everyone hushed as soon as he spoke. "We must first judge the claim of Bran, king of the Silures that Borvo, king of the Atrebates, is his *celsine* and has reneged on his obligations as such. We have heard the testimonies of the principals. We will now hear the histories sung and then the laws pertaining to such cases."

At a sign from Foxface, an elderly bard came forward and began to sing the story of the battles between the Silures and the Atrebates. After he sang one complete version, he launched into another. At that point I eased myself closer to the trunk of the tree and nestled against it. As the namesake of Queen Maeve of Connacht, not to mention as a bard-in-training, I ought to have been more gripped by tales of war and cattle raiding. But I could not keep my eyes open, which was perhaps pardonable after the day I'd already had, and even wise considering the night to come. I came half-awake when the rhythms changed from epic tale to law triads. But listening to recital of law is a wonderful soporific. I went back to sleep and did not wake until I heard King Bran's voice again. It was his passion that made me snap to.

"You have found against me," he was saying, "though it breaks your noble hearts to do so. Now that I have nothing to lose, I will freely confess. Yes, I picked the bones of an old quarrel for a scrap of meat that might nourish the *Combrogos*. And yes, I intended to question by any and every means the sovereignty, and, yes, the potency, of a king who surrenders his kingship, his manhood to Rome, then justifies this treacherous act by calling it 'merely a trade agreement with a civilized power.'

"I have lost my case." Bran's voice did not rise, but it deepened, widened like a great river, submerging King Borvo's outraged sputterings. "But that is nothing compared to what may yet be lost. And so I put it before you: What is a king's sovereignty? Is a king free to sell himself, his people, the very body of Anu into bondage? How answers the Law?"

Bran's speech was met with both cheers and angry shouts. The archdruid rose and the others with him. Then all twelve druids closed ranks and conferred in a huddle. They had given judgment; the case could have been closed. But the druids were well versed not only in law but in human nature. They knew a cauldron of deep feeling had been stirred and was rapidly coming to a boil. They weren't about to let it boil over into a useless mess. They were masters of the flame. They knew how to contain and direct raw energies.

In a moment, the other druids resumed their seats and Foxface came forward again, stepping into a shaft of afternoon light, so that his long shadow penetrated the crowd. The edges of his hair and beard glowed fiercely. By contrast, his face seemed ghostly and full of grim command.

"The Law is a living thing. It stands as a tree with its roots deep in time, even as storms rock its branches. It endures many winters and still puts forth new leaves to drink summer's fire."

I thought this speech very fine, despite the poor rating Nissyen gave Lovernios as a poet.

"When lightning splits the trunk or a branch breaks, the tree heals itself, growing around the wound, adjusting its shape to become stronger and wiser still. The tree grows to answer each challenge. Let the *Combrogos* stand beneath the tree. Let the *Combrogos* speak. Let the *Combrogos* understand that the Law grows like a tree, according to its own time."

It was an impressive non-answer. With our paltry human life spans, we tend to want everything settled right now. But the druids attuned themselves to deeper rhythms. They measured time by the widening circles rippling slowly from the unseen center of the Tree.

"I object vehemently to the extremist, insular, isolationist position that views all Roman clients as slaves," someone from the crowd spoke up. "Say what you will. In Gaul we enjoy peace and prosperity, an orderly exchange of goods and services." The man made the classic case for *Pax Romana*. "We have good roads and sophisticated plumbing. And we have protection from the kind of savagery that is here exalted as freedom."

"But you do not even have your own kings. You're ruled by Roman prefects!" an insular extremist objected. "You are the bastard, orphan children of a mercenary empire. You cling to your last shreds of pride and fancy that you are clothed. You gobble crumbs from the Roman tables you heap with your land and your labor and you imagine yourselves well fed!"

"That worn-out argument is both absurd and ignorant," said the Gaul, doing his best to seem unruffled. "We are still the *Combrogos*. We practice our arts unmolested. We worship our own gods in our own ways—"

"Oh, sure," someone sneered. "As long as you worship the emperor first. Your druids are geldings. They are not free to teach in their own colleges.

Why else do your tribes send candidates to the Holy Isles for training? Though what use they can make of that training I don't know, since Rome has outlawed the most sacred rites—"

"Only the most barbaric ones."

That was code for human sacrifice. In those days, the idea of human sacrifice was part of everyone's consciousness, whether deep or near the surface. But usually the whole subject was politely avoided, the way Victorians avoided the subject of sex (while secretly indulging in pornography) or the way people in your time, until very recently, avoided the subject of money, especially if they were sitting on piles of it.

"Who are the Romans to decree what's barbaric and what's not? Are their so-called gladiatorial games civilized? All those simpering citizens, who've never faced battle, sitting on their fat asses while men slaughter each other for their amusement?"

The debate wore on for quite a while, and I use the word 'wore' deliberately. Anyone who's ever been embroiled in controversy knows that the same passionate arguments repeat and repeat, slowly wearing each other away like grinding stones. As you know, this debate has never been resolved. Rome after Rome has risen, swallowing up smaller peoples, imposing an oppressive, often brutal peace, suppressing old beliefs and customs with a bland monoculture. Inevitably, the tensions become too great. The center, no matter what the political system, cannot hold. The empire breaks apart. There is an exhilarating moment or two of freedom. Then the tribes remember their old emnities and war with each other ruthlessly. Meanwhile, who is remembering the old songs and stories, the steps to the harvest dance, the remedies, the recipes?

Now Bran was speaking again. His throat was thick with tears and his voice the more powerful for speaking through them.

"I am growing old. I admit to the recklessness of my youth. Call it savagery if you will. Druids, I beg you, call me to submit to the discipline of some great vision. Let me be ruled, not by the steel of Rome, but by a wand of living wood. The *Combrogos* fight like the children of one mother, but we are hers. She gives to us and we give back to her our most finely crafted works of gold, silver, and copper, her substance, shaped by our hands, our art.

"But do you know what she is to Rome, this land, this lady of sovereignty?

"To them she is not alive. She is a carcass to be plundered. Call me to account if you will. Condemn me for my crimes, but do not sell the sacred body of Anu into bondage. Do not let our mother become a Roman drab."

King Bran's speech was like a mighty vessel, plowing through the waves, leaving a turbulent wake behind. Voice on voice rose, some in rage, some in passionate accord. Foxface remained still, his arms outstretched, palms towards the crowd, containing and calming the chaos. The sun slipped from view, and the ash grove turned grey. But Foxface's hair and beard held their color in the diminished light, and the western sky was streaked with red fingers, as if Anu had smeared it with moon-blood.

Then, when everyone else was quelled and even Bran and Borvo had sat down, one person stepped out from the crowd and stood before Foxface.

It was Esus.

Twilight is a dangerous time. It is the *Samhain* of the day. It is a dangerous time for time itself. Twilight is time's fault line. Past or future can open like a fissure in a rock. Foxface knew the dangers. He knew he was facing a danger that made the debates that went before mere squabbles, as Bran had said, between the children of one mother. I could see his jaw tense in anger, but I could also see in his face a truthful acknowledgment of the power that stood before him. Not a moment too soon, he motioned Esus to speak, thus preserving the illusion that he had some control. He might as well have said to a volcano: Go ahead. You have my permission to erupt.

"Woe!" Esus's voice tore the air. "Woe unto the inhabitants of the Holy Isles, even unto the druids of Mona, I say woe!"

He was speaking slowly in his accented P-Celtic. No need for me to hop down from my tree and translate. But if the words were Celtic, the rhythms were pure Hebrew in finest prophetic tradition.

"For you have sold your own kin into slavery, even your own brethren into the land of oppression as the brothers of Joseph sold him into Egypt."

Murmurs arose. "Not I. Not I. Only King Borvo has made a pact with Rome."

But I knew. He had seen the captives in their pens. He had not been able to forget them as I had. He turned from Foxface and began to pace among the crowd, confronting one person after another. Remember, he was a fourteen-year-old boy, slight, dark, not overly tall, a stranger in a strange land. Yet, though there were muttered protests, no one questioned an authority that seemed to grow with every step he took.

"Do you not deal in *cumals*?" Esus demanded. "One woman being equal to three cows? Do you not trade your captives for wine and fine goods? If the body of your sister is not sacred to you—"

"My sister? I never sold my sister," a man objected, but I could tell Esus's words were hitting home.

"— then you are already slaves, and your mother Anu is a childless widow. For even so do the Romans buy and sell human flesh. In Judea the Romans impose heavy taxes. Then they hire thugs and thieves to rob the people. When the people cannot pay the tax, they are sold into slavery—"

"Well, that's hardly the same thing as taking captives in an honest raid," people muttered, but Esus went on, relentlessly.

"Roman peace," he spat the words, "is for the rich, for the sycophants and hypocrites, the puppet kings, and the Sadducees."

"Now you're talking!" someone shouted.

"Just as freedom here is for the rich and mighty. Verily, verily, I say unto you, freedom that can be bartered and sold, won and lost as in a game of dice is no true freedom. You quarrel with one another over Roman rule, and you do not see: Rome has already cast its shadow on your countenance. Rome is not a place. Rome is not an army. Rome is cruelty and idolatry and slavery. Wherever these flourish, Rome is in your midst. And so I say unto the *Combrogos,* hear the words of the living God—"

Suddenly, he stopped. A stillness overcame him, an eye-of-the-storm stillness. Even in the dim light, I could see a greenish cast to his face. He looked as though he was going to be sick any minute.

"Repent," he croaked in a voice to rival any oracular raven's. "For the day of the Lord is at hand. Yea, the day is coming when the Menai Straits will run red. The black-robed priestesses of Holy Isle will stand in the turning tide and shriek their curses, yet devastation will come. A great host will ford the waters. Blood will spill. The groves will burn. The heavens will turn black with smoke, and the earth bitter with ash, and the druids will be gone forever from Mona mam Cymru—"

Without warning, Esus crumpled and fell to the ground. Before I could even get down from my tree, a swift flock of mixed Cranes and Crows swooped down on him and bore him away. Foxface remained where he was. Stern, unshaken. Even in the midst of my fear for Esus, I could not help admiring him.

27

EXAMS

Are you sold yet, or shall I say converted to, the concept of our cosmic twinhood? Just look at the two of us. Within the space of a few hours, we'd both managed to make public spectacles of ourselves. Wait a minute, you say: *He* was acting out of profound moral conviction, while *you* were merely acting out. Now listen, I'm not going to let you get away with writing me off as an exhibitionist while exalting him as a prophet. It comes down to the same thing: neither or us could stay out of trouble to save our lives. To lay on him a *geis* of danger and destruction was an act of sheer redundancy.

∞

Foxface contained the crowd with the stillness of his bearing until the old archdruid formally dismissed the court. People began to file silently out of the grove, their festival mood flattened by the prophetic words that hung in the air like heavy smoke. Because flow of traffic was in the opposite direction from the one the Crows and Cranes had taken with Esus's limp body, I struggled against the stream, ducking and dodging, with no other plan in mind than to reach Esus. Just as the crowd began to thin and I might have been able to run, I saw Branwen, sitting alone and sobbing. There was no way I could walk on.

"Branwen!"

When she heard my voice, she looked up, then got to her feet and ran to me, flinging herself into my arms. I had never seen her so upset. All her tense watchfulness was gone. She was beside herself.

"There, there," I murmured meaninglessly, stroking her long braid and rocking her. "It will be all right. Everything's going to be all right."

"No, it isn't!" she said, drawing apart from me. I'd never seen her angry before. "How can you say that? Father has lost his case before the *Combrogos*. There's nothing to stop the Romans from tearing us apart, piece by piece, tribe by tribe. And the Stranger!" (Even Branwen called him that.) "What he said! What he saw!" She shuddered.

"But you're all right, Branwen," I insisted. I needed to find Esus.

"No!"

She spoke with such force that I wondered for an instant if Esus's vision had shown Branwen not just any future but her own future. A future she could never forget. Then I dismissed the thought. I did not want to believe it. Besides, the present was too pressing. I had no time for the future.

"Branwen," I almost pleaded with her. "I've got to find Esus."

In an instant, Branwen got hold of herself; then she took hold of me. The strength of her grip surprised me. She was so small. But then, small, wiry people are often stronger than they look. What's more, she'd grabbed the arm Foxface had already bruised.

"Ouch, Branwen. You're hurting. Let go."

Gentle little Branwen held on tight. "I am not going to let you get into more trouble today, Maeve. I saw Lovernios's face when he marched you away. He was livid. You simply can't afford to draw any more attention to yourself."

"Branwen!" I tried to yank myself free. "I've got to go after Esus. I've got to find out if he's all right. He might need my help."

"What on earth could you possibly do for him that the Crows and the Cranes can't? The Crows are seers and healers. They'll know how to treat someone who has collapsed in a trance."

"But what he saw was horrible! They might punish him, they might—"

"Maeve," she reproached me. "They are not like the Roman emperors who pay people to flatter and kill those who speak the truth. If his vision was true...If his vision was true—" She broke off and began to weep again, releasing my arm and covering her face with her hands.

I could have turned and left her. Instead I just stood there feeling helpless and uncertain for perhaps the first time in my life. I didn't like it.

"Branwen!" It was King Bran's voice, sharp with anxiety, coming to us through the twilit gloom. "There you are, thank Bride. I've been looking all over for you. Why didn't you follow me out of the grove? Ah well, I've found you, and in good hands, I see. There, there, love." His voice softened as he saw her tears. With one arm, he drew her to him. With the other arm, he gathered me in. "Both my girls safe. That's all that matters now."

He held us close, this big man, with his manly bosom just made for soul-rocking. I nestled closer and breathed that heady male scent of sweat and musk. Bran had the wisdom and kindliness not to mistake my pleasure in his body for anything other than what it was: sheer sensual trust. I rested against him and let go my plan for immediate pursuit of Esus. I would wait until after I'd told my tale before the *Combrogos*, then I'd go to the Dark Grove as I'd planned.

"Hush, Hinny, hush now," Bran crooned to Branwen. "Save your tears for the crying time. And now both of you, come along. You need to be carefully fed. Enough to strengthen you, but not enough to give you indigestion. For there's nothing worse than a poet with gas."

With that, he bore us away to the feasting and fed us as tenderly as a mother bird.

∽

Surely you remember. Past lives or no past lives, this scene is engraved in your genes. Storytelling is an essential human act, what we did when we discovered we could use our tongues for more than tasting sweet and bitter, salt and sour, for more than licking wounds or other tender, throbbing bodily parts.

It is night. There's a fire answering the cold fire of the stars. We are sitting in circles within circles. Children curl into laps. People lean back against each other or against rocks or trees. A hush falls, and a human voice, singing or chanting, speaking or whispering, rises from the darkness of the body and makes its invisible miracle with the air. In the flickering light, in the connected minds of the listeners, images form. Worlds and lives come into being. Film is a mere technical re-creation of this old, old magic. So come. Join the circle. Tonight I am one of the magicians.

I was not the first storyteller of the evening. At the great festivals, a whole cycle of stories was told, beginning with *Invasions*, what the Celts have instead of creation stories. The first formers were responsible for recounting *Conceptions* and *Births*. Between *Invasions* and *Conceptions*, there were quite a few *Battles*, *Cattle Raids*, and steamy *Courtships*. Many seasoned and famous Bards performed before us. If you think essay exams are bad, imagine having to stand up before a huge audience and follow the act of the first century equivalent of a movie star.

Branwen was the first of our form to recite, and her performance was a shock and a delight. This shy shadow of a girl had an electrifying stage presence from the moment she stood and somehow fixed each person with her huge, doe eyes. As she told the tale, Branwen embodied Arianrod, the proud woman who kept her cool even as she stepped over King Math's magic wand, casually dropping the twins Lleu and Dylan from her womb (thus utterly failing her virginity test).

Others from our form followed. I noted, with petty satisfaction, that Viviane's rendition was lacklustre to say the least. She could not have looked any paler and still been alive. Who would have thought, after her confident recital at admissions, that she would have developed stage fright? I congratulated myself that I did not feel in the least nervous about my own performance. It was going to be a breeze. I told myself it was best not to overrehearse and gave my mind to more important matters, such as how I would conceal myself when I staked out the Mound of the Dark Grove. But when my name was finally called, I was so startled my cool abandoned me completely.

"Maeve. Maeve Rhuad. Maeve Rhuad, daughter of Manannán Mac Lir."

"That's you!" Nissyen hissed in my ear. He pulled me to my feet and gave me a little push.

I found myself standing in the center of the circle, staring out at hundreds of expectant faces bathed in flamelight, so different from the anemic bluish cast of television. Here I was, the next scheduled entertainment. If I didn't please, no one would simply tap the remote and change the channel. Nothing so benign as that. I stood in silence, but there was nothing deliberate or dramatic about my wordlessness. My gaze was not in the least enigmatic but plainly panicked as I ransacked my mind for the first line, the first fact about what's-his-name's conception.

Today I could tell you all about Lugh's mother Etniu whose father Balor of the Evil Eye imprisoned her on Tory Island in a crystal tower to prevent the conception of a grandson destined to slay him. (Impregnable towers, remote islands, Arianrhod tried those methods, too, and the moral of both stories is: No contraception works 100%.) That night I could hardly remember Lugh's name, though you could argue that Lugh is my foster brother, Manannán Mac Lir having taken him into fosterage after Balor failed to drown him along with his two brothers. You see, Lugh was a triplet; Etniu went Arianrhod one better. But I had never met Lugh—or my father for that matter. At that moment, Lugh meant less than nothing to me, and he didn't seem to be intervening to help me out of this scrape. Nor did Manannán Mac Lir or even Bride, who was supposed to watch out for poets.

I was on my own.

The crowd was getting restless. I wondered: what *did* the *Combrogos* do to poets who wouldn't put out, to female first formers who failed their first finals. (Say that five times fast.) I took a deep breath and opened my mouth.

"The Pleiades shone bright on the night Grainne of the Golden hair walked alone on the shores of Tir na mBan."

Zap! The words Tir na mBan hit the crowd, casting them instantly into an altered state of consciousness, even the druids on the examination board. (Foxface, to my intense relief, was not among them.) I warmed to my task. They wanted a tale of conception? I could deliver. They wanted the birth of a hero, with mystery, danger, and prophecy into the bargain? Not a problem.

So I stitched together the best elements of my mothers' many tales of my Otherworldly conception, tossing in a few fresh details of my own. When I was firmly implanted in my mother's womb, I invoked the Pleiades again and launched into a parallel tale of Miriam, a virgin of Galilee (virgin births were a popular theme) betrothed but not married to some old fart (another common feature of conception tales). In short, I decided to throw out Esus's patrilineage entirely and give him a conception worthy of a Celtic hero.

In my account of my own conception, Manannán Mac Lir ravished my mother in the form of a seal—or silkie, if you think that sounds more poetic and less kinky. So for Esus I thought okay some kind of bird. (Celts consider birds to be oracular, remember?) That would make for a pleasing balance: one fathered from the sea; the other from the sky.

You can hardly accuse me of being derivative in my choice of a bird father for Esus. I didn't know the story of Leda and the swan, and angels were not part of my cosmology. As for the Holy Spirit taking the form of a dove, well, it's never been entirely clear whether the H.S. is male or female—though when I was a dove, I believe I remained true to gender. In any case, this was no tender little dove but a *big* bird I invoked for Miriam. This bird of mine had fiery wings and a face with the bright, impersonal beauty of a star. In short, I outdid myself on Esus's behalf and only wished I could go back and spiff up my somewhat pedestrian silkie—if a sea mammal can be called pedestrian.

I was just getting to the birth scenes—in effect the beginning of this story you're reading, the story I've been wanting to tell for two millenia—when I was whisked off stage, so to speak. Picture the scene as Vaudevillian slapstick, if you like, someone yanking me with a crooked cane. It was a little like that, except in the wings waited a phalanx of druids, Nissyen among them, looking far more distressed than I had the sense to be, wringing his hands. Before anyone could inform me of the precise depth of the shit I was in, the crowd threatened to get completely out of control.

> We want Maeve!
> We want Maeve!
> Maeve Rhuad!
> Maeve Rhuad!

The chant rose louder and louder, accompanied by footstomping. The druids held a hurried conference in nose ogham.

"All right," said the grey-bearded Druid, who happened to be head of the literature department. "Go back out there, but make sure you bring your outrageous improvisation to a definite end immediately after the births. No *Heroic Exploits*. No *Wonder Journeys*. Is that quite clear?"

So I returned to the center of the circle and told the crowd all about the attendant animals at both our births and the eight sets of lactating breasts that greeted me. (The crowd loved that part.) I spiced up Esus's story by having him born in a cave, his family in hiding from a jealous Roman puppet king. (The tax plot twist, devised so as to have him born in Bethlehem, and the no-room-at-the-inn routine do not come from me.) Finally, as a sop to my teachers, I had three druids from the Holy Isles arriving to prophesy over him.

"And that's all for now, folks," I concluded. "The story continues even as we speak." Which gave my story an edge over all the others—or so I fancied in my naiveté.

The crowd gave me a standing ovation.

"Did I pass?" I asked the panel of deeply disconcerted druids.

"Your performance, indeed your status at the college, will have to be thoroughly reviewed," Greybeard informed me.

"Am I finished with exams for this evening?" I asked.

"You're finished."

That sounded ominous. But at the moment I couldn't summon much concern about my academic status. I was merely relieved that I could go at last, but when I turned to walk away, Nissyen followed me.

"Oh, Maeve, Maeve." His voice was tender and reproachful.

"Didn't you like my story, Nissyen?" I pleaded. "The *Combrogos* did."

"Maeve, that's not the point and you know it."

"I know," I admitted, and I managed to hang my head.

I was supposed to be learning the stories of the people. The mind and memories of bards and druids were not private property. They were store houses, story houses. If those minds were not full of knowledge, it was almost as disastrous for the *Combrogos* as an empty granary.

"Just tell me, Maeve, why did you do it?"

"Oh, Nissyen. I'm sorry. I couldn't remember anything. Now I can. It's all coming back. But when I stood there facing the crowd, I couldn't remember one thing about *Lugh's Conception.*"

"Well," he sighed. "At least you got the narrative structure of the *Hero's Conception* right. I'll see if I can get you credit for that."

"I'm sorry," I said again. And I hugged his body with its hollow bird bones.

"Where are you going now?" he asked, justly suspicious.

"Back to the hut. I'm not feeling too well." Neither of these statements was exactly a lie. Not exactly. I was cold and tired and intended to stop at the hut for a heavy cloak and some oatcakes before I went on to Bryn Celli Ddu.

"Then I expect to find you safely tucked into bed when I get back," Nissyen told me. "The truth is, I'd prefer not to let you out of my sight, but there's still more of our lot to recite. This ordeal is far more excruciating for me than for any of you. Here you've set the whole literature department on its ear. And Viviane, word perfect as she was, looking white and fey as some changling. I'm beginning to think it was a mistake to admit females," he grumbled.

And he turned back to the storytelling, leaving me at liberty to continue my own story.

I couldn't wait to find out what would happen next.

BOOK IV

THE ISLAND OF
DARK SHADOWS

28

LOVE YOUR ENEMY

I say I could hardly wait to find out what would happen next, and that is true. But whatever surprises awaited me, and all good story tellers are taken by surprise from time to time, my illusion that I was in charge of my own tale was still intact. I am sure I am not alone in this view of my life as a wonderful story, starring myself and a few select others. When you were young, weren't you the star of your story? Aren't you still? True, as we age, the genre often changes from pure adventure-romance to something riddled with irony at best, but it is hard to relinquish the hope that there is a more or less coherent plot that will resolve itself to our advantage. Every time we read a story or see a film we are bolstering this belief.

I was raised by mothers for whom reality was infinitely malleable—or anyway subject to endless revision. The New Age solipsism: "You create your own reality" was not new in the least to them. In all oversimplifications, there is an element of the more complicated truth. It is equally true that we are all victims of circumstance. In this apparent paradox lies the power of our stories and our lives. Here is the heart of the mystery: that moment when our own inner force meets forces beyond our control. That moment when the plot thickens or falls apart completely. Suddenly we find ourselves in an altogether different story; or worse, we begin to suspect that there is no story at all. In this moment, when we discover we are not the sole authors of our lives, what we choose matters. We shape this moment even as we are shaped by it. Forever.

∞

According to the story I was telling myself, I was now about to risk danger (though naturally I would triumph) in order to guard the one I loved, to be near him at his hour of need. Hadn't Anna said "Don't despise this shitty little dove. Someday you may need her?"

I didn't intend to stop at Caer Leb for more than the few seconds it would take me to grab my heavy cloak and some food. But when I neared our hut, I hit a wall of fear and pain so strong that it stopped me as surely as if it had been made of stone. I stood, stunned, confronted with a totally unexpected choice. I sensed—I use the word sense advisedly; I could practically smell the panic in that hut—that if I went inside I would be hopelessly deflected from my long-laid plans. If I wanted to find out what was happening to Esus in Bryn Celli Ddu, I had better walk on right now and forget about my cloak. My right leg was all for going. I could feel the muscles straining, but my left remained rooted.

Branwen, I thought. What if that was Branwen in there, sick or grieving?

I closed my eyes and tried to see who it was behind the hut walls and what was wrong. But sixth sense or second sight, or whatever you want to call it, doesn't work that way. It doesn't exist to let you off the hook. It doesn't make everything clear and simple. On the contrary, it often gives you information that you wish you never had. Now, instead of bursting into the hut and happening on whatever it was, I had to decide whether or not to face it. I tried to think of Esus at the Mound of the Dark Grove being prepared for some awe-ful rite, braving YHWH's wrath and his own fears. I willed him to call out for me in some way. Nothing.

Then I heard someone moaning in the hut. My left foot led; my right followed. I lifted the flap and stepped inside. The air was thick with the stench of sweat and blood. It took me a moment to spot her lying on the far side of the hut. Then she moaned again: Viviane, her face whiter than the moon's. Her eyes were closed. The way the blue veins stood out on her eyelids remains in my memory.

Viviane must have heard my indrawn breath or felt the draft that came in when I lifted the flap. Very slowly she rolled her head in my direction; just as slowly, she opened her eyes.

"Maeve, don't tell."

Her voice was so weak! I crossed the hut and knelt beside her. Even before I looked, I knew she was lying in a pool of blood. I felt cold all over. My hands were shaking. I had no idea what to do. Still, Viviane held me with her eyes, trying to bend me to some crazily persisting will. Then she shuddered, and her eyes closed again.

"Viviane, you've got to tell me what happened." I tried to take charge. "I've got to find a way to help you."

"Help me what?" She almost managed a sneer.

"Live!"

She opened her eyes again and we stared at one another, each acknowledging the other unspoken possibility.

"I tried to take it out myself," she said, barely whispering. "I took potions to make the blood come, and when it didn't, I opened myself with an awl."

As she spoke I picked up one of her hands. It was colder than a dead fish, but the rest of her was hot. I didn't know anything then about the fever from infections that complicated so many childbirths and abortions. We never had any sickness on Tir na mBan. Until this moment, death was no more to me than a plot device, a way to dispatch heroes when they'd had their full share of battles and exhausted their luck. Now I was confronted with sudden knowledge beyond Viviane's few words, beyond words themselves, since I lacked even rudimentary ones for what had happened.

"At first I thought it was all right. I could see that it had come out of me. You wouldn't believe how it hurt. But I didn't cry out. I didn't want anyone to know. I buried it. I won't tell you where. For a few days, I thought the blood was just the stored up moon blood. Then it got worse. I don't know how I made it through my recital, but I did. I did."

"Don't talk anymore," I said. "You're wasting your strength. Just lie still. Sleep if you can."

As quietly as I could, I stood up, fully intending to run top speed back to the festival to grab the first Crow I could find. The most terrifying female mystery was happening right here in this hut. The Crows had to do something.

"Maeve!" The fear in Viviane's voice was naked. "Don't go!"

"Viviane, I've got to get help. Look, I know you don't want anyone to know. I know you're afraid you'll get sent home. But that doesn't matter now. I've got to get the Crows. They'll know what to do."

"Don't go," she whispered.

She touched my bare leg with her hand. The cold went straight to my bones. And I understood what she did not have the strength to say: By the time you get back it will be too late.

"All right," I said. "But you've got to let me help you."

She closed her eyes. Some infinitesimal movement of her facial muscles indicated assent. I had no idea what to do, but some basic human response to crisis seems to be water. I got clean rags and fetched fresh water. Lifting Viviane's tunic, I began to wipe the blood away, a futile exercise. Soon I was drenched in blood up to my elbows. I stopped and stared at my hands in dismay. Then Viviane opened her eyes again and caught mine. I knew, without words, that we were both remembering our fight, my hands and her face smeared with my blood then. Strange as it may sound to you, I believe if we'd had the strength we would have laughed out loud. We didn't need laughter to seal the bond that formed between us in that moment, a literal blood bond. Don't get me wrong. We were still enemies, but now we loved each other whether we liked it or not.

It was then that I felt the fire of the stars beginning at the top of my head, flowing swiftly to my fingers. The blood on my hands dried instantly. Of course. Water was the wrong element altogether. We needed fire. Following the pictures forming in my mind, I placed one hand over Viviane's womb. With the other I reached right up inside her sex, coming as close as I could to holding her womb between the palms of my hands. Then I closed my eyes.

I was on Tir na mBan. There was my womb mother, Grainne of the golden hair, burning away the cold, the damp, the fog, calling the sun's brightness and heat, making herself a chalice for light. Now that cup of fire poured over me, through me into the dark, red sea. I don't know how much time passed. The fire kept flowing through me until I could see the sun, Grainne's sun, blazing inside Viviane's womb, drying the blood, burning away the fetid heat of fever.

One last image came to me and lingered. A smooth, sun-drenched rock by the sea on a hot, still day. You know what that feels like. Imagine it. You've just come out of sea water cold as a winter night. You lie down on the heated rock. It warms you right through. It's lightly crusted with salt like your own body. You drowse there on the rock, perfectly at peace.

When I opened my eyes at last, Viviane was asleep, breathing deeply. Her bleeding had stopped, and her hands were warm again. I took the bloody rags outside and tore away what I could of her ruined tunic. My legs and arms felt so heavy, as if they weren't part of me but were separate objects that I had to lift and maneuver. I had no strength left over for thought—not even thought of Esus. My last conscious memory of that night is of lying down next to Viviane and covering us both with a heavy plaid.

∞

I am moving slowly in some pitch dark, narrow place. Though my shoulders just clear the cold, sweating walls, I have the impression of being purposefully squeezed down a passage. Think of a snake swallowing a mouse. Think of contraction of vaginal muscles or bowels; only here, the direction is in, not out. When the passage opens into a larger space, I remember the sweet, salty walls and the warm spring I found beneath Bride's breast. But now there is no sound of water. And it's cold, terribly cold.

Suddenly, I know I am trapped. I turn around and around, feeling for the passageway, but like a throat, it has closed after swallowing me. I keep pacing round and round, dizzying myself, my breath growing shorter and shorter, the sound of it amplified by the cold, rock walls. A bizarre notion comes to me that I have somehow swallowed myself. Then a cry rings out, so loud, so anguished, I don't know how the walls of this place can contain it.

Eli, Eli, Lamasabactani.

Esus.

The darkness whirls around me, and I hurtle towards him, the center of gravity. We become the still point, the axis, cosmic twins curled in the womb. We lie with our heads crooked in each other's crux. I want to stay here, just like this, forever. Contained. The sweet meat of the hazelnut, safe inside the shining salmon.

Then the sheltering darkness splits wide open. Images, harsh with light, break in. I see that same strange, stripped tree I saw before. The tree pierces the empty sky and sends bleeding cracks splintering across it. No, it's not the sky that's cracked. It's the lips, the dry lips. They are my lips. Their pain is lost in the agony of every muscle, in the cruelty of my own hanging weight. Something touches my lips, wet, sour. My pain-blurred vision clears for a moment. Below me I see hair the color of fire and a strangely familiar face streaked with dirt and tears.

"Maeve!" I don't recognize the name, but I know I have heard the voice before. "Maeve Rhuad." It's the Cailleach. "Maeve Rhuad, come back to yourself."

Then I hear my own voice crying, "Come back! Come back!" I am standing on the slope of Bride's breast. I am standing before the Mound of the Dark Grove. I am standing in a garden crying into a gaping emptiness. "Come back. Come back!"

Someone's arms encircle me.

"Esus?" I whisper. "Esus?"

∞

I opened my eyes and found myself looking into a face as old and unyielding as a rock, a face made mostly of shadows but with a flicker of flame in the eyes. It was a Crow. I looked around in confusion, taking in the low roof and the close walls, the scent of smoking herbs. Then I saw Viviane lying not far from me, still asleep.

"We moved you and Viviane to our hut to keep you under observation. You'll both need some time to recover. You have done well, Maeve Rhuad," she added. "Better than you know."

"I have to go now." I struggled to get to my feet, but I was still very weak. The Crow easily restrained me.

"Drink."

She brought a cup of something hot and bitter to my lips and forced it between them. I swallowed and felt heat and calm seep through my body.

"You will sleep now," she commanded. "No more dreams tonight."

I had no choice but to obey.

29

UNDER THE CROWS' WINGS

I woke to daylight spilling through the open door. For a moment I remembered nothing of the night before, but when I looked at Viviane, still asleep beside me, everything came back. It was hard to believe that only hours ago, I had been drenched in her blood, held her womb in my hands. Now, except for the bluish tinge in the hollow of her eyes, she looked almost her usual self—which included looking elegant and composed even when she was sound asleep.

I was pleased to note that there were no Crows with us in the hut. I hoped they were busy doing whatever it was Crows did in the morning. It was not a time when we usually saw them. Certainly, no one would consider it strange for me to go to the trenches. After that, I could have a wash in the Afon Braint. Then I'd be on course again, moving slowly, casually upstream to the Dark Grove. Once I cleared Caer Leb, I could pick up my pace. It had been a long detour, but Esus remained my destination.

At the thought of him, I began to remember fragments of my dream—if it was a dream. I could not make sense of all the images, but one thing was clear: I would be waiting when he emerged from the mound. Whether or not I made a sound, I would be the one to call him back to life.

Taking care not to wake Viviane, I got up and wrapped myself in a Crow cloak, which would come in handy for warmth and concealment. As for food, blackberries grew in abundance along banks of the Afon Braint. They would suffice if I could not scrounge some leftover oatcakes at the cookfire. I cast one glance at the still slumbering Viviane; then I slipped out of the hut, excited and well pleased with my plan. It would be easier to find the Mound by daylight and, with the *Lughnasad* events still in progress, the Dark Grove was likely to be deserted in the morning. Caer Leb also appeared to be empty, but I had not gone ten paces before a Crow appeared at my side.

"You must take it slowly at first," she cautioned, grasping my elbow with a talon. "You're not as strong as you think."

"Excuse me," I said as politely as I could. "I think you must be mistaking me for Viviane. It's true we both have red hair. But she's the one who nearly died. Not me. I'm fine."

Yet even as I spoke, I found that my knees felt a little wobbly, no doubt because the ground beneath my feet refused to lie still but instead seemed inclined to spin. The Crow put her arm around me and began to walk me slowly towards the trenches.

"Just because you can't tell us apart, Maeve Rhuad, don't assume that we share in your confusion—or indifference. In any case, your outward appearance is of minor significance. We see and know a great deal more than that."

Considering how much I had to hide, I did not find her words at all reassuring. There is nothing more annoying to a young woman than a mind-reading, female authority figure—though to couple mind-reading and female is to risk redundancy. The druids might have to cast entrails on the ground in order to read them. All the priestesses had to do was take one, sharp glance at your midriff.

"We know, for example, what it costs a person to open herself to the fire of the stars as utterly as you did last night. You need rest as much as Viviane does, perhaps more. And we're going to see to it that you get it."

When we reached the trenches, the Crow made it her business to steady me as I squatted. In general, I don't mind pissing in company, but it is annoying to know that your stream is being inspected and sniffed—a basic diagnostic technique. I was glad I didn't have to shit.

"I have one question," I said, hoping to break her concentration. "If you know so damn much, why didn't you do something about Viviane before?"

"Ah," said the Crow, handing me a mullein leaf. At least I was allowed to wipe myself without assistance. "Well you may ask, Maeve Rhuad. Well you may ask."

Sure, I thought as I stood up, I could ask. Answers? That was something else again.

∞

So Viviane and I were forced to rest in the hut. (If you dampen the wattle and daub, a hut can be cool and comfortable even on a hot day.) The door was left open to let in the breeze, but we were not allowed out. One Crow was stationed just outside, weaving on a standing loom like a great, black spider. I grew more frantic by the hour, but as any fly will tell you, it does no good to kick when you're caught in a sticky web.

Viviane slept more than I did, and we didn't talk much when she was awake. We didn't know how. We had seldom been on speaking terms, so we had no history of friendly chatter. Our extreme intimacy of the night before did not offer much opening for casual conversation. To my discomfort, I found that I was a little in awe of Viviane, the awe the novice feels for the initiate, however terrible the initiation was. I was uncharacteristically subdued in my attitude towards her.

"I owe you my life, Maeve," she spoke once out of the silence.

"You don't owe me," I said. "I was just there. Life used me to come back to you."

"All the same, it couldn't have if you didn't let it," she said. "When the time comes, I will remember my debt."

Later in the day, people began stopping by to ask after us, but the Crows wouldn't let most people in. Ciaran of the blue-black hair was one of them. I recognized his voice, and, of course, Viviane did. For a moment her face was a battlefield, full of chaos and pain. Then whatever was hardest and most unyielding in her won, and all feeling was routed. When she caught me watching her, she frowned and turned her face to the wall.

Not long after that, the Crows admitted Branwen, who came with her arms overflowing with gifts from her father, bracelets and combs and some fine Gaulish wine that the Crows allowed us to sip. With Branwen there, and the wine flowing merrily in our bloodstream, Viviane and I both relaxed and listened to Branwen's account of the day's games and festivities while she combed and dressed each of our hair in turn. (I couldn't help noticing how much more easily managed Viviane's hair was than my wild tangles.) I also noticed that Branwen avoided any mention of the on-going claims. Nor did she give us any report of how our other classmates had fared in their recitals. Viviane's and my status at college was, at the moment, painfully uncertain.

In the early evening, Nissyen's long, skinny shadow preceded him into the hut. He brought us a large bowl of stirabout, sweetened with honey as a special treat, and he stayed to make sure we ate it. I believe he was somewhat disappointed that he did not need to spoon-feed us, so tender was his concern.

"And how are my two favorite redheads?" he inquired when he judged we'd taken enough nourishment to be allowed to speak.

Two favorite redheads? Ordinarily I would have bridled at his lack of discrimination. But at the moment I had more pressing concerns.

"I'm feeling fine," I stated emphatically. "As a matter of fact, I'd like to come back to our hut tonight."

"That's up to the Crow ladies, Maeve."

"Fat chance, then," sighed Viviane.

We exchanged a glance of sisterly solidarity and sympathy.

"Keeping you under close scrutiny, are they?"

"To put it mildly," I said. "They won't even let us pee by ourselves. At least I can go to the trenches. Viviane has to piss in a pot."

"Maeve!"

Viviane glared at me. I think we were both pleased to find that our mutual antipathy had survived.

"How much longer do you think they'll keep us here?"

I tried to sound off-hand, but I was becoming desperate. Tonight was the second night of Esus's ordeal. Tomorrow night would be the last.

Nissyen shrugged. "I'll tell you the only thing I know for certain: the pair of you need to be as meek and docile as little lambs."

"Sheep are notoriously stupid," I couldn't help remarking.

"And you're what's known as too clever by half, Maeve Rhuad. Use your brain to keep you out of trouble for once."

"Nissyen." Viviane's voice was low and strained. "Does everyone know what happened? I mean, do the druids know or only the Crows know...."

"That you were pregnant, dear?" Nissyen's voice was so gentle. "It's no shame. Don't take it as shame on yourself. Why, you were so close-mouthed and proud it almost killed you. I blame myself. I am the one who should be ashamed."

"How can you be to blame for what I chose to do freely?"

Yes, Viviane was proud. I had to admire her for that.

"Sure, you've all been sneaking out to your trysts all summer long. It was my duty to stop you or anyway warn you, and I did nothing."

He sounded so miserable, I wished I could think of some way to comfort him.

"But to answer your question, Viviane," Nissyen recovered himself, "I don't know what the Cranes know or how the Crows have presented the matter. I can tell you that there have already been meetings between the two bodies, meetings at which I have not been present. I believe my conduct is under discussion, and rightly so. Among other things, they are deciding how to hear my case."

"Oh, Nissyen!" Viviane and I spoke at once.

"Now, now. Don't distress yourselves on my account. They won't do anything more to me, given my astonishing age—I'm long-lived even for a druid—than relieve me of my present duties. If that buys the two of you a second chance, then I'll be more than glad."

"But we won't!" I declared. "We love you, Nissyen. We don't want any other druid or Crow in our hut!"

"What did you mean by the two of us?" Viviane was puzzled. "Maeve's done nothing wrong. She saved my life."

I have to admit, I was extremely touched by her defense.

"Indeed," said Nissyen. "And I hope that will weigh in her favor. I can tell you one thing for certain, Maeve, you're on academic probation at the very least."

I could feel Viviane's raised eyebrows.

"I blew my recital," I admitted to Viviane.

"Now that is not entirely true," said Nissyen. "You gave a rousing performance, but your deviation from the prescribed story-line was extreme. Between us, my guess is that you, Maeve Rhuad, are in much bigger trouble than Viviane is. Everyone understands that young people can get carried away by their desires. I've always said that training in sex magic ought to begin in the first year instead of the seventh. Viviane and Ciaran are guilty of nothing more than being overeager and inept."

I was amazed that after losing so much blood, Viviane could blush so furiously.

"Whereas you, Maeve, appear to be guilty of not taking seriously the primary reason you are here: to learn the stories of the *Combrogos.*"

That was not *my* primary reason, I thought to myself.

"So, my silly little sheep, if you love old Nissyen as much as you say you do, then keep out of trouble."

I did not think I could promise that, even for Nissyen, so I said nothing.

"You know what I mean, don't you?"

I had a fair idea, but I couldn't risk opening my mouth for fear I'd spill my sheep-brained scheme. Although it wasn't really sheep-brained. It was more the sort of thing a goat would think of, goats being notoriously willful.

"The Stranger—" Nissyen called him that, too. "—he is not a safe person to know. He has seen things no one wants to see. He has said things no one wants to hear. From what I understand, he is a more dedicated student than some I could mention, yet it seems unlikely, stranger that he is with his even stranger notions about the one true god, that he will ever serve the *Combrogos* as a druid. Yet even as we speak he is being initiated into the secrets. For what purpose? I am not privy to the reasoning of the V.I.D.s, but I can tell you, he is a dangerous person with whom to link fortunes."

"I have tried to tell Maeve just that many times before," said Viviane with enough self-righteousness to make me want to smack her.

It was becoming clearer and clearer to me that saving someone's life didn't make you like the person. You had to do it purely on principle.

"What if I have no choice?"

I spoke quietly, but not so quietly that they couldn't hear me. Neither of them chose to answer.

"Now that you've had your supper," said Nissyen, "how about I tell you a story?"

"Tell us a voyage story, Nissyen," said Viviane, lying on her side with her head cradled on her hands. She looked and sounded so young that I forgot for a moment how much she got on my nerves.

Nissyen began to half-speak, half-sing the tale of a king who sails to the West. On this voyage the king meets my father, Manannán mac Lir, riding in his two-wheeled chariot over the sea. My father describes Magh Mell, the

Plain of Delight, lying just beneath the prow of the king's skiff, beneath the curl of the wave. On Magh Mell of the many flowers, speckled salmon frisk like lambs, and trees laden with beautiful fruit crown the ridges. The longer Nissyen sings, the deeper I sink. Soon I am drifting through my father's land on a slow current of dream. High above me, golden sheep graze on broad, green swells.

∾

My first thought when I woke at dawn the next day was that I'd missed the second night of Esus's ordeal. Missed it entirely. I hadn't even dreamed of him. The second day of confinement under the Crows' wings was far worse than the first. I had recovered my strength, and I knew I was running out of time. Although we were now allowed out of the hut, the beady eye of a Crow was on us at all times. Then, unexpectedly, my chance came.

It was the night of the full moon, the last night of the festivities. At Llanddywn Bay, there was to be an enormous women's rite attended by a full complement of Crows along with all the queens and female tribal leaders, of whom there were a great many. Viviane was feeling well enough to be quite put out when the Crows informed us that we were to stay behind. I protested along with her, so that no one would suspect how relieved I was not to be taking a seven mile hike in the opposite direction of Bryn Celli Ddu.

I tried as subtly as possible, which was not very, to find out from Nissyen what the men would be up to while the women met alone.

"What do you think? They'll be drinking and fighting each other over the hero's cut of meat. When they're too drunk to stand, the bards will sing to them while they snore. Then, when everyone's bored with that, whoever is still on his feet will go spy on the women. What else?"

"What about the secret rite at Bryn Celli Ddu?"

"And who told you anything about that?" he asked sharply.

"Why, you mentioned it only yesterday, Nissyen."

"Did I? Well, don't fret yourself about the Stranger, if that's what you're doing. It will all be over tomorrow morning at dawn. He'll rise with the sun."

And I'll be there to greet him, I didn't say, though I still didn't know how I'd manage it. I was sure the Crows would not leave Viviane and me unguarded. Nor did they.

We were left in the keeping of a Crow of great antiquity, one of the ones who had come from Holy Island for the festival. She was no happier than we were about being stuck at Caer Leb. In fact, she was in a decidedly foul temper.

"Might as well watch the bloody moonrise," she muttered. "Come along, you two."

We all went to sit on the earth wall surrounding the caer. When you look towards the Menai Straits to the Snowdonia range, you face southeast. You can watch the moon rise and roll across the sky over the mountains. The light plays with the range, a ridge turns silver; a ravine is cast into shadow. When the light hits a rocky peak just right, it shines.

"Not a bad view," the Crow conceded grudgingly. "Though certainly not as fine as ours on Holy Head. From *there*, you can see the whole world."

She spoke with great authority, then took another swig from a flask of wine she did not seem inclined to share. I studied her profile. Her black hood kept her face in shadow, except for a distinctly beak-like nose that gleamed in the moonlight. She could not have looked more like a crow and still remained human.

On the other side of the Crow sat Viviane. She was not looking at the view at all but resting her face on her updrawn knees. All I could see was a solid wall of moon-struck orange hair. It occurred to me that there must have been a full moon when she and Ciaran made that life that was already over. I thought she must be remembering. I felt an unaccustomed urge to comfort her, but the Crow sat between us blocking any direct communication.

"If only they'd listened to me, none of this ever would have happened," the old Crow muttered. "Sex education. They don't even know what it means. What good is tell without show? If they'd let me, *I* could have shown them. But does anyone listen to me? No, they think I'm a crackpot. Now they're sorry. Now everyone's sorry. Worra, worra. You'd think I'd get more respect. Respect for elders. All talk, no action. No one listens to old Murna anymore. But believe you me, when it comes to friendship of the thighs, I could teach the druids a thing or three. All that schooling and most of 'em still have their heads up their ass. But do they come to me? No. They think I'm a shriveled old crone. Them and their damn votive wells they keep cramming with all kinds of junk. They don't know what a sacred spring really *is*, let alone where to find one. But then, they don't know much. I swear they wouldn't know Anu, if she sat on their face."

There didn't seem to be any call for response or any pause in the flow of her speech. In fact, old Murna was so absorbed in her grievance that I began to hope that she might not notice if I got up and slipped away.

"And do they listen now? Now that I've been proved right? No. They leave me guarding the girl. What good is that, now the damage is done? Said they wanted to spare my legs the walk to the straits. Spare my legs! Haven't I just walked here from Holy Head? Well, maybe I didn't walk all the way, but there's no law against that. Spare my legs! They're all too young. They don't remember. These thighs have held kings and warriors in their grip. The marrow of my bones is made of pure moonlight. When the moon is full, my bones remember the feeling of a fine stallion between my legs. Up then. There's no need for me here. I know my way to where the sea rushes in and licks the shore. It's not far as the crow flies."

Using our shoulders to hoist herself to her feet, the Crow began to walk down the embankment. The full moon can play tricks on your eyes, it's true, but I swear before she'd gone more than a few steps, the flapping of her black robe became the flapping of wings, and she flew off over the hedgerows towards the straits, her shadow gliding over the silver grass. Viviane and I stared after her. Then, turning our heads at the same moment, we stared at each other.

"Do you think we ought to go after her?" Viviane asked.

"No," I said, barely able to contain myself. "She was supposed to watch us. Not the other way around. Viviane—" I hesitated. Could I tell her? Could I trust her? No, I decided. She might try to stop me. And if she knew what I intended and didn't stop me, she could end up in more trouble on my account.

"What?"

"Nothing. I'm just tired, that's all." I forced a yawn. "Maybe we should go to sleep now." I couldn't think of any other way to rid myself of her as a witness.

Viviane looked at me, as if I were nuts. If she wasn't so absorbed in her own brooding, she might have been suspicious. As it was, she quickly lost interest in me.

"I couldn't possibly sleep anymore," she said. "But don't let me keep you up. No offense, Maeve, but I could use some time alone."

"All right then."

As I got to my feet, I touched her lightly on the shoulder, a small gesture of comfort I had wanted to give. She looked up at me, surprised.

"Goodnight, Maeve," she said. Then she turned her face to the moon's.

Yes, she was lovely, I admitted to myself, perhaps out of gratitude that she was making my last-minute escape so effortless. Hurrying to the Crow's hut, I bunched up some blankets to make my pallet look occupied at a glance. I was already well fed and cloaked.

At last! I exulted, as I scrambled down the other side of the Caer Leb's embankment towards Afon Braint. At last, there was nothing and no one between Esus and me.

30

WATCH

A **moon-flooded field is all very fine.** Moonlit water is lovely. In the open, moonlight looks like what it is. Moonlight filtered through thick leaves is another matter altogether. You lose all perception of mass and depth, all sense of direction. A patch of moonlight becomes a solid, glowing entity; the huge oak beside it, a mass of emptiness.

I knew, of course, when I crossed the invisible boundary into the precinct of the forbidden. Not only did I feel a tremor, like a not-so-mild electric shock, but the air around me became still and watchful. Even the Afon Braint seemed to flow more quietly, almost furtively. I had crossed the stream earlier, not wanting to risk splashing or slipping once I was in the Dark Grove. Now I walked along its left bank, peering through the trees, trusting that I would see or sense when to turn from the stream towards the mound. So disorienting was the moonlight that if it hadn't been for the water on my right I might have wandered aimlessly in circles.

I was beginning to wonder if I had walked too far and somehow missed the mound, when an owl cried so loudly and so close to me that the bones in my head vibrated. I couldn't tell at first from which side the cry had come. Then, winging so low I could feel the air fanned by its wings, the owl flew over my head. From right to left. A bad omen, very bad. But I forgot about the owl in the next moment, as, following the direction of its flight, I saw the mound through the trees.

The mound looked even more like a fallen moon by moonlight. It awed me to think that somewhere beneath that bright surface, Esus waited in the darkness. Hardly daring to let my feet touch the ground for fear I would make too much noise, I walked through the grove towards the mound. When I reached the outer earth bank surrounding the mound, I crawled on my hands and knees, then lay on my belly looking over. On its other side, the bank fell sharply to a ditch. Beyond the ditch stood a circle of stones—not very large stones, but each one had a distinct shape. Because of the way they leaned, some stones seemed intent on the mound, others watchful of any, like me, who might approach. I stayed still for a time, alert and listening for any sign of more animate guards. The night remained unbroken by any human sound.

The moon was behind me now, shining directly on the huge roundness, the lengthening shadows of the stones stretched towards it, making thick

232

bars of darkness on the silvery grass. Clearly there was no entrance on this side. I slipped into the ditch, climbed up between the stones and approached the mound. I had a strong urge to stroke its smoothness with my hands, to caress the great moon-belly that sheltered Esus. Standing with my feet at the base of it, I reached out my left hand and began trailing my fingers along its side as I walked around. When I found the entrance, I would go back among the trees and look for a hiding place that would also give me a good vantage point.

As I moved slowly towards the shadow side, I hummed to myself, to the mound, to Esus inside it. A happy little hum, and I decided that once I chose my watch, I would spend the rest of the night making a song to sing at Esus' rising. A sun song. Touching the mound, thinking about the morning to come, I was content. I knew that at last I was where I was meant to be. I was doing what I was meant to do.

Then, a harsh jangle of bells came out of nowhere, and I saw a flash of white feathers.

The owl, I think, the owl is swooping down on me. There it is: huge, as big as a man, standing before me, blocking my way. Its gold beak flashes. I shut my eyes tight. Then something seizes my ribs, and an overpowering scent envelops me. I know this smell, but I can't remember what it is. It stirs strange feelings in me. Terrified as I am, I lean into the scent. Sweat. A man's sweat. A man. I open my eyes. Inside the feathered mask, I see human eyes. The man's throat is naked; I can see his pulse pounding. Then a terrible sound tears from out of that throat and turns into words, crazy words.

"They ruined me. They ruined me. Do you hear me? Do you? Do you? Their magic, their lust destroyed me. But that wasn't enough for them. Nothing's ever enough. Is it? Is it? Is it!"

The hands grip my ribs so hard, surely my bones will shatter.

"I warned you!" he screams at me. "I warned you! But you're always taunting me, haunting me. Everywhere I go. Everywhere I look, you're there flaunting yourself at me, mocking me, making me remember. Why do you do it? Why? I warned you! I warned you!"

Then he rips off the mask. I see the face, the face I fear most in all the three worlds. My own face twisted, hideous, hating.

"See! See what they've done to me. See what you've done! Speak! Speak, you bitch. Bitch! Speak!"

I open my mouth. I can feel air straining to become sound, but no sound comes out. That's the last thing I remember clearly.

How can I tell you what happened? The images refuse to cohere. I am inside and outside of myself at the same time. Where do you want to be? Do you want to watch? Do you want to look away? Do you wish I wouldn't tell you any more? Listen. I have been too long without words. Listen.

I am being lifted through the air as if I weigh nothing, there is such strength in his fury. But when he hurls me to the ground all my weight comes back as the earth slams into me, knocking the wind out of me. He is still jabbering, but his frenzied speech is not as terrifying as his eyes. Suddenly, they roll up inside his head.

I can't see this anymore. Behind my lids the world is bright and pulsing. A spiral tunnel made of fire. Then I am not in my body anymore. There's a girl lying on the ground. A huge man heaves himself onto her, into her. Now. You. Look at the sky. See a long, jagged gash in the stars. See the full moon weeping like a great sow's tit. The spiral pulses and burns. Then I am back inside my body again. The ground is hard and cold. Something warm gushes on my thighs. I'm wetting myself, I think. I am so ashamed.

∞

I must have passed out then. The next thing I knew, someone was shaking me. I opened my eyes and saw Foxface kneeling over me, his face grey and drawn, framed by a feather head dress. I didn't remember anything then. But I remember thinking how dingy the feathers looked in that light. The sky was dull and lifeless, too. The endless grey between night and day. The air was stale and cold. I could hear drums in the distance, keeping a steady, monotonous beat.

"Get up," Foxface was urging. "Get up. You've got to get out of here if you value your life."

Did I? I wasn't sure. Besides I had come here for a reason, hadn't I? What was it?

"E-sus." My body remembered. The word rose from some deep place and formed on my lips. "Esus."

"He is none of your business," said Foxface sharply. "You should not be here. I warned you before. Get up now."

He shoved my ribs. Pain shot through me, and my head cleared a little. I managed to sit. I was here to see Esus. Wasn't I?

"Get up!" Foxface stood, then took hold of my arms and pulled me the rest of the way to my feet. "You have no business here. The Stranger is nothing to you. You are nothing to him. You are nothing to anyone. Do you understand? Nothing."

Nothing. I thought. Nothing. I stared at my feet. They were dirty and smeared with blood.

"Go," he commanded. "And never speak of this night. Never. The penalty for what you have done is death. If you speak of this night to anyone, I will see to it that the sentence is carried out. Don't deceive yourself that death would be easier than your miserable life. Not the death you would die. Pounded alive into a pit of earth. The death of slaves. The death of dishonor you deserve for desecrating this sacred place. The death of shame. Go!" He turned me from him and pushed me away. "And from now on stay out of my way. Or I might have to remember."

I walked past the mound without looking at it. It had nothing to do with me. Nothing. Somehow I found the strength to climb out of the ditch and over the embankment into the darkness of the trees. My feet took me the rest of the way. Just before the sun rose, I crept unseen into the hut and under my plaid.

I returned to unconsciousness like a baby to a mother's breast.

31

HYSTERIA

Are you feeling betrayed? Are you saying to yourself: Hey, wait a minute! I thought this story was supposed to be funny. I thought this was a *hysterical* novel (as distinct from strictly historical). Trust me, it is. But remember: hysterical doesn't just mean hysterically funny. Hysteria is derived from the Latin, which is in turn derived from the Greek, for womb. (I told you those Romans were derivative.) Hysteria was believed to be caused by disturbances in the uterus—another Greco-Roman word, same root.

According to Freud (Freud? Does she have to bring Freud into a novel set in 11 CE?), hysterics suffered because of their repressed sexual fantasies. They had those crazy notions about their fathers, remember? Or sometimes their fantasies fixated on their uncles or respectable friends of the family. And they had nightmares too terrible to remember, too absurd to be real. You're fantasizing. It's just a dream. Don't be hysterical. You're hysterical! Lie down. Take it easy. Lie down on the couch and stay there.

Contrary to the image you may have of an hysteric as a Victorian woman alternately shrieking and fainting, the symptoms of hysteria as a clinically de-fined neurosis include "a calm mental attitude" interspersed with episodes of hallucination, sleepwalking, and amnesia. It is the calm that may be mis-leading, a deadly eye-of-the-storm calm. Think of the calm as a disguise that cloaks the disturbed uterus. The womb remembers, even if the mind forgets. The womb remembers and does not forgive the disturbance of rape.

☙

For a long time after that night at Bryn Celli Ddu, which I could not remember at all, I was very calm. I somnambulated through my days and slept as though I were drugged every night. Sleepwalkers can be a danger to themselves, but I seldom left the confines of Caer Leb even on the finest autumn days. The skies were full of migrating birds. Wandering bards and warriors began seeking places to winter. People and animals scurried about gathering nuts, seeds, and berries, growing fur, weaving warm cloaks, storing fat. Amidst all the bustle, I stayed as still as I could.

When the first dark moon time came, I was sick at my stomach and passed only a little very pale, thin blood. I told the Crows that I had had my bleeding early. There had been blood, I remembered, when I was still with Viviane at the Crow's hut. I'd had a terrifying dream on the night of the full moon, and I'd woken to find I was bleeding. No wonder I'd had a nightmare. Bleeding at the full moon was a sign that I was badly off balance, out of kilter, out of sync.

The Crows took my word for it and attributed the early bleeding at the full and the pale blood at the dark to the lingering effects of strain. That was also how they explained my listlessness. I know, because I overheard them conferring with Nissyen, who, like Branwen, was alarmed at the change in me. Nissyen still had charge over the first formers, though he, too, was on probation. I was inside our hut, laboring under the stone, when the Crows and Nissyen held their conference just outside the door. Maybe Nissyen overestimated the insulating properties of the plaid around my head. Or maybe he wanted me to overhear, hoping to stir me in some way.

"Yes, Nissyen, we have noted her lackluster appearance. We are concerned. But consider, she may be going through a necessary phase, a preliminary to great change."

"Her behavior till now has been undisciplined, to put it mildly," said another Crow. "She's put the whole experiment at risk. She could not go on as she'd begun. She knows that. I'm inclined to agree that this withdrawal into herself signals a chrysalis phase."

"I don't know," sighed Nissyen. "I'd like to put it to down to an attack of good behavior, a heartfelt effort of the young reprobate to reform. The cocoon is a useful metaphor, as metaphors go. But to me she seems more like a sick horse. A high-spirited mare may need to be trained, but if she becomes docile and indifferent, you haven't gained anything, you've lost a fine horse."

"Why must men always compare women to horses?" grumbled a Crow.

"Your sister here was just comparing her to a caterpillar. Take your druthers," said Nissyen. "Any metaphor you care to choose, there's something wrong. It would take more than being put on probation to work such a drastic change in the girl."

"I don't suppose for one minute that academic probation has anything to do with it," said the Crow who had spoken first. "Are you forgetting that she pulled a young woman back from the brink of death? She is headstrong, a youthful fault, but we believe she has the makings of a potent healer."

"It is a dangerous time when the power first comes," cautioned one of the Crows. "Maeve Rhuad is untrained, untried. She had to respond instinctively, instantly to Viviane's plight. More power came through her than she was prepared to receive."

"How can that be?" objected Nissyen. "It did come to her, and she knew what to do with it. How can that be what's made her so quiet and empty?"

"Think of what happened to her as if she had been struck by lightning.

A fire raged through her. She gave herself to it and saved Viviane's life. But that doesn't mean she won't be charred and hollow inside. In our experience, the greatest healers often go through a period of life when they are sick almost to death. We believe some of them actually do die for a time. But if they survive—"

"If?" Nissyen moaned.

"—as we believe she will, then they are able to cross the boundaries of the three worlds. They can learn to open themselves at will to the fire. Maeve Rhuad may be such a one. Give her time, Nissyen."

"It seems I have nothing else to give," said Nissyen, uncomforted by the Crows.

The sadness in Nissyen's voice almost touched me. I heard it the way you might hear someone calling to you from a distance or over the sound of high surf or wind. I heard it, but I didn't fully acknowledge that I did. And anyway, it was too late for any voice to matter. After a moment I stopped listening, turned my face to the empty wind, and kept on going. Nowhere.

Branwen did not press me to tell her what was wrong. Instead she watched over me and stayed close to me in much the way an animal will who senses grief or trouble. Her devotion was silent and undemanding, and I see now that I took it so for granted that I hardly noticed it. I also took more comfort from it than I knew, especially at night when we slept curled together for warmth.

Of all the people I encountered on a daily basis at Caer Leb, Viviane was the only one who confronted me directly enough to cause a hairline crack in the bland smoothness of my calm. She intercepted me one day as I returned from one of my increasingly frequent trips to the latrines. Holding my elbow in a firm grip, she insisted we take a walk and have a private talk.

"I want to know what's eating you, Maeve."

I glanced at her. She did not look so much concerned as cranky. Once I would have snapped: what's it to you? or, mind your own business. Now I just shrugged and considered the sky, the gathering clouds fat with rain, the birds flying low seeking shelter.

"It's the Stranger, isn't it?" she persisted. "You've quarreled."

"Don't talk about him."

The words spat themselves out, sharp and stinging as sleet. I didn't know why. I just knew I could not think of him. I could not bear it.

"I will so talk about him," Viviane asserted, "whether you like it or not. Whatever happened or didn't happen between you two, I think it's time you got a grip. Don't get me wrong. I'm grateful to you for saving my life. Eternally." In fact, she sounded very cross about it. "But I am tired of the Cranes and the Crows and everyone else talking in reverent whispers about your marvelous feat and the toll it's taken on you. It's getting on my nerves, and frankly I don't believe saving my life has anything to do with why you're behaving like a deranged cow! Look at what *I've* been through." Viviane shifted effortlessly from scorn to self-righteousness. "I almost died, and everyone in the whole college knows why. Can you imagine how humiliating that is? But I'm not going to pieces over it. Life goes on. I'm not the first woman to make a fool of herself with a man, and neither are you. So just what is your problem?"

We'd reached the embankment where we'd sat that night of the full moon, the night of the dream and the blood. I didn't want to be here. I turned to go, but Viviane still had hold of my arm. She dug in her nails.

"Answer me, Maeve!"

"The Stranger has nothing to do with it." A shiver went through me. I had never called him the Stranger before. But it was true. He was. "He is nothing to me." Someone had told me that. Someone who knew. "I am nothing to him."

"Oh, really? Then why does he still go to the yews every day to wait for you? Don't kid yourself, Maeve. Everyone knew your little secret."

There was a roaring in my ears. Earthquake, tidal wave, fire burning at the root, raging underground.

"He goes there to study." Each word came out carefully, separately. "That's all. That's all he ever did."

It was calm again. I took small, cautious breaths. I didn't want to disturb the air.

"You," said Viviane, releasing my arm at last, "are even sicker than I thought."

In fact, I was sick at my stomach much of the time, not violently, but a lingering queasiness clung to me. Picture it as a ground mist, faintly green, hovering over a swamp. After awhile I grew accustomed to this condition and couldn't remember ever feeling any other way. By the same token, most people stopped remarking on my remoteness, though Nissyen continued to brood and did not take as much satisfaction as he might have in my improved academic performance. Learning by rote was easier in my somnambulant state.

Q: Where did you come from? What is your beginning?

A: I come from the great world, having my beginning in Annwn.

My responses to the catechism in Elementary Cosmology class were toneless and correct. I brought the same detached attention to the *Tales of Voyages and Frenzies* that made up the curriculum that term. Committing to memory other people's words and tales suited me just fine. According to the druids, memory is the mother of all learning. That meant she belonged in school, not wandering about at will.

As soon as the harvest was gathered and stored, the rains began. It had not been a very good harvest, I heard people say. Not long after *Lughnasad*, a freak hail storm had flattened much of the barley. Several fields of oats had inexplicably moldered, despite mostly fair weather. Though I was too cocooned in my calm to take much notice of the general concern, it crossed my mind that the Cranes and the Crows could have learned a thing or two from my mothers about climate control. Now sheets and sheets of rain billowed over the island, turning flat Mona into a sodden bog. People spent more and more time inside. The huts stank of damp wool. Experienced harpers and neophytes alike cursed as they tuned and retuned their warping instruments.

Despite the rain, I often quit the hut and sat on the embankment watching the clouds collide with the mountains. I liked to imagine myself dissolving, being taken up into air and scattered in tiny, misty droplets. Another full moon came, though thick clouds obscured it. I went through the motions of the dance with the others, but nothing in me rose to answer the moon. When dark moon time came, the skies cleared. I went out alone before the night of our blood rites and picked berries in a thicket near the straits. The birds had taken most of the berries, but I found a few, enough for what I felt compelled to do. Lifting my tunic, I crushed the berries on my thighs and smeared them with the juice.

You may be thinking: She must know, if she went to all that trouble to make it appear that her period had come on time. But if you suppose I understood my condition at any conscious level or that I was capable of making any cause and effect connections, you would be mistaken. I only knew that if I did not go through all the motions, including the involuntary ones, I would attract attention I did not want. Crows would descend on me in flocks. I would be prodded and poked and picked apart by sharp beaks and eyes. I did not think I could bear it. So I kept my secret safe, even—or especially—from myself.

The weather remained clear after the dark of moon. The new moon, slender and bright in the glowing west with the evening star as companion, troubled my calm with its loveliness. When everyone went out to greet the moon with hymns, *"Hail to thee, thou new moon, jewel of guidance in the night."* I stopped my ears with my fingers. I slept fitfully that night, rising time and again to go to the latrines. It was during my third visit to the trenches that it happened. I was squatting, vaguely amazed at the strength of my unspent stream, when I heard a voice.

"Maeve! Maeve Rhuad. It's me, Yeshua. Esus." Even in the dark, I could hear him grinning. "Got you back!"

Now you may have missed the reference to the alley in Jerusalem, but I did not. I tried to halt my flow, but I couldn't. So I let go completely and started to laugh. I laughed and laughed. Yes, hysterically. And pretty soon I was sobbing, standing there with my feet rooted on either side of the trench, the night wind drying my crotch. I might have howled, alerting the night watch and everyone in Caer Leb to my hysterics, except that Esus got to me first, braving the stench (and uncleanness!) of the trenches and pulling me to him, so that my cries were muffled in his neck. I wept and wept into that warm, pulsing place. One of his hands cupped my head and the other circled beneath my arm and held the small of my back, pressing me close.

At first my own sobs shook me so violently that I was aware of nothing other than his containing me. As I began to quiet, I noticed the heat in his hands, heat that was paradoxically cool and soothing. It was as if the softness of starlit mist flowed from his fingers into my veins, and the stars themselves with their own burning cold, sparks of it, like the bubbles in certain waters or wines when they burst in the back of your throat. As the cooling fire spread through my body, I let go and leaned my whole weight against Esus as if he were all of my mothers rolled into one.

After a time, Esus took my hand and led me away from the trenches to the embankment. On the way, we passed the night watch snoring peacefully.

"He'll wake up if any real danger threatens," Esus assured me, and I understood that the scourge of Hebrew school had struck again.

We sat down close together, looking towards the straits. The mountains looked like a wave rising against the stars, a black wave forever about to break. I was glad the moon had already set.

"Maeve, tell me what has hurt you."

Instead of answering him—I didn't know the answer—I tried to think why this conversation sounded so familiar. It was the same as trying to recall a word or name that you know you know, but it just won't come. At first you strain after it, frantically. Finally, you give up, let your mind meander. Minutes or hours later, you'll spy the word bobbing along, right on the surface.

"Oh, Maeve."

His voice was so sorrowful. I shut my eyes tight against tears, and behind my lids I saw the green light under the yews. I remembered the feel of Esus's hard skull under his springy hair, the fire of the stars pouring through my fingers. That time it was me saying: are you hurt? It was not that long ago, but that moment, indeed my whole life, seemed separated from me, left behind on the other side of some huge divide. No toss of a caber could bridge that chasm.

"I tried." I began to speak, not sure of what was coming next. "I tried to be there at Bryn Celli Ddu. I wanted to meet you on the third morning."

I stopped myself, feeling confused. Had the horrible dream been about going to Bryn Celli Ddu? I couldn't remember. It still wouldn't come clear.

"Viviane got sick. I had to help her."

My words felt heavy and furred, as if I were talking in my sleep. Maybe this was another dream, Esus being here with me. Well, if it was a dream, I would make the most of it. I leaned closer to him and breathed the scent of him, spices from another world still clung to his hair, mixing with peat smoke and salt, wet leaves.

"Then the Crows made me rest. I wanted to be there—"

"But you *were* there."

What did he mean? What did he mean? I broke into a sudden sweat, and a wave of nausea hit me.

"Somehow you were there with me, at least part of the time, inside the mound. I saw terrible things, Maeve."

I held my breath, as if that could stop everything. His words. The scream in my throat.

"You weren't there the whole time, but when it was so bad, I thought I would lose my mind, you came to me. Then," he paused, "then it was as if we changed places. I was you. You were me. I can't think of any other way to say it. I can't help wondering if that's what hurt you so badly."

I didn't answer. I was remembering that first dream, the first night. If that dream were true, then how could it be that we were nothing to each other?

"I'm ashamed," he said. "Ashamed that you took the pain for me."

"Why shouldn't I?" I blurted out. "I'm the one who placed you under a *geis*."

"No, Maeve." He put his hand on my arm. "The pain wasn't because of the *geis*. Or if it was, then the *geis* had to be pronounced. What I saw when I was inside the mound, what I saw is my life, what I'm meant to do."

"Tell me, Esus."

"I can't. I don't understand it yet. But you saw, too, didn't you? You were there. At the end."

The blasted tree. The cracked lips. The dissolving bones.

"Yes," I said. "Yes." I started to weep again.

"Is that what hurt you?" His voice was tight, almost angry. "Tell me, Maeve. I have to know what I've done to you, what I'll do."

I wanted to believe it was only that. Then everything would be clear, simple. I would die for him. Any time. Simple. But I had been called back into myself. I remembered that. I could still hear my own voice calling to him: Come back! Come back! But I hadn't been there on the third morning at Bryn Celli Ddu. I had failed. It wasn't just the Crows keeping me away. I remembered now. They had all gone away, and the old Crow had gone off in a flap. And then? And then? I saw myself walking beside the stream. An owl screeched and fanned my face with its wing. And then? Some huge chunk of that night was still missing. Without it, nothing cohered. The night lay in jagged shards.

"I don't know," I whispered. "I don't know."

"What don't you know?"

"I don't know what happened. I don't know what hurt me. I only know that you are good, and if anything bad happens to you, it's my fault. I thought I was like you. I thought we were the same." The words rushed on a torrent of tears. "You told me it wasn't true, but I didn't want to believe you. Now I know I was wrong. I saw my other face, and it was ugly, ugly, ugly!"

I covered my eyes with my hands, but I couldn't shut it out: the bird mask being ripped off, the naked hatred underneath.

It hadn't been a dream.

"Ssh, ssh." Esus put his arms around me, cradling me, murmuring the liquid, dove syllables of Hebrew.

When my sobs subsided, he stood up. For one sickening moment, I thought he was going to walk away. Instead, he took his cloak and spread it out. With gesture and touch, he guided me to lie down. Though he was gentle, my body cringed, remembering in every bone and muscle a harsher meeting with the ground. I lay rigid, staring at the sharp stars. Esus knelt so that my head was between his knees, then he placed his hands on my crown. The heat that came through his hands before had come spontaneously. Now he was deliberately opening himself to the fire—and opening me.

I closed my eyes and watched blue flame race through my every vein and capillary. I saw tight swirls and whorls of knotted muscle loosen. Light played on the sinews as if they were fluid as moving water. My bones glowed—not like the moon but like molten rock. I was that close to melting, and I didn't care. Let me be hot earth in his hands, let him make me like his god made dirt into a man.

Then he lifted his hands from my head and moving to my side began to make his way down the length of my body, touching me, not with his hands, but with their fire. I did not need to open my eyes to see where his hands floated like a bird's wings. His hands rested over my heart for a long time. I felt it grow huge and empty as a sky. No, not empty. There was the new moon and the star. I could look at them now. When his hands reached my womb, I felt a tiny flutter that made me think of hummingbird wings or a tiny spring bubbling underground.

Then his hands moved lower.

Someone was holding a burning torch, there at the crux of me. I cried out and tried to claw my way out of my body.

"Don't fight," a voice said. Esus. Esus. "Let the pain consume itself."

I had no choice. The pain exploded, so fierce and bright it obliterated all other light. Then it was over, swiftly, silently, the way a falling star comes to earth. Esus was holding onto my feet with his hands. His hands were warm, not burning, but warm, brown, human. He moved his hands to my ankles and pushed up my knees so that he could plant my soles on the ground. Then he covered my feet with his hands again.

"Come back, Maeve Rhuad," he said softly. "Come back to yourself."

I sat up slowly and looked at Esus. Behind him the sky began to brighten. It was almost morning.

"I'm here, Esus," I said.

And I was.

32

POP GOES THE HAZELNUT

All these centuries people have been arguing about his **words.** What did he really say? What did he mean? What must we believe? What must we force other people to believe? And all the while we've been arguing, not to mention torturing each other, all we really wanted was his touch. Only we don't know it. We can't allow ourselves to face the loss. The spirit is a consolation prize. We want his hands.

Love one another, he said. That's how it got written down. But love is so vague, and we have given it such monstrous meanings. This is for your own good. Whack! The snap, crackle, and pop of burned flesh and wracked bones.

Listen! It wasn't what he said that mattered, although I'll grant you, he had a way with words. He mattered; he was matter, the word made flesh. Touch one another, he should have said. Touch one another as I have touched you. It's that touch we're crying for, and we don't even know it.

His touch restored me and awakened me. I wasn't sleepwalking anymore. Now I could remember the night in Bryn Celli Ddu, though it retained its nightmare quality. No doubt, like the best and worst dreams, that night held a hidden meaning, but I couldn't crack the code.

You could argue that the clues were all there, the stage set for a disaster between me and this strange, tormented druid. If you knew the precise course of both the Titanic and the iceberg, you could have predicted that, too. Every plane crash has its logic. Unlike a plane crash, my disaster was still secret. There were no teams of investigators trying to reconstruct what had happened, what went wrong. I was my only witness. For all my prescient visions, Foxface's attack seemed to me to have come out of nowhere, the act of some angry, arbitrary god.

The memory of that night took up residence at the outskirts of my consciousness, a derelict neighborhood I didn't visit very often. Foxface had left Mona soon after *Lughnasad* to travel among the tribes, and so far he hadn't returned. Instead, Esus had come to find me. He had planted my feet on the earth. I was here, present to the present. That was enough.

Branwen and Nissyen were visibly relieved to have me back, but they didn't want to jinx it by saying anything to me directly. The Crows had noticed the change, too, but they seemed less trusting of it. Now when I went to meet Esus at the yews, I had the unshakeable feeling that I was being watched. I'd scan the sky for wings the way a sailor might watch for storm clouds. Out in the open I felt as vulnerable as a rabbit or mouse under a hawk's eye. Still, I refused to scurry and managed to saunter instead. No one had *said* I could not meet him at the yews. No one stopped me. Why did it never occur to either of us that we were being set up? We were too full of ourselves, I suppose. Too full of each other.

If I am giving the impression that, having been restored, I was unchanged, let me amend it. You can be made whole again, but it is a different, more complex whole than if you had never been broken. There are new fault lines, new weaknesses, new strengths. At the time, I did not reflect much on changes in my character; I was more intent on my body, which for reasons I did not understand, felt as though it did not quite belong to me any more. Its center of gravity had shifted subtly, throwing the rest of me off balance. And I was hungry all the time. No, hunger isn't the right word to describe the yearning I had for food, more like love longing than mere appetite. Even the simplest food, unflavored stirabout, astonished me and moved me, the beauty of it, the generosity. I particularly liked to forage and spent any free time I had picking the last berries and gathering nuts to hoard like any squirrel. Starting the day after *Samhain,* no one was allowed to pick anything.

On the day of *Samhain,* the students were given a holiday from classes. All the teachers and many of the advanced students were busy preparing for the night to come, the most important—and dangerous—night of the year. The gates were wide open between the worlds. It was all too easy to slip out of the familiar world and wander timelessly in another. The tribe needed to hold together, huddle with the cattle who would be driven from the far pastures to winter in the byres till *Beltaine.* Tonight was the night for prophesy, too. Halloween, as you call it, is a hologram. Look at it one way, you see one image; squint or blur your eyes, and you see another. To those with the seer's gift, past and future opened their vistas. Later, the tribe would gather to hear the predictions for the new year, who would marry and bear a child, who would sicken or die.

The seven female first formers (seven, like the stars in the Pleiades that would rise that night) had their own ideas. We had gone to the wood near the straits to gather hazelnuts for love divination, some complicated system— unfamiliar to me growing up on Tir na mBan—turning on whether the nut jumped, exploded, or burned in tandem with another nut. I hadn't paid too much attention. I wasn't about to trust my precious love luck to a bunch of nuts—however much wisdom they supposedly contained. I was going to eat them.

By early afternoon, having gathered more nuts than we needed, we emerged on the other side of the wood and sat down by the straits. Those wearing shoes took them off and cooled their feet in the water. It was a warm day. Summer was letting out one long, last, sweet breath before winter began to blast. It was so rare for us to have time off from our studies. None of us wanted to go back to the caer yet. It's hard to say who had the idea first, but soon we were daring and double-daring each other to go to Dwynwyn's Isle to consult the oracular eels that lived in her well. Rumor had it that these slippery creatures were the last word in love divination.

You remember Dwynwyn, dancing in the distance on the night of our full moon rites? The Crows, consistently inscrutable, had never told us anything more than her name, but we had soon discovered that she was a local legend. Before we knew it, we were laughing and shrieking as we raced each other along the shore.

Predictably, the journey was much longer than we remembered. Maybe the Crows took a more efficient route or made the trip shorter by magic. We fought our way through midge-ridden thickets, trudged endlessly over the dunes, and arrived at the beach tired and sweaty. The sea wind chilled us and the warmth of the day began to ebb. The curving shadows of Dwynwyn's Isle stretched toward us. The sandy neck joining the island to shore lay exposed. We'd be able to cross, but the tide was turning. We could hear the rush of currents meeting and crossing in the straits. We glanced at each other uneasily, but we all knew we'd come too far to turn back. Wordlessly we joined hands and went on.

Though the isle was small, it was easy to feel lost among its dips and rises. Some of the hillocks were grassy, some rocky. Late wildflowers grew in abundance, and spicy smelling sea-roses bloomed alongside the rose hips. Animals roamed free: two black goats, several spotted pigs, and some sheep with horns that looked like celtic knots. Overhead, birds wheeled and cried. We had no idea where to look for the woman and her well.

"As soon as we get to the end of the island, that's it, we're turning back no matter what," one of us said.

"We don't want to get stuck here overnight," another agreed. "Not on *Samhain*."

We all shuddered at the prospect. When we came to the island's tip, we stopped for a moment and gazed at the mountains. A few gauzy clouds settled just below their peaks as if they were shawls to keep off the evening chill.

"Let's walk back along the shore," someone said.

No one argued, and we fell into single file. No one cared about the eels or love luck anymore. We only wanted to get back to Caer Leb before night overtook us. Then, suddenly, as we rounded a rocky point, she was there. Or rather, we were the sudden ones. Clearly, she had been there forever watching the world take shape around her.

She sat on the ground, legs crossed, bare feet peeking out from beneath a tunic that was red as a fresh wound. She wore a black cloak and her hair was white as we'd remembered and so long that it pooled on the ground around her as if she sat in spilled milk or moonlight. Between her and the sea, a blackened cauldron hung suspended between three braced sticks. A fire that she prodded from time to time blazed beneath it, the flames leaping to reveal the cauldron's carvings: a confluence of fish and snakes—or were they eels?—birds and bees. Beneath the crackle of flames was another sound: the rhythmic roar of the sea washing in and out of a cave. These sounds alone—fire, water meeting earth, the wind moaning over the rocky point—were enough to put us into a trance. She didn't have to lift a finger. We would stand there forever if she wanted us to. We would dive unresisting into her pot if she commanded it or sink to all fours and graze on the sparse grass for the rest of our days.

Then without warning, she turned her head, the way an owl does, without moving any other part of her body. She fixed us with her dark eyes—or I should say eye. One eye was clear as a cold, starry night; the other veiled with a milky sheen.

"What have you brought for my pot?"

None of us had thought to bring an offering. We had only an oatcake (it had been mine) crumbled and shared between us. The eel divination required crumbs. Then I remembered the hazelnuts. I reached into my pocket and held out a handful. The others followed my lead.

"Hazelnuts!" she scowled. "What? Not a fish or a rutabaga for an old woman? Something to slide easy down the throat? I suppose you expect me to crack all those nuts, hard as they are. Hard as a young man's head, though with more wisdom inside. Hard as a young girl's heart, though with more sweetness inside. Don't give me that dewy, doe-eyed look. Of course you have hard hearts. All hearts are hard till they're broken. Then they're a bloody mess! Though not bad tasting if you cook and season them properly."

Abruptly she turned her head from us and poked at the fire again. We stood and gaped, our hard hearts pounding in our mouths, in danger of being snatched and roasted.

"Save your hazelnuts for the *Samhain* fires," she said. "Though for all the good you'll get of them you might as well stuff them up your pussies and let them pop there. Such a waste of wisdom. No one ever asks for wisdom, I've noticed. Just: what's going to happen? Will he, won't he be true to me—he," she warbled. "All depends on how frisky the eels are feeling, my dears. Yes, I know that's why you've come. I knew it was only a matter of time before you girl-druids learned the fame of my eel-infested well. I only wish the locals had thought to tell you that you're supposed to bring something substantial for the pot," she sniffed. "Perhaps they thought that went without saying. See? You're overeducated already. So busy cramming your heads you've forgotten your stomachs—or rather you've forgotten mine. You can eat your heart out forever, but it doesn't stop the hunger pangs."

Far from forgetting my stomach, I was getting hungrier by the second listening to her. The growls from my stomach rose to compete with the surf.

"I must say, the thought of eel pie is awfully tempting," Dwynwyn sighed. "But I have my living to get and a legend to perpetuate."

With an agility that belied her poor-little-old-lady act, she suddenly got to her feet, with no help from her hands, and stirred the cauldron with a long-handled ladle.

"We're sorry about having nothing for the pot," said one of us. "We could bring you something another day. But we did bring crumbs for the eels."

"Overfed little sods," she muttered. "It *is* a shame not to eat them. I'm sorry, my dears. But you won't be seeing the eels today. Never mind that you've neglected my pot, the eels are wanted at the bottomlessness today. They can't be bothered with raw girls. They have business with the Other Folk. Don't you suppose for one minute that paltry mortals have cornered the market on love trouble. Still, let me have a look at you girl-druids before I send you on your way—that is, if I do. I could turn all of you into swine," she considered. "Though it's sheep you most resemble. Good eating in that and wool besides."

Dwynwyn laid aside her ladle and approached us as we waited, standing in a semi-circle like the curve of the new moon. On this side of the island, in the shadow of the hillocks, it was already dusk. A ground mist began to rise and swirl at our feet. Even in the shadow, we could see, now that she faced us, that she was wearing a necklace of small skulls. I could feel fear emanating from the others like radiant cold. I was wary but not unduly alarmed. This woman was surely kin to the Cailleach. And after all, my mothers were prone to overstatement and partial to the preposterous. They had always taken pleasure in a well-turned insult, even if they were its object.

Perhaps Dwynwyn sensed my lack of fear. She paused in front of me.

"This one," she pronounced, "has the fire, all right, but she doesn't know what it's for. Fire in a few other places, too. Will she burn to a cinder or set the world on fire? That's always the question, isn't it?" she said to herself or whatever invisible audience she addressed. She certainly wasn't asking the girl-druids.

Then, all at once, she raised both her arms. "The rest of you, shoo! Go home! Come again another day with turnips and truffles, barley corn and cloud berries, goose liver and the balls of wild boars!"

Suddenly the air was alive with the frantic beating of wings. A small flock of birds rose into the light and disappeared over the dunes. Only Branwen and Viviane remained, one on either side of me.

"Ah," said Dwynwyn, "I see. The true friend and the true enemy. All right. Stay with her for awhile. You do her and yourselves honor. But soon you must fly away, too. There are things she must see and know and suffer alone."

There was little doubt that "she" meant me.

"Will they turn back into themselves?" I demanded. I wanted Dwynwyn to know that I was not overawed by her powers.

"Before they're halfway home," she said sadly. "Birds on the wing are such a pretty sight, don't you think? Much more uplifting than the spectacle of girls making fools of themselves."

"Why do you assume that we are going to be stupid?" Viviane was insulted.

Dwynwyn fixed Viviane with her eye. "You ask that?"

Viviane remained silent.

"Some people mend their hearts with pine pitch. There's more than one way to be stupid. Too smart for your own good is one of them. But never mind, girl-druid with the scarred, tarred heart. You have the makings of a fine *Brehon*. You will set precedents. Your judgments will shape judgments to come long after your bones have bleached and your fame has been forgotten. A word to the wise: Don't think the boy-druids know it all. Any knowledge they have worth knowing they sucked from the tit of the great sow. Be true to mother-right and you won't go wrong."

"Thank you, Mother," Viviane said with more respect and humility than I'd ever heard in her voice.

"And you, my dear." She turned to Branwen. "Your heart was broken a long time ago. And the wound, ah look!" she cried, as if she could literally see Branwen's heart. "The wound is open. It is becoming a gateway between the worlds, the mark of the poet and seer. Keep it open, brave heart. You will be sorely tempted to stuff the wound or seal it over. Yes, I know it hurts. Each beat a labor pain. But the words you birth will be passed from bard to bard to bard, a lodestar, a motherstone."

The great poet was speechess. I loved Branwen, and I have to admit that I felt jealous of her in that moment. I was not as dedicated a student as she was, but I wanted to be accounted a great poet— or, anyway, a great something. No doubt, you think my claim that I'm the cosmic twin of Jesus Christ is grandiose enough. But that's an identity, not an ambition.

Then it was my turn to have my fortune told.

"You," said Dwynwyn, putting her hands on my shoulders and breathing into my face. Her breath smelled like salt fish and roses all at once. "You, you, you precious, silly girl."

There was a mix of sorrow and exasperation in her voice. Both made me nervous. I wished she'd get to the point.

"You're going to have to live your story before you tell it. It will be a long, long, long time before anyone will believe your story even if you try to tell it. You're going to be too busy being in the thick of things to worry about that yet. You don't know the half of it. You don't know what's hit you. Should I tell her?" she asked herself.

As a soothsayer, I was finding Dwynwyn extremely unsatisfactory. Ambiguity is one thing—it's a stock in trade—but she was being downright vague.

"You told Viviane she was going to be a great *Brehon*, and you told Branwen she was going to be a great poet." I'm afraid I sounded petulant. "What about me? Aren't I going to be a great anything?"

Dwynwyn cackled. She did. There is no other word for it.

"Didn't I tell you, you have the fire?"

"Yes, but I don't know what that means."

"Of course, you don't know. No more than the stars know as they burn holes in the great cloak of night. No more than the fiery eye we call the sun. No more than wood there bursting into spark and ash. Of course you don't know. But the world around you will feel the heat. Some will love you and even want to worship you. (I'd nip that in the bud, if I were you. It's going to be a great temptation to you to allow it.) But some people are going to want to douse those flames. They'll fancy they've succeeded, but you'll keep coming back, rising like the firebird that you are. And the people who tried to quench you will be extremely angry."

"Do I have a talent for anything but fire and trouble?"

"You will be a great lover."

I thought at once of Esus. I could see him so clearly, I am sure his image showed in my eyes.

"That does not mean what you and your companions suppose," Dwynwyn cautioned. "There is not much the eels could tell you about it. It's not a matter of true or false, win or lose. It's a task, and it won't be easy. If I told you more now, you wouldn't understand."

"Try me!" I challenged.

Dwynwyn began to laugh. And laugh. None of us got the joke.

"By Anu!" She wiped her clear eye. "How well I remember. Old women always said things like that when I was a young girl. And I swore I wouldn't when my time came. Well, now I am. That's one thing you surely can't know. What a surprise it is to find yourself old and horribly wise. Well now, all right. There may be some things you do need to know, Maeve Rhuad. Yes, of course I know your name. I can read bird wings. But it's time for the other two to go."

Swiftly and gently, like a breeze turning in its sleep, she lifted her hands and two birds, bright with the last light, flew into the gloaming.

"You've chosen your friend and your enemy well," she commented. "That's a good sign."

"Viviane hardly seems like an enemy anymore."

"But you both do well to honor the antagonism between you. False friendship is dangerous, a coating of honey to conceal the poison. But now, down to business. Have those old Crows told you nothing?"

"What would they tell me?"

She sighed long and deep. I could hear the surf rush in and out of the cave.

"Sweet thing, you're going to have a baby."

33

GOD THE FATHER

Perhaps this was my cue to say, "How can that be, seeing as I know no man?" But Dwynwyn was no archangel, and this was the announcement, not the annunciation. Yet all conceptions, including the ones attended by calendars and thermometers, are miraculous. What is the vagina if not the way between the worlds? I'm sure I'm not the first woman to fall short of Mary's eloquence. Many before me and since have responded to the announcement with a single syllable.

"Huh?"

"A baby. You're going to have a baby. Near *Beltaine*, by the look of you."

I stared at her, still unable to connect this concept with myself.

"Maeve Rhuad, do you know how babies are made?"

"A god comes to a woman in the night," I said automatically.

Then I frowned, remembering that it could happen in other ways, as it had to Viviane and Ciaran. But how had it happened to me?

"If that's your story, then stick to it," said Dwynwyn. "You're going to need one soon, though with your build you may be able to hide it for another few changes of the moon. That is, if the Crows persist in looking the other way. Which god was it?"

"God?"

"Or rather which god do you want to name? Never mind who it was."

This is one problem monotheists and monogamists don't have.

"But I don't even know how it happened!" I protested. "If you're so sure I'm going to have a baby, why don't you tell me? You've been talking like you know everything that's going to happen till our bones bleach."

"I only know the general gist," she shrugged. "You have enough of the sight yourself to know that it's like the weather. Sometimes you can see a long way. Sometimes the fog rolls in, and the visibility is very poor. I can tell you're pregnant without the sight. And so could those silly Crow ladies if they weren't so busy misinterpreting the signs and looking for something more than meets the eye. That's another trouble with people who have the sight. They're so busy peering into the past and future or spying on the doings of the Other Folk, they miss what's in front of their nose.

"As to how you got into your present condition, when I try to look back I run into some very dense cloud cover, which no doubt reflects your confusion. But I can give you a hint. You conceived around the time of *Lughnasad*. Does that ring any bells?"

253

My chest tightened and felt too small for my heart which hammered as if it was desperate to escape.

"Do you remember now?"

I didn't want to open my mouth for fear that I would scream.

"I think I am beginning to understand," said Dwynwyn grimly. "Listen, Little Bright One." When she spoke my childhood name—how did she know it?—tears that I hadn't known were there spilled down my cheek. "It is not too late to send the unborn one back to the Otherworld. She will be all right there, rocking over the waves of the dark sea to the Shining Isles. She will play with moon-bright pebbles on the beach and feast on silver apples till time begins again. I know the way back. I can take your baby back. The child may have been conceived by force but no one can force you to bear it. To choose when to bear a child and when not to is Mother-right."

I had closed my eyes as Dwynwyn spoke, picturing a child rocking in her coracle, then crouching among the pebbles on the shore. For the first time, the idea that I carried life inside me became real to me. The changes in my body took on momentous meaning. I still could not quite fathom "baby." I pictured the child as a small flame burning inside the darkness of my body. I had made only the most tenuous connection between Foxface's attack and the baby Dwynwyn said was inside me. Visitation by a night god or an archangel seemed a lot more probable. The truth is, I didn't really care what had begotten this spark of life. Now it was mine. No one could take it from me.

"You said I was going to have a baby, and so I am."

Dwynwyn sighed, "That also is your mother-right. If that's what you choose, you've got some thinking to do."

"About what?"

I'm not dumb, but I was pregnant. I was at hormonal high-tide. Everything seemed elementary, elemental. Waves rolled in and out; the sun rose and set, and the moon went through its changes. People died and babies were born. Life didn't care what we thought about it. It just rip-roared through us.

"Think what it will mean if you bear this child. You may not be allowed to continue your studies."

I shrugged. "Branwen is going to be the great poet, and Viviane the great *brehon*."

"You have gifts, too," she said sharply. "And you need training, never mind if the Crows and the Cranes are the ones to do it. Of course, they may send the child out to foster and let you continue your studies."

"Send her away!" I was aghast.

"It's a common enough custom," Dwynwyn remarked.

"Not on Tir na mBan," I said.

I watched to see how those syllables acted on Dywnwyn. She just nodded thoughtfully.

"So you belong to the warrior witches of Tir na mBan. I should have guessed as much. Who do they say is your father?"

I didn't notice the carefulness of her phrasing.

"Manannán Mac Lir."

"I see. Impregnation by gods runs in the family. Well, why not? So which did you have in mind for yourself? Or will you name the man who forced you? You have the right, you know, the mother-right to accuse him."

I tried to imagine telling people—who?—that Lovernios, the v.i.d. had— what exactly? It was still unclear to me. I couldn't put together that sudden fear and pain with the lush, romantic tales my mothers had told of my own conception. It didn't make sense.

"Why do I need to name a father at all? What's the big deal about fathers? I've never even seen mine."

"The Cranes are going to want to know."

"What business is it of theirs?" I demanded.

"Get used to it. If you have a baby, it's going to be everyone's business. Surely, you know by now that the Cranes keep track of everyone's lineage."

"I wish it was Esus."

I spoke more to myself than Dwynwyn. Then I thought, maybe it is. The way he had touched me, with fire streaming through his hands, couldn't he have caused life to spring in my womb, the way spring sun calls forth the new grass from the earth and makes the buds burst into leaves?

"Esus," mused Dwynwyn. "Not the god I would have chosen for myself, but there's no accounting for tastes."

"Not Esus the god," I explained. "The one everyone calls the Stranger. Do you know who I mean?"

Dwynwyn didn't answer, just peered at me intently, her blind milky eye reflecting the late light like a small moon. For a moment I felt as though someone else stood next to me, visible only to her.

"I see," she said, without saying what she saw. "I wish he was the father, too. It would make things simpler, since no doubt people will assume he is, no matter what you say. But simple is not what your life is about."

"Are you sure he isn't?" I clung to my unlikely hope. "I thought maybe—"

"Come," Dwynwyn cut me off. "We must look in the well before the light is gone. Something about this whole business is still murky. Maybe it will come clear if we look into the bottomlessness. Between day and night, today of all days, is the best time for seeing."

For some reason I felt resistant, balky as a spooked mule.

"Come." She took my hand and pulled me along. "The water will know best what to show us. You won't need the crumbs for those little gluttons. We're way past worrying about simple love luck here."

She led me to a deep pool among the rocks. The water glowed, faintly red, reflecting the western sky—or maybe Dwynwyn's tunic. But when I stared into the depths, I saw the black bottomlessness I had seen in the well of wisdom between Bride's Breast. We waited, feathering the water's surface with our breaths. An image began to float up from the depths.

"What have we here?" muttered Dwynwyn,

A bird-mask, fox eyes. I closed my eyes. I didn't need to see this again, but I saw anyway: the mask being ripped away, my own face, grotesque, distorted, full of hatred, enough hatred to unmake the world.

"Shit!" said Dwynwyn. "A fucking druid. I might have known it. Worra, worra. And not just any druid but *that* druid. Oh, here's a pretty pot of eels. Yet, the way it happened, it would not be untrue to say it was a god. Not a very nice god, but then they often aren't. Maeve," she said. "Open your eyes. It's too late not to see. And I have a feeling there's more coming. Show some spine, girl. Be worthy of the one who named you."

For the sake of Queen Maeve the Brave, who, as I recalled, could not stomach the second sight, I opened my eyes. In the well, so clearly that I soon forgot it was only an image, I saw a hive-shaped hut. Flame-light licked the walls. A group of people knelt, their heads bent together over something. I could not see their faces, but suddenly I could hear their voices.

"I think he's too old to be trained."

"He's already been trained as something else. Just look at this torque. And he bears no weapons."

"You can tell that by his hands. He's no warrior."

The voices were familiar. Literally.

"Look, he's got a serpent's egg under his tunic."

"Shit. A fucking druid. Just our luck."

"We should let him go. Toss him back into the sea. There's other fish."

"How can we, after we wrecked his boat?"

"By the way, about that storm, who started it?"

"I don't recall that we ever reached consensus on the storm idea."

"Not to mention, nobody bothered to consult an oracle."

"Oh, come on! When was the last time we even saw a ship? When was the last time any of us had any? Myth or no myth, all of our biological clocks are ticking."

"Some a lot louder than others."

"Look, he was on *our* horizon, okay? Obviously the gods sent him to us."

"But they didn't tell us to half-drown the poor guy. That storm was a little heavy-handed, don't you think? We didn't need kindling so badly that we had to splinter the damn boat on the rocks. Honestly, Boann, what do you think we have a beach for?"

"So my aim was a little off, maybe. Like I said, it's been a long time. Why are you all being so fussy? He's here, isn't he? He's alive. And he may not be a hero, but he's got the right stuff for begetting heroes. Just take a look under his tunic."

Oohs, ahs, giggles, sharply indrawn breaths.

"Check it out, ladies. Check it out."

"Just think how happy he'll be when he wakes up," someone gushed. "Why, it'll be just like a dream come true for him!"

"Or a nightmare."

I caught a glimpse of the Cailleach staring into the pool between Bride's Breasts.

The image dissolved. Then I saw a slender man pacing a narrow beach at dawn. He was shouting into the wind. From time to time, he raised his fists, as if he were trying to pull down the whole sky. Then the sky changed color from grey dawn to bloody afterglow. The shore changed, too, lengthening out. The man's frame thickened. His hands were beseeching now. He was not shouting now but wailing.

"Holy mother!" said Dwynwyn, grabbing my arm. "This is happening now. *Now!*"

At that word, the pool went black, but the man's lamentation went on. "Quick!"

Dwynwyn grabbed my hand and, old as she was, raced with me toward the sand neck that was now almost completely submerged. There she stopped and pointed. From the shore to the west of her island, the man waded into the sea.

"There is something you must face here. You must go alone, but I will be behind you. I won't let any harm come to you. Still, be ready to fly when I say the word. Come to me again at will or need. Now, Maeve Rhuad, go to him. Go!"

Not looking at the man, I crossed the neck, thinking only how slippery the stones were, how sharp the barnacles. Cold waves licked at my bare toes. I tried to ignore the man's voice, but I couldn't. He was incanting something, roaring outraged poetry to the waves. But the sense was lost to me. The wind always moans, and the sea pounds out its grievance against the innocent shore. That was the sound of his lament.

I don't know how I knew when to stop and turn so that we were all aligned: the red rim of the vanishing sun, the man hip-deep in the sea, and me on the shore. Does destiny make invisible chalk marks on the stage? There I was, and here is what I saw:

A head on fire, a huge-chested man, with a magical crane bag flung over his shoulder, about to sink beneath the wave, to go back to Tir fo Thuinn before I'd ever seen his face or sat on his knee or heard him call me his child.

" Manannán! Mac Lir," I cried to him. "Father, my father! O my father!"

He stopped. The sun waited. I held my breath. The waves froze. Then he turned to face me, and I knew him.

This is my father.

The thought was curiously light, a leaf tossed on the wind, a splinter of wood tossed on a wave, swirling, eddying, going where some larger force willed.

This is my father.

For a moment that was all that mattered. I could forgive him any harm he'd done me, if only he'd call me daughter.

"Father!"

He stared at me, then he began to walk towards me, slowly, out of the sea. I did not feel afraid. I waited for him. He stopped some ten paces away, still ankle-deep in water. He was naked. It did not occur to me to look away.

"Father," I said again.

"What do you mean by that word?" he asked.

It took me a moment to remember that "father" could be a generic title of respect.

"I mean that you are my father."

"Who told you that?"

"No one. I just know."

"Witch." The word was not an epithet, just a statement. He was strangely calm, calmer than I had ever seen him. "How could you not be?"

"I'm at druid school now," I suggested.

"You are a witch and the daughter of witches. They stole my life from me to make yours. You are no daughter of mine."

I didn't get it. He had acknowledged me and denied me in the same breath. That's what a druid education can do for you.

"They told me Manannán Mac Lir was my father," I said to keep the conversation going.

"Then so be it. So be it. It makes a far better story." He seemed normal now, almost approachable. "It is terrible to be trapped in the wrong story. Mine was meant to take a different turn and have a different ending altogether."

"How do you know?"

"Because it's *my* story!" He seemed surprised, almost offended by the question.

"Don't you have to live the story before you tell it?" I borrowed from Dwynwyn's store of wisdom.

"There will be no telling," he said sharply. "No telling now. Now there is no story."

I thought he was being awfully picky. If what I'd seen in the well was true and he'd been shipwrecked by my mothers, what was wrong with that as a plotline for a *Voyage* story, with *Conception and Birth* thrown into the bargain? It wasn't as boring as *Cattle Raids*.

"I don't see why—" I began.

"There will be no telling," he repeated. "I wanted to make an end at last. To choose the ending, at least. Why won't they let me? But no, there you are, calling me back, back from the sea, the sea. And that's all I ever wanted, the wide, western sea and the land beyond where the sun lives. Instead it's my boat smashed on the rocks and now you. You! Calling, calling, calling."

Like the turning of the tide, the calm gave way to raving. Without having an exact word for it then, I understood that he was crazy. There was a rational Lovernios, V.I.D., expert on the Roman question, eloquent spokesman, just lawgiver. Then there was this Other, who had found his way to the Otherworld and returned not with gifts but ghost-ridden with murdered dreams.

"Look." He passed his hand over his face and seemed to recover for a moment. "Maybe it's not your fault. How could it be? You didn't mean...You couldn't know...I didn't mean.....It's not that I wouldn't be proud to have a—"

He stopped and stared fixedly at my womb where a little flame flickered and shrank from a sudden, cold blast.

"No," he said, too quietly. "No. It can't happen again. Not again. It can't go on and on. No."

I started to back away.

"There must be an ending, my little dove, don't you see?" His voice was soft, caressing. "I must make an ending, a sweet, sweet ending, don't you see?"

He kept crooning as he advanced and I backed, matching him step for step.

"Hush, hush now," he whispered, though I hadn't said a word. "Stay, just stay still. Wait now, and I'll come to you."

I hesitated, hypnotized by his voice. I *had* waited. I had waited so long for him to come to me.

It happened in a flash. Red and silver lunging at me. Huge jaws, wide as the sky.

"Fly!" a voice shouted. "Fly!"

I rose into the air, a few of my feathers fluttering below. Then I was winging through the sudden night, over dunes white as bone, by the light of the full *Samhain* moon.

34

THE NEWS OF THE YEAR IN PREVIEW

When my shape shifted again, how I got back to the confines of Caer Leb, remains a blur. Wing strokes, running strides, it was all flight, my heart, bird or human, smashing against my ribs. I have vague memories of Branwen and Viviane taking charge of me, washing and feeding me, then dressing me for the *Samhain* gathering. The other four girls hovered near. I retain the impression of being surrounded by a solid wall of female flesh. Keeping me in their midst, they bore me along to the field of the two stones where we became part of a huge crowd not only of students but cattle herders, tillers, craftsmen, as well as warriors—in short, everyone from miles and miles around.

We waited under the now high moon, our faces faintly blue in its light, for the druids to ignite the great fire. From this fire someone from every household would light a torch or take a coal to re-ignite the home hearths. So the fire of life spread from the center to the farthest reaches, like blood to each extremity, reminding us that we shared the same spark of life. We were the *Combrogos*, the companions, the people. So the archdruid assured us when he came into our midst wearing a crown of gleaming antlers. When he had paced the quarters and planted his staff at the center of the world, he gave a signal. Five masked druids brought their torches to the bonfire.

One of them was Foxface. I recognized him not only by the bird mask but by the turmoil in the air around him. My first blind impulse was to bolt. Branwen, feeling the tension in my muscles, put her arm around me. Viviane's hand closed over mine, not so much to comfort me as to have a good grip on me if I decided to do anything dumb. After a moment I realized I was safest exactly where I was.

The kindling smoked and hissed, tiny sparks jumping, rising a little high and a little higher. Then all at once, the whole thing caught. Flame leaped and licked our cold faces like a huge, eager dog. I glimpsed Esus partway across the circle with the other ovate students. He was staring into the flames intently, as if he hoped they would speak to him the way the burning bush spoke to Moses. It struck me then that Esus did not know my secret. I barely knew it. I closed my eyes and tried again to picture a baby growing inside me. But all I could see was the after-impression of the flames of the *Samhain* fire making patterns of iridescent green on my eyelids.

Then the wind hushed and the fire lowered its voice to a whisper. The druids had that relationship with the elements. They could hush the babble of the brook, and, if an earthquake wanted to happen while they were talking, they would simply say: Don't interrupt. Wait until I've finished. It was time for the New Year's predictions. Each Crane and Crow had an area of responsibility and expertise. What followed was something like an oral farmer's almanac: long-range weather forecasts for each moon of the year, which crops to plant when, which fields to rotate or keep fallow.

When practical matters had been thoroughly covered, the predictions became more personal and cryptic, things like: "Five sons will be born to the same man under the same moon." "A woman who has taken two husbands will wish she had none." The druids also gave oblique, oracular judgments on various quarrels that needed attention before the next court session. There were lots of messages from the recent and the celebrity dead. By the end of the session, it was a lot like reading *National Enquirer* headlines while you wait in line at the supermarket. In short, the predictions were, among other things, an entertainment. The carefully rehearsed show had been going on smoothly, no one missing a cue or a beat when, unbidden, an old woman came forward from the crowd.

"Disaster!" she cried. "Some disaster is hovering. I can feel it. I can feel it in my liver. I can feel it in my bunions. Stones have come rolling down from the craggy mountains beyond the straits and lodged in my gall bladder. My body is wracked as if for some monstrous birth. And as for my kidneys, not to mention my knees, they are crying out a warning, crying to be heard. Disaster!"

A Crow and a Crane descended on her, murmuring sympathetically as they escorted her from center stage. But she had succeeded in stirring the crowd's vague fears. Humans in the aggregate can become a fifth element, harder to control than the other four.

"I don't know about disaster hovering," shouted a man. "Seems to me it's already made itself right at home. What about that hailstorm that flattened the barley?"

"And what about the cattle. No one's talked about the cattle. Half of one herd was dead when we went to the far pastures."

"Yesterday a flock of birds blotted out the sun. They were moving from right to left, every one."

"What about the Romans? We heard there were Romans wintering on the Southeast coast of Cymru. How long until they're here?"

"Owls have been crying out every day at noon!"

The crowd had become a large, uneasy animal, scratching at bad omens as if they were fleas. And like fleas, bad omens begot more bad omens. Everyone now could call to mind some ominous sign or event. The druids had to find a way to soothe the beast.

"All these signs—and more that only we can detect—we note, we gather, we consider," said the archdruid, with his deep, rumbling voice that was also somehow soothing, like a mountain purring. All is well; everything is under control, his tone said. "We will take action at the precise moment that it is needed. Remember: Unripe action is as bitter as unripe fruit."

"And as bad for the bowels!" one of the Crows chimed in.

That brought everyone's mind back to the dead cattle. The archdruid stepped aside, and the Crows took over. They had performed autopsies on the cattle and had determined that the cattle had been munching Nightshade. Better a case of self-poisoning than contagious disease. Still, dead cattle, spoiled meat, things going wrong stick in people's mind, leave a stench in their nostrils. The crowd was not reassured. They were worried, and they needed something to worry about.

"These Romans to the South, people say they're merchants, but what if they're spies for the Roman army?"

"How do we know they're not planning a surprise attack?"

"Even if they are merchants, doesn't their very presence in the Holy Isles anger the gods? Look at what the Romans did in Gaul. They destroyed the great sacred grove of the Carnutes."

"The Gaulish gods have no home. Their druids are impotent. Are we next?"

No one had forgotten Esus's devastating prophecies about Mona.

"Speak to us, Lovernios! Are we in danger? Speak to us!"

"Lovernios!" The whole crowd took up the cry. "We want Lovernios!"

The archdruid nodded, and Lovernios stepped forward. For the second time that day I saw him framed by fire. He wore his hood now but some tendrils of hair escaped and caught the light, looking like flares shooting from an eclipse. He was still wearing his bird mask, though it was hard to see the details with the fire behind him and his face in shadow. I closed my eyes, but I could still feel the weight of his authority steadily increasing as the people poured their trust into him, and he absorbed it.

"To this sacred ground, Roman feet are as vile vermin."

The crowd roared agreement. I opened my eyes again. He had taken off his mask. But the face that so terrified me remained hidden. He was just a man, stern, proud, accomplished, but one of them, one of the *Combrogos*.

"We are aware of the Roman merchants, so-called, living among the Atrebates, who have become Roman clients. We are taking precautions. Each Roman is under watch. Kings loyal to the Holy Isles have warriors standing guard in the mountains."

He was soothing the people but without too many specifics, I noticed. There could be Roman spies on Mona.

"There will be no attack this winter. Winter is no time for moving armies. The great danger is that the Romans will conquer without armies, client by client, settlement by settlement. Some of our own people have forgotten that gold is not for gain but for the honor of the gods. The threat to our Holy Isles is more insidious than a foreign army. We must all be on guard—even against ourselves."

I fervently hoped he would take his own advice.

"Even now," he continued, "there may be strangers among us that we, in mistaken trust, have taken into our innermost secrets."

My heart pounded. Esus. He must mean Esus. I turned my head to look at him. My foster brother's attention hadn't budged from the fire. Was he even listening?

"And there may be those native to the Holy Isles who anger the gods with wanton trespass in places sacred to the gods."

Foxface had to mean me. I knew it, and Esus must have suspected it. He finally looked away from the fire towards Foxface.

"Just as a cowardly warrior saps the courage of his companions, so any one of us who violates the mysteries weakens the magic that protects us all."

The crowd was restless and riled. "Who?" they shouted. "Who has done these things! You must have had a seeing. Who are they? Show us! Show us! Let us give their blood to the gods. *Samhain* is the right time for sacrifice!"

"Yes!" A Crow's voice cut through the din. "Speak if you mean anything by it. Otherwise be silent. Ungrounded suspicions cause nothing but trouble."

Foxface just stood, staring. His whole face was in shadow, but I had the impression of his eyes sinking deeper into his skull, leaving huge hollows. Lovernios the v.i.d. had disappeared again.

"A child," he cried out, his voice strangled as if the words wrenched themselves from his throat against his will. "A misbegotten child of a misbegotten child will be born to the *Combrogos* this year. From this line—" He gasped and clutched at his throat, but the words would not stay inside him. "From this line will spring the last—" He began to sob. "The last one of us to stand against the Romans."

The hair stood up all over my body as I remembered Queen Maeve of Connacht's prophecy: *A great warrior queen will spring from your line.* And hadn't I glimpsed her myself in my time beneath Bride's breast? Not just seen her, but heard her battle cry. I cupped my hands over my womb, the tiny dark world where the line that would spring from me was still safely curled. For now.

The crowd was in full cry all around me. "What shall we do? Save us, Lovernios! Tell us what to do!"

Instead of answering, Foxface fell to his knees and wept into his hands. The Crows flew to attend him. The archdruid stepped forward, stretching his hands out, palms down, over the crowd. I don't know quite how he managed the illusion, if it was an illusion, but his hands seemed to grow huge, as if he could contain all of us. It was the same gesture, protective and finally futile, that I had just made.

"O my *Combrogos*," he said. "These are strange times of stirring, shifting powers. The stars predict the passing of one age and the dawning of another, but we need not fear it. We are not craven Romans, fearful of death. We are the *Combrogos*. We know that death is only a gateway between the worlds. The druids guard at the gate and gaze at the stars, unafraid."

"The stars are far away," someone cried. "They burn with cold fire. We need warm-blooded auguries in times like these. Warm human blood."

Shit! Were we going to go through this every six months? *Beltaine* and *Samhain*, the two hinges of the year. They had you coming and going, so to speak. I wanted nothing more than to go to Esus, grab his hand, and run. But I checked the impulse. To draw attention to ourselves would be tantamount to volunteering.

"It is the beginning of a quinquennial year," said the archdruid in his ruminative voice. "That is a propitious time for the Great Sacrifice. But the Great Sacrifice is a great—and I might add delicate—mystery. It is not like the sacrifice of animals—which we will make at the proper hour tonight. Nor is it like the sacrifice of captives and criminals, essential as such offerings are. For how can the earth nourish flesh and blood if the earth does not eat in turn?

"But the Great Sacrifice, the sacrifice of one who goes on behalf of the *Combrogos* to the gods, who becomes himself a god, this sacrifice cannot be arbitrarily decreed. It is a matter of watching for and recognizing certain significant signs."

"Seems to me there's been plenty of signs," someone bellowed. "What about that Stranger Lovernios talked of? We all know you druids have been teaching him your secrets. What if he betrays us all to the Romans?"

I had been waiting for that. I tensed and strained my neck to look at Esus, who had shifted position and gotten out of my direct line of vision. He didn't look as worried as he should have. He was back to flame-gazing, and if he knew that everyone was casting suspicious glances in his direction, he didn't show it.

"Yeah, what about him?" others took up the cry.

The archdruid summoned his considerable authority. His antlers seemed to lengthen. They became a forest growing over our heads. He stretched out his arms and encompassed us all. At last he spoke.

"A Stranger can be a curse from the gods or their finest gift. Either way, we cannot turn him away. He is as a *geis* laid upon us. He is a word that is pronouncing itself. We must all wait and listen. Listen. Listen."

We all held our breaths. All we could hear was the wind blowing cold sparks from the stars.

35

Sense and Sentences

I don't know about you, but I need to pause for breath. Even the best-trained bards, who could sustain a story all night, for days, even weeks at a time, took a break now and then, just to breathe for awhile without shaping air into words. They left silences for their listeners that later became the wordless stretches of white between one body of text and another. Listeners as much as storytellers need those pauses to empty the contents of the mind, to pick things up, examine, reflect, discard, or store away. That is how the story lives, becomes not just one person's but another's.

All right, you say, but we've had our chapter break. Well, just give me a moment, will you? I'm not ready to go on yet. I've just found out I'm pregnant. By my father. Who is not who I thought he was. Who has tried at least once to murder me. And who is to say he hasn't succeeded?

There's a stench of death in the air. Remember that cunt-sure little girl whose eight adoring mothers told her she was the daughter of a god? Where is she, now that she no longer has a divine, if absent, father? Where is she, now that one hard-hooved truth has trampled a whole pack of pretty stories? Where is she, now that she knows her mothers knew all along and didn't tell her? And did they also know that *he* was here when they left her motherless on Mona?

Maybe every child dies a thousand deaths. First, we're expelled from the womb, then the whole maternal world. Maybe every mother tries to create the world all over again for her child, according to her rules. Maybe every mother forgets the limits of her power. If she can create a life, why not a world? I had eight mothers playing that game competitively. Suddenly, all their stories had been broken off violently mid-sentence, participles dangling precariously over a cliff edge, not one of them substantial enough to grasp. In such a position, how do you begin to construct new sentences? Without sentences, how do you make sense? Without a story, how do you know who you are?

I had lost my mothers' stories, and my father had said: "There will be no telling. No telling now. Now there is no story." Like my mothers, he connected stories with control, and he was clearly not in control. The story had him in its grip as mercilessly as a hawk some hapless rabbit. It was tossing him about like the wreckage of his boat on the roiling seas of that fatal storm. Even as he tried to take charge again, setting that clever trap for Esus and me with carefully phrased warnings about strangers and trespassers, the story seized him and made him babble about the misbegotten child of a misbegotten child.

Now that prophecy was flapping about loose, its wings filling everyone's peripheral vision. It was only a matter of time till it settled on my head. Then everyone would know that I carried the misbegotten child. Next, they'd look for the misbegetter. I didn't need an oracle to figure that one out, though I was no more in control of this story than Foxface, maybe less. He, at least, had the protection of his public record and persona. Well, no matter whose story was unfolding (or unraveling); no matter who would (or wouldn't) live to tell it, I had to find a way to warn Esus. One thing I knew for sure (and maybe it's all anyone ever knows): When the shit hits the fan, no one goes unspattered.

Every day from that night on, I tried to get to Esus. Though no one confronted me in words, it seemed I was already under suspicion. Whenever I ventured off on my own in any direction, I soon encountered three Crows blocking my path. They didn't ask me where I was going. They didn't say that I was confined to Caer Leb. They were just there at every turn, silent and grim. Although in my spare time I rehearsed both convincing lies and defiant speeches, whenever I found myself face to face with them not a word would come out of my mouth.

Twice in my life, though one of those times might have been a dream, I had found myself flying through the air. It occurred to me that what happened willy-nilly could perhaps be willed. One day I sat out on the embankment and brought all my concentration to bear on shape-shifting. Just as I was mentally constructing myself a serviceable pair of wings, a mouse ran across my foot. I tried to get back to thinking bird, but the image of brown fur and pink scampering feet kept intruding. Then, without being quite sure how I did it, I found I was racing along on all fours. It was hard to have any sense at all of where I was from a mouse-eyed perspective. But when I sat and tried to collect my wits, I saw a gigantic fox moving towards me with terrible swiftness. I would have been mince mouse if three equally huge black birds had not swooped down to peck at the fox's eyes.

When I recovered my human form again, I was trembling all over and my tunic was soaked with pee. Seemingly out of nowhere, Crows appeared beside me. One of them handed me a hot drink.

"Don't try that again, Maeve," said one of them. Morgaine, I think.

"You don't have enough control," added another. Morgause?

"Give us a break," said Moira. "We didn't sign on to be your full-time body guards."

That was when I realized I wasn't being punished, I was being protected. It's hard to tell the difference sometimes.

After the mouse and fox incident, I gave up trying to reach Esus directly for awhile and attempted telepathy. After all, I had seen him in the well of wisdom when he was a world away. I had flown to him as a dove in the Temple of Jerusalem. Now he was only a couple of miles from me. Maybe that was the problem. The distance was not extraordinary enough. Or maybe the baby growing inside me somehow short-circuited the connection between us. In my mind I spoke to him every night, but I never felt any assurance that he had heard. Nor could I feel him reaching towards me with his mind.

Sometimes I managed to dream of him, but they weren't those lucid dreams, like the one of him at the Temple. They were ordinary dreams: jumbled, fragmented, and frustrating, as if I'd glimpsed him across a crowd and couldn't catch his attention, however frantically I waved and shouted. I must have cried in my sleep sometimes. More than once I woke to Branwen's murmured reassurance: It's all right, Maeve. It's just a dream. Just a dream. That's what I was afraid of: that this story I had been telling myself since the day I saw Esus in the pool was as flimsy as my mothers' gossamer web of lies.

Meanwhile, precious time was passing. Forget whatever philosophical notions you may have about time being an arbitrary human construct or about past, present, and future being part of one eternal moment. For all of us mortals, but especially for a pregnant one, time had a literal, organic meaning. In fact, ever since human beings stumbled upon the idea of time, they've measured it by the movement of heavenly bodies not so different from my own body. The moon waxes and wanes in shape; the sun waxes and wanes in strength. As the sun retreated further and further, my pregnancy advanced, though as Dwynwyn had noted, my husky build obscured my condition longer than a frame like Branwen's would have. Also, a tunic is a very forgiving garment, and the cloaks we wore almost constantly now covered everything. I pictured the hidden flame inside me burning brighter every day, a secret sun that would one day burst upon the world in a blaze.

Now that the berries were gone, I was faced with the problem of how to fake my menstrual blood. The way they were watching me, you could argue that the Crows had not only guessed my condition but also suspected that Foxface's prophesy resided in me. Still, they had not confronted me with their knowledge, and I had no intention of confiding in them. They were women in the collective, and since my mothers were not handy, the Crows stood in as representatives of treacherous maternal authority. Withholding trust was the only vengeance available to me.

During our bleeding times, I tried to go to the trenches when no one else was there. My old berry-stained cloths were looking less and less convincing.

One afternoon before full moon rites with the Crows, Viviane took me by surprise at the trenches. I might have heard her coming, but I was too absorbed in braving a nearby thicket of brambles. I had decided to scratch myself and smear the cloth and my thighs.

"What in the name of Anu are you doing now, Maeve!"

I whirled around, cloth in hand, one thumb already bloody, my tunic hiked up above my thighs. I experienced a rare moment of utter and complete embarrassment. With the deductive powers of what was to become one of the finest legal minds in the Holy Isles, Viviane assessed the evidence and reached a conclusion before I had time to think of a plausible lie.

"Give me the cloth," she sighed. When I hesitated, she snapped her fingers impatiently. "I'm going to help you, idiot."

Still tongue-tied, I came out of the bramble patch and handed it to her. Though her intent should have been obvious, I was nevertheless stunned by what she did next. Casually, almost contemptuously, she lifted her own tunic and pressed the cloth between her legs. She handed it back to me generously stained with her own blood. Then she dipped her fingers into the same source and came over and smeared my thighs.

"Why are you doing this for me?" I demanded ungraciously.

"You saved my life. What else?" She shrugged. "I'm not sure I've really done you a favor, though. I have to tell you, I think you're crazy to go through with this. For Bride's sake, Maeve! Dwynwyn could have helped you that day. That's why she sent the rest of us away, isn't it? Well, isn't it!"

I nodded.

"Then why in the three worlds didn't you let her take care of it for you? No." She changed her mind. "On second thought, don't tell me. I don't want to know how it happened. I don't want to know why you're being such a fool. The less I know, the better. I already know too much."

With that, she turned and stalked away.

⁜

One problem was solved—for another change of the moon or two. Would I *really* come to resemble that woman of the Atrebates who seemed eclipsed by the huge round protrusion she carried in front of her (or which dragged her after it)? Despite Dwynwyn's pronouncement, Foxface's prophecy, and the changes I'd already felt in my body, I still found the very idea of pregnancy strange. I wasn't just a person anymore. I had become a habitation, a cocoon for some unimaginable life form, a cave for some tiny, hibernating being.

As the longest night of the year drew near, we all slept more and dreamed more. On foul nights we kept to our hut and fell asleep listening to one or another of us sing or chant stories. When the nights were fine, we'd gather outside and hear older, more accomplished bards perform. Stories bled into dreams and dreams lingered longer in waking minds, working their way into poetry.

Though I didn't seem to be making any progress with telepathic communication, on each of the last three nights before the solstice I had a short, vivid dream. In the first one, the Cailleach appeared to me as a huge bear. (Don't ask me how I knew it was the Cailleach. You just know these things in dreams.) She was in her cave. With her huge claws, she scratched a series of ogham into the earth floor, but I couldn't read the inscription, no matter which way I looked at it. I begged her to tell me what she had written, but she just stared at me with her golden eyes, arresting as ever in her brown, furry bear face and just as inscrutable.

As soon as I woke up, I tried to reconstruct the ogham on the floor of the hut. I was sure if I could read them, they would reveal a vital secret. Every now and then a prickle of excitement would tell me I'd gotten one or another right, but no combination of ogham seemed to work.

I went to sleep that night willing myself to dream of the ogham again. Instead I dreamed of my womb mother, Grainne. She was sitting alone by the fire, carding wool and weeping. Her tears were more than tears. They grew bigger, heavier, colder. They mixed with sleet. The whole hut became grey and full of rain. The fire hissed, and the damp wool steamed and steamed until Grainne, the hut, and the fire all disappeared in vapor. I woke in a panic, crying over and over, "The sun is gone. The sun is gone."

"Of course it's gone. It's still night time," grumbled my hut mates. "Shut up and go back to sleep."

On the third night, the eve of the shortest day, I dreamed of Esus. He was wearing a druid's hooded robe. His eyes were so dark within the white, dark as the dark grove where he stood holding a golden sickle in his hands. In the dream, I knew he could see me, but he gave no sign of recognition. He just gazed at me, as if I were the water of a scrying pool. He looked through me, as if I were the space between two standing stones. When I tried to call out his name, my throat wouldn't open.

I woke that morning full of rage and vigor. I'd had it with dreams and visions. I made up my mind that I was going to see Esus that day. In the flesh. Nothing and no one in the three worlds was going to stop me. And although he didn't know it yet, Nissyen was going to help me.

At breakfast I sat down next to him and told him that I needed to speak with him urgently and alone. We both knew that the only way to have a private conversation was to take a walk. Under Nissyen's escort, I finally made it beyond the confines of Caer Leb Crowless. It was a cold, grey morning. Beyond the straits, the Snowdonia range was, indeed, being snowed on. Their peaks had disappeared in circling squalls. The ground on Mona was still bare and hard as bone. Our footsteps sounded sharp as the fall of hooves. Because of the cold, we walked briskly. I headed us in the general direction of Caer Idris where the ovate students lived. I was so bent on my destination, so exhilarated to be on my way that I forgot that I'd asked to talk.

"So, Maeve," Nissyen prompted. "At last."

"At last," I agreed.

"At last," he hinted again after a few more paces.

"At last?"

"At last you're going to tell me."

"Tell you what?" I stalled.

"Tell me what I already know."

"If you already know, why should I tell you?"

"Ah," he considered. "Well, you may be right at that. Not to tell, that is. Unwise speech is like a leak in a boat. Say too much and you're sunk. So we'll just turn around and say no more."

He did an about face and started back to Caer Leb. Wily old druid.

"Nissyen!"

The cold was so bitter, I could see my blast of breath on the air. He pivoted at once. Old softy.

"I need your help."

"I would gladly help you." He stood still as he spoke. "But not to get into more trouble. You don't need any help with that."

"Let's just keep walking, Nissyen. Please."

"Not too much farther." He gave in. "Have some consideration for my old bones."

"Your old bones are so tough, the Other Folk will be using them for hurley sticks."

"None of your cheek. Out with it, girl. You said you had to speak with me. *Ur*-gent-ly." He drew the word out dramatically.

"It's just this, Nissyen." I decided to come clean. "I've got to see him. Everywhere I go I'm surrounded by Crows. I don't stand a chance unless you're with me."

"Whoa, Maeve, slow down. First of all, who's him? Not that I don't have my suspicions, mind. But I might as well have them confirmed."

"Esus."

Nissyen stayed his steps and let out a long, low whistle. His exhalation turned to ice crystals in the air.

"I can't countenance it, colleen. I'm with the Crow ladies on this one.

After all, it was sneaking off to meet the stranger that got you into trouble in the first place. That makes two of you now. On my watch."

So Nissyen had already jumped to the obvious conclusion.

"No!" I spoke as forcefully as I could. My teeth had suddenly begun to chatter uncontrollably. "It's not what you think."

"Perhaps you had better tell me what it is then," Nissyen sighed.

I opened my mouth. Words rushed to my throat tumbling against each other. The Fox. Lovernios. Bryn Celli Ddu. Rape. My father. They stuck there. I did not know how to choose first one, then another to construct a sentence that might not make sense to anyone. And if it did?

"Don't tell me," Viviane had said. "I already know too much."

I looked at Nissyen standing patiently in the cold, light as the feathers of snow that were beginning to fall. Viviane was right. Anyone I told would be endangered. Nissyen, especially. However lax he was, Nissyen was a druid, a member of the college with two counts against him already. If I told him what had happened, he would be forced to choose between me and the Order that was his whole life and livelihood.

"Please just believe me, Nissyen. Esus didn't do it. But everyone will think what you just thought. I've got to warn him. Don't you see? I've got to!"

I grabbed hold of his skinny arm (to tell the truth, his bones would make better toothpicks than hurley sticks) and began dragging him forward again.

"Take it easy, Maeve! Warn him of what? Suppose everyone does think he's the one. What of it? It's all in the natural order of things. What did anyone expect," he grumbled, "what with you girls away from your mothers and your foster mothers, your grannies and your aunts? How did they think such a frail reed as I am was going to prevail against the hormonal equivalent of high tide at full moon? I ask you. Well, that's just the trouble. No one thought this so-called experiment through. If they had, they might have realized that opening the mind does not automatically close the womb. And why should it? All the orifices have their offices...."

Nissyen was off and running. His pace quickened. He was a druid all right. He liked to think out loud, to walk along with his head surrounded by a flock of words.

"But Nissyen," I interrupted, "what if it's *not* in the natural order of things?"

"Not in the natural order of things? What can you mean? You need more rest. I shouldn't have let you walk so far." As if he'd had any choice. "Come on now. We're turning around."

I planted myself. I knew I outweighed him two to one.

"What if I'm the misbegotten child who's carrying the misbegotten child?"

"You misbegotten!" he snorted. "A great, strapping, redheaded, gloriously breasted creature like you with a fine, if undisciplined, mind. You misbegotten?"

I was touched by his kind bluster, but I could tell he was uneasy.

"But if I am, or if people think I am, and if they think he...." Oh, forget complete sentences. "Anyway, I have to warn him."

"Maeve, Maeve." Nissyen stopped and took my shoulders between his hands. "If people are going to think you're the one and he's the one, then it's better for him if you keep away. Better for you both. Look at me, Maeve. Look me in the eye and tell me you don't see the sense in what I'm saying."

I did look in his eyes. They were kind and old and rheumy, tearing with the cold. Or I told myself it was only the cold. But I didn't see what he meant me to see. (Let that be warning to you. Eyes are like scrying pools and you never can be sure what someone will see in yours.) Instead, from their watery depths, a white deer swam into focus and raced across each retina. The next thing I knew, the frozen ground was ringing under my hooves as Nissyen's cries grew fainter. Huge trees rose before me and plunged into the sky. Then I found myself leaping among the oaks, my full belly swaying beneath me, each four-legged stride taking me deeper into the Dark Grove.

The once impenetrable roof of leaves had disappeared. Cold light spilled unchecked on the ground. But if it was less dark, the Dark Grove was no less forbidding and forbidden. The bare, intersecting limbs of the trees looked like ogham sticks some grim god had cast across the sky. The air retained its unnatural stillness. No winter birds sheltered in the branches; no squirrels raced from limb to limb. The only sounds came from trees contracting with cold and from the delicate (yes, delicate) fall of my hooves whispering through the dried leaves on the ground. Soon I leapt the Afon Braint and continued swiftly up the bank on the other side.

I did not think about where I was going. If it ever happens to you, you'll find that shape-shifting has its own momentum. When you're winged, you fly; when you're hooved, you run. Or at least I did until I came upon a gathering of druids and ovate students, their golden sickles casting the only warm light in the bleak grove. The grey-bearded druid held forth on the healing and mystical properties of mistletoe and why this day of all the days was the most propitious for gathering it. The students, who had their backs to me, listened intently, or so it seemed from the angle of their heads, all hooded because of the cold. No one had heard my approach, and, being a deer, I naturally froze in the presence of potential danger.

Then (who knows why?) one of the ovate students turned around and looked directly into my eyes. And I looked into his.

"Follow me." I willed him to read the words in my eyes. "Follow me."

I turned and began to lead the way, making no more sound than a bead of water detaching itself from a leaf and falling onto soft earth. The voice of the instructor droned on. Through my hooves I felt the infinitesimal trembling of the earth as he took one step away from the group, then another and another. Across the half-frozen Afon Braint, among the stillness of the oaks, I led him slowly to the edge of the Dark Grove. Once in the open, I broke into a run, glancing once over my shoulder. He followed at full speed, his hood blown back, his hair whipped by the sudden wind, fanning out from his head like the rays of a dark sun.

36

QUICKENING

When I reached the yews, I sank down and leaned back against the trunk of the tree. Under my cloak, I spread my hands over the roundness of my belly that grew larger and tauter each day. In case you're wondering, I did not think: Oh, I'm back in my human form again. I was too tired. If I thought anything at all, I thought: Good, I'm here. Just as the shade of the yews was cool in the summer, their shelter made the spot warmer in the winter. Or maybe I was just overheated from the long run in my condition. I closed my eyes and let myself drift in the brightness behind my lids.

"Maeve."

His voice. Have I told you about his voice? It could split the husk of a seed. It could make the dead want to dance. Beneath my hands, I felt a movement in my womb like the hammering of some Otherworldly smith deep in the earth. There it was again.

"You were the white doe!" His voice held both wonder and accusation. "Our form hasn't even begun to study shape-shifting. Why do you already know how to do everything?"

"Esus." I opened my eyes and a smirk spread over my face. "I'm a woman. Women are smarter."

"If you're so smart, why are you in so much trouble?"

"Who says I am?"

"You're under watch night and day."

"And you're not?"

"I seem to be able to move about freely—except when I try to see you."

"Oh, Esus. So you *have* tried."

"Sure."

He was still standing, making circles on the frozen ground with his toe, not looking at me. Why wouldn't he come and sit down next to me? Why was he making it so difficult? I was about to ask when I felt the movement inside me again, not just the faint hammering this time. Something hard and distinct sailed under my palm.

"Esus! Come here. Quick!" I shouted.

I wonder how many men over how many thousands of years have been called just like that to a woman's side. He kneels before her. She places his hands over her womb. Nothing.

"What is it?" Esus asked. "Are you ill? Do you have a canker?"

Maybe in response to his voice, it happened again: a good swift kick, then another, followed by what could only have been a half turn of a whole little body.

"What in the name of the Most High! How did you do that?"

"I didn't," I laughed. "It's the baby."

For just a moment, heartbreaking in its fleetness, we might have been any pair of lovers, awed by their miracle. Except that we weren't. Esus lifted his hands from my womb and sat back on his heels.

"How did it get in there?" he asked after a silence.

"Don't you know how babies are made?"

I knew he wasn't asking that. I knew something was wrong, but I didn't understand what it was yet. I started to feel afraid.

"Of course, I know."

His voice was as chilly as the air. I pulled my cloak closer and held myself tighter to keep from shivering.

"What I don't know is how you got with child. Who had knowledge of you?"

"Had knowledge of me?" I repeated.

In the midst of sudden bitterness, I could taste the sweetness of that phrase. Had knowledge of me. I could not connect those words with the jagged fragments of the night in Bryn Celli Ddu. Instead it called up the green-gold light of summer, Esus tracing the veins of my breast, naming them for the rivers of paradise. You, I wanted to say, only you have had knowledge of me. Now he wouldn't look at me. He sat scraping at the hard earth with a sharp rock. I stared at the lines he was making and hoped they would turn into ogham or some other clue that would tell me what to do.

"Went in unto you." He jabbed at the ground. "Does that make it plainer? Because I know it wasn't me."

No doubt you understand better than I did then how touchy men are about their girlfriends getting pregnant. How do I know it's mine? are often the first words out of a man's mouth (or in his mind) even if it couldn't possibly be anyone else's. Well, that is the question, isn't it? The one at the root of all patriarchy. How do I know it's *mine*? No matter how angry I was with my mothers, I was still virtually clueless about patriarchy. Though two millennia separate your time and his, I am sure you know more than I did then about how an upright first century Jew would regard a despoiled virgin. You are familiar with the epithet: *whore*. Things haven't changed all that much. In your time, politicians win points in the polls for proposing to punish unmarried teenaged mothers like me, not to mention our children. No father? No food.

Yet you are disappointed in him. Admit it. You wanted him to be perfect. All-wise, all-loving, all-compassionate. Hey, give the guy a break. Not that I was about to.

"I know it wasn't you." I tightened my voice to keep back the tears. "It could have been, but you were too afraid."

"That wasn't the reason. You know very well—"

"Anyway," I cut him off, waving his words away like so many gnats. "Everyone will think it's you. That's why I came to find you. To warn you. Excuse me for doing you a favor." I started to get to my feet, but it took more maneuvering than it used to.

"Why would anyone think it's me unless you say so?"

"Is that what you think I'm going to do!" I was furious now, all the more so because I had to roll to the side and get on my hands and knees before I could stand. "Don't flatter yourself!" There, I was up now, and he was still down. I could squash him like a bug. "The father of my child is no second-rate, second former who can't even figure out how to shape-shift without taking a class, who thinks he's such hot shit because he can cast a guard into a trance. The father of my child is no less than a god!"

I paused for breath and also because I had to make a quick decision about which god to name now that the god Esus was definitely out of the running. The other Esus was still sitting scratching in the dirt. I'd make him sit up and take notice.

"As a matter of fact, it was YHWH. That's right. You've never seen him. Even Moses has only seen his ass. But *I've* seen his face."

Esus was on his feet now, facing me, his face paler than I'd ever seen it. No doubt he expected a lightning bolt any minute. Or maybe the ground would gape and swallow me. Well, that was just fine with me. Let YHWH do his worst.

"Do you want to know what he looks like? Well, I'll tell you. He's a bird. A big fucking bird, that's all. With a horrible beak and talons that tear you to pieces, and—"

Suddenly I was screaming. The scream that wouldn't come out that night ripped from my throat and tore into the wind. I screamed and screamed until my whole body was nothing but sound. There was nothing else in the whole world but my voice.

Then there were arms. Someone contained me. My mother, Grainne of the golden hair, who could call the sun and hold it in her hands. The screaming air calmed. I let myself be gathered and rocked.

"Ssh," he murmured. "Ssh, ssh, my sister, my love, my dove, my undefiled."

I did not know what undefiled meant. I did not know the *Song of Songs*.

I only knew that Esus held me close even though I'd insulted his god, his precious god.

"Esus," I whispered, hoarse from screaming. "I'm sorry. It wasn't YHWH. I've never seen him. I just said that."

"Hush. I know. And I knew before that you had been badly hurt. I should have guessed what happened. I'm sorry, Maeve. I'm so sorry."

Somehow we were sitting down again. His arms were around me; my head lay against his heart.

"Esus, I want to tell you something." I waited for a moment, sorting out the words, ordering them with care. "The father of my child and my father are the same person."

I spoke into his chest, but I knew he heard me. He became very still. Incest was more horrifying to him—and to you—than it was to me. I didn't even have a word for it. I only knew that a man I wished I could have loved, hated me, wanted me and my child dead. That seemed quite bad enough.

"What are you saying, Maeve?"

"My father—"

I stopped. If I told Esus I would put him in danger. Then I realized: he was already in trouble because of me. Or would be soon. He'd better know just how serious this trouble might be. Maybe then, he'd agree to the plan that was taking shape in my mind.

"Tell me, Maeve."

"My father." I took a deep breath. "My father is the druid Lovernios."

Silence. What if he didn't believe me?

"I haven't known for very long," I went on. "I know I told you my father was Manannán Mac Lir. That's what my mothers always told me. They did not tell me the truth."

Even now the concept of lying was alien to me.

"How did you find out?"

He did believe me. I could hear it in his voice. So I told him everything, beginning with the nightmare vision I'd had beneath Bride's breast of my face turning into Lovernios's face and ending with the almost deadly encounter I'd had with him on the shore by Dwynwyn's Isle.

"But I still don't understand," I added. "Why is he so furious with my mothers and with me? I just don't get it. When King Bran hears the name Tir na mBan, he practically swoons with ecstasy. As soon as he retires, he wants to go there. To me, my mothers are just my mothers. But the way some men talk about Tir na mBan, you'd think my mothers were goddesses or something. My mothers clearly expected him to be thrilled when he woke up. Why wasn't he?"

I looked up at Esus, who was chewing his cheek the way he always did when he pondered something.

"I don't suppose Moses would have liked it either," he said at length. "King David might have. Maybe King Solomon, but I'm not so sure. Even with all his wives, seven hundred I believe, Solomon was in charge. The wives were *his*. That's the sticking point. You see, when a man goes to your mothers' island, he's theirs."

"I still don't get why that's a problem."

"It's a problem, Maeve. At least for some men it would be. Trust me on this one."

"Would it be a problem for you?"

"I don't know." He looked thoughtful. "To tell you the truth, I can hardly imagine it. I'd like to think we could work something out."

Never mind him, I suddenly realized. If my mothers took charge of Esus, it would be a problem for me.

"Well, we're not going to Tir na mBan. So don't worry about it. That's out. We've got the whole rest of the world. Where should we go first?"

"What are you talking about?"

"Us. You and me. Our escape."

"Escape?"

I sighed. How could somebody so smart be so dense?

"Esus, didn't you pay any attention to the *Samhain* prophecies? Don't you get it? I'm the misbegotten child who's going to give birth to a misbegotten child. Do you think Lovernios wants anyone to figure out that he's the misbegetter? No. So, who does that leave? Who's the Stranger that some people feel should not be initiated into druid mysteries? Who went into a frothing-at-the-mouth-falling-down trance on *Lughnasad* and went on about the Menai Straits running with blood? You may not remember what you said that day, but everyone else does. Trust me on this one."

"Wait a minute. Let me get this straight. You think that because of some garbled prophecies and some scattered hints, you and I should run away?"

I nodded vigorously.

"You can't be serious."

"Why not?" I demanded. "Don't try to tell me that you were seriously thinking of staying here for the full twenty-year course. What about your people? What about YHWH?"

"What about *your* people?" he countered. "You're not seriously thinking of running away and letting Lovernios get away with what he did to you. What about justice? What about truth?"

"Truth," I repeated.

No, I didn't say: What is truth? I just said the word, hard and sharp. Truth is a knifeblade of a word, a jagged shipwrecking rock of a word. A word that snags your cloak as you try to scramble. A word that can tear you open.

"Who would believe me?"

"Is that the measure of a truth?"

I held my head in my hands and rocked back and forth for a moment. I didn't feel equal to Esus's abstractions.

"What do any of us have but the truth, Maeve?" he persisted. "It is the one thing that can't be taken from us."

"Esus." I took my hands from my head and looked at him. "This is the truth: I want to leave here with you. Now."

"You want to let people go on believing that Lovernios is a druid paragon while you're a...."

He didn't say the word. He just shook his head. I didn't yet know words like slut. I didn't know enough to care about my reputation.

"Don't you at least want to confront him?"

"But I have confronted him, Esus. I told you. He wants me dead. And he'll want you dead, too, if you cross him."

As soon as I spoke, I knew I had lost my cause.

"I am not afraid of him. Or of anyone."

His boyish chest expanded with manly assertion. Then he turned to me, his eyes full of the sweetness and uncertainty that made his righteousness sufferable.

"Maeve, listen. I don't know what's going to happen. I don't know how long I'm going to stay. But I'm not going to run away. There is something I am meant to do here. Or to learn. I don't want to leave until I find out what it is."

I wanted to say: You came here to find me. Your task is to get me out of here alive. But I couldn't. I needed him to say it. I needed him to make it true. Truth was much more complicated than he thought. It wasn't just there waiting to be discovered and proclaimed. You had to choose it. You had to invent it.

"What could you possibly learn from a bunch of unclean, barbarian pig-eaters who worship false gods among trees and unhewn dolmen," I snarled instead. "Before you went into your little trance on *Lughnasad,* you made us out to be as bad as Romans. Slave-dealers, you called us."

"The *Keltoi* are no worse than other people. No worse than my own people."

He sounded so sad, I forgot my anger and touched his hand.

"You're right," he went on. "I'm not meant to be a druid. I can't stay here for twenty years. But the druids—not just the druids, but all your people—know things. About death. About life. Things I need to know. Things...."

His voice trailed off. He wandered into the wilderness of his own thoughts. I knew the signs. And I was left in my own wilderness, different from his. In mine there was always the sea: pounding, pounding, pounding. And a woman watching and waiting. Shit, I was born shipwrecked.

"I have no right to tell you what to do," he said, returning from wherever it was his mind had gone.

"You are telling me." I was relentless. He wanted truth? I'd give him truth. "By refusing to go with me."

He sighed. "Even if I agreed, we couldn't go on our own across those mountains in winter with neither of us knowing the way."

"Maybe I could get word to King Bran. He could help. He could send an escort."

"Maybe you could."

Maybe I could. His implication was clear. He was shifting the full weight of my destiny to me. I hated it. I preferred moral exhortation. Even unsolicited advice would be welcome. Then I could argue with him. I wanted to argue with him. Let me tell you something, Yeshua Ben Miriam. Destiny is like bread and wine. You're supposed to share it with your friends.

The baby kicked again. I put my arms around the small world in my lap and stared out across the straits. I didn't need him, I told myself fiercely. I would speak to Branwen today and ask her to send a message to her father for me. Then I realized that without Esus, I not only had no destiny but no destination. What I wanted was to go with him to his world, to sit in the sun with him eating salty, black olives and sweet figs, exotic foods that I knew only by his description. If you have ever been pregnant, you will understand that longing for this food, and knowing I could not have it brought tears to my eyes.

"Maeve, my dove."

At the tenderness in his voice, I broke down and wept.

"If you want to say the baby is mine, I won't deny it. I'll stand by you."

I turned towards him, but my tears blinded me. I felt as though I had just stumbled through some labyrinth and arrived unexpectedly at its heart.

"Esus," I managed. "What about the truth?"

"I am not abandoning the truth, and the truth will not abandon me."

"You can't save me," I found myself saying, though surely I had been asking him to do just that. "I will tell the truth. Or I will tell one of what you call my stories, but I will not name you."

"Why not!" he demanded, both peeved and relieved.

I couldn't help laughing. "Because you're not the only hero around here."

"Hero? Who said anything about being a hero?" He sounded cross. "Anyway, in your stories only warriors and kings are heroes."

"Don't forget queens," I reminded him.

"Well, druids and ovates aren't heroes. They just manipulate them. And poets just sing about them."

"If that's all you're learning at druid college, you might as well go back to Hebrew school."

I pushed him, then he pushed me and we started to tussle. Soon we were rolling around on the ground like two puppies in a litter.

"And what about you?" he teased. "Is there anything *anyone* can teach you?"

"Probably not. Anyway, I'm afraid I'll never be a great poet. That's what Dwynwyn said. Well, she didn't actually say I wouldn't, but she said Branwen would be."

"Who's Dwynwyn?"

"The old woman who lives on the island by the dunes."

"You and your old women. No wonder you know everything first. They give you the answers. You cheat!"

"I don't cheat. I just receive the wisdom they're itching to bestow."

"So did she give you any other useful information?"

"As a matter of fact, she did." I took a deep breath. "She told me I was going to be a great lover."

Sometimes you just have to wait, wait till the moment gains just the right amount of weight to fall like ripe fruit into your hand. I looked at Esus, then I looked past him at the green yew boughs reaching down to root again and again in the earth. I did not have to wait long. Soon I saw no branches, no sky. Only his eyes, dark and deep as the well of wisdom with my reflection swimming in them like the salmon. I reached up my arms and drew him down to me.

Beyond the yews a cold, stinging snow begins to fall, blown by a bitter wind. The tracks of a fox circling the yews are erased as soon as they are made.

Beneath the yews is gold and green and heat. Esus and I have gone to the Summerland of the Shining Isles. We have gone to the orchard of Tir na mBan with its impossible bloom and fruit. Then we go deeper, deep inside the fairy mound where the two snakes live. They twine around us, they rise inside us.

That night in the Dark Grove I was broken. Now I break like a wave. We break together, wave on wave pounding madly, joyously on the shore.

BOOK V

QUINQUENNIAL

37

CAUGHT IN THE WEB OF LIFE

So, how was it for you, I wonder. Do you take the it's-about-time-took-them-long-enough-to-get-to-it view? Or do you prefer to believe that I have an active fantasy life?

According to Christian orthodoxy, my foster brother was incarnate, meaning he lived his life in a mortal body and suffered death like all the rest of us. Though his conception was a little out of the ordinary, a mortal woman gave birth to him. (Never mind that she remained a virgin and was later lifted bodily to heaven. Hey, I'm not the only one with a fantasy life.) The church has always been skittish regarding his knowledge of the other mystery, the one that links life and death, the little death that makes life.

There have been rumors and speculation, but basically the church fathers come down firmly on the side of sublimation. After all, backed-up sperm can win battles and baseball games. A lifetime supply might lead to resurrection. Our Lord may have been incarnate, but he held on to his vital fluids. No begetting for the only begotten. No wife with swollen ankles. No squalling brat in soiled swaddling. No, sir. It's straight to the cross and into the tomb. After a brief tour of hell and a reprise with the apostles, it's up to the right hand of god. Then a dove (rumored to be female) descends to do all the dirty work.

I like my version better. Heretics and mystics (you know, the hysterical types) agree: He is the divine lover. His suffering has been well chronicled. Do you begrudge him a moment of joy? Do you begrudge me?

Because it is one moment we're talking about, however momentous. Maybe all moments are momentous, each one connected to all the others, each act setting the old web of life aquiver. I've noticed that the web is in vogue now as a metaphor for nonhierarchical inter-relationship. It's a healthy corrective to seeing life forms as isolated units of enlightened self-interest, just as the concept of free-wheeling atoms must have been a relief after seeing ourselves neatly stacked in hierarchical tiers somewhere between the earthworms and angels with almighty god sitting alone on top of the heap.

But don't forget: Those sticky, near-invisible threads are designed to be a trap. If life is a web, everyone is caught. You. Me. Him.

∽

After our idyll under the yew trees, I was deliriously happy. In the middle of one night, I annoyed my hut mates by sitting bolt upright and shouting aloud the P-Celtic equivalent of: Yahoo! No more *geis*! Esus had become my lover. Our lovemaking had beaten back danger and destruction to wherever it was they lurked while they waited for someone rash to invoke them. I pictured danger and destruction sulking in a hole somewhere, lamenting their lost opportunity. Nothing and no one could harm Esus or me now. We were eternally paired, hermetically sealed, forever protected by true love.

I was also enjoying the robust health and vitality that accompany the second trimester of a healthy pregnancy. I was all but impervious to the discomforts of the unusually harsh winter that held Mona in an icy vise. Ordinarily Mona's climate is mild, even in winter, with frequent thaws and an early spring. The cold that winter was so severe, people feared it must have an Otherworldy source. Some speculated that at *Samhain*, the veil between the worlds had not just thinned but torn. A wind unfriendly to humans blew through the tatters unchecked.

There was lots of illness, too, in the college and on the farmsteads. Many days classes were suspended because the Crows and Cranes were called to sickbeds. Out of desperation and to keep an eye on me, Moira—I had finally learned to distinguish her from the other Crows—took me on as her unofficial apprentice. I was pleased to be learning the arts of diagnosis and prescription that were usually taught only to ovates. I also had the chance to hone my other healing skill. At first Moira was reluctant to let me use my hands, but there were so many baffling cases that she came to rely on me more and more. Gifted herself, she taught me how to open to the fire of the stars without burning my own stores of energy. More than once on our rounds, we encountered Esus in the company of a Crane. His hands, too, were in demand. Best of all, the Cranes and Crows occasionally rewarded us for our extra labors by looking the other way when we slipped off to the yews.

So for Esus and me, the winter passed swiftly and sweetly. We worked hard, but we weren't weighted by worry. We had no families (yet) to feed. Unlike the Cranes and Crows, we had no populace holding us directly accountable for the well-being of the *Combrogos*. We slept soundly at night, unaware that our perplexed elders regarded us with increasing awe and suspicion.

Soon it was lambing time, and the sense of crisis intensified. Birth after birth went wrong, with lots of ewes and lambs lost. The ewes who survived with living young had only the scantiest of milk. Then the feast of *Imbolc* (the name means ewe's milk) dawned cold and grey, confirmation that the cosmos was seriously out of whack. As a child on Tir na mBan, I had always loved this holiday. *Imbolc* marked the quickening of the year, the first secret stirrings of green life in the softening earth, the rekindling of the Bride's sacred flame. Since the formal version of my childhood name was Bride's Flame, I had always taken the holiday personally.

Now, despite my almost unassailable sense of well-being, I felt troubled. *Imbolc*, later celebrated as St. Brigid's day or Candlemas, was a particularly female holiday, bright with flame but also sweet and rich with new milk. Snow melted on mountain breasts and mammal breasts became fountains. Bride was the inspiration of poets and smiths. She was also midwife, wet nurse, and foster mother. Now that I felt so far removed in every sense from my mothers, I needed her to be my foster mother. As I looked around on that bleak, frozen morning, Bride was nowhere in sight.

Despite the bitter weather (why, I wondered once again, were the Crows and the Cranes so inept at climate control?), the women who lived at Caer Leb gathered to begin the rites. Men would not be part of the ceremonies until later. We fashioned a Bride doll, dressed her in white, bedecked with shells and ribbons, then set her in a wicker cradle with an oak wand crowned with a shapely acorn lying across her. Singing songs of praise, we processed with her from Caer Leb towards a spring that welled in the lap of an ancient oak, both the oak and the well being sacred to Bride. On the way, we were joined by women and girls from the farmsteads and all their bony, female cattle. The maidens wore white (under their warmest cloaks) like the Bride doll. The women of childbearing age and older painted their faces with woad to honor the departing blue hag of winter. Except that she wasn't departing, and the pinched faces of the young girls looked almost as blue as the woad-painted ones.

What should have been a joyous procession was all too somber as we shivered in the cold wind, bruising our feet on the frozen hummocks of winter fields that should have been ready for the first planting. The almost-dry ewes and their spindly lambs did not have the strength to bleat back and forth to each other as they usually did. There were no new greens in the fields to encourage them. Still, we sang as loudly and bravely as we could, praising our Bride, invoking her power and protection.

> Early on Bride's morn
> Shall the serpent come from the hole.
> I will not harm the serpent
> Nor will the serpent harm me.
> This is the day of Bride.
> The Queen shall come from the mound.

When we reached the spring, all but a small hole was covered with ice. We gathered round and breathed over the water, as if we had Bride's power to breathe life into the dead. Some of the ice melted. Between songs, women spoke to Bride and importuned her to bring them safely through childbirth. They made offerings of torques and brooches to the half-frozen well. As unobtrusively as I could, I removed the brooch pin from my cloak and tossed it into the cold, dark water. I had not thought much about the actual birth of my baby. It sounded as though I was going to need all the help I could get.

At sunset (such as it was, there being no light or color) the men arrived at the spring, headed up by the Cranes. They formed an outer circle around the women's inner circle. We had been singing and offering devotion to Bride all day. Now, with the Cranes present, the ceremony suddenly became official and formal. It irked me, this presumption that a rite could not seriously begin until the druids were there. I deliberately unleashed my attention and let it wander while the archdruid sang the quarters. I couldn't see much in the gloaming, but I thought I glimpsed the red of Foxface's beard across the circle from me. And could that be Esus standing next to him?

Then one of the Crows from Holy Isle came forward with a live ember from the sacred fire the Crows tended in a cave among their cliffs. This fire was never allowed to go out and was never extinguished, even on *Samhain*. With the coal, the ancient Crow (possibly the one who had shirked guard duty on *Lughnasad*) lit the bonfire that had been prepared next to the spring. Bride's flame leaped toward the heavy, starless sky. Above a mass of dark cloaks, faces appeared, suddenly bright, glowing in the light. I was right; Esus was standing next to Foxface. Their proximity made my stomach knot. The baby, sensing my disturbance, twisted restlessly. Then Esus caught my gaze and held it. The heat from the fire felt like a cool breeze in comparison to that one look passing between us.

In spite of my preoccupation, I began to pay attention again when the old archdruid stepped into the circle again and rooted himself there. He stood until it seemed as though he had grown there like the huge oak he so resembled. Like any ancient tree, he looked storm-rocked, scarred, bereft of a branch or two after the hard winter. But he was there, his being a testimony to endurance. In the presence of that potent stillness, the crowd calmed, more than calmed. We fell into a collective trance.

At a sign so subtle it must have been no more than the flickering of an eyebrow, the crowd shifted and made way. Flanked by two Crows, a white cow with red-brown ears stepped into the circle and approached the archdruid. Like all the cattle on Mona that winter, she was gaunt and her udder looked shrivelled. Her horns had been decked with furze (the only live bloom to be found), dried heather bells, and rowan berries. Around her slack neck she wore a gold torque, specially fashioned for her, of twining snakes. No matter how much the winter had ravaged her, we knew whom she embodied.

A cry of greeting and beseeching rose from the crowd: Bride! Bride! Someone struck up a drum and we all began to sing to the docile (possibly sedated) cow as she came to stand before the druid, who greeted her ceremoniously. He bowed his head to her, then kissed her eyes and her nose. With a little help from the two Crows, he stooped and kissed her dry teats. Throughout his attentions, the cow remained calm, only flicking her tail now and again as if the archdruid were a pesky fly. When he straightened up, he came back to her head and began speaking to her in a low voice only she could hear. She appeared to pay grave attention, her head bent towards him, her tail perfectly still.

Gradually, the volume of the archdruid's voice rose so that we could all hear him addressing Bride, with consistent poetic meter, in formal Q-Celtic. He told her of the hard winter and the hard ground, the hard births and the hard, ungiving teats of the ewes and the cows. (As if she didn't know, being a cow herself at the moment.) At last he beseeched her for a sign. Tell us what is wrong, he begged her. What must the *Combrogos* do?

The old cow listened ruminatively—cows are ruminators, after all—moving her jaws in the same rhythm as the druid's speech. When he had done, she continued to chew thoughtfully for a time, apparently unmoved by all the expectation focused on her. Then slowly, serenely, she lifted her head, looking around the circle—until she locked eyes with me.

You must have looked into a cow's eyes before. You know how mild that gaze is, how benign and bemused. Bride, in her form as a white cow with red ears, looked at me that way, without urgency but steadily, leaving me in no doubt that she had a message, and the message was for me. Despite Bride's reputation as a poet, she did not speak in words. She sent images to my mind. I saw the bleak, grey cloud that had covered Mona all winter, the high, unyielding cloud that doesn't temper the cold but seals it in. Then I saw beyond the cloud cover to the clear, shining, near-full moon. That image dissolved, and I saw myself from the outside, as if I were someone else. I saw myself cloaked and concealed in my heavy, grey cloak. Just as I had seen beyond the clouds before, I saw though my garments to the round, glowing moon underneath. All the while these images came and went, I saw her eyes—the cow's, Bride's. The reflection of flame flickered in their depth.

I don't know how to describe what happened next, except to say that Bride communicated her whole nature to me: the divine and the bovine. I was myself, Maeve, fifteen-year-old girl, six months pregnant, and I was also the goddess. We had been singing to Bride and calling her all day. Now she was here, if I would let her be. That's what she asked of me, the mild-eyed, starving cow. I stepped into the circle. The cow, already looking in my direction, turned fully toward me. Just as on the day of the caber toss, my awareness narrowed and intensified. I could not hear the murmuring of the crowd or the sharp admonishments of Crows or Cranes. All human emotion was a flickering of energy on the periphery like silent heat lightning. I undid the knot of thorn that had fastened my cloak since I'd tossed my brooch into the spring. A droplet of blood appeared on my thumb, but I felt no pain. Then I reached for the hem of my tunic and pulled it over my head. It joined the cloak on the ground, a layer of green over the grey.

The holy cow gave a long, low moo, tossed her garlanded head and retreated into the crowd. The archdruid and the Crows backed away from me, perhaps inadvertently. There I stood, in the center of the circle, naked. All around me, there was what you might call a willing suspension of disbelief. Yes, think of me as a suspension bridge, spanning a great chasm, holding the tension of the moment in balance. Or think of me as one glistening thread of the web, suddenly illuminated, making the pattern visible for an instant. No one spoke, no one made a move to stop me. For an instant, I could do whatever I wanted—or rather whatever was wanted in that moment, by that moment.

I just stood for a time with the firelight playing over my body. I gazed at my breasts. They were fuller than ever, their blue veins matching the blue at the base of the flames. The nipples had the almost golden cast of bare mountain tops at sunrise. Round as my breasts were, my belly now was rounder. I could see its full-moon curve rising over their peaks. With the cold of winter and the necessity for concealment, I'd scarcely had a chance simply to marvel at myself. Now I did. Never mind that I was standing in the midst of several hundred people. Slowly I turned in a circle, looking at my belly in all lights and angles. As I turned, a fresh wind began to blow, a soft, warm wind. It smelled of wet earth. It bore the scent of blossom and fruit from the magical orchard of Tir na mBan. I recognized, too, the spicy smell of the Temple gardens where I had been a dove in Anna's hand.

Gently, the wind pushed the clouds aside. Overhead, the almost full moon echoed the curve of my belly. The *Combrogos* began to weep.

At the sound, my breasts tingled and burned the way my hands do when the fire of the stars pours through them, and my nipples began to spray a fountain of golden milk. Then, you might say, all heaven broke loose. The cows lowed and the sheep bleated loudly. A cry went up from the crowd.

"The ewes are in milk! The ewes are in milk!" And then someone shouted: "The snakes are awake. The snakes are awake!"

From the rocks around the spring, two snakes emerged, coiling and uncoiling and began gliding in my direction. When they reached my feet and began to twine themselves round my ankles, the crowd went crazy.

"Bride! Bride herself!"

They began to surge towards me, a huge wave of human passion that threatened to take me under or sweep me out to sea, far, far beyond my depth. It is dangerous to be adored. It can be fatal. The Cranes and the Crows acted quickly and no doubt saved my life. Linking arms, they surrounded me, a black and white barrier reef, and stood fast till the ecstasy began to ebb.

"My *Combrogos!*" said the archdruid, holding out his staff, then rooting it again. "As Bride is the goddess of the hearth's flame, go home now and celebrate her with laughter and song, with cakes and ale. Then rise up early tomorrow to sow the first seeds in the ready ground. Let the earth quicken. That is what Bride desires of you. That is why she appeared to you in this guise. To your hearths now, all."

When the last of the crowd had wafted away, like the last wisp of cloud or smoke, the Cranes and the Crows, who had been facing outward, dropped their arms as one and turned in on me. Then they linked arms again.

I was caught.

38

WHO'S THE FATHER?

"**N**o one can say that our Maeve lacks dramatic flair!" someone said. "What timing! What an entrance!"

It was Nissyen. As soon as I recognized his voice, something snapped or I snapped out of it, you might say. Suddenly, I was no longer the embodiment of a divine force. I was merely myself, Maeve, a first former on academic probation, standing naked in front of the entire faculty of the college. Now, the *Keltoi* were not overly modest. You wouldn't find them scrambling for fig leaves (even supposing fig trees were indigenous). Woad-painted warriors often rode naked into battle. But even so, appearing naked and pregnant in front of a host of robed authority figures does put one at something of a disadvantage. You may wonder why I did not put on my tunic or cloak. But think about it. I was surrounded. To pick up my clothes I would have had to bend over or squat, positions that would have exposed me even more. The Crows must have sensed my dilemma. One of them retrieved my tunic and gestured for me to lift my arms over my head and another Crane held out my cloak.

"Wait!" commanded the archdruid. "Do not cover her yet."

"But she'll catch her death of cold," objected a Crow.

"I think not," said the druid.

Indeed the air was warm, even balmy. The snakes continued to luxuriate around my ankles. Divinity had not altogether abandoned me.

"Haven't we seen all there is to see?" snapped the Crow who held my cloak.

Without waiting for permission, she put the cloak around my shoulders. (Let me tell you, the expression "cover your ass" is not an empty one.) Now most of me was modestly draped. Only my belly protruded, and, of course, that was the part of me under scrutiny.

"Between six and seven changes of the moon, wouldn't you say?" The archdruid deferred to the Crows' expertise.

"About that," agreed a Crow, grudgingly.

"That would put the conception in the vicinity of *Lughnasad*, would it not?" They could count well enough, those druids. "Is it just my imagination or do my colleagues agree that it was about that time when we began having a rash of freak storms and accidents culminating in this extraordinarily harsh winter?"

"She is the misbegotten one."

I started so when I heard Foxface's voice that one of the snakes nipped my ankle in protest. He was to the right in my peripheral vision. I could easily have turned my head to look at him, but I had the instinct of prey in the presence of the predator. I couldn't bolt, and I was vastly outnumbered, so I stilled myself. I scarcely even breathed.

"Lovernios," the archdruid acknowledged him. "Would you care to expand this theme?"

"She is the misbegotten child who will give birth to the misbegotten child."

"I am sure everyone here remembers the *Samhain* prophecy. Can you tell us more, now that this young woman stands before us? Let's begin at the beginning. We are told she is the daughter of a god. In what manner was she misbegotten? Treachery? Deceit? Violence?"

"Treachery. Deceit. Violence. All three."

"Are you saying Manannán Mac Lir suffered these or perpetrated them?"

Foxface didn't answer. I risked a glance at him. He wore that look of confusion I had seen so many times before. I realized he couldn't remember what he had just said.

"Who are we to understand the ways of the gods?" he managed at last. He was not called the Fox for nothing.

"Pardon me, but could we get to the point?" My mentor Crow, Moira, butted in.

"Which is?" The archdruid's voice was mild and unhurried. It reminded me of the cow's eyes.

"The girl is pregnant, and she's a first former. We have to decide what to do about her and the child. The college does not have a clear policy, which was sheer foolishness on our part. This was bound to happen sooner or later."

"What you say is true," soothed the archdruid. "And these practical matters shall be addressed in due season. We are concerned here with the larger aspects—or shall we say dimensions—of this pregnancy."

"For women, childbearing is first and foremost a practical matter," said another of the resident Crows, Morgaine, I believe. "In fact, it's practically the only thing that does matter, when you come right down to it. The rest is mostly wind."

"An essential element, though a changeable one," the archdruid murmured.

The mention of wind reminded everyone of the ill wind that had moaned all winter—until I stepped into the circle and stripped.

"If I might be permitted to rephrase my concern," resumed the archdruid. "Whatever we decide regarding her status at college and the fostering of the infant, we must take into account the *Samhain* prophecy. We cannot ignore the evidence of Otherworldly interest and influence in this case. We know that six months of ominous omens and misfortunes have coincided with this pregnancy. And tonight—"

"Tonight she brought Bride to us!" declared Moira. "The ewes are in milk and the air is soft and sweet as a baby's breath. Mark you, Maeve Rhuad is under Bride's protection."

"That is certainly one possible interpretation of tonight's events. But then why the preceding woes?"

"Because she was forced to conceal her condition! Because we all refused to see what was under our noses," Nissyen burst into speech. "When she bared her lovely belly, the clouds blew away and the waxing moon shone down on us all. Can't you see? It was the concealment that was all wrong."

"Which brings us to a critical question," said the archdruid. "*Why* was she hiding?"

You may have noticed that it hadn't occurred to anyone to ask me anything. For the moment, I was just as glad.

"Surely that's obvious," said another Crow, Morgause, I think. "She was afraid of losing her place in college."

Slowly, with an air of regret, the archdruid shook his head. "I think we must probe more deeply than that."

I didn't care for his turn of phrase. I placed my hands protectively over those parts most vulnerable to probing.

"For instance, leaving intact the veil of mystery surrounding her own begetting, we still might wish to inquire about the begetting—or misbegetting—of the child she now carries. We must consider the possibility that this concealment of her condition might have arisen from a mistaken wish to protect the misbegetter. Given her youth and inexperience, she may not have understood that hiding such a deed could put the whole college, indeed all the *Combrogos*, in danger."

"We don't know that for certain," said Moira sharply. "We don't know that she has anything to do with the hard winter."

"And yet as you yourself pointed out, the revelation of her condition has broken winter's hold—at least for the moment."

No one spoke for a time. The wind blew softly; the pores of our tight, winter skin opening to drink in the sweet moisture in the air. I gazed down at my belly, almost forgetting my predicament as I watched it ripple and heave with the baby's movements.

"Young woman," the archdruid addressed me at last. "You who are called Maeve Rhuad, you who claim to be the daughter of the god Manannán Mac Lir, I charge you, entrust us with your knowledge. We seek only what is best for the *Combrogos*. As must you."

Even though, I added to myself, what's best for the *Combrogos* might not be best at all for me. Entrust us with your knowledge, he said. I thought of Esus asking: who has had knowledge of you? Now the Cranes and the Crows wanted knowledge of me. Or they thought they did. Would they, if I told them the truth?

I looked up and met the archdruid's eyes, so like the cow's in their insistent patience. I glanced at the Crows' faces. They seemed more human tonight, as if their rock-like countenance had been shaken by some earthquake and settled into softer lines. There was Nissyen, his thistledown hair awash on the breeze. Above me, hovering, not quite visible, I sensed my own dove form.

"She does not remember." Foxface spoke with authority. "She cannot speak, because she cannot remember an event too strange for words, just as Arianrod could not name the father of Dylan and Lleu."

I flew, not away into the night, but into a rage. The dove was in my heart, wings beating madly against my ribs. My throat constricted. Then, suddenly, it opened. I gave a cry that rang in the hollow of every bone.

"You!" I rounded to face him. I seized his gaze and held it. "You will not take my voice from me. You will not take my words from me. You—"

Talk about a sense of timing, good or bad I'll never know. Just when I had the spotlight, just when I was about to speak the unspeakable, Foxface shifted his gaze and pointed beyond me.

"Behold the man."

Like everyone else, I turned to look. O shit. Esus.

"No," I shouted. "It's not him."

Esus, my lover, my brother, my cosmic other turned to me with that sweet, secret smile of his and spoke to me alone.

"Who else am I, Maeve, if not myself? I am that I am."

"Esus," I said severely. I was the only one who knew enough of Jewish theology to be shocked. "That is blasphemous."

I spoke in Aramaic. The closest Celtic translation would have been: you've broken a *geis*. The situation was dicey enough already without introducing an extraneous theme.

"Since when are you worried about blasphemy?" Esus laughed. We were both a little punch drunk.

"Anu knows YHWH is not my god, but I don't think you should risk offending him right now. What are you doing here anyway?"

"I'm standing with you. I told you I would. You could try being a little appreciative."

"You see," said Foxface. "They speak together in a secret tongue."

"It takes more than talk," said a Crow tartly.

"Esus is not the father," I said in plain P-Celtic.

My words were lost as Esus sprang in front of me, planting himself between me and Foxface, shielding me with his body.

"There is danger to her here," he informed the archdruid.

"There is danger to us all," said the archdruid gravely. "Tell me, Esus ab Joseph of the interminable lineage, stranger from a strange land, foreteller of disasters, if you are not the father of the child Maeve Rhuad carries—and I must tell you, I am not yet satisfied on that point—why are you here? Why do you protect her body with your own? What is the nature of your bond with her?"

Esus didn't answer. I wished I could see his face, but he was standing in front of me. He was not much taller than me. I could easily peer over his shoulder to catch a glimpse of Foxface whose eyes were guarded, his expression carefully controlled.

"Are you under some *geis*, that you refuse to answer me?"

"As a matter of fact, I am under a *geis*," he said thoughtfully.

I pinched his arm. "You are not under a *geis* to tell anyone about the *geis*," I hissed in Aramaic, except for the word *geis*, which no doubt all pricked ears picked up. "Besides, you're a Jew. No *geis* need apply."

"Or I was under a *geis*," he continued. "Does a *geis* become moot once you've honored its terms?" He sounded genuinely interested in this fine point.

I pinched him again, harder.

"Well, now, that all depends." The archdruid was quite willing to take off on a technical tangent. "Often a *geis* is a chronic condition. For example—"

It was the Temple of Jerusalem all over again. I thought longingly of my dove form. A druid's hood is not the same as a yarmulke, but I felt confident that I could spatter one just as thoroughly.

"I see no point in discussing *geasa* in the abstract," a Crow cut in, Morgaine, I think, "unless the stranger's *geis* has a bearing on this case, which is, may I remind you, the pregnancy of Maeve Rhuad."

"And its effects on the general population, not to mention the prevailing weather conditions," added the archdruid.

"Putative effects," insisted Moira.

"Whatever," said the archdruid, showing his first sign of impatience. "Esus ab Joseph, I charge you, tell us what you know of this case."

"You are not telling about the goddamned *geis*," I muttered in Aramaic.

"Maeve, my dove, if we tell the whole truth, we are invulnerable."

"That is such bird crap, Esus. Besides, what is truth?" Okay, I did say it. "The truth, as I recall it, is that you forgot all about the *geis* when we finally did it that day under the yew trees. What is the point of bringing up how I tried to force you to be my lover? Can't you see they're trying to pin this pregnancy on you?"

"Well, what if they do? What if they don't believe me? Where's the harm in that now? The hard winter is over. You may not believe in him, but YHWH has shown his favor to you by vouchsafing you a miracle, Maeve."

"You can't be serious!"

"Maeve Rhuad, Esus ab Joseph. Speak to us all in our common language."

"Esus is not the father of my child," I said again.

"Are you saying that you have not been lovers, that you have made no ill-advised, premature practice of sex magic?"

I thought of how we had made summer come in the dead of winter.

"They have been seen together under the yews," said Lovernios, his face expressionless.

"Have...been...seen?" the archdruid repeated, stressing each word.

"I myself have seen them," Foxface amended.

"Do you deny that you have held lovers' trysts under the yews?" the archdruid asked us.

"No," said Esus.

"But we were never lovers until the shortest day of the year!" I cried out. "At *Lughnasad* Esus ab Joseph was sealed in Bryn Celli Ddu."

The druid's mild gaze sharpened. No doubt he was remembering what Lovernios had said on *Samhain* about people who angered the gods with wanton trespass in sacred places.

"Well then," the archdruid said smoothly, "supposing what you say is true and putting aside—for the moment—the matter of how you came to be in possession of information no initiate is permitted to divulge, then tell us, Maeve Rhuad, tell us truly, who is the father of your child?"

I stepped out from behind Esus. As I stood face to face with Lovernios, I started to shake. Holding myself as still as I could, I looked at him, trying to fix in my mind who he was: fox, druid, bird of prey. Beyond all his changeableness was the face I had glimpsed beneath Bride's breast, the face that was mine and not mine. I saw this face not as a distorted reflection of my own but as another version, another telling of the same story. Another truth. Silently I pleaded with him: Go on, speak. Tell your story. But he just stood very still, looking past me at something no one else could see.

"Maeve Rhuad," the archdruid prompted. "You will name the father of your child."

"He is," I whispered.

"Who is? Speak up."

Lovernios's face swam before my eyes. I felt the dark waters close over my head as I sank down to the land beneath the wave where my father lived.

"My father is the father." I spoke slowly, my words swimming through fathoms of water to reach the surface.

"The child is raving!" said a Crow. "The strain has been too much for her. We should never have kept her standing under question. Look, she's about to swoon."

I was swaying in the cold, cold undersea currents, but Esus held me fast. The night air was warm, but he was warmth itself, the warmth of the sun, of the earth steeped in sun. He was the dry land. As long as I was rooted in him, the angry riptide could not carry me away.

"In my own country of Galilee there was once a wise and learned man, a rabbi, a great teacher whom everyone respected." Esus began to speak.

My head cleared a little, of necessity. What was he up to? I opened my eyes, which I had not realized till then I had closed. Foxface was paying close attention to Esus. Everyone was.

"Whenever this rabbi went out of his house to teach in the square or to pray in the synagogue, all the people would cry: There goes a righteous man. The rabbi was particularly revered by the young men and warriors who were trying to free the holy city of Jerusalem from the domination of Rome. Whenever he was not at home, he would travel from village to village preaching against the Roman occupation and encouraging the people to do whatever they could to resist. So great was his reputation that kings and warriors sought his advice."

I was standing so close to Esus that I could feel the vibration of his voice, the tautness of his muscles. I watched Foxface. I saw the very moment when a bead of sweat appeared on his brow and caught the light of the moon, now brighter than the dying fire.

"And yet I say to you that though this man was revered, the honor he received tasted bitter to him and the word of small victories against Rome rang hollow in his ears."

Esus paused, perhaps for effect, and perhaps to consider a fine point of translation. He was speaking P-Celtic.

"Why? What was his problem?" his listeners urged him on, caught up in the story. For the moment everyone was more concerned with what happened next than with anything else.

"He had broken a great *geis*."

The audience nodded. It happens to the best of us.

"But that is not all. Only he knew of the *geis*. Only he knew that he had broken it. And when disasters followed, he kept his secret and did not tell the people of his transgression."

"But how can that be?" Lovernios interrupted. His voice was calm and reasonable in contrast to his face that had turned pale with a greenish cast like the air before a thunder storm. "When someone breaks a *geis*, disaster, destruction, or death come upon him alone."

"Usually," someone added. Throats cleared as the faculty prepared to debate the point.

"Perhaps that is a difference between your people and mine." Esus jumped in quickly. He knew all the pitfalls of learned discourse. "Among my people it often happens that not only the wrong-doer suffers but the innocent suffer." He waited exactly one beat. "The lambs suffer."

I shifted my weight and drew aside so that I could look at Esus. He stood silent and intent. It was the silence of sap rising in a young, straight tree, the silence of surging green life. My foster brother directed all that vibrant power towards Lovernios who seemed at once to yearn towards Esus and to shrink from him.

"It is true," mused the archdruid, "that when a king is wounded the land is barren. But your story is not about a king. Tell us, Esus ab Joseph, what finally happened to the wise man. Did he ever tell his secret?"

"I don't know. Yet."

"Then what is the point of your story?"

"That is the point. The wise man must choose."

The blood that had drained from Lovernios's face flooded back in a sudden rush. His jaw tightened.

"You have said you are under a *geis*, Esus ab Joseph," said the archdruid. "Perhaps you will choose now to speak."

Esus said nothing.

"You will at least show me the courtesy of facing me when I address you," the archdruid commanded.

Obviously reluctant to break his connection with Lovernios, Esus slowly turned to obey. But I was quicker. Whirling around, I placed myself between Esus and the archdruid.

"I myself laid a *geis* upon Esus ab Joseph. It's none of anyone's business what it was. Far from breaking it, he has honored it fully. This I swear on my own life and on the life within me. I swear it on my mother's womb and on the sixteen breasts of the eight mothers who gave me suck. I swear it on the Cailleach who initiated me into the mysteries. And—" Inspiration struck. "—I swear it on the Shining Isle of Tir na mBan."

The air could scarcely grow sweeter or balmier, but suddenly it was full of sighs and low, sensual moans. One of the Crows began to sing a wordless song in a deep, quavering voice. Even the old archdruid closed his eyes and swayed rhythmically. Only Esus and I were unaffected. Only we saw Lovernios turn away from the circle to vomit.

I grabbed Esus's arm. "Let's get going while the going's good."

"Don't be ridiculous, Maeve, where could we possibly go?"

"What were we saying?" The archdruid came to, looking a bit muddled, looking, in fact, like an old man longing for his bed, bone tired of this tedious business of probing, divining, and uttering wisdom.

"We were saying...." A new voice spoke. I turned and saw Dwynwyn elbowing aside a couple of druids as she entered the circle. She wore her usual blood-red tunic, her necklace of small skulls gleaming on her breast, her white hair floating all around her like moonstruck sea mist. "Or were about to say or might have said long since, if we weren't so long-winded, that Maeve Rhuad, the daughter of a god, has conceived by a god, which makes perfect sense, coming as she does from the, uh, let's just say, Otherworld."

"The ways of the gods are strange. They come to us in many guises. Often in the guise of a Stranger."

"Who speaks?" Dwynwyn shaded her eyes with her hands, as if the light were very bright, and peered around the circle. "Ah, Lovernios. The famed fox. Hear this, and take heed: A man can be a stranger to himself."

Then she rounded on the archdruid. "As for you, you and your whole flock of Cranes and Crows, next time you need someone to help you locate the noses on your faces, call me. Sooner rather than later. I may have only one good eye, but it sees clearer than any pair of yours. Now I will take Maeve Rhuad back with me to my island. I am the best midwife on all of Mona mam Cymru. I will receive the god-begotten child into my own hands, and I will mediate for the *Combrogos* with the Otherworld."

"Not so hasty, not so hasty, my dear Dwynwyn for whom I—and I believe I speak for my colleagues as well—have only the highest regard and esteem—"

"Pigs' testicles," spat Dwynwyn. "Get to the point."

"I will endeavor to do so. As I was saying, accepting your rebuke as perhaps deserved, I must nevertheless inform you that I cannot allow you to take Maeve Rhuad into your care. She is a student of the Druid College of Mona, and, as such, she is under our jurisdiction."

"Does anyone want to know what *I* want?" In fact, I wasn't sure myself, but I thought it was about time I raised that point.

"Hush, Maeve," said everyone in concert, and they went on arguing.

I felt as if I was back on Tir na mBan with my mothers united only in ignoring me while they ranted about childrearing. Suddenly, I was so tired. I wished some mother would pick me up and carry me to bed. I leaned against Esus who put both arms around me and held me tightly.

"Look! The child is asleep on her feet," cried Moira. "We are taking her with us to Caer Leb this instant."

Then I was enfolded in Crow wings.

"Esus," I called. "Dwynwyn."

I looked over my shoulder to see them standing next to each other.

Maybe it was the moonlight, maybe it was the growing distance between us, but Dwynwyn's white hair looked like a purple shawl. The red had drained from her dress. She held a white dove in her hand.

39

SPRING BREAK

At the Druid College of Mona, students did not have a spring break in the sense that college students do now. We did not pile into overloaded cars and drive all night to some overcrowded mecca of sun and booze. But after *Imbolc*, with the weather continuing mild and the living infinitely easier, a party mood prevailed—especially at Caer Leb. And guess who was life of the party, the hub of the bub, the queen of a carnival that would not give way to a dreary forty-day Lent? That's right: the old cosmic M as in me, M as in miracle worker, M as in Maeve Rhuad.

Now that my pregnancy had been publicly revealed, and under such dramatic circumstances, my growing belly became an object of attention and affection. Dwynwyn had effectively settled the hash of the child's paternity—some god or other. For the moment, everyone seemed content to leave it at that. In the absence of an ordinary father, the unborn child belonged to everyone. She became the class mascot; we had names for her: Little Moon, to commemorate the moment of her unveiling when the clouds parted and the big moon shone; and also Moon Calf, in honor of the white cow with the red ears.

Naturally, the fame of my pregnancy spread beyond the college. Lore grew up around me. People came from all over to touch and stroke my roundness for good luck. The Crows had the added responsibility of scheduling and supervising these audiences. Though I am sure they found their new duties onerous, the sight of my great belly had a softening effect on them, too. They made up for months of "ignoring what was under their noses," as Dwynwyn put it, by now sticking those noses into every minute detail. They brooded over my every bowel movement; they constantly checked the rims of my eyes for anemia. (They didn't call it that, but they knew what to look for.) They kept track of what I ate and often forced the chopped livers of various creatures down my throat. No one had more painstaking or painful prenatal care than I had in the last few months of my pregnancy. I accepted their excessive interest with as good a grace as I could muster. Their vigilance in monitoring every detail of my pregnancy was matched with a laxness regarding everything else. As long as they could examine me to their hearts' content, they didn't much mind what I—or anyone else—did.

Every night after we'd labored under the stone—(Except for me. I did my memory work but had weight enough pressing on my internal organs)— we'd gather outside around a fire. I'd hoist my tunic and let my hut mates, and anyone else who was hanging out, take turns placing their hands or heads over my belly. Moon Calf responded to this attention by performing amazing antics in her increasingly cramped space. No doubt her leaps and turns were encouraged by the chief harper who often came to play at Caer Leb while others drummed and the rest danced. The ground quivered and the whole earth quickened. I usually danced a turn or two myself, though I was easily winded these days. Most often I lolled, sipping the minuscule amount of mead the Crows allowed me.

Branwen was never far from my side. Maybe because I was uncharacteristically silent, content in my magnificent being, she was uncharacteristically talkative. It troubled her that no one appeared to be considering what would happen when the baby was born. To reassure herself, she made plans and went over them obsessively. Her favorite was that first form should keep the baby and raise it collectively. The child could get a head start on her studies while, by sharing her care, the rest of us could keep up with ours. Since this solution was so unprecedented, she felt obliged to have a contingency plan, which was that the child should be fostered among her own kin. Without being quite sure why, I tuned out most of Branwen's talk. Her voice became background, like the crackle of flames, or the endless, soft moan of wind.

The only person at Caer Leb who kept her reserve and refused to worship the great sacred mound was Viviane. One day when we found ourselves alone—(again at the trenches; for once, I had managed to sneak away without a Crow on my tail)—I asked her outright if the sight of my pregnancy caused her pain.

"It's not that," she said, stiff with pride. "Well, I suppose it is, at least in part. Don't we always wonder about the course we didn't choose? Isn't that part of what makes life so hard?"

Life hard? Oh, no. Despite my exposure to violence and rage, I rejected her words. From now on, life was going to be all honey on the lips, mead singing in the blood.

"But it's not just that. I'll swear it," she went on, her tone horribly earnest. "Remember how Dwynwyn said I'm your true enemy? Maybe that means I can see some things more clearly than Branwen or Nissyen or the Stranger or even the Crows. Anyway, I do know one thing: I was with you right before it happened. At moonrise, remember? When you and I were left alone at Caer Leb. That's the night it happened, isn't it? That's the night you conceived."

"You told me before that you didn't want to know anything about it," I said coldly. "Why are you asking now?"

The truth was, I didn't want to think of that night. I had almost forgotten about it. Not forgotten in the sense of being unable to remember, but forgotten as if it didn't matter any more. I was angry with Viviane for bringing it up.

"Believe me, I don't want to know. But I still owe you a debt."

"Drop it," I said shortly. "You've helped me enough. The blood on my thighs—"

"I haven't saved your life." She was dead serious.

"Sorry, but I don't think that will be necessary," I said airily.

"Don't be so sure," she cautioned. "Maeve, I have to tell you: I'm worried. Something's wrong. And I can't help feeling in some way responsible. If it did happen that night, then I let you go. I let you deceive me."

"I didn't mean to deceive you. I just didn't want to involve you."

"You mean you didn't want me to interfere with you. So, you admit it. Look, whether or not I want to know, why don't you just tell me what happened that night."

I shook my head and bit my lip till I tasted blood. She waited.

"Viviane," I finally said, "I got through that whole ordeal with the Crows and the Cranes on *Imbolc*. You weren't there, but believe me, it was no picnic. Dwynwyn came along and told everyone that a god fathered my child. If that was good enough for the Cranes and Crows, it should be good enough for you. Besides, what difference does it make how it happened, anyway? That part is all over now. It doesn't matter anymore."

"I think you're fooling yourself, Maeve."

"And I think you're jealous, if not of my baby, then of all the attention I'm getting because of her. And maybe you're jealous because I made the hard winter go away, and everyone knows it."

"If you want to insult me, Maeve Rhuad, go right ahead. We wouldn't want to jeopardize our precious enmity. Ha! Fat chance of that. So I'll tell you straight out, I think you're stupid to talk that way."

"What way?"

"Putting on airs, getting above yourself, saying you brought winter to an end."

"Well, it did end. I'm just stating the obvious."

"Yes, it did. And if you had anything to do with it, it's that you made yourself an opening for something greater than your silly little self to come through, just the way you did when you saved my miserable life, thank you very much."

"If I was just an opening, why do you persist in pestering me about the bloody debt you owe me?"

"Because you did not have to open yourself," she said, ruthlessly honest with herself. "Well, that's all I have to say. I've warned you. Maybe you'll be able to take in some of what I've said when you're not so...so full of yourself."

So full of shit, I bet she meant. And she turned and flounced away.

There is no denying that Viviane's warning marred my pleasure, at least for an evening. I felt listless as I lay back listening to the music and laughter. Perhaps sensing my mood, Branwen for once did not review her postnatal plans. Instead, she silently massaged my belly with oil. Now and again one of her long braids slipped over her shoulder and tickled me, but I didn't laugh. I was staring at the stars. They seemed a bit wan and peaked, as though they were weary of shining.

∞

The best and worst part about this time was that I was allowed to see Esus—more or less. Excursions to the yews were out of the question. We were both under scrutiny, and even if no one stopped us, we could never feel safe or private there again. But as I've noted, Caer Leb had become a hot spot and rules, in general, had relaxed. Whenever the ovate students could spare time from their studies, they came to our caer to party. So we had time together, of a sort, in the midst of a crowd. Often he sat near me, but not near enough to touch me. People were always coming up to talk to me— or rather to prattle and coo to Moon Calf. It was hard to have a private conversation. Our most intimate exchanges were made with our eyes, and I suspect many of these speaking glances were intercepted by watchful Cranes and Crows.

Lately I had noticed that something was bothering him. His brows almost met, they were so tightly knit, and he chewed constantly at his cheek. I tried to tell myself that he was merely frustrated by the lack of privacy. But after my encounter with Viviane, I began to suspect that he, too, thought something was wrong. One night when almost everyone else, even the Crows, were dancing a reel, Esus came and sat closer to me than he had in a long time. Little Moon leaped, and I laughed and reached for Esus's hand, placing it on my bared belly.

"Little Moon is happy to see you."

"It can't see me," he stated, and he removed his hand.

"How do you know?" I demanded. "Anyway, she feels you near. You could return her greeting. There now. You've hurt her feelings. She's turning her back on you."

I was still absorbed in watching her maneuvers.

"People are worshipping your belly, Maeve," he said in Aramaic. "You shouldn't let them."

"Why not, if they enjoy it?"

"It's like the Israelites worshipping the golden calf."

"Moon Calf is not a golden idol!" I was still speaking more to the baby, than to Esus. "She's alive. What's wrong with worshipping life? Besides," I added, turning towards him, "I never did understand why stone tablets with rules carved on them are a better thing to worship than a golden calf."

"I've explained this to you before, Maeve." He was thoroughly exasperated with me. "My people don't worship stone tablets. They don't worship rules, written or unwritten. They worship the living God."

"A god they can't see or touch," I countered. "Look, Esus, look!" I pointed to my belly. "Here is a wonder people *can* see and touch. You could, too, if you'd let yourself. Why do you have to spoil everything by bringing YHWH into it? If that's all you can think of all the time, why don't you just leave me alone and go back to his country?"

We were spoiling for a fight. What young lovers wouldn't be, under the circumstances?

"You said it yourself, Maeve: There is nowhere that the Eternal One is not. Besides, regardless of whether or not you believe in YHWH—and I know you are a thoroughly unregenerate gentile, despite the mercy and favor the Most High has shown to you—"

"Oh, give that a rest."

"—no matter what you believe or don't believe, you are making an unseemly display of yourself."

The reel had ended, but hearing raised voices speaking a foreign tongue, the crowd held back, giving us a few feet of privacy. Not that we cared, at that point.

"You're jealous." This seemed to be my all-purpose counterattack. "Just like your god. You don't want anyone else to see me. You don't want anyone else to touch me. Well, I've got news for you, brother. I don't belong to you. I am not a slave. My body is mine. I do with it as I please. I belong to myself."

I took my eyes off my holy belly long enough to glare fiercely at Esus. I was momentarily taken aback. His eyes were hot with anger; the set of his mouth, cold. It was one thing to be outraged and imperious myself and quite another to realize that he was even more furious with me.

"No one belongs to himself, excuse me, or herself." His voice was rich with scorn. "Whether or not I am jealous is beside the point. Have you no shame? Have you no modesty?"

Had we not been speaking Aramaic, he might not have been able to ask those questions—or not in this context. Shame for the *Keltoi* had nothing to do with how many clothes you did or didn't have on. And modesty was decidedly not a virtue. So I didn't actually know what Esus was talking about.

"Um, no," I said in some confusion.

Esus laughed. He didn't want to, but he couldn't help it. Once he started, he surrendered fully, and all the tense, rigid lines in his face and body released. Think of a spring river in full sunlight. His laughter was strong and bright and swift like that. You didn't have to know what it was about. It just carried you along, the sheer joy of it. I laughed, too, and by the time our laughter subsided, we were lying in each other's arms.

We held each other for a long time, without speaking. Surely beyond the curve of our backs, people were watching, waiting. Or maybe they had already reached their conclusions. Inside the circle of each other's arms, we had made a little world, a secret world of warmth and darkness and shared breath. I drowsed peacefully. Little Moon settled down to sleep.

"Maeve."

I snuggled closer to show that I had heard him.

"There's something I need to ask you."

"Ask, *cariad*."

"What did I say that day?"

"What day? There have been lots of days. You're not exactly known for keeping your opinions to yourself." Him and his god, I added to myself. Big mouths, both of them.

"You know, at Arbitrations. When I went into a trance and spoke some sort of prophecy."

"Oh, that day. But don't you know? Has no one ever told you? Have I never told you?"

"Tell me again, if you have."

I felt my whole body stiffen with resistance. If you have ever been pregnant, you will understand. I was bringing life into the world. I needed to believe it was benign—or would be for my baby. No shrieking, black-robed priestesses, no burning groves, no rivers running with blood. Not in my child's world.

"You prophesied the ruin of the college," I said tersely. "But, Esus, it's not going to happen now. Everything's changed now."

Against my will, I suddenly remembered Branwen's face that day, her wild grief, as if, instead of merely prophesying, Esus had actually transported her, for an instant, to that terrible future. But now Branwen would never have to live it. Never. It was changed now. All changed.

"How can that be, Maeve?"

I could barely hear him. He had curled himself closer, his head between my breasts, his mouth at the top of my belly. Through veils of water and layers of flesh, Moon Calf probed him daintily with her foot.

"Because." I took his head between my hands and made him look at me. "Because we have loved, *cariad*. You know it's true. You saw. My belly. The moon. The melting. The spring. Everything's all right now."

He wanted to believe. I wanted to believe.

"Ah, Maeve, if only it were our baby. Yours and mine."

"But she is, Esus, she is, if you'll let her be. The rest doesn't matter."

"Maeve, please understand me. I do not mean to speak unkindly of the child you carry beneath your heart."

His description touched me. It was more tender and intimate than any of the nicknames my classmates had made for her.

"But I am troubled," he went on. "The child was conceived in violence and sin."

I hated it when he talked about sin, but I checked my anger. Maybe because his head still rested between my breasts, the impulse to comfort and reason was stronger than the urge to smack him.

"Esus, listen to me. I didn't sin. I may have broken the college rules, but I didn't sin."

"No, you are innocent," he agreed. I could feel him chewing his cheek. He wasn't through. "But Lovernios is not. He has made you the scapegoat, the sin eater, the one who carries the sin for others. Ssh, don't interrupt. This is important. Remember I told you about the dream I had in Bryn Celli Ddu? How you bore the pain for me? Now you are carrying his sin for him."

"That is the silliest thing I ever heard, Esus. Truly. I'm carrying a baby, for Anu's sake, not a sin. How can you carry a sin, anyway? It's invisible, without form or substance, just like your god."

"You're wrong, Maeve. Sin is the heaviest thing in the world. And you are carrying his."

"I'm not!"

He was quiet for a time.

"Then maybe I am carrying his sin."

"What do you mean?" Something about his tone alarmed me. "Do the Cranes still think you're the father? Oh, Esus, I tried to tell the truth, but I should have tried harder. I should have said his name. If anything happens to you because of me—"

"Hush, my dove," he said. Now he cradled my head. "That's not what I mean. That's not what I mean at all. I don't care who thinks I'm the father. I told you, I wish I was."

"Then what is it?" I drew apart so that I could look at his face.

"He follows me. Not all the time. Not to Caer Leb. But whenever he can, he follows me."

I didn't need to ask who he was. My whole body knew. My heart slammed against my breast bone. My palms sweated. The baby kicked frantically.

"Esus, you've got to be careful. He must have guessed that you know what happened that night. Don't go anywhere alone. He'll try to kill you!"

Esus shook his head. "It's not as simple as that. I almost wish it was."

"Why else would he be following you?"

"I don't know. It's almost as if, well, I get the feeling that he worships me, reveres me. He seems to be waiting for some sign or revelation. In class, he defers to me, asks me questions about my people, tries to get me to hold forth. He knows I don't eat pig meat. He's taken to bringing me delicacies I can eat. Sometimes he just stares at me, silently, for hours. Whenever he corners me alone, he tries to tell me things, only he never says anything outright. Just hints at mysteries and secrets that he claims only I can understand. The others are not worthy, he says. And he keeps referring to the prophecies I made."

"Has he ever said anything about that night in Bryn Celli Ddu?"

"Not in so many words."

"Have you ever told him that you know he's the father?"

"No, I haven't. Maybe I'm being cowardly. Maybe if I could get him to confess the truth, it would help him. It would heal the terrible sickness in him. The sickness in his soul."

"You, a coward? You who stood beside me in front of all the Cranes and Crows? You gave him his chance that night. You said it yourself: It's his choice. You can't force him. It would be dangerous to try to force him. Haven't you noticed? He's crazy half the time. One part of him doesn't know what the other part is doing."

"All the same, I can't help wondering if that's what I'm meant to do, if that's why I've come to Mona, to help this man face himself."

"Esus!" I sat up, appalled. "Are you telling me that after all this time, you *still* don't know why you're here?"

"Oh, and you do, I suppose." His tone had lightened. "So tell me, already."

"No," I said, relieved but keeping my back to him. "I'm tired of telling you. This time you tell me."

"Hmm, let's see," he teased.

Then he drew me back into his arms.

"You," he said. "I came here to find you."

⁂

Come. Stand apart with me for a moment. Look at them, the young Maeve and Esus, wrapped in each other's arms. Rapt in each other's arms. I see brightness all around them. The sweet, rich darkness of the body, then the blaze. Call it a halo, if you want to, but it's not confined to the head. Let them have this moment. Let it charge every cell of their beings. Never mind what happens next. He said it: There is enough trouble for each day.

Bliss has to keep.

40

CANDIDATES AGAIN

hen the bad news came, no one was prepared for it. Are any of us, ever, no matter how many oracles we consult? Go ahead. Read the entrails. Intrepret the patterns of bird flight. Cast the ogham sticks. When the news comes, it still knocks you flat.

It arrived at a prosaic time, not dawn, not dusk, not midnight but mid-morning. We were just taking a break after genealogy class, all of us standing and stretching beneath the oaks, when we saw a band of horsemen riding from the straits towards the tree-crowned ridge where classes met. Their pace was not leisurely, and, as they drew nearer, we saw that they were warriors fresh from some skirmish. Their hair, limed for battle, stood out from their heads, stiff but battered looking. Dried blood, dirt, and sweat overlaid their swirls of woad. When they saw us under the trees, they slowed their pace and one of them cried out: "Where can we find the archdruid?"

Before any of the Cranes could answer, Branwen surprised us all by rushing forward.

"Owain!" she greeted the warrior by name. "Do you come from my father?"

He looked at her, this massive, spike-haired, blue-whorled warrior, the very sight of whom struck terror into his enemies. His face suddenly puckered and he began to bawl. His comrades joined him and the whole grove resounded with their wails. Branwen stood still, a column of silence, the blood draining from her face. Viviane and I moved simultaneously to support her. The warriors wailed on.

"Shut up!" I finally shouted.

Amazingly, they stopped as abruptly as they had begun.

"You must tell me," said Branwen, her voice faint but commanding. "I am Branwen, daughter of Bran." She went on to recite her full lineage; it seemed to strengthen her. "If my father has set sail for the Shining Isles of the Blest, you must tell me."

"Branwen, daughter of King Bran the Bold, your father and my king is still living."

"Anu!" Branwen let out her breath. For an instant, her muscles relaxed. Then she braced herself.

"King Bran has been taken captive. Unless—may the gods give him strength and cunning—unless he has escaped, he is on his way to Rome."

I will never forget Branwen's single cry. Yet in my memory it is not so much a sound as a sight. In the meadow below the ridge, a lapwing, unperturbed by the passing of the warriors' horses, suddenly dove into the sky, echoing Branwen's cry as she strove to call attention away from her nest to her own unprotected breast.

∞

None of us heard the full story until that night when the chief bard and harper had a rough draft ready to present to the college. Then, of course, you had to wonder what details might have been added or sacrificed to meet the demands of poetic form. The long of the story took several hours to recite. Since I never had the chance to memorize the poem in full, I'll give you the short of it.

King Bran the Bold had spent the winter, along with a number of chieftains from both the Silure and Ordovice tribes, guarding the mountain passes and making a series of raids on the Atrebates and on the Roman trading settlement. The narrative included a long description of the Atrebate king's new Roman-style villa, complete with under-the-floor heating. What is more, the king had built a temple over a spring and placed in it a carved Roman image of the goddess Sulis, whom the Romans claimed was the same as their Minerva. Thanks to the Roman genius for plumbing, this statue of Sulis spouted water from its mouth and breasts. You might think this a clever device; apparently the king did. But most of the *Combrogos* thought it vulgar and as close to blasphemy as anything we were able to conceive: to take the living goddess of the spring, close her in, and make her literal and personified.

Bran did his best to send a message to the Roman settlers: You won't like it here. It won't be worth the trouble. Go home while you still can. He made a hard winter even harder, stealing stored grain, cattle, even carrying off hostages—most of whom he eventually returned. Bran had no stomach for killing, except in battle, and the hostages only made more mouths to feed. He hoped the freed hostages would unintentionally join his cause and urge their fellows to make a swift and permanent departure from the Holy Isles.

Bran's raids on the trading settlement were not without effect. But instead of saying the hell with this and packing it in, the business community called for protection of the empire's investments. The Holy Isles were too rich a source of gold, tin, and meat to be left unmolested by a sprawling empire that had to keep conquering to support itself in the manner to which it had become accustomed. The Romans certainly weren't going to let a few pesky raiders stand in their way. As soon as the weather permitted, the Romans sent military aid. Instead of raiding civilians, Bran found himself facing

Roman troops in battle. What's more, the ranks of his warriors were dwindling as heads of *tuaths* returned to their homesteads to plant fields and move herds. Bands of roving warriors, stationary for the winter, took to roving again, and Bran could not count or count on his followers from one day to the next.

So he did what any great Celtic warrior king would do: he challenged the Romans to send their best man to meet him in single combat. (Here the chief bard warmed to his subject, and Bran's challenge went on for a good hour.) Whether it was cross-cultural misunderstanding or deliberate Roman deceit, when Bran went alone in good faith to meet his opponent, he was surrounded and captured, though not before he lopped off a few Roman heads. His companions rushed to his defense and fought fiercely, though they were greatly outnumbered and outmaneuvered. In the end, not only was King Bran taken captive, but two hill forts were lost to the Romans. The remaining Silure and Ordovice chieftains had now scattered.

The chief bard ended his poem with a heart-rending description of Bran's attempt to kill himself rather than submit to the shame of captivity. But the Romans prevented him, binding him like a slave. I wanted to throttle him. Branwen didn't need to hear any more. Clearly, he was giving the nod to poetic convention rather than relaying an eyewitness account. Yet we all knew it was true. Bran would kill himself if he got the chance. If he had the misfortune to survive, he would be exhibited in chains. A noble savage. A titillating side show in the ongoing Roman circus.

All during this excruciating recital, I'd sat next to Branwen, who insisted on hearing it to the end. She had allowed me to hold her hand. It was so cold, I doubted she had any feeling in it. Several times she gripped my hand and dug her nails in. Other than that, she was perfectly still, though no one would have blamed her if she had screamed or torn her clothes. In fact, I sensed that everyone expected some display. But that was not Branwen's way. She just sat with her back straight, her face immobile, her tears silent.

When the last strain of the harp quivered on the air, Branwen rose and bolted. She tried to shake off my hand, but I wouldn't let go. She ran all the way to the latrines with me puffing behind her. (I was almost full-term.) She sank to the ground, and I held her braids and stroked her brow while she was violently sick.

The Crows arrived in short order. Two of them tried to shoo me away, but Moira overruled them.

"Branwen will want her. They are foster sisters."

At that moment, Branwen did not want anyone but her father. As the Crows bore her away to the hut, her restraint finally gave way and she fought the Crows with all her slender might.

"Let me go! Let me go! I must go to him. I must find him. He needs me," she screamed.

At last Moira slapped her across the face. I might have sprung at the old Crow, if I had not glimpsed the sorrow in her eyes. Branwen quieted at once and stared at her in shock, which, of course, was the intended effect.

"Branwen, daughter of Bran," said the Crow, and she recited Branwen's paternal lineage. "What is your father's wish for you?"

Branwen rallied, standing up straight and lifting her small chin.

"That I should be poet, priestess, and lawgiver. Druid and wise woman. Keeper of peace among the tribes and counselor in times of war."

"And so, he would not want you to follow him in mad, futile pursuit. He would want you to go on serving his cause, our common cause, the protection of the Holy Isles, the honor of the *Combrogos.*"

"That is what he would want," Branwen whispered. "What I want."

But I knew what she really wanted: her father's arms, the sweet, sweaty scent of him.

"Branwen, daughter of Bran the Bold." The Crow's voice was almost tender. "Do not be ashamed to grieve. But also do not forget that to meet misfortune bravely, as your father has done, is greatness. It is the poet's work to see that such greatness is never forgotten."

We went into the hut and Branwen let me hold her while she wept. The Crows bustled around, heating water to bathe her face, and preparing her a hot sedative drink. Finally she went to sleep in my arms. I held my hands over her heart and felt the fire of the stars flowing through them. Branwen's heart was already broken, Dwynwyn had said. Maybe the fire would help keep it open so the poems could be born from it.

Gradually, the heat ebbed from my hands as Branwen slept more and more deeply. Though I was exhausted, I was also wide awake. I'd had trouble sleeping lately. The baby was now so huge, no position I found was comfortable for long. My cramped bladder needed frequent relief. Yet it was not discomfort that kept me awake now, but the stirrings of my own grief, which I'd ignored before, Branwen's grief being so much greater.

When I was sure Branwen would not wake if I moved, I got up and went to the trenches. For once no Crows attended me. I guess they knew I wouldn't go anywhere tonight with Branwen needing me. She was still fast asleep when I got back, so I decided to sit outside the hut for awhile. It was a starry night, not too cold. I thought of how just a year ago I had set out across the sea with Boann and Fand. I relived the day of our arrival, our meeting with King Bran, his kindness and gallantry. I remembered the feel of his arms as he lifted me to my feet, the shock of his maleness. He was the first man I'd ever seen. Isn't that what a father is: the first man? Before Bran, *father* only meant the man I had never seen. Bran was my first father, my foster father, who had adopted me with such casual generosity and delight.

For Bride's sake, for Anu's sake, for all our sakes, why couldn't King Bran have been the one to be shipwrecked on Tir na mBan? He wouldn't have wasted time (or timelessness) railing against his fate. There would have been parties every night, sword play, *laigen* casting, and chariot races every day. All his life Bran had been longing to go wonder-voyaging to the West. Now he was being dragged in the opposite direction to a world where time was measured by the years of some emperor's reign. I wept for Bran. I wept for Branwen. I wept for myself. Without my foster father, my first father, who would stand between me and the other father, the one who refused to claim me as his, the one who wanted me dead? Who would protect my child?

I must have dozed sitting up for a while. Someone was shaking my shoulder and hissing my name. I opened my eyes and saw Viviane kneeling beside me.

"Maeve, I've got to talk to you. Alone. Is Branwen asleep in there?"

"The Crows gave her a brew."

"She'll be out for hours, then," said Viviane. "Poor thing. There's no other comfort for her."

I nodded. There didn't seem to be much more to say. I started drifting off again.

"Maeve, listen." The urgency in Viviane's tone jerked me awake. "I've just come from the teaching grove. They're having a *major* faculty meeting. They've been going at it for hours, and it's not over yet. Everyone is there, including the archdruid and the rest of the priestesses from Holy Island. Someone must have sent for them."

"It's not that far as the Crow flies," I quipped.

"This is serious, Maeve. Some of the others from our hut are still there, hiding in the trees. I didn't want to wait any longer to warn you."

"Still trying to discharge that old debt, Viviane?" I actually yawned.

I don't know what had come over me. Was it just drowsiness or a much deeper fatigue that left me with a strange indifference to my fate? I felt as though I had a thin film of stickiness all over me. My reactions were slowing down. It was harder and harder to move. But you know what was happening, don't you? I was caught, caught in those fine, invisible threads.

"Do you want to hear what's going on at that meeting, or not?" Viviane demanded.

"Truthfully? I just want to go back to sleep."

"Oh, fine!" Her sigh of disgust was so gusty it no doubt disturbed the leaves in the thickets near the straits. "May the children of Don be my witness, may the standing stones and the ancient groves of oak bear witness, also, that I have done all I can to warn this—"

"Oh, you haven't tried all that hard," I interrupted querulously. "If anything happens to me, it will still be all your fault."

"Maeve Rhuad, you are impossible!" To prevent herself from screaming she whispered; her utter exasperation with me resulted in a lot of spit. "I don't know why I or anyone else should want to save your ridiculous carcass. Perhaps I'd better not interfere any further. Maybe you were made and meant to be a sacrifice. Anu knows you're fat enough!"

"It's not all fat," I pointed out. "After all, I'm due to have a baby any day—"

Then, suddenly, what she had just said went home. Winning a spat with Viviane no longer seemed so vital.

"What did you say about a sacrifice?"

"Oh, do I have your attention now?"

"If you insist." I was keeping up a good front, but my heart was pounding. Inside me, Little Moon, sensing the change, shifted uneasily. "Begin at the beginning. Please," I added.

Viviane set the scene, and I could picture it clearly: the orange of firelight, the black and white of the Cranes and Crows; the shadowy trees, magically stilled, so that it seemed as if they attended, too; Viviane and the others, hidden behind trunks or high in limbs, scarcely breathing. Together the Cranes and Crows dissected the latest disaster to the *Combrogos*: one of the strongest kings, with the power to lead and unify tribes, was now captive. The rest of the resistance had disbanded. Roman soldiers occupied two hill forts. Though no one invoked it, Esus's prophecy of the ruin of Mona hung in the air of the grove, vivid in every mind's eye.

"There have been strange omens for almost a full-turning of the year," the archdruid observed. "Even before their feet touched the ground of Mona, the wings of the Cranes announced their coming." Everyone knew which *they* he meant. "Let us consider the two: One bright; one dark. One female; one male. One from the north and the west; one from the south and the east. Can anyone doubt that the gods are among us and that mystery walks in our midst? Moreover, it is a quinquennial year. It may be time, indeed it may be exactly the right time, to consider making the Great Sacrifice. All signs indicate that the *Combrogos* face grave danger, maybe even destruction at the hands of our enemies. We need someone to carry a potent message for us to the great protectors of the Holy Isles. Here are these two: one from the Otherworld; one from another world. If they submit to three-fold death in the fifth year... well now, two and three makes five. Hmm. Very pleasing. Very propitious."

I'm telling you, arithmetic was a lot more dangerous in those days.

Vivane didn't wait to hear what the other Crows and Cranes thought of the archdruid's math skills. She slipped from her tree and ran to warn me.

"I don't get it," I said, more dumbfounded than frightened. "If they think Esus and I are so mysterious and powerful, practically gods ourselves from the sounds of what the archdruid said, why would they want to sacrifice us? You'd think they'd want to keep us around, maybe offer a few sacrifices to us, but—" I gestured, at a loss for words.

"I'm not sure I get it either," Viviane admitted. "I mean, we're still learning genealogies. But I get the impression that it's not that you are a god now; the sacrifice makes you one. Having representatives in the Otherworld can only help the *Combrogos*."

"I don't see how," I said. "Even if I became a god after death, why would I want to help the people who strangled me, stabbed me, and drowned me? Does that make any sense to you?"

Viviane looked nonplused. In every religion there are questions you are simply not supposed to ask. If you're properly indoctrinated, it won't occur to you to ask them. But my background had been a little irregular. As you may recall, I had always wondered how that skull got in the well. Looked like I might be about to find out.

"Ideally, you're supposed to want to, you know, offer yourself."

"But what if I don't!"

"They might have ways of persuading you."

"Such as?" I certainly drew a blank.

It was just before dawn and the warm night had turned chilly. I shivered. I was so cold and exhausted, everything seemed unreal. I could hardly believe I was having this conversation. Maybe I wasn't. Maybe I'd wake up soon.

"Well," Viviane pondered, taking the question more seriously than I liked. "Wouldn't you consider sacrificing yourself if it could stop the Roman troops, if it could save King Bran?"

Despite the chill, tiny beads of sweat broke out on my forehead. The whole picture changed, becoming at once more simple and more complex. If my death could save King Bran's life, would I, should I.... But my baby! What about my baby? Didn't that skew the archdruid's neat little formula? Three and three makes six. So there. He needed to do the problem over. The *Keltoi* had no doctrine of archdruidical infallibility. Took the Romans to invent something as stupid and arbitrary as that. I gave myself a shake and lightly smacked my own cheek to rouse myself. It wasn't a done deal yet.

"What about the barley cake?" I asked. "The burnt piece of barley cake? I thought everyone was supposed to have a shot at the big one?"

"I suspect that may be a formality." Viviane furrowed her brow. "Especially in a case like this one, where it's so clear—"

"I don't think it's so clear," I objected. "What about the gods having a say in who they want? I thought that was the point of the burnt piece. How can the Cranes and Crows be so sure the gods want me? As for Esus, he's not even one of the *Combrogos*. He doesn't believe in our gods. If he met any of them, he'd start right in by telling them they were false idols."

"Don't ask me, Maeve." Viviane threw up her hands. "I don't know about the Stranger, but it's beyond me why the gods would want anyone as pig-headed as you. I'm just telling you what I heard."

I found Viviane's insult oddly comforting.

"Viviane, why did you come to tell me? I mean, apart from your owing me your life and all that. If you really think having me sacrificed could save the *Combrogos*, why would you want to warn me?"

"To be honest, I didn't take the time to think it through. As soon as I heard you might be a candidate for sacrifice, well, I didn't think about the *Combrogos*. I just thought: Maeve. I've got to tell her. That's all. I don't know if what I did was right or wrong."

"Well, thank you," I said awkwardly. "No more debt now, okay? I just want to ask you one more thing. Do you think, do you really think I, we, well, the sacrifice could save King Bran? Or anyone?"

I tried to grasp it: My body, Esus's body killed three times over. Did the blood seep into the ground to become part of some underground river, some secret, vital artery that connected everything, linked and changed all fates?

And my baby. What about my baby?

"I can't answer you, Maeve," Viviane was saying. "Talk to the Crows. Talk to Nissyen."

But I knew who I needed to talk to. I had wasted too much time already. Grasping Viviane's shoulder, I hoisted myself to my feet. The first light reddened the eastern sky.

"Stay with Branwen, Viviane."

"Don't rush off and do something crazy, Maeve. Haven't you learned yet not to be so rash?"

"I'm not sure I'm going to live long enough to learn anything more. You know I have to tell him, Viviane, just the same as you had to tell me."

"Let me go, Maeve. I can reach him faster."

Would it have made any difference if I had heeded her?

I had already started to run, moving as fast as I could with a rolling ungainly gait, racing the sunrise. I had some foolish, unformed notion that if only I could find him in that soft, malleable time before light made everything hard and harsh, we could hold the blear-edged world in our hands and change the shape of our fates.

∽

Without stopping to think, I headed straight for the yews. My instinct was right; he had gone there, too. Or had intended to. I came over the last rise in the fields and saw the yews, black and spidery against the southeastern sky that now brimmed with gold. Then I stopped in my tracks.

Between me and the trees was a knot of druids, white robes gleaming against the darkness of the yews behind them. They were moving slowly in my direction. I say knot, but their formation was more a circle. They walked surrounding someone in the center, someone slight with dark, springy hair. Who else? To Esus's immediate left, in this ringed procession, walked the archdruid. I recognized his staff. On his right—I knew by the chill in my bones even before I could see the gleam of the red beard—was Foxface. As they drew nearer, I could see that Esus was not bound in any way, but I could not help feeling that he was a prisoner. Now they were close enough that I could hear the sound and rhythm of their voices. No one was angry; I heard no fear. The tone of the conversation was speculative, philosophical. I did not like the sound of it. I liked it even less when I could finally see Esus's expression. He appeared interested, engaged, curious. A look I knew all too well.

Esus was the first of the men to notice me. The others were all too intent on him. He looked straight at me, his mouth curving almost imperceptibly in a smile for me. His name was on my lips. Before I could call to him, he shook his head, ever so slightly, never breaking his stride. Plainly he hoped the druids would pass by without seeing me. Before I could decide what to do, Foxface, attuned to Esus's every nuance, glanced back in my direction. When he saw me, he stopped and stared, whether involuntarily or not I'll never know. Then everyone turned towards me.

At that moment, the sun spilled over the horizon. The long, twisted shadows of the yews stretched towards us.

"Ah, Maeve Rhuad." The archdruid spoke to me pleasantly, as if he were some benign old man out for a morning walk, pleased at the sight of a fresh young thing.

"Take me, too!" I blurted out. "Wherever you are taking Esus, take me, too!"

The archdruid made sorrowful clucking noises that were soon drowned out by the scream of Crows. Great black wings sent shadows wheeling over the landscape and across our upturned faces. All at once I was surrounded, too. The Cranes and the Crows nodded to each other politely, then led Esus and me away. From each other.

Esus went quietly. Me they had to drag, kicking and screaming. Pregnant as I was, I weighed a whole lot more than he did.

41

DOUBLE OR NOTHING

L et the image of me being hauled off by the Crows fade away. And let the picture of Esus corralled by the druids dissolve.

See instead the huge, radiant sky as the time of Shoots-Show becomes the Time of Brightness. Now look at the new green in the fields and the groves, the buds in orchard and hedgerow about to explode. Coaxed by the strong, young sun, the whole earth quivers on the brink of its long, exquisite orgasm.

Esus and I are small, small. We are dancing particles in the great pattern. Short-lived as mayflies, as May flowers. Try to see for a moment the way the druids saw. Tide going in, tide going out. See the earth ablaze with green life. Life that sustains the *Combrogos*. Now see the bright blood spurting, arcing and pouring into the earth. Glory in it. Glory in the great meeting and mating of life with death.

By the time the tribes had gathered for *Beltaine*, only two days away now, I had almost persuaded myself of that larger, impersonal perspective. How can that be, you ask, when I was last seen pitching a fit among a murder of Crows? When the Crows got me back to Caer Leb, they forced a brew down my throat. To calm me, they said, so that I wouldn't harm the child. (No one seemed to worry about whatever was in the brew crossing the placental barrier.) I'm telling you, drugs are nothing new. They've always been used to help people accept the unacceptable—or the inevitable, if you prefer. Drugs can be a mercy. But you should always ask yourself, who's administering them? And why? Who is being relieved? Of what?

I think the Crows intended mercy, albeit with some side benefits to the powers that be. And if you have to face the possibility of going to a three-fold death, it's easier to contemplate if you're stoned out of your mind. In fact, in my youth and strength, my own death, threefold or not, did not seem very real to me. But the loss of Esus did. If the only way for me to be with Esus was to die with him, then on with the sacrifice. Despite my irregular background, I was Celt enough to see death not as a dead end but as a doorway. When we passed the portal, maybe we would be gods. Maybe we would find the Tree of the World and twine beneath it as the snakes twined in its branches, while its golden leaves drenched us with light.

It was easy to make these pictures as I drifted in a drugged haze. Besides, listen, I was a teenager in love. Larger than life. Romeo and Juliet hadn't been dreamed of yet. But they had nothing on Maeve and Esus. Double sacrifice! What a story.

But as the drugs wore off, my doubts revived. There was one literally pressing matter that troubled me, one major boulder in the narrative flow. Though I was staying in the Crows' hut—supposedly because of my delicate condition—I had the freedom of the Caer. So when everyone was busily preparing to decamp for the *Beltaine* festivities at Llyn Cerrig Bach, I sought out Nissyen for a talk.

"I don't dare walk with you," said Nissyen. "Let's just sit on the embankment."

"All right," I agreed. "But I'm not going to run away this time. I doubt I could even if I wanted to."

"That was an impressive bit of shape-shifting, fine as any I've seen. I've always said you were a natural. Watching you bound away in your doe form was worth all the grief I got for letting you give me the slip that day."

"I'm sorry, Nissyen. I didn't know you got into trouble on account of me."

"It's no matter, Maeve, my heart. Pay it no mind. I am the one to sorrow."

He meant my impending tragic death, I supposed. One tear pooled at the corner of my eye. I did not let it fall. I would be brave.

"I have failed you," he went on. "We all have, but especially I have. I failed to protect you. Then, when you tried to tell me the truth—"

"The truth?" I wasn't sure what he was talking about.

"About who got you with child."

"I don't think you could have done anything about it even if I had told you then," I said.

"No, I don't suppose I could have," he said ruefully.

"But I do want to ask you something. It's about my baby."

"Due any day now," he remarked with forced cheerfulness, as if I were any expectant mother.

"Yes, but what if it isn't....well, born on time?"

"Babies are notorious for choosing their own time, Maeve. Best let nature take its course."

I supposed some people did regard human sacrifice as natural, but I wouldn't have expected Nissyen to be one of them.

"I mean, what if it isn't born before *Beltaine*. Before the sacrifice."

"What are you getting at, Maeve? What sacrifice?"

"What sacrifice!" I exploded. "*The* sacrifice. The Great Sacrifice. The quinquennial sacrifice by triple death. I know the Cranes and Crows had a meeting about it. Weren't you there? Didn't you know?"

"By the paps of Anu, Maeve Rhuad, were you there? We all thought you were watching over Branwen."

"I wasn't there, but I have my sources."

"I don't know why the august faculty of this college doesn't take the simple precaution of beating the bushes before confidential meetings."

"Nissyen, please. You have to tell me before someone drugs me again. I need to know. Will they sacrifice me on *Beltaine*, even if my baby hasn't been born yet?"

"Sacrifice you! Who says anyone's going to sacrifice you?" Nissyen blustered.

"Oh, come on, Nissyen. Don't try to spare me. I know that's what the meeting was about."

"Listen to me, Maeve Rhuad." Nissyen took my face between his hands and made me look at him. "You must hear me and believe me. You are not going to be sacrificed. I swear it on the very ground of these Holy Isles."

"I'm not?"

Have you ever woken from a dream of death? I don't mean the frightening kind where something awful pursues you, but the kind where you feel you're on the verge of some great adventure, about to discover all the secrets life keeps hidden. You're a little disappointed, aren't you? When you're about to die, everything is pure, simple. When you know you're going to live, you have to answer the same relentless question over and over: Now what?

"No, you're not." Nissyen patted my cheeks, then let go of my face.

"But Viv—that is, my source."

"You can say Viviane. I won't report her."

"Well, was she lying then? She said the Cranes and Crows kept talking about the two, the dark and the bright, the male and the female. Esus and me. Who else could it be?"

"She wasn't lying to you, but that discussion wasn't conclusive."

"You mean they changed their minds?"

That flicker of disappointment was giving way to vast relief. This might be a decision I could live with, so to speak. I'd have the baby. Then Esus and I could quietly leave when the festival crowds began to disperse.

"You may be the misbegotten child carrying the misbegotten child," Nissyen was saying. "There seems to be general agreement on that point, always excepting myself. But the prophecy said a hero would spring from this line. Never mind if it's the last hero to stand against Rome. If the Romans are coming, the death of this child will not stop them. Better a last hero than no hero."

"But, Nissyen, what if I had the baby today? Then I would just be myself, the bright half of the pair, the one from the Otherworld," I quoted.

"Indeed, your origins were a consideration and, in the last analysis, a sticking point. How can we send you to the gods when they have already sent you to us? Manannán Mac Lir is your father; the warrior witches, your mothers; the mantle of Bride is about your shoulders. Would it not be ingratitude to send you back?"

I preened a bit. A gift from the gods to mere mortals. That's me.

"That's the high poetical version," Nissyen chuckled. "The other way to look at it is that they couldn't handle you in the Otherworld, so they sent you here, and they're not in a hurry to have you back again. Either way, the conclusion is: better to leave well alone where you're concerned. If you apply yourself to your studies, you'll keep your place in college. If not, you can have your pick of chieftains, be a warrior queen like your namesake."

"Did it ever occur to anyone that I may have plans of my own? I don't need any old lime-dipped, woad-painted hulking warrior. I have Esus! I'll go where and when he goes."

Nissyen sighed and reached for my hand, covering it with his own.

"Maeve, my heart, I am not at liberty to tell you more. But my loyalties, which should belong to the college alone, are all askew where you're concerned. You with your hazelnut eyes and the bright salmon swimming in them. I never had a daughter in all my wandering—not one that I know of. You are the daughter of my heart. What do I care what happens to me now? What do I care if they set me out to sea in a tiny corracle? Let the gods take me—"

"Nissyen!" I felt he was getting a little carried away with his poetry of his own fate. "Tell me. Whatever it is. Just tell me."

"Maeve, the Stranger—"

"Esus."

"He is the one. Or he will be if the gods so choose and the burnt piece falls to him."

"No!"

"Dear heart, the oracles have been consulted. All the signs point to him. He is the one with the power to bend time, to change the ending of the story. If he submits to the threefold death, untold power will be his. It may be that he is or will become the god whose name he bears."

Viviane had been right. It's dangerous to be named for a god.

"And if he refuses?"

Nissyen shrugged. "Maeve, he's a foreigner. Not one of the *Combrogos*. His admission to the college is unprecedented. That he's been initiated into druid mysteries is controversial to say the least. Despite his remarkable aptitude, it seems unlikely that he will live out his lifetime in the Holy Isles serving the *Combrogos* as a druid. He has indicated no intention of doing so.

A druid education is an enormous investment. You must understand that, Maeve. It is the bestowing of the greatest treasure. It is a high and sacred trust. If the Stranger were to leave the Holy Isles and take our secrets to other lands and peoples—"

"You talk as if he were a thief!" I said, outraged. "And as for your precious druid wisdom, what makes it so precious apart from your hoarding of it? If it's so wonderful, why not let it flow freely into the world, like the sacred rivers?"

"To *Rome?*"

"Esus would never betray the *Combrogos* to Rome."

"If he were captured and tortured?"

"So why didn't any of you think of that before you accepted him into your bloody college!" I demanded.

"The auguries—"

"The auguries say whatever the druids want them to say."

"Maeve, Maeve," Nissyen lamented. "I won't say you're not right insofar as you are able to understand. I am merely telling you that to them—us—the druids, I mean, this sacrifice looks like the best solution to a sticky problem. No one means any disrespect to the Stranger. We all agree that he is a remarkable young man with great powers. The Great Sacrifice, if you can bring yourself to see it that way, is the highest honor, the greatest tribute the druids can pay."

"And an easy way out for everyone but Esus."

"Perhaps for him, too, dear heart."

"I don't call the triple death an easy way out."

"No, I don't suppose you would, but as you yourself might tell us, things are not always what they seem."

He was right about that. I sure could tell everyone a few things. Maybe I would. Maybe it wasn't too late.

"Nissyen." I decided to change tack. "What part did Lovernios play in this decision?"

"He is a senior and distinguished member of the college," Nissyen hedged. "Naturally he had his chance to speak."

"And?"

"And what?"

"What did he say?"

"Maeve, am I a first former, spying on secret meetings and spreading misinformation based on my limited understanding of matters over my head?"

"No, you are not. Your information should be much more reliable. Go on. What did he say?"

"Maeve, you are asking me to break confidence."

"So? Haven't you already done that? What about how you never had a daughter, and I'm the daughter of your heart and never mind if they put you in a boat?"

"You wouldn't really want that to happen to me, Maeve," he reproached me. "On the other hand, I did say that, yes, and I meant it, too. All right, I'll tell you, but don't repeat what I say. Lovernios believes the Stranger to be a god. He is the one who made the strongest case for sacrifice."

I nodded. Esus had suspected as much. "What did he say about me?"

"Of you he will not speak."

"It doesn't make sense," I said. "I'm the one he should want sacrificed. I'm the one who knows. Knows what happened to Lovernios. Knows what he did."

"Child, child!" Nissyen put his hand out in front of me as if to stop me from hurtling over some cliff.

"What if I told!" I plunged on. "I tried to at *Imbolc* but no one would listen. No, I blame myself. I didn't try hard enough. I didn't speak loud enough. But it's not too late. I could tell the archdruid. I could tell everyone."

Nissyen put his hands over his ears.

"Listen!" I shouted at him. "You said you were sorry you didn't listen before. Well, listen now!"

He took his hands from his ears and covered his eyes. "Go on," he said.

"Lovernios. Lovernios is my father. Lovernios is the father of both misbegotten children. There is only one misbegetter."

Then I told him the story from the beginning. When I had finished, Nissyen let out a long, long sigh. It was hard to believe he had that much breath in his slight body. Despite the hot green of the new grass and leaves, despite the cloudless blue of the sky and the warmth of the sun, it suddenly felt like summer's end, not its beginning. Everything seemed old and dry and wind-tossed. Lost. Gone out with a tide of grief.

"I suppose I've always known," he said at last. "I suppose we all have."

"Then why—"

"Because we cannot know," he answered before I could finish asking. "It is not the story we want to hear. It is not the one we are telling."

"You said Esus had the power to change the ending of the story. Why not me? This is my story, too. Why can't I tell it? Why can't I change the ending? What if Lovernios were to say: Yes, I am the misbegetter, take me. Let me be the sacrifice?"

"Think about it, Maeve. Lovernios has offended against the Otherworld, despising its gifts to him. How could he be acceptable as a sacrifice?"

"Well, what better way to apologize? Besides, criminals are often sacrificed."

"Not that way. Not the god-making way. For the fate-changing sacrifice, the gods must have the finest we can offer."

"And I'm not good enough! Esus is, and I'm not?" I huffed. Call it cosmic sibling rivalry. "As far as I'm concerned, it's double or nothing. If they won't have me, they can't have him."

"Maeve, listen to me. If you're concocting some rabbit-brained scheme for saving the Stranger—and I have no doubt you are, and personally, I don't like the idea at all—let me tell you one thing right away. Forget about going to the archdruid."

"Why?"

"Think, girl, think. With your head for once. The archdruid could have forced Lovernios's story from him, if he chose to. He didn't because it suited him not to. And there's an end of it."

"What about the Crows? Would they believe me?"

"The Crow ladies have your best interests at heart, Maeve. Who do you suppose pleaded your case, besides my poor self? I don't have much clout."

"Couldn't they help me save Esus?"

"I don't think anyone would help you do that, Maeve." He sighed again. "Not even me, dear heart. Not even me. I love you too much to encourage such a rash course. And, Maeve, it may pain you to hear this, but has it ever occurred to you that the Stranger might not *want* to be saved?"

In fact, it had. But if Esus thought it was his destiny to be sacrificed without me, well then, he was going to have to think again. And, one way or another, I was going to make sure he did.

"Nissyen, you've got to tell me. Where is he? I saw them all surrounding him, talking to him, taking him off somewhere. Is he a prisoner?"

"Imprisonment would be unnecessarily crude. Where, after all, would he go? A stranger in a strange land. But you, Maeve Rhuad, if you were to draw attention to yourself in any way, they would not hesitate to put you on an even shorter tether. Your best chance of seeing him at Llyn Cerrig Bach is to say nothing to anyone. Don't run about making rash accusations about senior members of the college. It will do no one any good."

We sat in silence for a time. I looked at the mountains, deep blue today against the bright sky, a huge, unbreaking wave of earth. I called up the maps the Cailleach had made me memorize and imagined the land beyond the mountains, the channel that divided the Holy Isles from Gaul, all the mountains, valleys, and rivers between here and Rome. King Bran was being forced across them. How could Esus's death reverse his steps?

And hadn't Anna the prophetess said he would return to his own people? She had also told him: Don't despise this shitty little dove. Someday you may need her again. No matter what happened, he needed me now, whether he admitted it or not. There must be a way I could get to him.

Then, all at once, I knew who could help me. The only one who would.

"Nissyen, would you do something for me?"

"Oh, Maeve, how can you ask?"

There was a double meaning in his answer. Well, I'd go easy on him.

"It's almost my time. I want Dwynwyn to be there when my baby is born. Will you send word to her? She could meet us at the camp."

"I don't know what the Crow ladies will say."

I placed his hand on my belly to let him feel the baby stir. My hazel eyes with the salmon sparks did the rest of the persuading.

Nissyen sighed. "Maeve, my heart, will you promise to be good?"

"I am," I said, an ambiguous statement, subject to broad interpretation.

42

Hag

At first it seemed my plan had backfired. My request for Dwynwyn's presence, which Nissyen had worried might offend the Crows, delighted them instead—or anyway lightened them. I had become, in every sense, a heavy charge. Dwynwyn, on her remote, tidal island, struck the Crows as the perfect baby-sitter for an unpredictable mother-to-be. They'd had enough difficulty keeping track of me at Caer Leb. No one wanted the responsibility of minding me while on the move to a tribal gathering where the closest thing the *Combrogos* knew to a city would spring into being. The Crows unanimously ignored my pleas that Dwynwyn be asked to accompany me to the festival, and promptly set off with me to her island. Their only worry was that Dwynwyn might have been angered by the college's previous refusal of her services and would turn me away. But when we reached the narrow spit of sand and pebbles that led to her island, we saw Dwynwyn was waiting for us on the other side.

"Took you long enough," she called out. (She did say it rather snottily.)

"All right, all right. So you told us so," a Crow crabbed back.

This rancorous exchange between elder females was at once immensely comforting and maddening to me. In short, I felt right at home.

"Almost missed the tide," Dwynwyn added unnecessarily. "Hurry up."

I had started to cross to the island when Moira surprised me, almost knocking me off balance on the slippery stones, by grabbing me and whirling me into a black-winged embrace.

"Courage, Maeve Rhuad. You are in skilled hands. We'll be back for you in three days."

Then Moira and the other Crows were gone rather suddenly. There was nothing for me to do but walk between the waves to Dwynwyn who stood with her arms outstretched in her blood-red tunic, her wild hair whitening the wind.

※

It was late afternoon when I woke from the nap Dwynwyn insisted I take after she fed me something unidentifiable (and awfully slippery) from her pot. Only now did she permit me to speak. So I told her everything that had happened since *Imbolc*, including King Bran's capture, Viviane's warning, the rejection of me as a candidate for sacrifice, the likelihood of the lot falling to Esus. Then I poured out my doubts and confusion.

"I don't understand. How could it be—*could* it be?—that Esus's dying could save King Bran and even stop the Romans from coming to Mona?"

Dwynwyn did not answer for a time, just gazed across the straits. At last she turned her eyes on me, the clear one and the cloudy one.

"Without blood, there is no birth," she said in a singsong voice. "Without death, there is no life. Without the salt of bitter tears, the sweetest cake will lose its savor. But," she cautioned, "between this world and the Other, it is never simply tit for tat. Give me this, I'll give you that. It's give all you've got or nothing at all. Give what you want for yourself, not what you want gone. That's where the druid boys might have made a teensy little mistake."

"You mean because it doesn't matter to them whether Esus lives or dies? But it matters to me. And it also matters to me whether King Bran lives or dies. If they wanted both of us, or just me, it would be so much simpler."

"Oh? Did I miss something? Did someone put you in charge of life and death when I wasn't looking?"

"But if I could find a way to save Esus, does that mean Bran will be lost to Rome and that the straits will run with blood and the groves burn to the ground?"

"My, my," Dwynwyn clucked. "Such responsibility."

She was laughing at me.

"But I need to know!" I raged at her.

"You can't know, my sweet honey cake, my hot eel pie." Her terms of endearment were somewhat alarming. "That would be cheating, now wouldn't it, my plump, spitted piglet." She got up to stir the pot. Good grief, we'd only eaten a little while ago. "One eye sees what the other doesn't. Choose blindly with your eyes open. Walk and whistle in the dark. You're not the whole story, only a part. Even the teller is changed in the telling."

"What's the use of your being old and wise if you can't tell me what to do!" I cried out in frustration.

"I am old and wise enough to know that when people say, 'Tell me what to do,' they mean, 'Tell me to do what I want to do.' Of course they don't always know what that is, and they want you to do the work of figuring that out for them, too. But I'm too hungry and cranky. You'll have to figure that out for yourself, my overgrown cabbage. Now concentrate. Close at least one eye while you think."

It didn't take me long. Behind my lids, in my blood, in my bones, in my flesh, he was there.

"I want to see Esus," I said, and thick, messy tears began to fall. "I want to see him in this world, in the flesh. I don't know what he thinks or what he wants. I don't know if he is a god or could be one or not. I only know I love him. Nissyen says he might not want to be saved. I don't know what is right or wrong. I don't know what to do. But I need to see him. I must see him."

"Well answered, Maeve Rhuad, well answered." I could just hear her over my sobs. "And a wiser answer than I looked for. If you had been certain what to do, I couldn't have helped you. Or I wouldn't have. But now...."

She stopped speaking and regarded me thoughtfully. My tears ebbed as I began, willy-nilly, to hope again.

"There may be a way, but it won't be easy. It won't be what you or anyone expects. But yes, I believe it can be done, and will do nicely." She cackled to herself. Not a very reassuring sound. "Entertaining for me. Instructive for her. Yes, I like it. I like it a lot."

⁂

An old woman walks along the shore in the last light. She is cloaked in grey. You can't see her face and eyes. She blends with the rock or with the light reflecting from the swells when a cloud passes over the sun. She is a flapping, grey rag, wiping away the colors of the day as she passes, leaving shadows in her wake.

An old woman walks along the shore. Her back is bent, her ear cocked to the murmur of water meeting earth. Her breasts brush her belly, and her dry thighs whisper. Her breath whistles in and out, blown away behind her with the west wind. She walks on into night. Her flesh is thin over bones sharp as the sudden stars.

Meanwhile, to the East on a tidal island, a young girl takes her ease. Lying back on a heather bed at the mouth of a dry cave, she looks out at a round of starry sky. She drums with her fingertips on the round of her great belly and sings snatches of old songs between bites of honey cake. Now and then she gets up to heap her bowl with another helping of whatever bubbles in the pot. At last she curls on her side and falls into a cat-like sleep.

At least this was what I imagined Dwynwyn was doing with my shape.

"Don't worry," Dwynwyn had said when I fretted that I might miss the birth of my child while I was off being a hag. "I won't have your baby for you. Not on your life. I'm just going to eat and sleep, maybe comb these gorgeous, flaming curls. Not that my own hair isn't a wonder and a glory."

It was. I wished I could wear it loose and windswept as Dwynwyn usually did. But not only was I disguised in her flesh, I also wore her cloak of invisibility. That did not mean I could not be seen, only that I would appear to others, not as Dwynwyn, who would be recognized by Cranes and Crows, but as generic old woman—or, when need be, as the Hag herself. In other words, no one would mess with me.

The disguise, from my point of view, left a lot to be desired. I had wanted to be turned into some animal, preferably swift of foot or wing, and be restored to my own shape when I reached Esus. But Dwynwyn said she could not be troubled with zapping me from one form into another, long distance, and that I was not experienced enough to do it myself and would only end up getting caught. Take it or leave it, she finally said. When I agreed, she laid a *geis* on me for good measure.

"As long as you are in the shape of the hag, you will not reveal that you are Maeve Rhuad. If you do, I call upon the power of the three worlds to keep you in the shape of a hag forever."

Then faster than you can say holy shit, we changed shapes.

Now here I was, an old lady on a twelve mile hike to Rhosneigr. Despite my suddenly advanced years, I moved more quickly than I might have in my own shape, being much lightened. In fact, I felt lighter altogether, as if I had hollow bones. My blood felt thin, like the last trickle of an autumn stream before the rains. But I also had new aches. The call of the earth to sit, lie down, stop, let go, was like the constant drone of the pipes.

Gradually my new, old shape began to shape my thoughts, too. They slowed and became essential. No more tugging and bounding ahead and running circles around the rest of me. As I left the shore for the wood, my thoughts amounted to *one foot forward, then the other. There's a root rearing up. Listen, an owl calling. No, I won't rest now. Keep going. One foot, and then the other.* When the prevailing wind shifted and blew at my back, I spread my arms and the cloak of invisibility became a sail. I scudded the remaining miles, blowing into the festival camp just before dawn.

∝

At first glance, camp was much as it had been the year before, with its colorful, makeshift shelters, strolling musicians, and raucous reunions. But the absence of King Bran as a jolly, unifying force was palpable. His son Caradoc's leadership of the Silures was only tentative. Some felt Caradoc should be made king; others felt that he could not be while his father's fate was unknown. Still others thought there should be a king-making rite with a druid wrapped in a bloody bull hide till the identity of the next sovereign was revealed to him. This matter was the subject of much debate and not a few brawls.

The other hot topic was, of course, the quinquennial sacrifice. There were rumors that a candidate would be chosen that night in a secret rite. I began to appreciate my disguise as I drifted from campfire to campfire, always greeted with respect and given something to eat, then forgotten as people went back to their gossip or debate. By midafternoon, after sorting through some contradictory information, I had determined the likeliest spot for the ceremony of the lots: Bryn Du, a thickly wooded hill a mile or so inland from Rhosneigr where the druids traditionally made camp before the opening ceremonies beside Llyn Cerrig Bach. As the afternoon shadows began to lengthen, I left camp unnoticed and made my way through field and marsh towards the black hill.

For most of the way, I heard nothing but bird song and marsh water percolating and the occasional burble of a tidal stream pushing through the grasses towards the sea. Then, just as the marshes ended, voices drifted towards me, female voices, engaged in what sounded like competitive cursing. I stopped to listen.

"By the power of Badb, I invoke hail to hound him and hurl itself upon his head."

"Ha! That's nothing. By the power of Nemain, I call upon the crows to pluck out his eyes and swallow them and excrete the remains upon his head."

"You always bring shit into it."

"And why not? Shit to the shits, I say."

"It shows a want of imagination, that's all. Now listen. By the power of Macha, I call the great night mare to trample his tenderest parts. And may the Fomorians make his remains into haggis."

"It's my turn again. Let's see. By the power of Badb, I call into his bed all biting bugs and slithering slugs. Wait. I'm not done yet. And let him be soaked in the sputum of toads."

"And by Nemain's power, I call forth pulsing sores on his manly protrusion and bursting boils on his behind."

"By Macha, boils are much more painful when they don't burst."

"Let them not burst then. Now don't interrupt. It's still my turn."

Curious, I followed the sound of their voices into a thicket. There, imprisoned in a wicker cage, I saw three women, their hair unkempt, their bodies naked except for a ragged plaid they shared between them. Most horrifying to me were the iron neck rings, each one linked to the others by a massive chain. They were doing their best to keep up their morale by calling on the Mórrígan to curse their enemy. I could not help but be touched.

"Daughters," I hailed the women, all older than me—or they had been.

They started. The one on my left made the sign for warding off danger from the Otherworld.

The one on my right said, "It's just an old woman."

"No," said the one in the middle. "It's the Grey Hag herself. Are you come to prophesy over us? So, is it into the drink or sold for drink? No one tells us anything, and we don't know which is worse: to be sold as slaves? (For where there's life there's hope.) Or to be fed to the fishes."

"You mean the Lady of the Lake," said one of her companions. "Which end might be more fitting to our rank, though not necessarily more pleasant."

I turned a prophetic eye on them—surely one of Dwynwyn's eyes had the Sight. I lost my focus on the future when I noticed the comet-streak of white in the black hair of the middle woman.

"I know you!" I burst out.

"Flattering, I'm sure, to be known by the Grey Hag. But do you know my fate?"

"Give me a minute." An idea was beginning to form in my mind. "And meanwhile tell me how you come to be caged. I thought you were married to a Brigantian chieftain of some importance."

"So I was. But we had our little disagreements. I'm from Hibernia, the Wicklow Hills. He thought he was marrying a goldmine, so he did. But more and more, the druids control the route. That suited my husband, but it didn't suit me. It's not that I'm greedy, but I like to call my own shots. He'd taken over my mines, and the druids had taken over the trade. So I formed an all female warrior band and started raiding. About a month ago, my husband ambushed us and took us captive. I'm ashamed that I haven't died of shame, but here I am. We are reduced to calling down curses on his head. But I don't think they're having much effect. Perhaps yours might?" she concluded hopefully.

"I've got a better idea," I said. "How would you like to escape?"

Three pairs of eye widened, then narrowed in skepticism.

"Meaning no disrespect to yourself, Old Woman of Beara, but we're after needing Goibnu the Smith. Or had you not noticed the latest fashion in torques we're sporting?"

"Don't dismiss my powers out of hand," I said severely. I felt my hands beginning to pulse and burn. "Before I free you, I must have your solemn oath that you will do something for me in return."

A little while later I left them with their shackles melted in strategic places. According to their sworn promise to me, they would maintain the appearance of captivity until nightfall. At that time they would slip away and steal some horses. Or liberate them, as the Hibernian woman put it. Then they would wait, hidden in the thickets, till dawn. If I hadn't come by then, they were free to go.

I walked on up Bryn Du, strains of the women's voices following me a little way. They were composing hymns of praise to me and arguing about the rhyme scheme. It was obvious that none of them had had much formal poetic training, but their hearts were in the right place, which counts for a lot with us Mighty Ones. (I'm afraid being taken for a deity had gone to my head a bit.)

The wood thickened, though it was largely free of undergrowth, the trees being mostly copper beech. They were not in full leaf yet, but when they were, the hill would indeed look dark from a distance and be dark under the canopy of leaves. Although I had been climbing gradually for some time, I still hadn't seen any sign of a druid encampment. I was beginning to wonder if I was on the wrong track when I heard voices ahead, male voices. I darted as swiftly and silently as I could from tree to tree. When I caught the glint of a red beard, I hid behind a massive tree trunk and listened.

"I repeat," said an all-too-familiar voice. "No one can see the ovate students now. They are in the strictest seclusion, preparing for the most solemn of rites. You will see him tomorrow night at Llyn Cerrig Bach."

"Ah, but that's just it: will I? Let me be frank with you, Lovernios, most renowned of all druids in the Holy Isles. There are rumors abroad that the candidate for the quinquennial sacrifice has already been selected and that the rite is for form's sake only. Now I paid honest gold for my young friend's place in college, and I found eleven men to stand surety for him with me. You are answerable to us."

"Let me assure you then that your charge is well, and your gold has not been wasted. He has proven himself an able student, and we have observed that he is wise beyond his years. As for the Great Sacrifice, only the gods know how the lots will fall out. If the lot falls to him, I say again, your gold has not been wasted."

The merchant cleared his throat. "I would expect no less than justice and honor in all matters from the druids of Mona, whose fame spans the continents and the worlds. Still, as a much-traveled man, I feel bound to point out that many other peoples have abandoned this particular form of sacrifice—"

"And have fallen to Rome," said Lovernios.

"Now don't misunderstand me. I am not saying anything in favor of Rome. And I am appalled by their suppression of druids in Gaul. But I still fail to see how such bloodshed can—"

"It is a mystery." Lovernios cut him off. "It is not for you to understand. I am afraid I must order you to leave now."

I peered around the tree as I heard the merchant's footsteps coming my way. I wanted to intercept him, but I heard no movement from Foxface. I supposed he was watching to make sure the merchant did not double back and try to sneak into camp. As the man passed my tree, he happened to glance my way. I put my fingers to my lips and motioned for him to keep walking. To my relief he did, or he might have revealed my presence to

Foxface. A few moments later, I heard a rustle of leaves and snapping of twigs as Foxface moved off in the other direction. I hurried after the merchant.

"You," I called softly when we were well out of Foxface's range of sight and sound. "You who seek Esus ab Joseph, turn and speak to me."

He obeyed. Perhaps he, too, thought I was a supernatural being, though I'd sensed he was a bit of a skeptic.

"How do you know whom I seek?"

"The Grey Hag sees and knows all."

I figured I'd try it on for size. It was a certainly a more impressive answer than, "I was eavesdropping, stupid." He eyed me critically. I glared back at him.

"Tell me then, you who know all, will the lot be rigged?"

"I tell nothing for nothing," I said craftily. "You tell me: If you knew the lot was going to be rigged, would you help Esus ab Joseph?"

"Help him what?"

"Help him escape."

"Escape the will of the gods?" He began to look nervous.

"We are supposing the lot to be rigged," I reminded him.

"I can't go against the druids of Mona," he sighed. "Bad for business. Damn shame if they do sacrifice him. There's something about that boy—"

"His blood will be on you if they do," I hissed. "And upon your children."

Now he looked upset. (I've noticed that skeptics are often more scared of curses than other people. They have no recourse.)

"But I don't have any children," he remembered. "Can't. Had a fever when I was a young man. Fried my scrotum. The druids said there was nothing they could do to help me. That's why I took such an interest in the lad. Still, I don't see what I can do now—"

"I will tell you what to do." I decided he wasn't trustworthy enough to involve directly. "On your way back to Rhosneigr, you will pass by three women in a wicker cage. Trust me: they are the Mórrígan in disguise. They hold the fate of Esus ab Joseph in their hands. Give them all the gold and jewels you have on your person. Tell them the Grey Hag bids them keep it safe until the hour of need. Then go your way and keep your mouth shut. Tight. Do all that I say and your hands will be clean of his blood. Fail, and not only will your seed be boiled but your appendage will shrivel and fall off. More, you will never again hear the sweet clink of one gold piece against another. Do I make myself perfectly clear?"

"Perfectly." He gulped. "I will do all you say. I swear it on the sacred ground of the Holy Isles and all their precious metals."

I nodded, satisfied, and watched as he scurried away to do my bidding. I turned and walked on, jubilant, until I remembered that Esus's fate was not so easily secured. It was not in the hands of my trumped-up Mórrígán or in my hands—yet. My immediate challenge was to slip past the watch into the druid camp. The weather was on my side. The Time of Brightness notwithstanding, clouds cloaked the sky. Fog rolled in from the sea and began to swirl among the trees. (Were the Cranes calling for this fog to shroud their mystery—or were they as inept at weather magic as I'd long suspected they were?) In either case, the change in weather suited my purposes at the moment. No one saw the Grey Hag gliding silently through the mist.

I soon found the camp, with its bright pavilions and cook fires, and observed it from the edge of the clearing. Only druids and ovate students appeared to be in residence. I spotted Esus moving about camp freely, not restrained or drugged or set apart in any way. As I watched for a chance to signal him, he and the other students began making trips, back and forth, carrying firewood and various supplies to some other place. I edged around the clearing and followed Esus on his next trip to a smaller clearing within a perfect ring of beech trees.

As soon as I saw the glade, I knew it was the site of the secret ceremony. A fire was already blazing, heating a flat cooking stone beside it. Ingredients for the cake had been ceremoniously laid out. I recognized what must be the last unground sheaf of barley from the harvest tied with red yarn. Near the grain was a golden vessel of some sort, a chalice or a basin; I wasn't sure which. There were also several lengths of iron chain I did not like the looks of at all. I decided to take up my post here, where the action would be. When the students went back to the camp, I climbed up into one of the trees. Grey mist, grey bark, grey hooded cloak. I was as good as invisible. I hoped Esus would come alone on his next trip, and I could call him over to my tree.

Someone did come alone, but it was not Esus. Robed in ceremonial white with his birdmask and headdress of feathers, Foxface entered the ring of trees. Then he crouched, took up the barley and began to grind it in the quern. Grinding was usually the job of a female servant, but there were no women on Bryn Du, not even a Crow.

Except for me.

I sat in my tree, hardly breathing. Dusk deepened. The fire blazed brighter. I watched the arrhythmic leaping of flame and listened to it crackle and hiss. I watched the rhythmic motion of the druid's arm, and I listened to the repetitive sound of grain being slowly, surely ground.

Grey Hag or not, I was an old woman who had walked a long way and missed a night's sleep. My eyes closed. The arms of the great mother tree held me secure.

43

THE FINGERPRINT OF A FILTHY GOD

When I woke, they were all there standing in concentric circles around the fire, the students forming the inner circle. It was an eerie sight: the young faces lit from beneath by firelight, the outer circle of white-robed druids like a ring around some secret sun, the immense darkness crouching over all, thick clouds hiding the bright eye of the almost full moon. I might almost have thought I was dreaming, but the pain in my every bone and muscle soon cleared my head. I scanned the students and found Esus standing opposite my tree. Like everyone else, he had his eyes fixed on the round, flat barley cake, now cooling on the stone. I was perched high enough so that I had a good view of it, too.

After what seemed like a long time—but may have been only moments—the archdruid stepped into the circle and stood over the cake, his hands held palms up to receive it. Lovernios and the grey-bearded druid, who had presided over admissions, knelt and carefully eased the cake from the stone, placing it in the archdruid's hands. When his two assistants were standing again, the archdruid held the cake aloft so that the round side faced out. Reflecting the firelight, the cake glowed, a honey moon. Except for a black mark that looked like a thumbprint.

I looked from the cake to Esus, who gazed at it with interest. I bet he was thinking of the unleavened bread his people had taken when they fled from Egypt. There had been a mark in the passover story, too, a mark made on the houses of the Jews from the blood of an animal without blemish. That mark told the angel of death to spare the lives of the Jews. The sooty mark on the barley cake would mark the one to die. I wondered who had made it.

Now the archdruid began to parade slowly around the circle, holding the cake at chest-level. When he had completed the circumference, he held the cake over his head once more for a long, suspended moment. Then, without warning, he let out a loud cry, striking just the note that held triumph and agony in equal measure, and he broke the cake in two. Foxface and the grey druid each took a half and began to break off smaller pieces, which they placed in a wicker basket at their feet. When they had finished that task, they set about blindfolding the students and the other druids. Would they blindfold themselves in the end?

They did not.

Still sighted, the two druids rejoined the archdruid in the center. Though no one but his two assistants (and me) could see the ritual gesture, the archdruid raised the basket and began to chant. Then, circle by circle, so that the sound seemed to ripple, the others added their voices. It was a strange, wild chant. I kept straining to hear the words, but they were not in any language I knew, perhaps not in any human language at all. The deep, rhythmic rumble of male voices throbbed like the earth's heartbeat, pulsing through the roots of the tree that held me, rising and singing in the sap. Not all the sounds were low. There were harsh, high cries that made me think of predatory birds. There were the grunts and bellows of rutting boar and deer as well as long, piercing howls.

When the chant reached a certain pitch of intensity, the archdruid handed the basket to grey beard, and he and Foxface began making the rounds. I looked as hard as I could with my one clear eye. One was all I needed to see that it was Lovernios who reached into the basket and placed the piece of cake in each man's hand.

"The gods, my ass," part of me wanted to scream. "Just who the fuck do you think you're fooling here!" My limbs quivered with the urge to swing down out of my tree. But the rest of me was held in the grip of the rhythm. The scene rolled on inexorably.

At last the rounds were done. Foxface and Grey Beard returned to the center with the empty basket. When the chant ceased, the silence was louder and more awful than any sound that went before.

"Raise up the broken body of the god," the archdruid commanded.

A forest of hands rose into the firelight. I looked at only one hand: long, lean, and brown. His hand was darker than the other hands and more beautiful. What his hand held was darker still: the blackened piece of barley cake, the fingerprint of a filthy god.

Slowly my vision widened as I watched Foxface untie the blindfolds. Now the air was full of breaths being let out, hysterical laughter and sobbing. Only Esus remained still. Foxface removed his blindfold last of all. As Esus confronted the charred piece of barley cake, there was a faint twitch at the corner of his mouth. Then he lifted his eyes. I knew he couldn't see me, yet for a moment he looked straight at me. My heart pounded louder than the chant; a cry rose in my throat. Before it could break free, he shifted his gaze. His eyes swept the circle, coming to rest at last on Lovernios, whose face was bone-white and beaded with sweat.

No one spoke. Everyone, including the archdruid, seemed to be waiting for Esus to make a move. He was the chief celebrant now. He turned away from Lovernios and stepped into the center of the circle. He cupped the blackened cake in his hands, held it up and out. Though everyone watched him, it seemed a curiously private gesture. Then he uttered one word:

"Eat."

He raised his hands to his mouth and ate his piece all at once. The vision of my clear eye was so acute, I could see little particles of charcoal in the spittle at the corner of his mouth.

When all the others had eaten, too, the archdruid picked up the golden vessel. Suddenly I recognized its shape, and a flash of cold lightning struck my spine and raised every hair on my neck. A skull. A gold-plated skull. It had been filled with some dark brew. The archdruid handed it to Esus.

"Beloved of the *Combrogos*. Chosen of the god. My own dear son. Drink. Drink deep."

Esus drained the skull with a slight, uncontrollable grimace and handed it back to the archdruid. Then everything happened very quickly. Lovernios and the grey druid came forward, took hold of Esus's wrists and chained them behind him. If I had been in my own shape, with my own impulses unbridled, I would have hurled myself into the scene and done my best to start a riot. But my disguise seemed to have come complete with a measure of wisdom, and I heeded an inner voice that cautioned: Wait.

"Why are you binding him!" Ciaran of the blue-black hair had the grace to protest. "He's not a criminal."

"These chains are no shame to him," the archdruid soothed. "No shame at all. They are merely part of the rite."

Yeah, right, I thought.

Sensing the dismay of Esus's classmates, the archdruid swiftly pronounced a dismissal and the other druids herded them out of the grove before their shock could wear off any further. As it was, some of them wept and broke ranks to embrace Esus. But that was the extent of their rebellion, and I saw no potential for full-scale insurrection.

At last Esus was alone with the three (and me). I slipped out of my tree and followed as they led him deeper into the wood. The sky was still overcast, but the wind had risen again, and I had no need to muffle my footsteps. As near as I could reckon, we were heading down hill towards the marshes, though off the beaten path. About halfway down, they stopped before an oak tree (what else?) that dwarfed all the trees around it. I was relieved to see that they merely bound him to the tree instead of hanging him from it—a traditional pose of the god Esus. Perhaps they were saving that for later. When they were satisfied that the chains would hold, the three walked back up the hill, passing within spitting range of me. (I restrained myself with difficulty.) I was a little surprised that no one had remained to stand guard, but then I supposed leaving the victim drugged, bound to a tree, and utterly abandoned was all in a night's rite. I watched till the three were out of sight, then I turned towards Esus.

I thought I heard him moaning, but it might have been the wind, shifting and tossing like someone too restless to sleep. I couldn't see his face clearly; everything looked soft-edged in the milky darkness under the moon-soaked clouds. Then the clouds overhead thinned. The moon caught in the branches of the oak tree, and I saw him plainly. Just him. Not the druid's mysterious, oracular stranger. Not even my lover, my twin, my other. Just a young man weeping, a young man, not quite full grown, who might die without ever seeing his own bit of earth again.

Without thinking what to do or say, I went to him, murmuring comfort in his mother tongue. "There now. It will be all right." I lifted a corner of my cloak of invisibility and wiped his eyes and, yes, his nose, too.

"Anna?" he said.

Even with the thinned clouds and the brighter light, my face was hidden by the cloak. Also, the drink he'd swallowed was no doubt laced with mistletoe and other drugs. So it did not seem strange to him that an old Jewish woman he'd last seen at the Temple of Jerusalem should have found her way into a druid grove. No more surprising than that he should find himself there. I didn't see any point in setting him straight. It would only confuse him more. Besides, I was under a *geis* not to reveal myself as Maeve.

"Yes, dear," I said.

As I spoke, I thought of Anna, the deft touch of her hands, the rambling, authoritative way she spoke. If he had not heeded her, we might never have found each other. Silently I thanked her and asked for her help.

"Anna," he said again. I sensed he was struggling, trying to find a clear passage in his drug-clouded mind. "Anna, you sent me here to Anu's country. Are you Anu? When I said your name before the druids.... No, now I remember. I didn't say your name. Maeve did. Maeve." My heart leaped to hear him speak my name as if it sweetened his tongue. "Do you know Maeve?"

"Maeve. Ah, yes. You mean the cheeky little redhead. Not so little anymore, I hear."

"Little was never the right word for her," he said severely. "She is almost as tall as I am, and she has a great heart. Her breasts are like two fawns feeding among the lilies. Their veins are like the rivers flowing from Eden."

I would have liked him to go on in this vein, so to speak, but there was enough of the hag in me now to call my wants to heel. "You were going to tell me what she said," I reminded him.

"What she said." He strained to make the connection. "Oh, yes. She cried out: Anna sent him, and they all thought she meant Anu. Are you Anu?"

"Anna, Anu. Don't trouble yourself about it. Leave that to the Old Ones."

"Not that I believe in Anu, if that's who you are," he added, as politely as he could. "There is only one God."

"Whatever," I said. The night was not so young anymore. I was not going to be sidetracked by theology.

"But you did send me here, Anna the prophetess," he persisted. "You said: Take ship with the *Keltoi*. Step outside your tribe. The world is a big place, Yeshua, and it's small, small as a mustard seed, small as a hazelnut."

"Nice turn of phrase," I murmured.

"Anna, I don't know why you sent me, but I'm afraid I've failed. Or else I'm very stupid. And I always thought I was so smart. Always at the top of the class, unless the rabbi threw me out. You know how it was."

"You were a smart-ass kid, all right," I said tenderly. "Always kicking up a fuss at the Temple."

"Tell me, Anna. Please. Why am I here? What was I supposed to learn? What am I supposed to do? Maeve always says I came to the Holy Isles to find her. But I don't know. I can't believe it's that simple."

Simple! He wanted more complications in our lives? The Maeve part of me was feeling huffy, but the hag had hold of my tongue.

"The young are always absolutely sure they know everything," I heard myself say.

"Then you tell me, Anna, Anu. You are old and wise."

"The old are wise, because they know they don't know," I cautioned. But he wasn't listening.

"Is it for this? Is it to die here like this? A sacrifice like their god Esus? They call me Esus. Did you know that? Anna, Anu. Yeshua, Jesus, Esus. Does it make a difference?"

He laughed and his voice cracked. His throat sounded parched, no doubt the effect of the drugs. But in my mind I saw those cracked and bleeding lips again.

"They initiated me, you know. I was in the earth for three days like one dead. When I was inside, I saw my death, Anna, Anu. Is this it? Was I born only to die? Will my death save their college and their king, even if they don't change their ways? Can that possibly be why you sent me here? Or did I just fail? Maybe this death is a punishment. The Most High has abandoned me, because I have forsaken him. Here among the *Keltoi* I have kept the laws of Moses as best I could. I have eaten nothing unclean, but I have been with them where they worship in their groves and among the unhewn stones. And Maeve. I have loved Maeve. I love Maeve, a gentile I cannot hope to marry, who carries her own father's child. Eli, Eli—"

His voice broke and he sobbed.

I did not try to stop him. I did not know how to answer him. For once, I let myself not know. I let both of us be. In time he quieted. Clouds shrouded the moon once more. A drop or two of cold rain fell. I listened to the wind. I thought I could hear the sea in the distance. I breathed the scent of damp earth and leaves. I pictured rivers flowing over the earth and under it. I listened to my breath and felt it connecting me to Esus. I waited. Let it be as you will, I spoke silently, though I had no idea who or what I meant by *you*. Then my mouth opened, and the words came out:

"I sent you here, Yeshua ben Miriam. Now I have come to send you home."

Without another word, I set about loosing his chains.

My fingers were in fine fettle, full of fire and not in the least arthritic. Sooner than I might have hoped, I had him free. I grabbed his hand and pulled him after me, moving quickly and with more sureness than I felt, so that neither of us would question my authority. Exhausted and still drugged, he stumbled now and then, but movement and the scattered raindrops were waking him up.

"Where are we going?" he wondered.

"Don't ask questions now." I spoke just above a whisper. "And try not to make so much noise. You don't have to snap every twig. Think with your feet."

For awhile we did just that. I was glad we were on a hill. The cloud cover was disorienting, and the occasional flash of lightning didn't help much, but I figured if we kept going down, we would reach the marshes. Or if we had come down the far side of the hill, we could always walk around the base. So far, I sensed we were heading the right way, and soon this sense was confirmed by other senses: I could smell the salt of the marshes, and biting insects began to swarm. Best of all, not too far away, I heard the whinny of a horse. Since horses don't usually hang out in swamps, I reckoned the Hibernian woman and her sister warriors were keeping their word and waiting for us. The footing was a little trickier now. I was so preoccupied with keeping us out of the bog that none of my senses, common or extra, registered an obstacle ahead until a flash of lightning revealed it:

Foxface, in full regalia, standing foursquare in front of us, so close that with another two steps I would have run into him.

Darkness fell again, but before I could even think of making a move, Foxface's hand closed on my arm in a furious grip. I could feel the blood vessels shattering. I would be marked like the barley bread with his fingerprints. Or Dwynwyn would. I suddenly remembered I was hidden in her shape. I was so grateful, if I could I would have bent over and kissed the bunions on her toes.

"Who is it that flees through the night with the holy one, the chosen of the gods? Who dares!"

His voice was terrible. But mine, I decided as I drew a deep breath, would be even more terrible.

"As you value your life, Lovernios, as you value your druid's hood and your poet's branch, as you value your feathers and your beaked mask, stand aside. I am about the business of the gods."

My voice did indeed strike a deep, gritty note, as if the earth spoke, or a mountain.

"Who are you?"

"It is not for a mere mortal to know. If you knew who I was, your terror would be so great, your bowels would boil and burst their bounds." (A suitably poetic way of saying you would shit your pants.)

Foxface was not as impressed as I could have wished. His grip did not relax. His palms did not sweat.

"Esus ab Joseph, if I saw you truly, who is this hag, and how do you come to be in her clutches?"

Clutches! Foxface was the one doing the clutching around here. I was merely holding Esus's hand.

"She would not tell me her name."

'Atta Boy, Esus. And it was true, too. I had never said whether I was Anna, Anu, or anyone else for that matter.

"But why do you go with her, a man of your honor and greatness?"

Foxface was sincere. He wasn't flattering. This could present complications.

"She has great powers."

"That's right," I asserted myself again. "Very great powers. Now get out of our way before I have to use them."

"Not greater than yours, surely." Foxface ignored me utterly. "Think about it. Would you choose to be a common fugitive? A no one? A nothing? And if I bring you back by force, think how your great offering will be debased. How can you, Esus, chosen of the gods, how can you allow an old hag, whoever she may be, to drag you from your destiny?"

"Destiny!" I said. "What do you know about destiny? Are you the Mórrígán that you know the hour of a man's death?"

"Save your breath, old woman. No matter what you say, he knows and I know that he is the chosen one. His hand raised up the blackened barley cake. His tongue tasted it. He is the one."

"Sheep's pizzle!" I roared. "Answer me this, Lovernios. Answer me this, if you have testicles enough to tell the truth: From whose hand did he receive the burnt barley cake? From whose hand: the god's or your own?"

The words went home. I could feel the tremor that shook his body. I could smell the sudden sweat of fear even in the rain.

"Who are you?" he asked again.

"One Who Knows," I said in my most ominous tones.

At that moment the elements decided to get into the act. A terrific gust of wind blew back my hood and my white hair (or Dwynwyn's) tumbled out onto the wind just in time to be illumined by another flash of lightning.

"Now I know who you are, Dwynwyn!" cried Foxface. "One who knows. Ha! You're just a meddling old woman, and your talk is old woman's talk."

"Old woman's talk indeed," I agreed. "And if I chose to talk, ah, what tales I could tell, Lovernios, what tales. All the better for being true. All the better for being kept secret for so long. Would you like to hear a story?"

"Why would I want to listen to an old woman's stories? Come, Esus. I will take you back to the tree. No one need ever know you were gone."

"Because, Lovernios, it is not my story I would be telling. It's your story, Lovernios. And everyone wants to hear his own story, even if he also fears it."

"My story," he repeated.

"Listen, Lovernios, listen. Once upon a time, not so long ago, there was a young boy of great promise, who became a druid of even greater promise. He was ambitious, this druid, and he set sail for the vast western land beyond the the Isles of the Blest, the land where the sun goes each night. He dreamed of ruling there, no kings, just him, the greatest druid of all time. But he never got there, did he, Lovernios? He was shipwrecked, dashed on the rocks of one of the Shining Isles. It is called Tir na mBan."

I felt that name take hold of him. He stood silent in the cold rain, his life passing before his eyes. I went on, making the most of what I knew, until the story of his life also became the story of mine. When I got to the night at Bryn Celli Ddu, he could not bear to hear it.

"No!" he cried out. "No!"

"Yes," I insisted.

"Esus!" His voice was anguished. "You told her!"

"He did not."

"Then it was *her*. That bitch. That's right. It all fits together now. I saw her on your island before, and she was just now sent there again to be kept out of the way. That was a mistake. The two of you are in it together against me. Ever since she came here, she's been out to destroy me. The bitch! The treacherous, vicious bitch—"

I could feel Esus tense. He would have struck Lovernios, but I gripped his hand harder and jumped in before he could make a move.

"Your daughter," I said. "Your daughter. Do you hear me, man! Your daughter!"

"My daughter," he wailed. "My daughter. But you can't tell me she is not trying to destroy me, like her bitch-mothers before her. They sent her to destroy me. I know it! I know it!"

"You know nothing," I said. "If you knew anything at all, you would have known that all you had to do was call her daughter, and she would have answered with joy: father. As for destruction, she has no need to destroy you. You are destroying yourself."

There was nothing more to say. The rain fell. A man wept.

"Let us pass, Lovernios."

His hand fell from my arm.

44

BEARING DOWN

We are riding, riding, riding through the rainy night, the horses making swift work of the ground I covered so painstakingly by foot. Not that there is an absence of pain here. My jouncing bones are so ill-padded, I know that I am still in Dwynwyn's shape. One of us is going to feel this ride tomorrow.

I am riding behind the Hibernian woman; Esus behind one of the others. We are heading southeast towards the straits, Abermenai Point to be exact, a spit of tidal land five miles past Dwynwyn's Isle where the Hibernian woman hopes to cross and hightail it into the mountains—if the tide is right. For awhile I worry about the tide. I strain my ears for sounds of pursuit. I wonder if Dwynwyn knows what's happening and how and when we will resume our shapes. But there comes a point in our dark, wet flight when I cease to think about anything. The ride seems endless.

Then the rain stops, and the air changes. As we splash across Afon Cefni onto the Maltreath sands, I see stars in the eastern sky just before they begin to fade. The open ground gives the horses a fresh burst of energy. The speed, the dawn, the smell of the sea come together in a rush of wind. Now Dwynwyn's isle rises before us. I scan the hills for a glimpse of my own shape but see nothing as we race by and on and on, unimpeded, towards the silvery light outlining the dark mountains.

Soon Abermenai Point lies exposed before us, reaching towards the sands on the other side. The tide is at its lowest ebb. The first rays of sun shoot up behind the mountains as we race down the neck. A torch or maybe a stray spark of sun waits at the end of the land. Not sure what it is, the Hibernian woman begins to rein in her horse, but we are going too fast to stop abruptly.

Then suddenly—so suddenly that the earth and sky tumble one over the other as my stomach sails skyward and my knees buckle under me—I am back in my own shape, standing or struggling to stand on a spit of sand as three horses thunder towards me and come to a splashing halt in the straits. In another moment, Esus slips from his horse and runs to me. We are in each other's arms, holding each other as close as we can with my belly wedged between us, both of us trembling and sobbing.

"Maeve," he said when he could speak, "how did you know to wait for me here?"

"It would take a long time to explain."

345

I wondered if I was still under a *geis* not to reveal that I had been the hag now that I was no longer in disguise. A glance at Dwynwyn told me nothing. She just stood, white hair gleaming in the growing light, staring at nothing with her seeing, unseeing eyes.

"Time," said the Hibernian woman, dismounting and approaching us, "is exactly what we don't have." I noticed she had liberated some fine new clothes as well as her horse. "It won't take long for our escapes to be discovered and our trail to be traced."

"I was going to be the quinquennial sacrifice, Maeve," Esus explained. "But Anu, Anna...." he hesitated.

The sun was rising; the drugs had worn off. He was starting to think again, and the Hibernian woman was right. We didn't have time for that.

"I know, Esus. I know."

"The only thing we've got going for us is the tide," the woman urged. "We've got to cross the straits and get into the cover of the mountains as quickly as we can. With any luck, they'll miss this tide. Of course, they can cross by boat, but that will take longer. Say your goodbyes and let's be off."

Esus and I stared at one another.

"But Maeve is coming with us!"

"Now wait a minute." The Hibernian woman turned to Dwynwyn. "Old Woman of Beara, you told me nothing about hauling a woman-child about to whelp. The weight alone would slow us down, not to mention I'm no midwife."

"It is true," said Dwynwyn. "I told you nothing."

During this exchange, the world collapsed around me. No one else could hear it. But I did, in the lap of each wave, in the cry of the first bird. How had I failed to foresee this moment?

"Maeve comes with us!" Esus's voice broke. "Or I don't go. I can't leave her here alone. To face them alone."

Still, I did not speak. I looked to Dwynwyn again, who now looked back at me intently but gave me no sign. The Hibernian woman, with her warrior's discipline, reined in her restlessness, sensing that there was something here she did not understand. Her companions waited silently.

Then we heard the sound of hoof beats, still in the distance but moving closer.

"Go, Esus." I bore down and pushed the words out. "She is right. You can't outrun them with me about to have a baby."

"No, Maeve."

"You must, Esus. Anna says so." I appealed to Dwynwyn for help, though now she no more resembled Anna the prophetess than any old woman does another. But she said nothing, and Esus paid no attention to her.

"Maeve, my dove, aren't you the one who told me I was sent here to find you? Aren't you the other half of me?"

The sun shot over the rim of the world and caught in my tears, blinding me. Still, I could hear the sound of hooves, pounding, pounding.

"Maeve, we are lovers."

"You are lovers." Dwynwyn finally spoke, coming to stand beside us, one hand on each of us. "You are lovers, but not just of each other. You are the lovers of the world."

"We can't love if we're apart!" Esus insisted.

"We can't love unless we part." (I had no idea what I meant by that.)

"Not to put too fine a point on it," the Hibernian woman interrupted, "but it's now or never."

"Go without me," said Esus shortly.

"As you will." The Hibernian woman turned to remount.

I took a breath of air so deep I felt as if a whirlwind had entered me. Then I spoke in Aramaic: "Yeshua ben Miriam. In the name of the unnameable one, the god of your forefathers, the god of Abraham, Isaac, and Jacob, I command you to go."

We were both stunned, our tears stopped in their tracks.

"Maeve" was all he said.

He kissed my mouth, a kiss that was as much a blow as a kiss, yet no less tender for that. Then he hurled himself onto the black horse behind the Hibernian woman.

I watched them gallop into the straits, Esus, no equestrian, holding on for dear life. I had to stuff my fist into my mouth to keep from crying after him. I would have stood watching till he was out of sight, hoping that he'd become sure enough of his seat to look back and give me one more glimpse of his face, but Dwynwyn had other plans for me.

"Quick!" She grabbed my arm. "We've got work to do."

She dragged me from the point back across the sands.

"Don't look back," she commanded.

As if I were leaving instead of being left. As if I were Lot's wife from one of the stories Esus had told me. O let me be a pillar of salt. Let me dissolve on the next tide. A little more salt in the great salt sea. Let me go. Let me go.

"Hurry!" Dwynwyn urged. "Hurry!"

I stumbled after her.

"Now." Dwynwyn halted after we'd climbed a high dune more than half a mile from the point. "This should be far enough."

We turned. I strained for a glimpse of Esus, but the horses and riders had disappeared into the morning mists on the opposite shore. Then I caught sight of the pursuers racing full tilt towards Abermenai Point.

"Call the tide," Dwynwyn instructed. "And the wind."

"What?" You can hardly blame me for being a little slow on the uptake.

"You are the daughter of the eight greatest weather witches in the world. You can do it. The women and your Esus have already reached the other shore. You'll win them precious time if you can stop those riders from crossing. Don't think. Just do it. Call the tide. Call the wind. Call the rain. Now! Let it rip!"

And I did. I don't know how I knew what to do. I don't even know what I did. Somehow I opened: my mouth, my arms, my heart, every orifice and pore, every cell. Standing there howling on the dune, I met and mated with the elements. They took on my passion; I took on their power.

Now. Look. The riders wheel around to confront the source of a terrible sound. In an instant they see they are no longer the pursuers but the pursued. The tide is coming in, not slowly, inch by inch, but as a huge, black wall of water, a tidal bore driven by a furious wind and a sobbing rage from the depths of the sea. They turn inland and ride as fast as they can towards higher ground.

All but one rider. Dismounting, he sends his horse after the others. For one moment, he stands still. Then with his arms open, he walks straight towards the bore. As if his eyes are mine, I see the black water blot out the sky. Then the ocean inside me bursts its bounds. Hot tears course down my thighs.

∽

I don't know where I am. But that's not true. I do know. I am inside my own body, deeper than I've ever been before. I am imprisoned in it. My body is the earth, and we are surrounded by it. There's Dwynwyn and Moira on either side of me. The air is thick and close with Crows' wings. It is always night inside my body. A fire burns; water steams; herbs smoke. My body rocks crazily, almost colliding with the moon and the stars as tidal bores of pain rush through it and then ebb, then rush again. Don't fight, they are saying. Don't fight. Who would I fight anymore? Take me, take me. Finish me.

But it doesn't end, not the night, not the waves. Then I start to ride them. Wave after wave after wave. They are taking me home to the Shining Isle of Tir na mBan. That's why it's so dark. I am sailing the sunless sea, and that bright light on the shore is Grainne of the golden hair. Now I see the others, less distinct, but there, surrounding her. And behind them all, the great woman-shape of Tir na mBan, Bride's breasts milky with cloud, the sloping thighs and the dense, perfumed garden between them. Look. The water lapping at the shore is thick and red. My mothers crouch and dip their fingers into the blood. They paint the rocks. They paint themselves with the blood, my blood.

"All right, Maeve Rhuad. It's time."

I am being gathered in Crows' wings. Some of them are holding my arms, others my legs. I am squatting without having to bear my own weight.

"Bear down," Dwynwyn says. "Look at the fire. Let your body open like a flower."

She has it all wrong. The flames flutter like petals, butterflies feeding on flowers, soft, delicate. The fire is inside me. The sun is inside me, huge, hard, burning. I am the earth heaving; I am the sky torn by lightning; I am the husk of the seed splitting open.

"Push, bear down. Push."

"Grainne," I scream. "Grainne!"

I see her face in the fire. Her lips form words: Little Bright One, Little Bright One. In the flickering of a flame, I remember pushing through the dark river inside her to the mouth of the world, through the soft, opening petals.

"Little Bright One. Little Bright One," she calls to me.

I am opening wide, torn, bleeding, blossoming, a bloody, blown rose.

"She's crowning! Bear down once more, Maeve Rhuad. There!"

The hard head slides free, and the body slips after it. Before I see, I hear the robust squalling of a tiny, new storm.

"Praise be to Bride."

Moments later that strange, purple, undersea creature, the afterbirth, is born. The Crows ease me back down. Then in my arms Dwynwyn places the little flame, the little flower, red, wrinkled, utterly lovely. My daughter. Mine.

"Don't," a Crow hisses. "Don't let her nurse the child. It will only make it harder for her."

"Let them have this moment," Dwynwyn countermands. "Let them drink deep of it. There will be more than enough thirst to come. Let this memory be a secret spring."

I barely hear her words; I don't consider their meaning. I am stroking my daughter's fiery hair. She latches fiercely onto my breast as if she will never let go. I whisper in her ear her secret name. As she suckles, we fall into a deep sleep.

∞

When I woke I was alone. That was the first thing I knew. My baby was gone. Every mother knows this particular kind of terror and desolation if only in nightmare. *Where is my baby? Where is my baby?* That is what I mean by alone: without my baby. For a long while I didn't move. I didn't want to know what I knew. Anything I did—sitting up, crying out—would only make it more real: my baby gone.

As I lay still I began to notice thin lines of light leaking into the darkness through chinks in the stone. I did not want to consent to any reality, but my mind began to organize information anyway. I must be in a chambered cairn. It was probably the nearest shelter from the storm. They'd brought me here because I was having a baby. *My baby. Where is my baby?* I had fallen asleep with her in my arms, and now she was gone. I couldn't not know anymore.

I sat up, and when the dizziness cleared, I tried to stand, but my legs buckled under me.

"My baby!" I wailed. "Where is my baby?"

Moira must have been waiting outside. She rushed in and tried to put her arms around me. I struggled and screamed until exhaustion overcame me and I collapsed against her. She held me and stroked my hair.

"You're going to have to be very brave, Maeve."

She spoke to me as if I were a child. But I was a woman, a mother.

"Where's my baby?" I asked again.

"She is well and safe, Maeve. That's all I can tell you."

"Where's Dwynwyn?" I changed tack. Dwynwyn would know. Dwynwyn would help, as she had helped me rescue Esus. *Esus, Esus.* I couldn't think about him yet. I had to find my baby first.

"Dwynwyn has gone back to her island."

I rubbed my eyes with my fist to keep the tears back. How could Dwynwyn desert me now?

"Ah, no," said Moira. "I see what you think. Let me spare you a little pain, at least. She fought as hard as she could to stay with you. She was removed by force."

"I don't understand. How could anyone force her?" I did not welcome the discovery that Dwynwyn was not all-powerful.

"Dwynwyn is a great sorceress, to be sure, but, in the end, only flesh and blood, for all her Otherwordly connections. And the druids are not without powers. Dwynwyn did all she could do for you, more than she would have for any other. Take what comfort you can from that. Now listen, Maeve, there are some things I think you'd better know."

"Where's my baby?" I repeated without hope.

"Maeve, the druids believe you helped the Stranger to escape. You are being accused of meddling and interfering with high mysteries."

"High mysteries like rigged lots," I spat.

"They don't think you acted alone. They are almost certain Dwynwyn had a hand in what happened. But she is outside their jurisdiction. You are not."

Nothing she said moved me much. Esus was free. There was at least that: an aching throb of sweetness in the midst of pounding loss.

"Where's my baby?"

"She is well, I tell you, and will be well cared for."

"Who! Who will care for her? Who?"

Moira didn't answer. I waited, sensing that she was debating with herself.

"I am under orders not to tell you anything at all. But that seems unnecessarily cruel. I will tell you this much: Your daughter is on her way east, as we speak, away from this strife, away from the burden of prophecy and the confusion of rumor. She is to be fostered by a proud, strong, wealthy tribe, the Iceni, rich in horses and known for their strong, beautiful women. Believe me, Maeve Rhuad, your daughter will be well-treated and honorably raised."

"She's gone?" I whispered. "Gone?"

"It will be better for the child, Maeve." Her voice was gentle but inexorable. "The college would never have let you keep her. You are in too much trouble. Maybe mortal trouble. Pay attention, Maeve. As soon as you're strong enough, you are to appear before a court made up of the druids of Mona and the priestesses of Holy Island. You will be questioned about the Stranger's escape as well as the escape of three female prisoners. The archdruid will make a judgment concerning what is to become of you. You must begin to think clearly, and when the time comes, you must answer the court's questions very carefully. Your life hangs in the balance, Maeve."

What life?

"Do you understand?"

I nodded, just to stop her words. Then I turned away my head and was sick. *Gone. My baby is gone.*

My whole body wept.

45

BEYOND THE NINTH WAVE

Have you noticed that we're nearly at the end of this book? Are you getting worried? Are you wondering how I'm going to pull off a resolution, let alone a happy ending? Listen, I never promised a happy ending. You can laugh your way to a tragic end, just as you can weep for a night and find joy in the morning. Comedy, tragedy. It's we who named them and separated them into two distinct masks. The western version of yin and yang. But life is messier than that. It won't resolve itself into neat symbols you can wear around your neck or hang from your ears.

While we're on the subject of symbols, I have something I've been waiting to say for two thousand years. Thanks to the cult that's grown up around my foster brother's life and death, we've gotten used to thinking of the male principle as the prototype of the human: the god who shares our humanity, who suffers and dies with us, who harrows hell for us. We've forgotten those voyagers to the underworld, Inanna and Persephone, and poor, suffering Rhiannon falsely accused of murdering her own son. Even with the revival of interest in feminine archetypes, we tend to think of the female as other than human. The old crone doesn't die; she is death. The maiden is forever young; the mother eternally squatting to give birth or suckling with her many breasts.

Listen: I am a woman. I am flesh. I have been to hell and back more than once, like many a woman before me and since. I have lost my lover. I have lost my child. I am about to stand trial for my life. I want to tell you, whoever you are, male or female: When you are in the place of no hope and no comfort, I am there with you, just as surely as he is. You can call my name: Maeve, Magdalen, She who Suffers. Call on me. I will be with you.

I thought at first that justice (so to speak) would be swift and simple. The *Beltaine* festivities were still going on, the tribes still gathered. I was delivered of my baby. What were they waiting for? I'd cost them a sacrifice. Surely they would demand that I pay in kind. To me it seemed the most obvious—even desirable—solution. But the days passed, and nothing happened. I stayed in isolation at the cairn—not Bryn Celli Ddu but a small cairn halfway between the dunes and the college. The three resident Crows took turns tending me. I was allowed no visitors. Apparently the date of my trial had not been set.

"We have all agreed that you must regain your strength first," Moira explained.

Fattening me up, I thought to myself. No fun sacrificing someone who was half dead already. But I began to wonder. The cosmic moment for the quinquennial sacrifice had come and gone. The days passed; the moon waned; the tribes dispersed. Against my will, I was recovering, the young, green life within me putting out root and shoots, taking hold, making it harder for me to sustain my death wish. My bleeding tapered off. The Crows made compresses to ease my aching, engorged breasts. Still, several times a day, with a great, tingling rush, my milk would let down. In fact, what happened was more like the eruption of a fountain, tiny jets of milk shooting out in all directions. Whatever released the milk also unstopped my grief, and, at those times, I would weep until I had wept myself dry again.

Finally, late in the afternoon before the night of the dark moon, the druids sent for me. As soon as I realized that I was being taken to my trial, I felt more relieved than anything else. I rode on horseback behind Moira. We headed west, and somehow I was not surprised when we arrived at dusk in the very grove where Esus had received the blackened barley cake. When the trial was over, would they lead me away and tie me to the same tree?

As was their custom on windswept Mona, the druids stilled the air. (They were capable of that much weather magic, at least.) There was silence in the circle of trees except for the crackling and hissing of a small fire. I stood alone between the fire and a semi-circle of Cranes and Crows, my shadow dancing before me to the rhythm of the flames. Beyond the Crows and Cranes, I could see the beech tree where my old woman self had sat concealed. A smile tugged at my lip and laughter bubbled in my throat and threatened to explode. I wondered why I had so little fear.

Then it hit me: there was no russet beard and eyes under any of the white hoods. Before I had a chance to consider the implications of that conspicuous absence, the archdruid planted the world tree and sang the quarters. He was impressive by force of habit, but he seemed a little shaky tonight, more like the old man that he was. After a rambling preamble about why we were assembled, he turned to me. Apparently he was going to conduct the questioning himself, which meant, I reckoned, that I was a V.I.P. (Very Important Prisoner).

"Maeve Rhuad, is it true that you took it upon yourself to meddle with the sacred mysteries of divine sacrifice?" he began, his tone more sorrowful than stern.

"If you want to put it that way." I shrugged.

"You will please confine your answers to yes or no, unless otherwise directed."

"Yes."

"Did you conspire to contrive the escape of the chosen one?"

"You mean the one chosen by the druid Lovernios in a rigged lot?"

You would think the archdruid would have blanched or blushed. But it has been my experience, then and since, that people don't get very far in the ecclesiastical business—or any other—if they are overburdened by shame. The archdruid traveled light.

"Was that a yes or a no?" the archdruid inquired politely, completely ignoring my reference to Lovernios. Where was he, I wondered again?

"Yes."

"How did you accomplish your aim? You may expand your answer here," he encouraged me. "The court wishes to know how you, er, pulled it off."

"The court may wish to know, but I may not tell. I am under a *geis* not to reveal my methods."

I wasn't sure that was strictly true but it sounded good to me, and it frustrated them. There were regretful sighs and disappointed murmurs, but everyone had to respect a *geis*.

"Pity," said the archdruid. "I will say for the record—and please don't misunderstand me; I don't wish to encourage behavior such as yours—but I will say that though the court is appalled by what you admit you have done, we cannot help but be impressed. You managed to convince a perfect—and perfectly willing—sacrifice to shirk his fate. You got him clean away right from under our noses. We suspect you also had a hand in the escape of three important political prisoners, and I take it you are not denying responsibility for that tidal bore?"

"I am not." I'm afraid I could not suppress a grin, and I'm afraid the grin did not help my case, supposing there was any help for it, which I doubt.

"Well, then, my dear young lady," (Don't you hate that term?) "we can only grieve, grieve and deeply mourn and lament that you did not see fit to apply your considerable talents to your studies at this College; that you lacked the grace to offer your great, natural gifts for the good of the whole *Combrogos*. But, no. Green, young, and callow as you are, you defied the wisdom of your elders, setting yourself up as judge of what was best, and put your will above the good of the *Combrogos*." He paused to take a rasping breath. "In so doing, you have upset the delicate balance of the cycles, on which all life depends; you have put in jeopardy the safety and survival of the *Combrogos*, which a willing sacrifice might have ensured. Moreover, out of a blind, foolish, selfish passion, you have interfered with the divine destiny of an extraordinary young man who might have joined the Mighty Ones."

The charges against me did sound serious. Had I been as bad as all that?

"And finally—"

There was *more?*

"—though you may not yet know it, you are responsible for a man's death. Yes. The great druid Lovernios, whom you have falsely accused of manipulating the lots, is dead—or so we fear."

Foxface, dead? My father dead? And yet...hadn't I already known?

"Lovernios fell from his mount and was overtaken by the tidal bore you so recklessly raised. He was swept out to sea."

As the archdruid spoke, the scene played itself again in my memory: the rider dismounting and turning to meet the wave. *My father. My father lives in Tir fo Thuinn, the land under the wave.*

"His body has not been recovered. We may not even give his remains the rites and honor due so great a man, who tirelessly served the *Combrogos,* whose loss is incalculable." Here the archdruid allowed his voice to break. "Therefore," he went on, tears standing in his eyes, "although you may not have killed him knowingly—we will give you the benefit of the doubt, however undeserved—we are forced to regard you as a murderess."

"No!" I don't know how I found the strength to shout that word, but I did.

"No? What do you mean, no?" For the first time the archdruid was thrown off stride. "You have already admitted that your raised the bore."

"I mean no. No, I did not kill Lovernios. I called the wave, but I was there. I saw. While the others galloped to safety, he stopped and got down from his horse. He walked straight towards the bore. On purpose. He wanted to die."

There was a shocked silence, then an indignant sputtering.

"Oh come, come now, Maeve Rhuad," said the archdruid. "You can't seriously expect us to believe that. Why would Lovernios, a renowned druid upon whose counsel famous kings depended, a great and mighty druid whom I favored as my successor, why would such a man cut short his life?"

I looked at the archdruid's cold, closed expression, repeated on so many other faces. Nissyen was right. No one would believe me. It was not in their interest to believe me, or, as the archdruid might say, it was not in the interest of the *Combrogos.* It was not the story the druids were telling themselves. It would skew the plot line, make chaos of the cast of characters. What was left of my heart (a few jagged pieces) sank to my feet, then deeper, into the earth itself where dead things are buried.

"Because," someone was answering for me. I looked up and saw Nissyen tottering towards the archdruid, trembling from the wisps of his hair right down to his gnarled toes. "Because the great druid Lovernios fathered a child on Maeve Rhuad, his own daughter whom he denied, and he could not face the College, the *Combrogos,* or himself."

A heartbeat of silence gave way to outraged whispers that soon rose to gale force.

I looked at Nissyen through sudden tears. In my eyes, this little light-weight druid had taken on the stature and sturdiness of an oak. He smiled at me and gave a little sideways nod. I knew what he was saying: "It's all right, Maeve Rhuad. It doesn't matter what happens to me now. I am at peace."

"Silence please. Silence everyone." The archdruid took command. "The late, lamented Lovernios's honor and reputation have been impugned. We must determine the truth of the matter. Maeve Rhuad." He turned to me again. "Do you hold what Nissyen says regarding your paternity to be the truth?"

"I do."

"Then I am confounded. Do you have as many fathers as you have mothers? How many more fathers will you name?"

"I have...had only one father." I had a lump in my throat. How could I mourn the loss of a father who had hated me? Yet it seemed I did.

"Perhaps my memory deceives me, then. Did you or did you not present yourself to the College as the daughter of Manannán Mac Lir?"

"I did, but—"

"Then how do you come to make this wild claim that the late, lamented Lovernios is your father?"

How, indeed? What was I to tell them? Should I explain that Dwynwyn's magic well had revealed to me a key episode in Lovernios's mysterious past? Should I describe my mothers' glee as they surveyed his shipwrecked form? That was just the beginning. Would the druids really sit through an account of what happened that night in Bryn Celli Ddu?

"Can either you or Nissyen offer any proof whatsoever for this allegation of paternity?"

Nissyen and I exchanged a helpless glance. Of course Nissyen knew nothing but what I had told him and believed it only for love of me. Dwynwyn was a prisoner, of sorts, on her own island. Esus, who had heard Lovernios break down and admit the truth, was long gone. Lovernios was dead. I had no witnesses. It was my word against his eternal silence. Then I remembered my first vision of him, the one I'd had beneath Bride's breast.

"My proof, archdruid, is in my face and in the face of the child you have stolen from me."

There was a collective gasp, followed by a scrutiny so intense that it scoured my every pore. In a flash everyone saw what no one, including me, had wanted to see. My face echoed his. He was gone, but the shape of his bones remained in the set of my eyes and jaw.

"She speaks truly!" cried Moira, and the rest of the Crows added their voices to hers in triumphant ululation. "The rest of the story must be true, too. He was the father of the child she bore."

The old archdruid was nothing if not nimble. He had proclaimed Lovernios's greatness. He had even (now that the man was safely dead) proclaimed his preference for Lovernios as his successor. In short, he was out on a limb, but he had no intention of letting the bough break under him.

"Ah Lovernios, Lovernios! whom the Mighty Ones have used in their implacable, inscrutable way. Did not he himself prophesy the birth of the misbegotten child? Did not the Mighty Ones speak through him proclaiming that a great hero would be born of this line, a hero who will stand, win or lose, against Rome, who will bring the *Combrogos* fame for all time in all memories? Think how his great heart, dedicated to saving the sovereignty of the *Combrogos*, must have broken. Ah Lovernios, Lovernios, you have played your part, offering yourself in bitter and lonely sacrifice to the gods. But your name will live. Generations of bards will sing your praises!"

The court gave way to weeping and lamentation. The archdruid went on sounding his theme, adding meter and rhyme (*He was good!*) and by the time he was through, the plot was rescued, the main character rehabilitated, and the story could be told as the archdruid deemed best for the good of *Combrogos*.

"But what about Maeve Rhuad?" Moira recovered first. "What is to become of her? That is what we are here to decide."

The archdruid focused on me once more. He sighed and shook his head, back in his sorrowful mode.

"Despite what may—or may not—have come to light concerning the, uh, paternity in this case, the fact remains that Maeve Rhuad has defied the collective authority of this body. She willfully stopped the quinquennial sacrifice and has therefore threatened the survival of the *Combrogos*. None of us fears his single death. But the *Combrogos* must live. Maeve Rhuad has betrayed us all and therefore deserves to die a traitor's death."

There was an awful silence. In it, my will to live was born again. It wasn't so much that I feared death—though who doesn't. I would have died for love. Hadn't I already proved that? I might even have considered dying for King Bran or the *Combrogos*. But dying for the archdruid's convenience, so that he could tell the story *his* way, galled me. My story wasn't over yet. One way or another, one day or another, I was going to be the one to tell it.

"For Anu's sake!" Moira burst out. "She's only a young girl! Give her a chance. Consult the oracles! It is our sacred responsibility as druids and priestesses to act, not according to our own will as you accuse Maeve Rhuad of having done, but according to the will of the gods!"

The archdruid stroked his beard and made ruminative noises.

"You are right, sister," he said at last. "Druid law was not made by human beings for petty human purposes; it was merely interpreted and understood by those trained to have discernment. Druid law is the law of the gods and the elements, the law of life itself. It shall be as you say. We will consult the oracles. We will cast the *coelbreni*."

There was a stir of excitement and whispering in the court. Somehow from within the folds of archdruid's cloak a bag of ogham sticks emerged. (And if he had wanted to pull rabbits or doves or trick cards from his fluttering sleeves, he could have done that, too.) Then everyone grew still again as the archdruid squeezed his eyes shut and (without peeking) drew five sticks from the pouch, then cast them into the air.

To me the sticks appeared to fall in slow motion. I watched them spinning and wobbling through the air, bouncing a little as they landed, then skidding to their resting places. Five flat sticks carved with ogham lay on the ground between the archdruid and me. The three in the middle clustered, almost forming a triangle. The last one pointed directly at me. I tried to read the markings, but I was not close enough.

The archdruid waited for a moment, eyes still closed, arms outstretched in a rather stagey gesture intended, no doubt, to indicate his openness to divine inspiration and guidance. Then he opened his eyes and proceeded to the stick closest to him. Bending down, he examined it, then he moved on to the central three. He looked longest at the last stick. Everyone waited. You could hear occasional gasps when someone who'd been holding his breath had to breathe. Finally, the archdruid finished his scrutiny and returned to his place, where he stood for a time letting the suspense build to an intolerable pitch.

"The whole story is here," he spoke at last. "Laid out on the ground before us. This stick," he said approaching the one nearest him, "is the past, the foundation."

Though I was supposedly the subject, he read the sticks in relation to where he stood. The closest stick represents the past, and the farthest, future. I wondered about that, but no one else seemed to notice.

"It bears the inscription for *quert*," he went on. That's apple to you. "*Quert* means choice. Since it is in the position that represents the past, this ogham indicates that a choice has been made, a fatal choice. On this choice rests everything that follows."

That's what the archdruid saw. But *quert* called up for me the magical orchard on the Shining Isle of Tir na mBan. I could almost smell the heady mix of blossom and fruit. I remembered how the scent of the orchard had followed Fand, Boann, and me far out to sea.

"These three sticks," he continued, moving to the cluster, "will tell us the nature of the choice and its consequences. Here is *Ioho*." That's yew to you. "The tree of death and rebirth, the tree that links the worlds of *abred, gwynedd*, and *ceugant*. Maeve Rhuad chose to tamper with these mysteries. She skewed the pattern; she disrupted the flow between past and future."

I heard the archdruid's voice, but I was seeing the green-gold light under the yew trees. Beyond sight, I felt the heat of Esus's embrace. Esus, Esus.

"Next we come to *Koad*. The central stick, the heart of the story."

The grove. A chill came over me. It was true what had happened at the Mound of the Dark Grove was at the heart of the story.

"The grove is a sacred place; the grove is all the knowledge of all the trees. The grove is also the collective wisdom of this body of druids and priest-esses. When she stole the Stranger, Maeve Rhuad violated the grove. She scorned its wisdom."

The wisdom that had left Esus alone, tied to a tree, waiting to die.

"And so it will come as no surprise that the third of these three sticks is *straif*."

Straif, strife, blackthorn, crown of thorns. The skull anointed with blood. The baby crowning, crowned with the burning circle of my sex.

"*Straif* is the mark of ruin, of bitter fate. Maeve Rhuad has brought ruin not only to herself but to Lovernios and, it may be, to us all."

He let the heinousness of my crimes sink in as he slowly approached the last stick.

"This stick," he said as he came to a stop, "represents the future. It is this ogham that will answer the question: What are we to do with Maeve Rhuad. Are we all agreed to that?"

It was not really a question, and he did not wait for an answer in case anyone made the mistake of thinking it was.

"*Mor*," he pronounced.

Mor. The only ogham that does not stand for a tree, the ogham of the great, wide sea.

"Esteemed sisters, beloved brothers, the judgment of the *coelbreni* is plain. Maeve Rhuad once claimed to be the daughter of Manannán Mac Lir, son of the wave. She now claims as father the druid Lovernios, who was swept out to sea by a wave she herself raised. Therefore, not this court, but the sea itself shall decide whether she lives or dies."

The Crows and Cranes grasped, before I did, what the archdruid meant. There was a sound in the grove, like the rustling of leaves when the wind shifts or like the subtle change in the sound of surf when the tide turns. Then Nissyen began to sob out loud. Though her face remained immobile, tears streamed down Moira's cheeks.

"Maeve Rhuad." The archdruid turned to address me. "Having broken the laws of this college, which are the laws of life, having meddled in high mysteries, having willfully endangered the *Combrogos*, you shall from this moment forward be excluded from all our rites and sacrifices. You shall furthermore be exiled from the shores of the Holy Isles and sent beyond the ninth wave, there to meet the judgment or mercy of the sea."

❧

Now let the archdruid's words echo in your ears and ring through the rising wind as the firelit grove fades, giving way to the vast, rolling sea. I am standing on the shore. My small, flat-bottomed boat is waiting for me. The sky is purple, and a young crescent moon drifts down the West, a little boat, tiny in its own sea of sky. It is twilight, one of the magical times when the way opens between the worlds.

You have to admit, the druids have flair. Like all great performance artists, they know that timing is everything—especially if you have to catch the ebb tide so that it will take the exile's boat out to sea to meet the current that will take the boat farther still. It would be anti-climactic to have your exile wash up a few miles down shore—armed with a knife.

A knife is all I am allowed to take with me—(no one tells me what I'm supposed to do with it)—no other provisions of any kind. No food, no water. I am being launched from Porth Dafarch, a tiny beach on the south-western shore of Holy Island. The beach faces open sea uninterrupted for miles and miles and miles by any point of land.

At this moment, the beach is crowded with Crows and Cranes. Further back, perched among the rocks and cliffs that rise on either side of the beach, the entire student body of the Druid College of Mona is assembled. No one is saying personal farewells; the occasion is too formal, but I am allowed a moment to scan the crowd. I find Viviane first. Her hair catches the light and glows. She and Branwen are standing together on a ledge partway up a cliff. Nissyen and the other first formers are clustered nearby. I try to catch everyone's eye, saving Branwen for last. When our eyes meet, Branwen lets go of Viviane's hand and stretches out her arms towards me. I lift my arms to her in return, and suddenly the cliffs come alive with upraised, out-stretched arms as if some enormous flock of huge birds were about to take flight.

With tears in his eyes—(real enough, I suppose, though I can tell he's enjoying them)—the archdruid comes to me and places the knife in my hand. It's a beautiful knife, with a shining blade, and a bone handle carved with swirling birds and fishes. Then he and Moira, whose eyes are red-rimmed but dry, hand me into the boat.

"It's not that we don't love you, Maeve Rhuad," begins the archdruid.

"I know, I know," I cut him off. "It's for my own good."

He shakes his head sadly. "No, Maeve Rhuad. For the good of the *Combrogos*."

Then everything happens very quickly. At the very moment the tide turns, the archdruid begins intoning the words of excommunication and exile. Six brawny men push my boat through the breakers to the swells beyond. As I glide out on the tide, the archdruid's voice follows in wisps and fragments on the wind. Then another sound, higher and wilder, wings across the water: women's voices singing a hymn to the new moon, singing a hymn to me:

> Hail to thee, thou new moon,
> Jewel of guidance in the night!
> Hail to thee, thou new moon,
> Jewel of guidance on the billows!
> Hail to thee, thou new moon,
> Jewel of guidance on the ocean!
> Hail to thee, thou new moon,
> Jewel of guidance of my love!

Their voices follow me out to the open sea, into the deepening night.

∽

I can't tell you how many days and nights I survived in that boat. I suppose I could have made notches with my knife, but it didn't occur to me to keep count while I still had my wits, and later I was delirious. At first it wasn't so bad. I was well fed and watered before I left. I even slept comfortably that first, mild night. In my dreams I saw women, women everywhere, women I knew, and women I didn't know, keeping watch: My mothers grouped on the beach at Tir na mBan, the Cailleach bending over the pool between Bride's breasts. The Crows watching from the crags of Holy Island, Branwen and Viviane with them. Dwynwyn standing on the tip of her island. Then I saw others: women on the top of a tall promontory that rose abruptly from flat land, women on shores and islands I'd never seen. All watching, eyes trained on some distant point.

In the last dream that first night, I saw a woman on a marshy shore. She was pacing back and forth with a bright-haired baby in her arms, singing softly: *Jewel of the night, thou new moon.* I somehow knew that the baby was my daughter, and that the woman loved her. In that knowledge, my pain did not lessen, exactly, but it loosened, holding me gently as the woman held my child.

Day after night after day I rode the billows, which seemed to me like the strong, rippling muscles of my father's arm. Manannán Mac Lir, Lovernios lost to the wave, they were the same being now. And I woke every morning to Grainne's touch on my face. I did not struggle to survive. I surrendered to survive. Orphaned, exiled, the sea and the sky became my mother and father. I drank the rain, and I milked my own breasts with one hand, licking the drops that fell on the other. Often my boat was surrounded by dolphins. They sang and talked to me, and I had no difficulty understanding their language, or they mine. I chanted—word perfect!—all the stories I had learned laboring under the stone. I told them my mothers' stories, too. I told them the story of Maeve and Esus, which they liked best of all. Once or twice a day the dolphins tossed fish into my boat, which I cleaned with my knife and ate raw.

Then—and this is my last distinct memory of the voyage—I heard a voice: the Cailleach's, Dwynwyn's, my mothers', Moira's. In different ways, the voice belonged to all of them.

"Lie down, Maeve Rhuad, Little Bright One. Cleave to the bottom of the boat. We've got to step up the pace a little. There's going to be some weather, honey, but you'll be all right. Lie on your back. Trust us."

Then the storm began. Day and night were lost in each other as the sky was lost in the huge, black waves that towered over my boat. If I had lost consciousness face down, I would surely have drowned. As it was, I kept my nose above water and merely lost what was left of my mind. And a good thing, too. A mind is no asset under such circumstances.

Then everything stopped. The whole world lay still as if it had died. At some level of myself, I registered that stillness like a shock, even though I was inert and unconscious. When the warmth came, I felt that, too. Something hard and muscled and rich with scent lifted me and gathered me to itself. The world moved again, plodding steadily. That went on for a long, long time.

At last I was lowered onto something soft. I felt the tickle of many breaths close to my face. Someone touched my lips with something. Instinctively, I put out my tongue and tasted. I remembered the word. Honey. Women's voices began to speak in a dialect I did not know. Yet I understood what they were saying. It was simple.

"She will live."

ACKNOWLEDGMENT OF SOURCES

When I began research for *Daughter of the Shining Isles*, my knowledge of things Celtic was limited to an amateur appreciation of Celtic music, art, and the writings of W.B. Yeats and James Stephens. When the idea came to me that Mary Magdalen was a Celt, I thought, What fun! Then I began to read scholarly works about the ancient Celts' reverence for severed heads. I learned that the Celts ended up in the misty, magical British Isles after sweeping across Europe in warrior hordes, sacking cities as they went, leaving the odd sacrificial body in the bog here and there. Are you *sure* you want to be a Celt? I asked the Magdalen. She was.

I studied the Celts for months before I began to write and continued to do research through first draft and revisions—a period of about five years. I learned about the Roman and Greek accounts of the Celts from traditional scholars like T.G.E. Powell, Anne Ross, and Stuart Piggot. I was most affected by Tacitus's description of the Roman general Suetonius's hair-raising crossing of the Menai Straits to the sacred Druid Isle of Mona where his troops were met and temporarily halted by the sight–and sound!–of shrieking, black-robed priestesses. From Robert Graves's classic, *The White Goddess*, I gleaned knowledge of the ogham alphabet and its wealth of meanings. Jean Markale's *Women of the Celts* was helpful in deepening my knowledge of Celtic myth and literature, its recurring images and themes, as were Alwyn and Brinley Rees's *Celtic Heritage* and the many books by John and Caitlin Matthews. And of course I read the famous *Tain Bo Cuailnge (The Cattle Raid of Cooley)* starring Maeve/Magdalen's infamous namesake, Queen Medb of Connacht. For an understanding of Celtic religion and ritual, I am particularly indebted to lectures and articles by Alexei Kondratiev, Tom Cowan's *Fire in the Head: Shamanism and the Celtic Spirit*, John Sharkey's *Celtic Mysteries*, and Anne Ross and Don Robin's *Life and Death of a Druid Prince*. Peter Berresford Ellis's *Dictionary of Celtic Mythology* was a great resource. I continue to keep *Carmina Gadelica, Hymns and Incantations collected in the Highlands and Islands of Scotland in the Last Century* by Alexander Carmichael close at hand.

Part way through the first draft, I took a trip to the Hebrides and Anglesey (Mona) Wales. Although you will not find Tir na mBan (The Land of Women) on a map, the Hebrides seemed the nearest thing to those mythic isles. I wanted to get a feel for the contours of the land, of its air and light. I did much more specific research on Anglesey. Using an Ordnance Survey Map and mindful of Tacitus's account of the Roman attack, I chose a site for the Druid college. Caer Leb, Caer Idris, and Bryn Celli Ddu are all real sites along the Afon Braint within walking distance of each other, the

Menai Straits, and the two standing stones (still standing) described in the book. I also explored Holy Island, where I imagine the priestesses to have lived, and the environs of Llyn Cerrig Bach, now an airstrip, once a shallow lake chock full of votive offerings. I asked local inhabitants where first century boats might have safely landed. The most exciting discovery on that trip was a tiny tidal island called Llanddwyn, home of Dwynwyn, a fifth century hermit-saint whose oracular eels could predict a maiden's fortune in love. As many saints have pre-Christian roots, I did not think Dwynwyn would mind having an earlier incarnation. She gave the book a climax that surprised me as much as it did our Maeve.

As for researching Maeve's cosmic counterpart, Esus/Jesus, I refreshed myself about his background by reading Harry M. Orlinksky's *Ancient Israel* as well as large chunks of *The Jerusalem Bible*. Stories of Jesus's childhood come from *The Apocrypha*. For information about the Temple of Jerusalem, which appears in Maeve's dream, I consulted The Rev. Bruce Chilton of Bard College as well as reading his book *The Temple of Jesus, His Sacrificial Program within a Cultural History of Sacrifice*. I also thank The Rev. Chilton for directing me to *The Mishnayoth*.

I often despaired of my ability to retain information, so I wrote amidst a sea of books, gradually absorbing a worldview. Head hunters or not, it is hard not to love the Celts, a flamboyant people who loved to hear themselves talk and who revered the power and magic of the spoken word.